THESE
FLEETING
SHADOWS

THESE FLEETING SHADOWS

KATE ALICE MARSHALL

VIKING

Viking
An imprint of Penguin Random House LLC, New York

First published in the United States of America by Viking,
an imprint of Penguin Random House LLC, 2022

Visit us online at penguinrandomhouse.com.

Library of Congress Cataloging-in-Publication Data is available.

Book manufactured in Canada

ISBN 9780593405116

10 9 8 7 6 5 4 3 2 1

FRI

Text set in Apollo MT Std

This one's for El: sibling extraordinaire, crafter of curiosities, and best of friends

I PROMISE I will tell you the truth. But first, I need to lie. It doesn't make sense yet. It will. Be patient.

My name is Helen Vaughan, and I was born at Harrow.

This is Harrow: A house waits, tall and still, in the cleft between wooded hills. The forest rushes toward it and then stops abruptly, as if it has hit an invisible barrier. Not one root strays over the edge of this strict demarcation between the wilderness of trees and the well-mannered lawns, bordered with low square hedges and flower beds.

The house stands three stories tall. It is built of dark gray stone shot through with curious veins of white, which is found nowhere in the surrounding hills. The stone edifice is brutish, squared-off, every angle precise and unimaginative. A flawless symmetry defines the footprint of the house—east and west wings, perfect mirror images with no variation tolerated. Above this monument to predictability, the gabled roofs rise abruptly, so steeply angled that it makes the viewer uneasy to look at them. They make some people think of teeth, and others of falling.

As long as Harrow has stood, the Vaughan family has lived there. As long as the Vaughan family has lived there, Harrow has stood. Scientifically speaking, this is what is known as mutualism. Two organisms, each benefiting the other. A closed and balanced system. Orderly and stable.

There is another relevant scientific principle: entropy. All order eventually succumbs to disorder. No system can remain stable forever.

All things fall to ruin.

1

THE NIGHT HARROW found me, I was digging up a fox's bones. The ground was hardened with an early frost, and I had to throw all my weight into each hacking strike with the shovel. I should have waited until it thawed, but the bones were ready and we wouldn't be staying here long. I'd seen the way the neighbors were starting to look at me, and I'd seen the balance in our bank account. Both suggested it was time to move on.

I tossed aside the last shovelful of earth and knelt, brushing aside the rest of the dirt before peeling back the blue tarp. Beneath, the bones shone pale in the darkness, flesh and fur rotted away.

I'd found the fox on the side of the road months ago, mangled and twisted. Now I cradled the skull in my hands and looked into the empty eye sockets. A few stray bits of dirt clung to it, but the bacteria and beetles and worms had taken care of the rest.

I didn't know what I would use it for yet—what it would want to be and how I would craft that out of wire and river stones and scraps of cloth. Something so beautiful deserved to be transformed, not thrown out like waste. I trailed a finger along the center of the skull, then turned it over in my hands, checking for damage.

I froze. On the roof of the mouth, a spiral wound sharply inward, bisected by a single straight line.

My heart thumped. A thousand times I'd woken with a scream in my throat and that spiral blazing like an afterimage in my mind as I thrashed free of a dream. *The* dream.

Harrow.

My hand shook. It shouldn't be here. My dreams were just that—figments of my sleeping mind, the echoes of a childhood I didn't remember. I rubbed my thumb across the spiral, hoping it was a trick of the light or some smudge of dirt, but it was etched deep in the bone.

The weight of a hand settled onto my shoulder. I didn't move. Couldn't. My limbs were pinned in place, my jaw welded shut. I tasted damp earth.

"Harrow waits," a hoarse male voice croaked by my ear as my fear juddered through me.

Wake up, I thought. *You're dreaming. Wake up. Just wake up.*

"Beware the spiral. Find its center. Harrow—"

"Helen!" My stepfather, Simon, burst from the back door and charged toward me across the yard. "Are you okay?"

I lurched forward as whatever force had been holding me released its grip. I spun around. There was nothing there. No man, no reaching hand—nothing except the fox skull in my hands, still bearing that impossible spiral of carved bone.

"Helen?" Simon repeated.

Had I screamed? I must have called for help. "I thought I heard . . . I . . ." I gulped, stopped myself. "I'm fine."

I'd learned a long time ago not to tell Mom and Simon about

the things I saw or heard or dreamed. It only worried them, and there was nothing they could do.

"Where's Mom?" I asked, forcing my words around my calcified dread. If Simon had come running, why hadn't she?

"In the living room. She got a phone call," he said.

A feeling of deep wrongness swept through me. I hurried toward the back door, then straight through the kitchen, following the quiet murmur of my mother's voice. Mom sat curled against the corner of our rust-colored easy chair in the living room.

"Yeah. No, of course," she was saying. She had her thumbnail between her teeth, not quite biting it. "I have to go. I'll talk to you in the morning."

"Who was that?" I asked.

"That was your uncle Caleb," she said. She tapped her nail against her teeth. "He finally did it. Dad finally found a way to get me back to Harrow."

"What did he do?" Simon asked, stepping into the room behind me.

I knew the answer before she spoke.

"He died."

The house was officially named Harrowstone Hall, but I didn't think I'd ever heard my mother call it that. It was always Harrow, a name that encompassed the house and the grounds and the family and everything else bound up with that place.

We'd left when I was seven years old. My mother never gave me a straight answer about why. Sometimes I thought even she didn't know. All she could tell me was that we had to. It wasn't safe.

And yet we had returned.

One week after my grandfather died, we sat in the car, idling before the open wrought iron gates of Harrow. Beyond, a single-lane road slithered away among the trees. The house was hidden somewhere in that thicketed wood. I could almost feel it. I could almost hear it, a whisper in the back of my mind, a voice I half remembered.

"We don't have to do this," Mom said. She gripped the steering wheel like she was trying to strangle it. "If we turn back now, we'll be home before nightfall."

I swallowed, uncertain. I'd gnawed on my lip until the skin was raw, and my body still hummed with unspent energy. I hated sitting still this long, and I'd been in the car for hours already, drowning in the silence of my mother's stress and my apprehension.

"Helen?" Simon prompted, twisting in his seat.

"It's your dad's funeral," I said, voice hoarse. "Of course we should be there."

Mom's eyes met mine in the rearview mirror. People always said we looked alike, but it was mostly the eyes. Vaughan eyes, so dark they were almost black. Hers were framed with a sweep of dark lashes and indifferently smudged eyeliner. My lashes were thinner, lighter, my hair a muted brown, chopped off at jaw-length, in contrast with her rich mahogany waves.

"Your nightmares . . ." Mom began.

"They're just dreams," I said, and it felt like lying. "Besides, could you live with yourself if you didn't go?"

She sighed. "No, you're right. I have to do this. If only to make absolutely sure he's really dead." She gave an unconvincing laugh. "You two. Always taking care of me."

"Always," Simon said, his hand on her knee. I nodded. Always. That was our pledge. The three of us against the world.

The car rolled forward. As we drove, the land rose to either side in steep hills until I couldn't tell if we were descending or if the forest was rising. The trees, hemlock and birch and oak, wove a thick carpet of shadow over everything, the gray veiled sky gleaming between the branches. And then, suddenly, we were out of the trees, spilling from the cleft between the hills, and Harrow stood before us.

I didn't know when the dreams had started. I couldn't remember a time before them. I would wake in the night screaming and clawing at my throat, babbling about shadows and about being buried, about a spiral that wound endlessly inward. The dreams always began the same way: damp earth all around me, holding me down as I stared up at a dark looming house.

This house.

I would have known it anywhere. The windows were blank eyes, reflecting the overcast sky, and the dark stone drank in the light, swallowing it down. The flower beds lay fallow in preparation for the winter and were already scabbed over with frost, and though I'd expected a crowd of funeral attendees, there was no sign of another living soul.

"Welcome to Harrow," Mom said drily.

I had gone completely still—an alien state for me. I always had to be moving: my leg jittering under a table, my fingers tapping out random patterns on my thigh. But beneath the gaze of that place, I froze like a rabbit on a road at night, surrendering to the deadly velocity of the thing bearing down on it.

Simon whistled. "So this is where you grew up. The pictures don't do it justice."

"They really don't," Mom said. Her shoulders tensed, like she was thinking about flooring the gas and peeling out of there.

I knew that if I asked her to, Mom would turn around—but she needed this. I was going to be there for her at her father's funeral and support her and not make her life any harder than I already had just by existing. I wasn't a normal kid. I didn't have friends. Couldn't be in school. Couldn't be in one place for too long, or . . . things started to happen. Things we didn't talk about.

And there was another reason not to leave. Harrow had haunted me since I left its gates ten years ago.

I wanted to know why.

And so I didn't say anything as she wrenched the parking brake up. We clambered out of the car, all stiff limbs and stumbling. I tilted my head back to look up. The peaks of the house stretched toward the sky, and with my head tilted back, all I could see were gray clouds and those slashes of roof. It left me dizzy, like there was no ground at all, just a sky to fall into.

"Have you ever seen such a spooky old house?" Simon asked. I fell back down to earth and looked at him. He gave me an easy smile. "Gives me the heebie-jeebies for sure." He was the sort of guy who could say "spooky" and "heebie-jeebies" without a trace of irony and thought *Jumanji* was "a bit on the scary side." I loved him for it.

The front door opened, and a man in a black suit stepped out. His hair was peppered with gray, and his beard had patches of white at the jaw, but all the lines on his face only made his smile look warmer. Uncle Caleb, Mom's older brother.

"You made it," he said. "I wasn't sure you would."

"It's not that long a drive," Mom said. Her fingertips brushed the back of my elbow, just a soft touch to say *I'm here. You're here.*

"You know what I mean," he said gently. He stepped forward. They didn't hug. They did an odd sort of forearm clasp–cheek kiss combination that was smooth and practiced but still intensely uncomfortable. I fixed a smile on my face and prepared to stumble my way through this ritual, but Caleb put out his hand instead. "Helen. I'm Caleb."

"I know." When I shook his hand, something in his firm, friendly grip eased the tension in my shoulders.

"I wondered if you'd remember me," he said.

"I don't. Remember you," I said. "But I've seen pictures." Was that rude? I couldn't tell. I didn't exactly have a lot of practice talking to people.

"Well, it's very good to see you again," he said, gracefully ignoring my fumbling. His expression was friendly and open.

It wouldn't last, I reminded myself. It never did.

"And, um. This is my—this is Simon," Mom said, gesturing. Simon stepped forward. He and Caleb shook hands, nodded at each other, and stepped back. And then we were done with introductions, and there seemed to be nothing else to say.

Caleb cleared his throat. "We've got rooms made up if you want to claim a couple before things get started."

"No," Mom said immediately. "We're staying in town. Heading home in the morning."

"At the Starlight?" Caleb asked skeptically. "You'd be a lot more comfortable here."

"I'm not spending another night under this roof," Mom said. "I'm here to pay my respects. Then we're gone. You can't ask anything more of me, Caleb. You can't."

"I won't," he said reassuringly, hands upheld in surrender. "But it's been a long time, Rachel. It might be time to make peace."

"When has this family ever been able to let something go?" Mom asked.

He rubbed the back of his head. "Fair point. Change isn't easy. But it's possible. At least I have to believe so."

"We'll see," she said tightly.

A young man in a suit vest trotted down the steps. For a moment, I thought he must be family, but then he spoke in a deferential tone. "Ma'am, I'll take your car around back for you," he said. Right. This place had *help*. We didn't even have a functioning dishwasher.

"Hold on!" I said. I scrambled back to the car and grabbed my backpack, a green canvas bag that had been scuffed, ripped, and patched over the years. It didn't exactly go with the subdued blue dress and pumps I'd chosen for the funeral, but I didn't go anywhere without it.

I slipped my hand inside, feeling for the bundle of cloth nestled there and the skull wrapped protectively within it. It was like an anchor, a tiny piece of *me* that I could be certain of.

I walked back over to Mom, wobbling when my foot landed wrong. I was remembering why I never wore heels. This place better not be haunted. If a ghost chased me down a long shadowy corridor, I was going to break an ankle.

"Everyone's inside," Caleb said as the car pulled away. "But you can take a moment if you need it."

"Better just get it over with," Mom said. Her fingers knotted together. "Ready to meet the family?" she asked me.

"Too late to back out now. That guy stole our car," I said with false bravado. Mom chuckled. And then she leaned close to me and dropped her voice.

"Be careful," she said. "Our family is not like other families. They will test you, and if they find you wanting, they will make you miserable. If you give them any power over you, any at all, they will carve you up to fit whatever mold they've made for you. Don't let them."

They were words she'd said to me before. Not all at once, but in bits and pieces—when I asked why we didn't talk to her parents, why I'd never met my cousins. But now there was a frantic edge to them, as if she were realizing this was her last chance to warn me.

"We're not staying," I reminded her. "Besides, I don't care what these people think of me. I'm here for *you*."

She nodded, but she looked troubled. Her hand on my shoulder gripped hard enough to send little jolts of pain into the joint. Caleb gestured, motioning us to follow. I ignored my fear, every instinct screaming at me to run. I walked forward.

Harrow drew us in.

2

BEYOND THE HUGE oak doors lay a brilliantly lit entryway, a massive chandelier hanging from its vaulted ceiling. A pair of staircases rose at the back of the foyer, leading to a balcony on the second floor.

"This way," Caleb said, walking straight through toward the hall at the rear. Caleb led us down a thickly carpeted corridor, both expansive and claustrophobic with its wood paneled walls and poor lighting. It smelled of dust, but I couldn't see a single speck on any surface. Maybe houses this old always smelled of dust.

We came to a set of double doors, and Caleb flung them open, revealing an opulent blue-carpeted room. At the far end, somberly dressed strangers stood in a small clot, talking among themselves—but as soon as the door opened, conversation died. Everyone turned toward us. I resisted the urge to step behind my mom.

"Well. You made it, then," came a voice, thin with age but with a core of iron. An old woman sat in a wingback chair, one hand resting atop a polished black cane. Her hair was snow white and expertly coiled on top of her head, and a three-stranded string of pearls fell to her sternum.

"Mother," Mom said uncertainly. She reached over and gripped my shoulder. "Helen, this is your grandmother."

Iris Vaughan. The matriarch of the family. I knew next to nothing about her, except that she had cut her daughter out of her life swiftly and thoroughly. She crooked a finger, summoning me closer. I glanced at Mom, who gave me a short, sharp nod.

I walked toward my grandmother woodenly. Everyone was silent. Vaughan eyes stared at me from faces I recognized only dimly.

A young man at the edge of the group caught my eye. He was Black—the only person in the room with skin darker than a store-bought tan—and wearing thick-framed, hipsterish glasses. The corner of his mouth quirked in a sympathetic smile, and I mirrored it instinctively. I took the last few steps more confidently. I stood in front of my grandmother and spread my hands.

"What do you think?" I asked, chin tilted up. "Am I good enough?"

I heard someone give a little gasp behind me, and someone else murmur disapprovingly. But Grandma Iris's mouth twisted in wry amusement. "You certainly look like a Vaughan," she said. She peered at me intently. "Yes, I know that face." She settled back into her chair. "Welcome to Harrowstone Hall. It's good to have you back where you belong."

"She doesn't belong here," Mom snapped before I could think of how to respond.

Iris only regarded me with her unflinching gaze. "How does it feel being back?"

The answer was "inexplicably terrifying," but I didn't think calling my estranged grandmother's house creepy was a good opener. "It's very impressive," I said.

"I didn't ask whether the house is impressive. I asked how you feel."

If this was a test, I was failing it already. Whatever brief moment of confidence I'd seized dissolved into my usual social floundering. I resisted the urge to fidget. "I feel overwhelmed," I said.

"Hm." Apparently, this was an adequate answer—but not a good one. She tapped a finger against the head of the cane, then turned her gaze on Simon. "And this is the husband, then."

"Partner," Simon said amiably, waving generally at the room. "Nice to meet you all." Simon had no talent for handling subtext, and his unease was plain on his face.

"Interesting," Iris said. Much as I loved Simon, that wasn't usually the first word people chose for him. "Very well. We're all here, then."

Tension eased in the room, accompanied by the faint rustle of clothing as people shifted and relaxed. Maybe I hadn't failed that test quite as badly as I thought. I hadn't been escorted off the premises at least.

Iris seemed to be done with me. She turned her attention to Caleb, and I took the opportunity to fade back toward the wall.

"Hey," came a voice at my shoulder. I turned to discover the young man who'd smiled at me. He was tall and large-framed, with medium-brown skin, his round face wearing an expression balanced between friendliness and a slightly alarming level of curiosity. His hair was buzzed close to his scalp, and he wore a blazer with a school crest embroidered over the pocket, which, combined with the glasses, made him look both polished and hopelessly nerdy. He stuck out his hand. "I'm Desmond."

"Helen. But I guess you knew that. Are you . . . ? I mean, are we related?" I asked, knowing how awful it sounded that I had no idea. He had the right eyes, so black the pupil and iris were almost indistinguishable, but I couldn't be sure. I didn't recognize him. Or anyone else, for that matter.

"You don't remember? I'm Desmond. Your favorite cousin," he said, layering on the humor in an obvious attempt to gloss over the awkwardness.

"I have a favorite cousin?" I asked. "Sorry, I have a terrible memory."

"No need to apologize. Honestly, I always thought you were pretty annoying, anyway," he said with a crooked smile.

I laughed—too loudly. A man with pale blue eyes shot a glare at me, and I clapped a hand over my mouth.

Desmond leaned in conspiratorially. "Don't worry. We already know you're the black sheep of the family. We can't possibly think any worse of you, so there's no need to keep up appearances." He said it all with such smooth assurance that it took me a beat to realize he was joking. I laughed again, managing to keep it at a normal volume this time, and he grinned.

A blond girl with a short bob and freckles appeared at Desmond's elbow. She was petite in every dimension, with a delicate energy about her. She wore the same blazer as Desmond, though she'd paired it with a skirt rather than slacks.

"This is Celia—my sister," Desmond supplied.

"You don't remember us?" Celia asked curiously.

I flushed, mortified. It was one thing to be the estranged cousin coming for a visit, another to admit that I had no idea who they were.

"Oh! It's all right. I don't remember you either," Celia said quickly.

"Yes, you do. You were just saying—" Desmond started. Celia gave him a death glare, and he shook his head ruefully. "Celia has a compulsive need to make people feel comfortable," he explained.

"So do you need the full family tree, then?" Celia asked, as if she hadn't heard him.

"Please," I said gratefully. She beamed and turned on her heel so that she could point around the room.

"Right! So obviously you know Grandma Iris. That's Grandpa Leopold's brother, Eli, next to her." She'd pointed out a white-haired man who I'd hardly noticed before. He seemed to recede into the background of the room, even standing in the middle of it. "Then Caleb, obviously, and his wife, Sandra."

Sandra was blond like Celia, but hers clearly came from a salon. She held a glass of white wine with a lipstick-stained rim in both hands, fingers laced over it. Several other people had wine, but she was the only one who looked like she'd had more than a few sips.

"Then there's your aunt Victoria, aka our mother," Desmond said, taking over. "And that's her husband, Roman—"

"My father," Celia interjected. "Desmond and I are half siblings."

"Which I'm sure comes as a shock to her," Desmond said, and

she rolled her eyes at him. A pang of jealousy zipped through me at their gentle needling.

Celia's father was the one who'd glared at me for laughing. He stood by himself now, one hand in his pocket and the other clutching a glass of red wine tight enough that I worried it would break.

"That brings us to your parents, who I *assume* you already know," Desmond concluded. As if hearing him, my mother looked over her shoulder. She looked worried, but when she saw me chatting with Desmond and Celia, her expression eased.

"We're acquainted," I assured him. I watched his face and Celia's, searching for the familiar signs that something was wrong. The twitch of the lip, the flare of the eyes, the faint expression of disgust that came over people's faces. Or, worse, the vacant smile, the puppy-like adulation that swept people up when they first met me. At least when people hated me from the start, I knew what to expect. It was the ones who loved me I couldn't bear.

It was always one or the other. As if they could sense something was wrong with me. It repulsed some people. Others were drawn in—temporarily. Until they got some distance and seemed to wake up.

I couldn't see any of that now. Desmond had a sharp, perceptive look, but he didn't seem put off. Celia's eagerness to please didn't have the vague, placid feel I was used to. Caleb hadn't looked at me like that either—and certainly Iris hadn't. The realization filled me with a strange kind of excitement—almost hunger.

Was it possible things could be different here?

I realized I'd gone silent for a beat longer than was normal. I cleared my throat. "So, uh, you go to the same school?" I asked, indicating the crests on their jackets.

"Atwood School, yeah. It's a boarding school. Our family has pretty much always gone there," Celia said. "Or I mean . . ." She seemed to realize she'd just excluded me from the definition of "our family" and stammered. "What school do you go to?" she asked quickly, recovering.

"I'm homeschooled," I said, trying to sound casual about it.

Celia flushed. "Oh, right."

"Had some trouble at school, didn't you?" Roman asked in a low rumble. I jumped—I hadn't realized he was listening or that he had moved to stand only a few feet away.

My shoulders stiffened. I hadn't been sure what the family knew. Clearly, they knew enough. What had happened.

What I'd done.

"We don't have to talk about that," Desmond said, not even glancing toward his stepfather.

"I don't do well in a traditional school setting. I'm not good with rules," I said, fixing Roman with a flat look. My direct gaze always made people uncomfortable, and sure enough, Roman looked away.

"You won't like Harrow, then," Desmond said lightly. "It's nothing but rules."

"Have you picked a room yet?" Celia asked, the shift in subject graceless but welcome. "Ooh, you should take the Willows. It would suit your complexion."

I didn't know how to respond to the idea that you should pick a room like you'd pick a foundation shade. "We're staying at the Starlight," I said.

"That grungy motel in town?" Celia asked, faintly horrified. "But you can't. Everyone has to stay at Harrow."

"I'm sure it'll be fine," Desmond said, but he sounded nervous. "Did you tell Caleb?"

"Yeah, we did. Why would it be a problem?" I asked.

"It's nothing. Just kind of a superstition," Desmond said, waving a hand dismissively. But his eyes were still troubled. "What did Great-Grandpa Lawrence used to say? *Harrow is a jealous mistress.* We were always warned to return to Harrow every night while we were here or . . ."

"Or what?" I asked.

Desmond shrugged. "Who knows? Probably an old-timey thing from when this place got built. The locals didn't exactly love us. They even accused Nicholas Vaughan of being a vampire and tried to dig up his grave. Gnarly stuff."

"If Uncle Caleb says it's okay, it's okay," Celia said, as if to herself. Her fingers twisted together, pressed against the folds of her skirt.

"Chill, Celia. It's not the end of the world," Desmond told her, but she bit the inside of her lip and didn't reply.

I glanced over at Mom. She was talking to her mother and siblings. Simon was with her. I felt a surge of gratitude that he was here. We'd been on our own for years. I'd known my mother was lonely. It was one thing to be a single mom, another thing to be cut off from your whole family with a daughter who was—well, *troubled* was putting it mildly. Then Simon appeared, and he was just—perfect.

"So, Simon, what do you do for work?" I could hear Caleb asking, halfway across the room.

"Oh, I'm a homemaker," Simon said with a chuckle. "That is, I'm between jobs."

The hair on the back of my neck prickled with that sense of being stared at, and I glanced to my right. Roman was looking at me again, though he'd moved over to the clump of conversation that included my aunt Victoria and the older man—Eli. Roman's jaw tensed, a tendon flaring, and his dark brows drew together.

"For god's sake, Roman, you look like you're going to go after the girl with a cleaver," said Sandra, Caleb's wife, punctuating this with a swig of her wine. Silver bracelets clinked at her skinny wrists.

"Sandra," my aunt Victoria said chidingly, but didn't follow it up.

Sandra snort-laughed, a startlingly unsophisticated noise in the stiff atmosphere of the room. "Don't you know we're supposed to make the girl feel welcome?"

Caleb laid a gentle but restraining hand on her wrist. She twitched it away.

"Get out while you still can," she hissed in my direction, and then laughed, a braying sound that cut off as Caleb murmured something sharply to her. She reached for the wine bottle on the sideboard to refill her glass.

"Maybe you've had enough of that," Victoria suggested.

"Not nearly," Sandra shot back.

Victoria shook her head. "This is a difficult time for all of us," she said apologetically, and it seemed like she was talking to me but couldn't quite bring herself to look in my direction. My mother narrowed her eyes but said nothing.

"What I find difficult to understand is pretending that girl is in any way part of this fam—" Roman began in a voice clearly used to being the loudest in the room, but Iris clicked her cane against the floor, a barely audible sound that somehow commanded the room into utter silence.

"It is time," she said simply.

Time for the funeral, she meant. Time to put my grandfather to rest.

Somewhere above us, a bell rang, deep and sonorous. The sound permeated the room, filled my body until it overtook the beating of my heart. I could feel it vibrating in my bones. It felt as if it were lifting me, pulling me upward—and dragging me down.

"Helen?" Simon said.

I staggered, blinking. Everyone was already heading out of the room, conversation a low tumble of noise. I had no idea where the last ten seconds had gone. "Sorry. I'm a bit out of it," I said, shaking my head to clear it.

"The funeral is in the ballroom," Mom said, sounding distracted. "Let's head in." She put an arm over my shoulders, and we trailed after the rest of the guests. We went deeper into the house, down a wide hall to a set of double doors. Beyond the doors was a huge room, the walls pale cream and gold, a crystal chandelier glittering above. A modest set of chairs had been arranged in the center of the room facing the casket.

It hadn't occurred to me that the funeral might be in the house itself, but somehow, it made sense. The Vaughans and Harrow—they were entwined, inseparable. Even in death.

Mom touched my elbow gently and tipped her head toward some chairs near the back on the right. I headed toward them, but Iris's voice stopped me. "You'll sit by me, Helen." She stood at the front row.

I froze. I looked over at my mom—but she only tightened her lips. I swallowed and plodded over. My heels clicked dully on the parquet flooring, and I felt everyone's eyes tracking me. Iris took a seat. I sank down next to her, picking up the program that had been left on it. From my chair, I had a perfect view of the casket. And the body.

Leopold Vaughan, my grandfather.

Your grandfather is a man with high expectations, and he doesn't tolerate people who don't live up to them, Mom had once told me on a rare occasion when she let slip something about her family. Even now he seemed to scowl, his cheekbones jutting out from a face made gaunt by age.

I looked away quickly, dropping my eyes to the floor. I didn't want to see something I shouldn't—or rather, that I shouldn't be able to.

Eli walked up to stand in front of the casket. He was probably in his seventies—a strangely colorless man, with thin hair and papery skin that made him seem like a pale copy of a person. He cleared his throat. I glanced at the program.

The Recitation of the Masters it said. The what now?

"Today we mark the passing of my brother, Leopold Anthony

Vaughan, the sixth Master of Harrow," he said. His voice had all the warmth and character of wet concrete. "He was born in the winter of 1953. He was guardian of Harrowstone Hall for twenty-one years and sacrificed so that it might stand and so that his family might flourish. His father was Lawrence Eustace Vaughan, fifth Master of Harrow, born in August of 1931. He was guardian of Harrowstone Hall for thirty-three years . . ."

Were they going to list everyone who'd ever owned this place? Old dead men who didn't mean anything to me. I tuned out the droning voice, my eyes fixed on the casket so that I wouldn't look at the body—but my eyes strayed, and I couldn't help but see.

Someone had gone to a great deal of trouble to make my grandfather look natural, like he was sleeping, and it should have worked. Yet I knew every detail of what they'd done.

His eyes weren't just closed—they were glued to keep them from staring glassily. His jaw was wired shut so it wouldn't gape, so his purpled dead tongue wouldn't shove between his dried-out teeth set in withering gums. Gloved fingers had pinched and smoothed and arranged his lips into that stern line and caked his face with makeup.

They'd slit his skin at the arteries, slipping needles in. Tubes had carried his dark thickening blood out of him to the whirring accompaniment of a pump, and all that lifeless liquid had been replaced with a slurry of chemicals, leaving the meat of him unfit for even worms and beetles.

"*What a waste,*" a hoarse voice whispered at my back. I sucked in a short, sharp breath.

Eli's eyes flicked to me, and his words hitched, an almost

imperceptible pause. I dug my fingernails into my palms. Kept my expression blank. *Don't let them see,* I told myself. My tongue worked slowly behind clenched teeth, as if I was the one whose jaw had been wired shut.

"*You are already wasting time,*" the voice grated. Fingers I knew weren't real dragged across my neck. "*Don't fight it. Don't dismiss the truth simply because it cannot be true.*"

That voice—it was the voice I'd heard before. *I'm dreaming,* I thought. *This is all one of my nightmares, that's all.*

"*You are entirely confused. What you think is a dream is not. It's everything else that is suspect. And if you don't find a way to wake up, they'll devour you. Pay attention. Look.*"

I stared at the body and through the body. The bones sang. Not as clearly as the fox's bones, muted as they were by the unnatural preservation, but still I heard it, a low thrum I couldn't interpret.

As I stared, flowers bloomed, cradled within the cage of my grandfather's ribs. Long stems of pale bell-shaped blossoms, their interiors speckled with dark purple. *Foxglove,* I thought, and something twisted deep within me, like a memory almost surfacing.

"*There,*" the voice said. "*Now you begin to see.*"

I tore free of my paralysis with a half-swallowed cry. I jolted to my feet, and Eli finally paused in the midst of his litany, blinking slowly at me. Everyone was staring.

"I'm sorry, I need to—" *Run,* I thought, and had the sense not to say it.

Caleb stood, too. "It's all right," he said. "Go get some air. It happens." His voice was gentle.

I nodded convulsively and stumbled past the casket. I didn't look. I was too afraid if I did, I would find those eyes open, filmed over but staring at me.

I made a beeline for the French doors, fumbled with one, and got it open. I strode out blindly, gulping down air that seemed too thin to fill my lungs. I almost smacked into the stone railing that lined the veranda outside. Panicky energy roiled through me.

It had never been this bad before. The things I saw—the things I knew—they were impossible, but most of the time, I could ignore them. Most of the time, people had no idea what I glimpsed just under their skin.

I didn't know how I saw the things I did. Only that whenever it happened, I had this same taste in my mouth—damp earth. Just like in the dreams that chased me from house to house, town to town. Now I stood on Harrow's grounds, and if I turned around, I would be looking up at the spires that loomed over me in my dreams. I'd thought that coming here would give me—what? Clarity? Insight?

Answers?

But there was only a dead man and a family of strangers.

3

I FORCED MYSELF to go back in after a few minutes. I sat stiffly through the rest of the service, but there were no more spectral voices or ghostly fingers on my neck.

The burial took place in a small graveyard on the grounds, tucked back among the trees. I stood tensely beside Iris, but if anything, it was the most normal part of the whole affair. A motorized pulley system lowered the casket; everyone cast a ceremonial shovelful of dirt into the hole. As we left, a pair of laborers set to work filling in the grave.

Leopold was buried and gone. With that, our time at Harrow was over, and it was just as much of a mystery as it had been before.

I caught up with my mom as we walked back toward the house. She pulled me close and kissed the top of my hair. "You okay?" she asked.

I didn't answer at first. "I'm not sure," I admitted.

"I know we can be a lot," she said. It took me a moment to realize she was talking about her family. I'd never really thought of her as part of that *we*. It had always been us and them.

"They don't act like everyone else," I said slowly.

She frowned a little. "How so?"

"With me, I mean," I clarified. "When we met Caleb outside, and then Iris, and Desmond and Celia—we were just *talking*, and they didn't . . ." I trailed off.

"I know it's always been hard for you to make friends," she said carefully.

I made a choked sound, halfway to a laugh. "That's one way of putting it." I'd never had a friend. Not since I left school. I hadn't needed to learn that lesson more than once. "They don't look at me like other people do. Like they know there's something wrong with me."

"That's because there's nothing wrong with you," Mom said fiercely.

"You know that isn't true," I replied. "It has something to do with Harrow, doesn't it? The reason I'm like this. It's why we left."

"We left because it wasn't safe," she said, staring straight out ahead.

"What wasn't?" I pressed.

"I don't know," she confessed. She spoke slowly, each word considered. "Harrow is not like other places. Our family is not like other families. But it's different with you. It's always been different. I don't know why. Like the house was . . . more awake, maybe."

"You make it sound like it's haunted," I said with a nervous laugh.

"No," she replied, soft and distant. "There are no ghosts at Harrow."

I slowed to a halt. She stopped as well, turning toward me.

"Something happened to me here, didn't it?" I asked. "And we left, but it wasn't enough."

"I don't *know*," Mom repeated. She shook her head in frustration. "Helen, I don't *remember*." She put her hands to her face. "I never should have come today. It was selfish and stupid."

"It's not selfish to go to your own father's funeral," I told her, my voice cracking.

"Well, I'm fixing my mistake. We're leaving. Now," Mom said.

"Already?" I asked, surprised.

"Don't you want to leave?" she asked.

I hesitated. All day I'd felt that push and pull—fear of this place pitted against the hope that, by coming here, I would finally find some answers. "I don't want to stay," I said. "But I'm afraid that if I leave, I will never know what's wrong with me. Or how to fix it."

This time, she didn't tell me that there wasn't anything wrong with me. She pulled me in tight instead, her hand on my hair, my cheek pressed against her sternum. "I'm so afraid, Helen. I don't know why. I just have this sense, like—like this place will devour you, if it can," she whispered.

I squeezed my eyes shut. I could hear her heart beating, fast and frantic. "Let's get out of here," I said, and felt her sag with relief.

We went back in through the ballroom and made our way to the foyer, where everyone was shedding their coats and chatting among themselves. Caleb, Iris, and Victoria stood apart from the others.

"It's time for us to go," Mom said as we approached them.

"He's barely in the ground. You could stay for dinner, at least," Victoria said. She was like a softer, shorter version of Mom, with less color in her hair and less light in her eyes.

"I've done what I came here to do," Mom said. She started toward the door.

"Wait," Iris said. She stepped into our path, her cane clicking once on the marble tile.

"What, Mother?" Mom asked, sounding exasperated. "Are you going to order me not to go? I'm not a child anymore."

"You never did what you were told when you were a child, either," Iris said, and I was surprised at the amusement and affection that came through the words. "I can't force you to remain, Rachel, but there is something that you need to hear before you leave. You and your daughter."

"Whatever you have to say, you can say it right here and now," Mom said.

"It's a matter I think we would all prefer to discuss in private," Iris replied.

"Please, Rachel," Caleb said with an imploring look. "It's important."

She hesitated, looking between them. I saw the moment she surrendered, like a small vital piece of her had crumbled away. Her shoulders slumped. "Fine," she said, voice brittle.

"This way, then," Iris said. Simon started to follow us, but she stopped him with a look. "This is a family matter," she said.

"And they're my family," he said, plainly but firmly.

"Simon." Mom put a restraining hand on his arm. "It'll be all right. Wait for us here."

When Mom said it, he didn't object. He squeezed her hand once for support, and then hung back as we trudged after Iris, Caleb following in our wake. She led us to a study, the walls covered in sturdy shelves, a huge oak desk at the center. An ashtray sat on the desk, a single half-spent cigarette balanced on its edge. I imagined it pinched in Leopold's fingers, smoke curling from its end.

"What is all this about, Mother?" Mom asked as soon as the door closed behind us. "What more do you want from me?"

Iris didn't answer at first. She crossed to a deep leather arm-chair and sank into it with a sigh. Her face was lined and weary. "Believe it or not, this isn't about you, Rachel. Not everything is," she said. Caleb frowned, but he didn't intervene. Iris's gaze shifted to me. "Helen. Helen Vaughan. You only have that name because you're a bastard."

"Don't talk to her that way," Mom snapped.

"I'm merely stating facts," Iris said, waving a hand. "If you had married, she would have another name. But she is a Vaughan. Helen, this house is held in trust. The terms of that trust state that only a Vaughan can inherit."

"Why does that matter?" I asked. "It's not like I'm in line for the throne, or whatever."

"It matters, as it turns out, a great deal," Iris said. "Leopold altered his will shortly before his death. I have been granted a generous share of Leopold's monetary assets. But because of the trust and because I do not have Vaughan blood, I own nothing of the house. Nor, as tradition would normally dictate, does Caleb."

"Who does?" Mom asked, confusion written on her face.

"Your daughter," Iris said flatly.

For a moment, I couldn't process what she'd said. Then I gave a choked laugh. "That doesn't make any sense."

"No, it doesn't, does it?" Iris asked. "And yet it is so. The house and a sizable portion of Leopold's assets are yours."

"But why?" I asked, my mind trying to pick up the information and put it together in a way that was anything but completely absurd. "I don't even remember this place."

"This is a joke," Mom said.

"It isn't," Caleb said. He leaned against the edge of the desk, his arms folded loosely. "Rachel, he wanted to make things right. But he didn't know how to reach out. This must have been his way of fixing things."

"His way of controlling me," Mom spat back.

"Your father is dead. Whatever his motivations were, they hardly matter now," Iris replied. "What matters is that Harrow belongs to the Vaughans, and the Vaughans belong to Harrow. And that means you and your daughter."

"Helen. We're talking about millions of dollars, even aside from the house," Caleb said, leaning toward me with an earnest expression.

"I know." Did I? A million dollars wasn't even a real number in my head, just an image of Scrooge McDuck diving into his coins. "How much, exactly?"

Caleb looked at Iris. Her lips pursed briefly. "You are to receive Harrowstone Hall and assets equivalent to approximately forty million dollars," Iris said, almost reluctantly.

I rocked back. Forty. Million. That was forty Scrooge McDucks diving into forty swimming pool vaults of gold.

Forty million dollars, and this house.

Not for the first time since driving through the gates, I had the sense of a trap beginning to close around me.

"Tell her the rest," Mom said, voice tight. "Tell her what it means to inherit this house."

Iris looked at her for a long moment, then turned her unflinching gaze on me. "You are not merely inheriting a house. You would be Master—Mistress, in your case—of Harrow. And that comes with certain conditions."

"What conditions?" I asked, certain I wasn't going to like them.

"According to the traditions of Harrow, as codified in the trust, in order to become the Mistress of Harrow, you must remain in residence at Harrowstone Hall for a period of one year," Iris said. "Once you accept, you cannot leave the grounds for any reason until the year is up."

"A *year*?" I asked. Any fleeting excitement curdled at her words.

"One year in which you must prove yourself worthy of being the Mistress of Harrow," Iris continued, as if she hadn't heard. "If you make it through the year, you will undergo a ceremony called the Investiture. Only then will we learn if Harrow accepts you."

"If the *house* accepts me?" I asked. "You realize that sounds . . ."

Iris's eyes blazed. "It has been this way since Nicholas Vaughan built Harrow. The traditions have always been followed, and now is not the time to break them," she said.

Caleb looked frustrated. "We didn't even know about the new will until a few days ago. I know it's ridiculous. It's a relic of a different time. One that needs to be left behind." He grimaced at me. "But . . . that's a discussion for tomorrow."

I felt dizzy. Wealth beyond anything I could have hoped for in my lifetime, the ability to buy any kind of comfort my mom and Simon might want—but to stay in this place?

If something had happened here, I didn't remember it—or *anything* about the house, which was strange in itself. I was seven when I left. Old enough that I should have recalled *something*. But I only had the dreams.

"What if I refuse?" I asked falteringly.

Iris's mouth got small and hard. "My portion of the inheritance is protected. However, the rest of the terms are contingent on you. If you refuse, it all goes away. The house is sold. The remainder of the estate is distributed among any number of worthy and unworthy causes. You, your aunts, your uncles, your cousins, your mother—all receive nothing."

Mom shook her head. "You can't put this on her."

"I didn't," Iris said. "Your father's decisions are what led us here."

"Please," Caleb said. He stepped toward me and took my hands, holding them gently, and looked into my eyes. "I know this is strange and overwhelming. My father was a deeply flawed man. But this house has been in our family for nearly two hundred years. Please don't let this take Harrow from us."

I could barely breathe. The walls seemed to seethe closer every time I inhaled. I yanked my hands free of his. "I—I can't—" I said.

Mom grabbed my hand. "We're leaving," she snarled. She strode out, dragging me with her. Her face was pale with fury. "I am not letting them—I am not letting *him* drag you into this. That bastard. That rotten-hearted scum-sucking bastard."

She marched us through the foyer. Where was everyone? The whole house seemed empty, our footsteps echoing loudly. We reached the front door and stepped out into the gray light, and the openness made me stumble. Mom turned to me and pulled me into a tight embrace.

"I don't understand what's happening," I whispered.

"This is what they do, Helen. They'll do anything to control you. And you can't let them." She brushed her thumb across my cheek, and I realized that, at some point, I'd started crying.

The car was already waiting out front, Simon standing beside it. "I had them pull it around," he said. "Thought you might need a quick getaway."

"Oh god, how do you always know exactly the right thing to do?" Mom said. She got into the driver's seat, and I had just opened the back door when I heard Caleb calling.

"Helen. Your bag," he said. He was holding the backpack I'd somehow left behind.

"Thanks," I said automatically as he trotted over to me. I folded my arms over the bag.

"Helen—I'm sorry," he said. "That wasn't the way I meant things to go. I want you to know—whatever you decide, you belong at Harrow." His voice was kind and sincere, and in his eyes, I saw nothing but hope.

"It was nice to meet you," I said. "Goodbye, Uncle Caleb."

I fled.

4

MOM DROVE SLOWLY down the lane as deepening shadows dappled the road. I watched the light play across the car window, trailing my fingertip down the cold glass.

"Why don't we ever talk to them?" I asked as car tires crunched on gravel. "Caleb and Victoria and the rest. I've never even met them before."

"Leaving Harrow and leaving the family was the same thing, as far as my father was concerned," Mom said. "He made that clear, and I took it to heart. They felt like I'd abandoned them, and I felt like they'd abandoned me. I guess none of us was ready to be the first to forgive and reach out."

"Mom. The reason we left. Do you think . . ." My voice broke. "Was it something that happened to me, or was it something that I did? Was it like . . ."

She looked back at me sharply. "No. It wasn't like what happened at school."

"How can you be sure?" I asked miserably.

She let out a breath between her teeth. She didn't remember, which meant she couldn't give me the reassurances I wanted.

Simon reached out, resting his hand on her knee. She'd lost her family because of me, and now it was happening all over again.

"Forty million dollars is a lot of money," I said. "Staying here a year might not be so bad. I'm already homeschooled. And it's not like you'd have to worry about your job. I'm pretty sure Madison Street Copy and Print can survive without its assistant manager."

"We're doing fine," Mom said.

"No, we're not. It's starting again. Isn't it?"

She didn't answer, but her jaw clenched. "It isn't your fault," she said.

"But it is because of me." Everywhere we went, it was the same. At first people were friendly. Mom was gregarious, beautiful, charming. But eventually, they started to avert their eyes when they saw me. Hurry past our house. "She gives me bad dreams," one woman had said when she thought I couldn't hear.

That was when things would start to happen. Like the rats scrabbling in the walls that the exterminators couldn't find. Or the time we came home after only an hour away to find every surface of the house covered in fine black mold.

Like what had happened to that girl in second grade.

Sooner or later, it always caught up with us.

It all came back to Harrow and what had happened here. But I still didn't know what that *was*—or how I could escape it.

We were at the gates now. They were open as they had been when we arrived, and beyond them the road was wide and empty. But we weren't moving.

"Mom?" I asked. "Are we leaving?"

"I can't," she replied tightly.

"You don't owe them anything," Simon said. "Let's just go and leave this all behind us."

"No, I mean I *can't*." She pressed the gas pedal. The engine revved, but the car didn't move an inch. She threw the gear into park and then back into drive, but still the car acted like it was in neutral. "What the hell is going on?" Mom demanded.

At that moment, the engine sputtered and died. Mom swore. She turned the key in the ignition but got nothing—not even a whine of the car attempting to start. She threw her door open and got out. Simon and I followed.

"What's wrong with it?" I asked.

"Well, according to my extensive automotive knowledge, the problem is that the go part isn't going," Simon said, hands on his hips.

Mom pulled her phone out of her pocket. "Let me call Caleb. We can borrow a car, or . . . Damn it. I forgot—there's never any signal out here. We'll have to walk back to the house."

"It's not that far," I said, trying to sound upbeat in the face of Mom's distress.

She looked at me, face a wreck of worry. "I'll go. You stay here," she said. "I don't want you going back there. Simon, you stay with her."

I wasn't really eager to go back to that strange house. But I definitely didn't want her going alone. "I'll be fine by myself. The gates are right there. I can always make a run for it," I joked. Twenty feet to freedom.

Mom agreed reluctantly. "Stay put," she ordered, giving me a quick hug before the two of them headed back. I watched as they made their way down the narrow lane, vanishing swiftly behind the trees as it bent.

The wind stirred the branches, making leaves shiver and branches rasp. I shifted from foot to foot, then started to pace back and forth. I almost didn't see it—that slip of white among the trees. My gaze snagged on it as I turned, and I paused, trying to work out what it was.

A person.

The girl was about seven or eight years old, blond, wearing a simple white dress and no shoes. She crouched down just off the lane, her back to me. She seemed to be looking at something on the ground.

"Hey," I called, frozen at the edge of the lane. She didn't look up. Her shoulders moved, and I realized she wasn't just looking at something—she was digging at the ground in front of her. "Hey, are you okay?" I called again and drew closer, uneasiness prickling at my skin.

The girl scraped up handfuls of dirt from the ground and shoved them aside, moving with frantic efficiency. I approached cautiously, a hard lump in my throat. The ground was stiff with frost, and yet she kept digging, her hands red and chapped, one nail torn and bleeding.

"Your hands!" I said, reaching for her. She turned, and I balked.

She had no face—none that I could see. There was only the crazed distortion of an ocular migraine, like a jagged crack in glass shot through with strobing light.

"*We're not safe here,*" she said. Her voice was distorted, too, like I was hearing it underwater. *"Please. You have to find me."* She sprang to her feet and dashed away along a deer track that shot through the trees.

"Wait!" I called, and without thinking or hesitating, I plunged after her. The path snaked ahead of me. A flicker of white flashed around a bend in the narrow trail, out of sight. "Stop!"

"Find me," the girl said—and her voice was a whisper, but it echoed through the trees. I ran after her. *"Hurry."*

I spilled out onto a wider path, this one lined with gravel that crunched under my heels. White bell-shaped flowers were scattered here and there. I caught glimpses of the girl flickering away at each bend in the path, but no matter how much speed I put on, she kept darting out of sight.

I came around a bend and halted abruptly. I was standing at the edge of the cemetery. My grandfather's grave was a rectangle of brown earth among the green.

A young woman stood with her back to me, beside a worn headstone that was covered with clumps of moss. She wore a long gray dress and had a leather satchel at her hip. Her hair fell in waves around her shoulders, dark as the shadows among the trees. With a small hooked knife, she scraped some of the moss into a little glass jar before tucking it into her bag.

She twisted, looking over her shoulder, and spotted me. She scowled. Her face was sharp, almost fox-like. Not a comfortable face to look at for long, even from this distance. My heart beat fast in my chest, but I couldn't tell if it was fear or something altogether different.

I drew forward, step by faltering step, and stopped short of the gate. "Hi," I said weakly.

She arched an eyebrow. "What do you want?" she asked.

"Sorry. I didn't mean to—there was this girl," I said. "Blond, maybe seven or eight? I think she might be lost, so I was following her, but . . ." Except I hadn't really thought she'd been lost, had I? Why had I run after her? I couldn't remember now, and that sent a cold shiver of dread down my spine.

"It's not a good idea to follow strange things into the woods," the young woman replied.

"She's a girl, not a thing," I snapped.

The young woman gave me an appraising look. "She's not lost. She's not dangerous, but it's still not a good idea to let her lead you around," she said, as if this clarified things.

"She's . . ." I took a deep breath and dropped my voice to a whisper. "Is she a ghost?"

She gave a sharp, startling laugh, like a bark. "No. There are no ghosts at Harrow."

I flushed. "Right. Ghosts aren't real. Obviously."

"That's not what I said," she replied with exaggerated patience, as if I were a small child or a dimwitted pug. *There are no ghosts at Harrow.* My mother had said that, too. The girl sighed. "Haven't they told you anything?"

"I'm just—my name is Helen. I'm here because—I'm Leopold Vaughan's granddaughter? And there was a funeral, and . . ." I wasn't sure exactly what it was I was trying to explain.

"Yes. I know. You're Helen Vaughan, Mistress of Harrow.

Waltzing in and claiming what you think is yours, just like the rest of your family."

I blinked. "I'm sorry, what? Who told you that? I didn't—who *are* you?"

She peered at me. "They should have told you that, too," she said with a frown.

"Well, they didn't. And I'm not Mistress of Harrow. I'm not mistress of anything. I turned it down. I'm leaving," I told her with more confidence than I felt.

She studied me, considering. "It's got a hold on you already," she murmured. "You've got that look. If you walk away now, maybe it lets you go. But I doubt it." She seemed to come to some conclusion. She reached into her bag and pulled out a small leather pouch bound with twine. She held it out over the iron gate. "Here. Take this. It's not much, but it might help."

When I hesitated, she shook the pouch impatiently. I drew forward and stretched out my hand. She set the little pouch in it, and as she drew her hand away, her fingertips brushed mine. A shock went through me, quick and sharp, and I drew in a hiss of breath. It felt—

I wasn't sure. It had been so quick I couldn't tell if it had hurt.

"Don't run. It won't do any good," she advised, then turned away, done with me.

"Wait," I said. She looked back, annoyed. Repulsion, disgust, and instinctive anger I was used to, but annoyed was new. And I had no idea what I'd done to earn it. "Did I do something to offend you?"

"Not yet, but give it time," she said. With that, she turned on her heel and strode away, head held high, dark hair flung out behind her on the wind.

I looked down at the leather pouch still gripped in my hand. I picked apart the knot that held it shut and spread the square of soft leather out on my palm. In its center lay a dog's tooth, a sprig of dried yellow flowers, and a curl of moss.

And a small circle of metal the size of my thumbprint, stamped with a spiral.

A shadow fell across the grass. A pair of black dress shoes, polished to a shine, stood in front of me. Slowly, my eyes tracked up to the black slacks, the tailored jacket. The delicate queue of bell-shaped flowers pinned to the lapel. To the face obliterated behind a hooked sliver of broken light, like a migraine occlusion. I didn't need to see his face, though, to know who he was.

Leopold Vaughan.

Maybe I was still asleep, still dreaming, I thought, in my normal life, far from here. But, of course, that wasn't true. I was wide awake.

"*No. You aren't,*" my grandfather said, and I couldn't tell which he meant—dreaming or awake. No matter how hard I tried to focus on his face, I couldn't see it, that fishhook of fractured light concealing all but a wedge of jaw and throat.

"What do you want from me?" I asked. I tried to step back, but I couldn't move. The taste of damp earth filled my mouth.

"*You cannot escape this place by running,*" he said. "*The only way out of the spiral is through its center. Find the heart of Harrow, or it will devour you.*"

I'd always been able to hold on to a scrap of belief that the things I saw were only my imagination. That they weren't real. But this . . .

"Find the heart of Harrow," my grandfather said again, his voice shredding apart with every word until it was only the low moan of the wind—then even that was gone.

All that remained of my grandfather was a sprig of foxglove, lying where he had stood.

5

I STUMBLED FROM the woods, my heart hammering and my mind spinning, and stood for a moment, dumbfounded at the sight of Harrow towering before me, its cold gray stone radiating indifference. I'd come back here without meaning to, my steps carrying me surely, inevitably, back to the house.

"Helen?"

I almost screamed, managing a ladylike yelp instead, and rounded on Desmond. He was sitting at the base of a tree right beside me, writing in a notebook, a silver pen hovering just above the page. The paper was covered with small, precise script, but not in any language I knew—tiny symbols, dots and dashes and curlicues. "Sorry," I said. "You startled me."

"You're good. I mean, you're a complete mess, but no harm done." He took a closer look at me, brow creased. "*Are* you good, actually? You look . . ." He was polite enough not to finish his sentence.

"I don't know. I just—there was—" I gestured helplessly at the woods. It already felt less real. Maybe because Desmond seemed so grounded in reality, as if in defiance of this place.

"Harrow can be a bit unsettling," Desmond said carefully. "People say they see things."

"What kind of things?" I asked, hoping and fearing that I would recognize the answer.

He seemed reluctant to say. "You hear stories, that's all," he said. "Did *you* see something out there?"

I almost answered. Then I thought of how insane I would sound, babbling about vanishing girls and spectral voices and a strange woman collecting grave moss and handing out magic charms. "Nothing. Just spooked," I lied.

He nodded slowly, as if deciding whether he believed me. "Can I ask you something?" he said. I gave the tiniest dip of my chin. "Did you really hurt that girl at your school?"

I flinched. He knew then. And any hope I'd had that he might be a friend withered. "They told me I did."

"But did you?"

"I don't know," I admitted. All I remembered was the sound of screaming. The blood on my hands. I looked away, fingers curling into fists. "I don't want to have done it, but I can't be sure that I didn't."

"I'm sorry to bring up bad memories," he said, and I looked at him in surprise. He wasn't leaving. He wasn't looking at me in horror. If anything, there was sympathy in his eyes. "I only ask because I feel like I should know what kind of person you are. If you're going to be Mistress of Harrow and all."

"You know," I said. It came out as more of an accusation than I meant.

"About the will? Yeah, I overheard my mom and Caleb talking about it."

"Do you think everyone knows?" I asked.

"I doubt it. Roman would not have been able to keep quiet about it, at the very least," Desmond said.

"I haven't decided if I'm going to accept," I confessed.

Desmond looked surprised. "Don't you want to be rich?"

"I don't know. Has it solved all *your* problems?" I asked.

He laughed. "Fair point. I mean, given the chance to join this family, my dad ran the other way, so it's not like you're the only one."

"I'm sorry," I said, stricken.

He looked startled. "Oh, no. Not like that. We're really close, he's a great dad, he just doesn't want anything to do with"—he gestured—"all of this."

"I don't understand any of it," I said, shaking my head. "Leopold didn't even know me."

"Yeah, but your mom was his favorite," Desmond said. I gave him a puzzled look. "Seriously. He doted on her. Caleb and Victoria might as well not have even existed. Absolute golden child, to hear the stories, until . . ."

"Until I came along," I said. He shrugged, uncomfortable. "So, what, he felt bad about disowning her? Then why not leave everything to Mom?"

"Because Leopold was a manipulative son of a bitch," Desmond said.

"He was your grandfather," I said cautiously.

"*And* a son of a bitch," Desmond responded cheerfully. "Maybe he felt bad about cutting your mom off. But my guess? He wanted to punish her. Force her to come back by dragging you into everything."

"So she couldn't escape," I said.

Desmond grunted. "Grandpa Leopold used to say that Harrow was a spiral."

"What?" I asked, startled.

"It's the symbol of Harrow, actually," Desmond said. He turned the page in his notebook and began to draw—a curve winding inward. "It pulls you around and around, tighter and tighter. You try to escape, but the gravity of it won't let you go. The only way out is to find the center." He reached the innermost point of the circle and made a sharp downward slash—a straight line breaking free. "That's what Harrow feels like. No matter how far away you get, you always get turned back around."

Harrow was a spiral. Harrow was a spiral, and Leopold was a manipulative son of a bitch. He'd wanted me here. He could have just left me money, left me Harrow, whatever he wanted—but he went further than that. He made sure that if I refused, everyone *else* would suffer. I didn't have any idea why. But I knew I couldn't walk away without knowing the answer.

My grandfather's hand gripped my shoulder. "*There is only one way out of this,*" he said.

Desmond kept drawing in his notebook, tracing the spiral again, wearing a deeper groove in the page.

I was dreaming.

"Yes."

And if I left, I would never wake up. Harrow would always have this hold on me.

"Ah. Now you understand."

I didn't. Not really. But I would.

"Helen?" Desmond asked, all curiosity and concern, looking up from his page. "Are you okay?"

"I'm fine," I said, aware that I didn't sound fine at all. "I need to go."

I was barely aware of my body as I walked back around the side of the house. I followed a curving path as it led me inexorably to the front doors. The sky was growing dim.

Harrow's gravity pulled at me. I surrendered. I stepped over the threshold, and I thought there should have been some moment of change, some sensation that stole across my skin, but there was nothing except a shift in the light, the electric glow of the chandelier instead of the gray, fading light of evening.

Harrow had haunted me all my life. I'd thought that I could outrun it. But I couldn't. The ghost—or whatever it was—had told me as much. And so had Desmond, and so had that strange girl in the graveyard.

I couldn't run from Harrow. Not until I knew what it was and what it was doing to me. The only way out was to find the center.

Find its heart.

"Helen." Caleb had spotted me, standing there in the center of the foyer, and he strode across the floor. "I've got everything arranged. You can head straight—"

"I'll stay," I said.

Surprise flashed across his features. "This is a big decision. Don't let us pressure you."

"You're not," I said firmly. "I want to stay. I'm choosing to stay."

He stepped forward slowly. "You need to say it. You need to say that you accept." Something flickered in his eyes—worry, doubt, maybe even fear—but I took a deep breath and said the words.

"I accept," I said. With the words came a feeling of pressure in the air, as if something vast had turned its attention toward me.

"You agree to become Mistress of Harrow, with all that it entails?"

"I do." The feeling of pressure grew, and with it the sense of movement, and I had a strange thought, an image—Harrow, overgrown with dark tendrils like vines, growing up through the floorboards, behind the walls, twisting and grasping. Growing around me.

"You will belong to Harrow, be bound to it, and serve those that dwell here," he said.

"I will," I said, the words hard to force out through the thickness of the air. I felt transparent, as if there were no barrier anymore between the air and my body. It was all Harrow.

"Then it is done," Caleb said, and he slumped with relief. "It's done."

"*Good*," my grandfather said, as if he stood just behind me. "*Now the work can begin.*"

Deep in the heart of the house, a bell began to ring.

6

I ENDED UP in the Willows room after all. Celia would be pleased.

The walls of the Willows were covered in a dark green wall-paper textured with trailing leaves and vines that stretched vertically, from ceiling to floor. The room was at least twice as big as my bedroom at home, with plenty of room for the king-sized bed, a writing desk under the window, an armchair, and a wardrobe large enough to hold every piece of clothing I owned in triplicate.

The walls in this place were thick. I couldn't hear anyone moving around or hear the murmur of voices, the noises I was accustomed to at home. Our house was too small to ever truly feel alone. Here, the silence was oppressive, and I found myself pacing in a tight circle, my toes scrunching in the thick rug.

Finally, I grabbed my backpack and slung myself into the chair in front of the writing table. When I got this twitchy, there was only one thing that could settle me.

I dug through the backpack until I found a leather case with a bone toggle. I set the stiff, shoebox-sized container on the desktop and opened it, checking briefly to make sure that everything was in place and intact: wire clippers, pliers, spools of wire, tiny plastic cases of beads and fasteners, embroidery floss, a carefully packed hollowed-out robin's egg . . . the list went on.

I took out the piece I'd been working on. The scapula had come from a fawn and was the size of my palm. Into its surface I had already carved twisting lines, curlicues that defied any kind of order or sense but gave the impression of endless movement. I had begun the work of twisting silver wire around the scapula, decorated with beads and other collected objects.

I never knew what a piece was going to be until it took shape under my hands. The scapula was an easy one—it was already most of the way to what it wanted to be, and so there was only the quiet centered focus of twisting a wire, threading a bead, securing a bit of feather or bone—a flow of decisions I was hardly conscious of making. Life and movement turned to the stillness of death, made to sing again of running.

The fox skull was harder. In the days since Grandpa Leopold died, I kept thinking that I had the glimmer of an idea, and I'd get out a length of wire or a paintbrush or a chisel, and then sit there staring, the shape of the piece gone from my mind like so much wind-scattered smoke.

I twisted the last bit of wire into place around the scapula, hiding its sharp edge, and sat back. The roil of nervous energy within me had settled, and cold, clear purpose remained.

Find the heart of Harrow.

A tentative knock sounded on the door. Mom entered without waiting for me to reply. "Hey," she said. She took a seat at the end of the bed and leaned her head against the post.

I folded my hands in my lap and looked down at the carpet, digging my stockinged toes in and leaving dimples in the pile. "I should have talked to you before I said yes."

"You shouldn't have said yes at all." She looked too drained and exhausted to be angry.

"I know it's not fair to you." I hadn't been thinking about Mom at all, and now guilt settled in my chest like a stone in river mud. I wanted to tell her about what I'd seen, but how could I begin? We'd lived a careful life, speaking of certain things and not of others.

"All I want is to protect you," Mom said, her face crumpling.

"You don't have to," I told her.

"Of course I do. I'm your mom," she said. She picked at a stray thread on the bedspread, twisting it back and forth. "There's so much about this place you don't know."

"Because you never told me."

"I couldn't. I can't," she said. "There are things we don't talk about, and things I don't remember, and things I remember that I can't be sure are true."

She rubbed her temples, then sagged with a sigh.

"I used to love it here, you know. Victoria and Caleb and I would go swimming in the pond every day during the summer and roam all over the woods. I used to play with . . . I can't remember her name. Laura? Lena?" She trailed off. "It was so long ago. Maybe Caleb would remember."

I caught her hand. "It's going to be okay, Mom. But I need to stay. I have to find out what this place is," I said.

"I know what it is," she replied, head tilted, gaze unfocused.

"What?" I asked.

She looked at me with hooded eyes. "A cage."

The dream always began the same.

I was looking up—and up and up—at Harrow. The spires tilted dizzyingly above. The taste of soil filled my mouth, and I could not move. Then the dreams wandered their own paths—through corridors of stone or among the twisted trees, where things of shadow and sharp teeth waited for me.

Tonight, I wandered the house. I watched its occupants playing out nighttime rituals. My mother curled with her back against Simon, sleepless and staring at the wall as he murmured sleepy words of comfort into her hair. Caleb sat at his desk in his study, an old, handwritten leather book open beside him, a glass of whiskey in his hand, untouched, with the ice slowly melting. Grandma Iris slept alone in a bed far too large for one person. Celia whimpered fretfully as dreams convulsed through her while Desmond snored, a book abandoned next to him on the bed.

In the woods, shadows moved with nothing to cast them, darkness within darkness. Their fingers were long and sharp, their necks stretched, their limbs distended. They were looking for something, but I didn't know what.

On a forest path, the girl in the gray dress walked slowly and sang softly.

>*"There was a maiden, golden-haired,*
>*Came to the fold, came to the fold.*

She walked among the shadows there.
Her bones are white, her blood is cold."

She paused in her singing. She looked behind her. Back at Harrow. Back at me. "Is that you?" she whispered. She sounded bewildered. She sounded hopeful. "Where have you been?"

But I was rushing away, rushing down, falling and falling and falling beneath Harrow's stones, and I looked down. Below me opened a spiral, an endless seethe of movement, dragging me in. A voice whispered in my ear.

"Find the heart of Harrow."

Then I woke, that familiar taste of soil making me gag. Harrow's bell was ringing. And I wasn't in my bed like I should have been.

Instead, I stood on the lawn with frost-rimed grass crushed beneath my bare feet, a pale mist of rain prickling my skin and leaving drops trembling in my hair. The morning sun stretched my shadow out along the grass. My hands were caked with dirt, and more was packed under my fingernails. I shivered, my breath a plume from my lips, confusion and fear swirling through me.

"What the hell are you doing out here?" a rough voice asked. I jumped and turned. Roman, Aunt Victoria's husband, scowled at me from a few feet away. He'd ditched his funeral attire for a brown woolen sweater over a button up and slacks. His jaw-length hair must have once been black but was now mostly gray, parted in the middle. He was the sort of guy who seemed to have the twenty-year-old version of himself superimposed over him, and I could picture the arrogant prep school kid he'd been, his jaw sharpened, his hair jet black, but the haughty sneer the same.

Something about the sight of him scraped the fear from my skin, left me raw and prickly. "What do you care?" I snapped.

"It's not safe to wander these grounds," he said, but the scorn in his voice belied his apparent concern.

"I'm not wandering. I'm on the front lawn," I said, head cocked. Harrow may have terrified me, but Roman did not. I focused on him, on that sneer. I focused on hating him, because that was so much safer than the question of how I'd found myself standing out here in the cold. "Everyone keeps saying it's dangerous here. No one will say why."

"Since you're not staying, you won't have to find out," Roman replied.

"I am staying, though." I should have shut up. But I couldn't help it. "Didn't you know? Grandpa Leopold left the house to me. So I live here now. Can you believe that?"

For about half a second, the satisfaction of seeing the expression on his face made it worth it. And then the bafflement turned to rage, and I realized I'd made a poor calculation. His face crumpled into anger, his hands knotting into fists.

"What are you talking about?" he demanded, reaching for me.

I stumbled back. Once upon a time, my mom had promised that I'd outgrow the clumsiness of puberty, but she'd been wrong. My heel caught against something—a rock, a delicate blade of grass, an air molecule—and I thumped flat on my ass with a squawk, the dew and rain soaking through my cotton pajama bottoms instantly as Roman loomed over me.

"Get away from me!" I shouted. Or at least, that was the intent. It came out as more of an angry mutter.

"I'm not going to hurt you, idiot," he said, and bent down to grab me by the arm. He hauled me roughly to my feet. He marched toward the house, dragging me at a loping stagger beside him. My mom and Simon were already in the foyer.

"Caleb!" Roman roared as we entered.

"Roman? What are you doing?" Mom demanded, rushing toward us. Roman jerked me back behind him. I yelped.

"Let her go right now," Simon commanded. It was the fiercest I'd ever seen him. It was like watching a goldendoodle growl at a rottweiler.

Caleb appeared at the head of the stairs, carrying a newspaper and a mug of coffee, and when he saw us, his eyebrows shot up. "Let her go," he said at once. He didn't raise his voice at all, but his tone was commanding.

"What is she talking about?" Roman asked. Footsteps sounded in the hall—Victoria appeared, Celia at her heels.

"What's going on?" Victoria asked, taking in my disheveled state.

"Would you *please* let me go?" I said, tugging on my arm.

"Not until—"

"Roman," Caleb snapped, and Roman relented. I tucked my arm against my side, rubbing it even though it didn't actually hurt. I wasn't afraid—just pissed—but I was also unsettlingly aware of the strength in Roman's grip. If he'd wanted to hurt me, he could have.

"Now," Caleb said, "Roman. What on earth do you think you are doing?"

"This girl is claiming that Leopold left her the house," Roman said.

"Ah," Caleb said, descending the stairs. The shouting had drawn the rest of the household. Desmond appeared to our right. Sandra stood at the banister on the landing above us, and as we all waited in expectant silence, Eli stepped in from behind me, carefully wiping his shoes on the mat. Simon had a restraining hand on Mom's shoulder. She looked ready to tear Roman into tiny, bite-sized pieces and feed those pieces to feral cats. I was all for it at this point.

"Well?" Roman prompted.

Caleb had gotten halfway down the stairs, and there he paused. "I intended to make a formal announcement at breakfast. It's true. Leopold altered the trust. He left the house to Helen."

Pale fury snapped in Roman's eyes. Celia bit her lip so hard I was worried she would draw blood. Not a fan of conflict, I guessed. Desmond just watched me, curious and unconcerned. But then, he'd had warning.

Sandra was the first to break the silence—with a high, sharp peal of laughter. "Oh lord," she said. "What a fucking loon. Well, cheers. Welcome to the family." She toasted me with an imaginary glass and, still laughing and shaking her head, went back the way she had come.

"This has to be a mistake," Roman said. "How can the other—"

"Roman," Caleb snapped, and this time he was out of patience, glaring openly. His rebuke was so sharp that, for a moment, I didn't even notice what Roman had been saying, and once I did,

I couldn't make sense of it. The other what? Whatever he'd been about to say, Caleb really didn't want him to. "Let's all take a beat, and we can discuss this after we get some caffeine in our systems."

Roman paused, and for a moment, I thought he might refuse and we'd have a shouting match right here in the foyer. Then he shook his head, and I recognized it as defeat. He stalked off, but before he did, he cut me a look. "You're not Mistress of Harrow yet," he said, under his breath.

His words sent a shiver of anxiety through me. He was right. I wasn't Harrow's mistress just because Leopold had said I should be. First, I had to survive the year.

A year suddenly felt like a very long time.

I showered and dressed, and by the time I was done, I had almost shaken the chill of the outdoors. The skin around my wrists was oddly tender, like a sunburn, and when I pulled on my shirt, the same not-quite-pain lanced across the skin at my sternum and my neck. But the sensation faded quickly, and I told myself it was my imagination.

That excuse was wearing thin.

Looking to hunt down Caleb or Mom, someone who might actually *talk* to me, I walked out into the hall. I checked Mom's room, but it was empty. I didn't know where else she would have gone, so I set out toward the entryway, figuring I would eventually run into *someone*.

Quickly, I discovered that I had no idea where I was going. I'd thought I was heading for the foyer, but I must have taken a wrong turn. I was on the ground floor, at least, in a hallway with a carpet the color of a three-day-old bruise. In the distance I heard the strains of a piano. At least that meant there was someone there. I followed it and soon found myself stepping into a room adorned with jewel-toned peacock wallpaper and rich red cherry furniture.

A piano the color of old bone sat in the center of the room. Celia perched on the bench, coaxing out a melancholy tune that shivered with the kind of hope destined to be shattered. The last notes slipped into silence, and her fingers stroked the keys on their way to curl in her lap.

"That was lovely," I said.

She jumped and twisted, snatching something off the seat beside her—a silver pen. A look like guilt flashed over her face before she beamed. "Thanks," she said. "I'm not really supposed to be in here, though."

"Why not?" I asked.

"It's Jessamine's piano," she said.

"Who?" I asked, puzzled.

She pointed toward the wall, so I turned—and sucked in a breath. A portrait hung on the wall: a young girl with honey-colored hair and a white shift dress. It was the girl I'd seen outside. There was no migraine haze to hide her face from me now. I could see the dark eyes that marked her as part of the family.

In her hand was a stalk of white foxglove.

"Jessamine," Celia repeated. "Caleb and Sandra's daughter. She passed last year. I guess she was too young for you to have really met her," she said, biting the corner of her lip.

"I didn't even know she existed," I said, shaking my head. "How did she die?"

"A heart thing?" Celia said uncertainly. "It happened really suddenly."

"I'm sorry," I said, struggling under how utterly insufficient the words were. *A heart thing.* Like Leopold.

A thought came to me, born of panic and the increasing conviction that I had made a mistake coming here.

Harrow had devoured them both.

Celia offered a fragile smile. "She was a prodigy. I like to think that if she could hear, she would be happy someone was making music with it. But it was her special thing, you know? And hearing someone else play, it just makes everybody sad. Especially Uncle Caleb." She drooped. "You won't tell, will you?"

"I won't," I assured her. She didn't respond at first, and before I could think of something more to say, the silence started to teeter on the edge of awkward. I wasn't good at this—conversation. Human interaction. I scrambled for something to say. "Maybe you can help me. I think I'm lost. This place is a bit of a maze."

"Literally," she said with a little laugh.

My brows drew together, uncomprehending.

"Oh, um, the house is supposed to remind you of a labyrinth," she said. "It's not actually—the corridors connect up with each other and everything so you can get through, it's just a feeling, but Nicholas Vaughan was obsessed with the whole idea. Where were you trying to go?"

"I'm not actually sure," I confessed. "I don't really know what to do with myself."

"I can show you around," Celia offered. "At least the basics. A full tour would take days."

"That would be really helpful," I said with feeling. I paused. "You don't seem to be upset about me inheriting the place."

She shrugged. "It doesn't really change anything for me."

"But your dad was angry," I pointed out, cautious, not sure if she'd turn defensive.

She frowned, her chin tilting up in a way that made her nose look even shorter than it was. "I guess he thought Mom might have gotten the house? Uncle Caleb and Grandpa Leopold—well, they hadn't really been talking for a while."

"She didn't change her name when she got married?" I asked, remembering what Iris had said—only a Vaughan could inherit the house.

"Dad changed his name, actually," Celia said. "He's very progressive."

Roman didn't strike me as progressive. The sort to buck tradition in the hopes of a chance at inheriting though? Possibly.

I nodded, accepting her explanation, and let her lead me down the hall.

"It's just about impossible to find anything, so you have to memorize the rooms you have to go to a lot," Celia told me as she showed me around. "Unless you're Desmond. He says it's all really regular patterns if you look at it right, nested inside each other, but I can't see it. So either I stick to the rooms I know or I find Desmond."

Desmond was right, I thought. There was a pattern here. A strange sameness to the turns, like the same shape rotated in different arrangements. That sameness made it impossible to tell where in the pattern you were. Walking through the house felt like a recurring dream. Like you knew you'd been here before and something dreadful waited just ahead, but you couldn't stop yourself from walking toward it.

I was glad when our tour brought us out on the back veranda, into the cool air and away from the tightening gyre of corridors.

We weren't the only ones finding refuge under the open sky. Desmond sat on the stone railing at the edge of the veranda, his notebook balanced on his knee, this time scribbling with a cheap ballpoint pen.

"Morning," he said.

"So it is," I replied. Celia hopped up on the railing next to him, her heels swinging. "Celia was just giving me the tour."

"What do you think of your kingdom, then?" Desmond asked.

I spoke carefully. I had the feeling that direct questions weren't going to get me too far, but maybe I'd learn something if I came at it sideways. "It's all just so weird. I haven't even seen most of this place, and it's mine. I don't even know how big it is. The grounds, I mean."

"Forty-six acres," Desmond said immediately. "So you at least have plenty of room to wander."

"It's not like I ever go out anyway," I said. Though I was already feeling the difference between wanting to stay at home and not being allowed to leave. I leaned against the railing of the veranda and looked down the cascading levels of patios that led to the lawn.

"And it's not like there's anything in Eston worth leaving for,"

Desmond said. "Unless you want to watch last season's movies in a theater with sticky floors. And hey, at least you'll have the witch for company."

"The witch?" I echoed, eyebrows shooting up.

"*Desmond*," Celia chided him, but he ignored her.

"*Beware, beware, the Harrow Witch, with soul as black as blackest pitch*," he intoned with a grin that said he knew he was annoying her. "The witch is a local legend. It goes back all the way to when Harrow was built. Nicholas Vaughan was a weirdo, and he liked the locals being afraid of him, so I think he encouraged all the stories about this place. Then they kind of took on a life of their own."

"They're not just stories," Celia said quietly.

Desmond shook his head. "You don't really think Harrow's haunted, do you?"

Celia's cheeks turned pink, and she didn't answer.

"So there isn't really a witch?" I asked, still puzzled.

"No," Desmond said at the same time as Celia said, "Yes." They looked at each other, and Celia got pinker.

"There's this girl," Desmond allowed. "She's just the groundskeeper's daughter, but Celia started joking that she was the Harrow Witch a few years ago and I guess it stuck."

"I wasn't the one that started calling her the witch. You were," Celia objected.

"No, it definitely wasn't me," Desmond said. "Maybe it was . . ."

He stopped himself, biting back the words. *Maybe it was Jessamine*, I thought he'd been about to say.

I thought of the girl in the graveyard, with her knife and her withering stare. The way her eyes had seemed to slice right through me—as if she could see below my skin, the way I could see.

I hadn't been able to see her that way, though. It wasn't like I had been trying to, of course. But there had been something about her, something that made me think that even if I did, I could never peer within her. Never know her secrets unless she let me.

"I think I met her," I said softly. "She was in the graveyard yesterday."

"You talked to her?" Desmond asked, sounding intrigued. I nodded, and he looked impressed. "I don't think she's said more than ten words to me, ever."

I hardly heard him. I touched the pocket where I'd stowed the pouch she'd given me. I couldn't get her face out of my mind—that narrow chin, those gray-green eyes, the dark freckles scattered across her cheeks. She wasn't pretty. She was too harsh, too strange, to be pretty. She made me think of the skull still resting on the desk back in my room. That unsettling beauty, those sharp teeth. "What's her name?" I asked.

"Bryony. Bryony Locke," Desmond supplied. It felt like I'd known it all along. *Bryony.*

Behind us, a bell rang, making me jump. "That's the bell for lunch," Desmond explained.

Lunchtime already? I was startled to realize how much time had passed while Celia and I wandered the halls.

Desmond hopped down from his seat on the railing and headed in. Before I could follow, Celia grabbed my sleeve. She didn't look at me, fixing her eyes on a point on the ground instead, and her voice was so quiet I had to strain to hear it.

"They say the witch knows the names of all of Harrow's shadows," Celia said. "If you want to know Harrow's secrets, you should talk to her."

"You know something, too," I said softly. "Don't you?"

She looked up sharply, her lips parted as if she was about to say something. But she only shook her head once. And then she was gone, scurrying toward the house with her shoulders hunched forward. I watched her go, and then I turned, looking back toward the trees, which rippled slowly in the wind.

"Beware, beware, the Harrow Witch," I murmured. And then, to myself, I whispered her name. "Bryony." Like an incantation, like a charm.

In the woods, something moved: a long and ragged shape that flowed unnaturally from tree to tree. As if the shadows had heard me and had stirred at her name.

But surely that was only a trick of the light.

7

SOME PEOPLE SAY houses are like living things. It had never felt true in the houses we rented, with their dull brown carpets and popcorn ceilings. I understood it now, though, among the hallways splaying out like veins and arteries, the rooms like organs. When people began to leave Harrow, it was like watching an animal drained slowly of blood.

Roman went first; he had some incomprehensible but vitally important job in finance, and the way he talked, the global economy would collapse if he wasn't there at nine o'clock sharp on Monday morning. Sandra vanished around the same time. Then the teens left, chauffeured back to their lofty private school, and then Victoria. That left me, Mom, and Simon, along with Caleb, Eli, and Iris. Eli and Iris were permanent residents of Harrow, and Caleb was staying to "ease the transition."

The house felt dead with half the family gone, but you could learn a lot from a corpse. It was time for me to perform an autopsy. If I was going to spend a year in this house, I had to understand it. I had to know what Leopold had meant—what lay at the heart of Harrow.

So I set out to explore. There were an unfathomable number of rooms—studies and sitting rooms, libraries and bedrooms, storage rooms and rooms with no discernible function.

I kept getting turned around, finding my course folding back on itself so I was back where I started. Once I opened the door to what I was absolutely convinced was my own room only to find a tiny, closet-sized chamber, the walls covered with bizarre paintings: strange creatures rising behind mountains; a woman greeting a sunrise, the sky filled with writhing tentacles; six-legged hounds coursing after a distant fleeing figure. They were all signed the same way: *Annalise Vaughan.*

It would have been tempting to call the house random or mad or jumbled, but it wasn't. It was precise in its confusion, careful as clockwork. The whole house felt like a machine, but what purpose it had, I couldn't say.

I spent every day alternating between stiff, formal meals with Iris, keeping up with my homeschool curriculum, and exploring the house. It wasn't getting me anywhere. I wasn't anywhere closer to understanding why Leopold had left Harrow to me or what it meant to find Harrow's heart. But the house had an obsessive hold on me. Every free minute, I found myself walking the corridors. Even when I wasn't, I pictured their turns, counted doorways in my mind.

Find the heart of Harrow. Find the heart of Harrow.

Every time I thought I'd explored all of it, I found another room that I was certain I'd never seen before. One morning, wandering out of habit more than purpose, I came across a hall that I didn't think I'd been down before. I noticed it mostly because of the words painted in gold leaf on the lintel above the door on the left side of the hall. EX ALIIS MUNDIS VERUM.

I tried the knob. It turned only a quarter of an inch before stopping. Locked. I was about to turn away when the door suddenly opened, and Eli peered out at me. "Yes?" he said.

I blinked, feeling like I was trying to think through a fog. "I'm sorry. I was just exploring," I said.

"And you've discovered the promised land," Eli replied with a chuckle. I stared at him blankly. "The Vaughan family library. My preferred haunt," he amended.

"Oh. Right." Haunt was a good word for him. He didn't seem much more alive than a ghost. I'd never met someone with so little presence. It was like he was a tissue paper tracing of a man. Colorless and thin, with a care to his movements, like he thought he might snag on something and rip if he moved too quickly.

"Are you all right, dear?" he asked.

I put a hand to my cheek. The skin of my palm felt shockingly cold. "I don't know. I feel weird," I admitted.

"Come in a moment," he said, and stepped aside to usher me in. Beyond him was an expansive room covered floor to ceiling in packed bookshelves. I could make out a handful of titles on the shelves nearest the door. *The Book of the Words, The New Revelation, The Sea of Stars, The Magus,* and *Transcendental Magic, its Doctrine and Ritual.* They looked old—nineteenth century, at least.

My head was suddenly pounding, and nausea roiled in my gut. Eli herded me over to a leather armchair, and I sank down into it with a groan.

"I think I have a migraine," I said. "It came on suddenly."

"You said you've been exploring," Eli said. He pressed a glass of water into my hand. I managed a sip, but my stomach rebelled. I pressed the glass against my forehead instead.

"Just a little bit each day," I said, but that wasn't quite true, was it? Once I actually thought about it, I couldn't remember doing much of anything *other* than exploring. "I thought I'd poke around for a few minutes after breakfast," I said falteringly.

"And you've been wandering the house this whole time?" Eli asked. I looked at him blankly. "Helen, breakfast was at eight. It's three o'clock in the afternoon."

"That's impossible," I said, but he held out his watch for me to check, and it was 3:07. I gave him a baffled look. "I thought it had been fifteen minutes."

"I'm sorry, Helen. I should have noticed you were wandering the halls. It didn't occur to me . . ." He sighed. "The halls of Harrow have unique properties. They'd give *anyone* a headache, but some people are more sensitive than others."

"You're telling me that Harrow gave me a migraine?" I asked. I wished it didn't make perfect sense.

"As I said. Some people are more sensitive. Annalise Vaughan herself wandered the halls obsessively at night."

"Annalise Vaughan. I think I saw some of her paintings," I said. The headache still had a solid grip around my skull, but the cool glass helped at least a little bit. "Who was she?"

"She was the wife of Nicholas Vaughan, the founder of Harrow," Eli said. He stood with his hands behind his back in the pose of a history professor giving a lecture. "They were occultists—dedicated to their belief in the supernatural. Annalise Vaughan was a medium. She claimed to be able to visit other worlds via astral projection. Nicholas Vaughan believed that her abilities were the key to unlocking vast realms of knowledge and power. Thus, the words above the lintel: *Ex Aliis Mundis Verum*. From other worlds, truth. He believed that this valley was a place of particularly powerful connections between the worlds. That's why he built Harrowstone Hall on this spot."

"And made it into a maze?" I asked.

"A labyrinth," Eli said. I couldn't tell if he was agreeing with me or correcting me. "He worked with a friend of his, Dr. Samuel Raymond. Dr. Raymond had some unique theories about the brain. He believed that he could use architecture to influence the mind."

"I see," I said carefully, not sure how I was supposed to react. A medium—wasn't that a kind of psychic? Maybe Annalise Vaughan had been like me, and my ability to see things that I shouldn't was inherited somehow.

"Nicholas Vaughan believed some very strange things," Eli said, not without humor.

"But there are strange things at Harrow," I said, and stared at him, trying to see beneath that papery skin. But I had only the sense of old sorrows and bitter guilt, and then even that slipped away, leaving an old man in front of me with hooded eyes and an unreadable expression.

"These old houses will play tricks on you," was all he said.

Eli helped me find my way back to my room after that. I dragged myself into bed, barely getting my shoes off, and pulled the blankets over my head.

I'd had migraines all my life, but rarely like this. The dimmest light sent a needle through my eye, and I felt like I was going to vomit if I moved at all. All there was to do was curl up inside the pain and wait.

Gradually, I became aware that I wasn't alone. I sat up slowly, opening my eyes reluctantly.

My grandfather stood by the door.

I shrank back against the bed, fear fluttering like moth wings against the skin of my throat, before steeling myself. "What do you want?" I asked. He only glared at me from behind the fractured glass pattern that blurred out half his face.

"Bryony said that there aren't any ghosts here." Still no answer. "If you aren't a ghost, what are you?"

The mattress sagged, weight settling beside me. The edge of my vision cracked, strobing with the crazed rainbow of migraine aura. Jessamine. She hummed softly, brushing her fingers through my hair.

"I'm lost in the woods. I want to go home. Help me get home. I want to go home."

"What *are* you?" I asked, desperate.

Leopold's mouth opened as if to answer, but flowers burst from it instead of words, stalks of bell-shaped blooms that blackened and fell to the floor in a silent rain of decay. His whole body collapsed, spilling to the ground in a tide of earth and dying flowers and scuttling beetles, and I sat on the bed, alone, and the ghosts that weren't ghosts were gone.

Only the pain remained. I shut my eyes and tried to breathe through it. Time would pass. The pain would fade.

I didn't sleep, but the agony was a kind of unconsciousness—the rest of the world shut out, irrelevant. Time became a meaningless slurry. I couldn't tell if minutes or hours were passing. My mother came in at some point—spoke to me; pressed cool, wet cloths against my forehead; tightened the curtains so no traitorous light could invade.

I must have finally fallen asleep because when I heard voices outside my door, they seemed to be in the middle of a conversation that I hadn't heard the beginning of.

"Of course I am concerned," Iris was saying—though she sounded as calm and composed as ever. "If it doesn't accept her, we could be in a great deal of trouble. But I am *more* concerned about the house sickening her."

My breath was loud in my ears. I held still, straining to hear.

"We ought to have anticipated that," Eli said. "She's been gone a long time. Harrow is rigid, and she's grown beyond its boundaries. Its attempts to fit her back into its patterns are proving too much for her. We should slow down."

"And risk running out of time," Caleb countered. "If Harrow is set against her and the Other doesn't recognize her, she'll be torn apart come the Investiture. Integration will be impossible."

The Other? Hadn't Roman been about to say something like that when Caleb interrupted him? What was *the Other*?

And what did he mean, "torn apart"?

"Perhaps if we told her more . . ." Eli began.

Caleb made a frustrated noise. "Maybe it would help. Or maybe it would draw the Other's attention before she's able to withstand it or sever their connection completely. I still think that the safest thing is to allow her to learn on her own. For now—"

"For now, we leave her in the dark," Eli said, resigned.

"It's for the best," Caleb replied, not sounding much happier. "I'll go check in on her." There were a few more words exchanged, and then the door creaked open all the way, and Caleb's footsteps thudded toward me, impossibly loud. I kept still, my breath deep and even.

Caleb touched my shoulder. "Helen, wake up. I brought you something."

I eased my eyes open a crack, not having to feign the difficulty of focusing on him. He helped me to sit up before putting a white pill and a glass of water into my hands.

"What's this?" I asked, my voice a croak.

"A remedy Eli makes," Caleb said. "It should help."

"It's a migraine cure?" I asked skeptically.

Caleb shook his head. "Not exactly. But like Eli told you, you aren't the first person to have a bad reaction to Harrow. We've had the chance to experiment a bit."

I looked down at the pill in my hand. It seemed like a bad idea, taking unknown drugs from a man I barely knew. But they'd been talking about helping me. That had to be a good sign.

I swallowed the pill and drank a couple more gulps of water before the nausea caught up with me. I handed the glass back. Caleb held on to it a moment, looking down at me. "You've got the whole year to settle into your role here," he said. "You don't need to figure out everything in your first two weeks. Take it easy, okay?"

I gave a tiny nod—but he had it wrong. I had to survive a full year, and I didn't know if Harrow would let me. The faster I found answers, the better armed I would be.

Caleb patted me on the shoulder one last time and left me to rest.

The pain eased gradually, either time or Eli's remedy loosening the migraine's grip on me. I sank back against the bed, my thoughts swirling.

They had talked about Harrow, but they'd also spoken of *the Other*. I didn't understand what that meant—and my family clearly wasn't going to tell me. I was on my own.

One person *had* talked to me about Harrow, though. Bryony Locke, the Harrow Witch.

If my family wouldn't tell me the truth, maybe she would.

8

OVER THE NEXT few days, Mom and Simon fretted, Caleb made up endless excuses to get me out of the house, and even Iris went out of her way to check up on me. It was the end of the week before I had the chance to slip out alone and make my way into the woods.

I didn't have to search for Bryony. Somehow, I knew where to go, charting a sure course along a gravel path among the trees. I found her sitting on a small stone bench and reading a tattered paperback, her satchel resting on the ground beside her. The sun shone on her dark hair, sending darts of red along the strands. The wind caught it, creating half-wild waves around her sharp face.

"You're still here, then," she said, friendly as a puff adder. She didn't look up from her book as I crunched along the gravel toward her.

"I decided to stay," I said. My tongue felt clumsy. There was a strand of hair caught at the corner of her mouth, and I found my eyes fixed on it.

She looked up at last. The animosity in her eyes was so fierce I took half a step back. "Congratulations," she said dryly.

"Why do you hate me so much?" I blurted out. What had I expected? She hadn't exactly been friendly the first time we met.

She arched an eyebrow. "I don't hate you, specifically. I hate you, a Vaughan."

"Not really better."

"Yeah, that really sucks for you," she said, but the corner of her mouth quirked. "For what it's worth, I don't think leaving would have done you much good."

"Why not?" I asked.

"People don't escape Harrow unless it's done with them. Trust me, I've tried," she said. Her voice had a wounded edge.

"You tried to leave?"

"I was afraid. Aren't you?" she answered, her eyes searching mine. "Aren't you afraid that, eventually, Harrow will turn on you and you'll have to pay for the things your family has done?"

"I might be if I knew what any of that was," I said, spreading my hands.

As before, my utter ignorance seemed to knock her off-balance, and she squinted at me. "Do you know *anything* about this place?" she asked.

"Not really," I admitted. "Look, the last time I was here, I was seven. My mom never talked about it, and no one will tell me anything. But you did."

"That's because I don't belong to it. I don't have to follow its rules," she said, tilting her head back as she examined me like a weird bug she was getting ready to pin to a specimen card.

I didn't know what to make of her. I was used to people not liking me, but she didn't seem unsettled by me—it was almost the opposite. Like she was daring me to surprise her, and I hadn't managed it yet.

"My mom took me away from here because she didn't want Harrow to have me. But it didn't work. It followed us, and it drew me back. And now I'm trapped. You're the only person who's been honest with me, as far as I can tell, and I know you hate me, but I need your help," I said, all in a rush.

She sighed and stood abruptly. I was struck by just how much taller than me she was. She seized her bag from the ground and threw the strap roughly over her shoulder, then grabbed my hand and started dragging me down the path. I squeaked. Actually squeaked. If I wanted to impress her, I was not doing a good job of it.

"Where are we going?" I asked.

"Shut up," she told me, without particular animosity.

She walked so quickly I had to practically run to keep up. We hustled down a twisting path, between trees that loomed and rattled their branches disapprovingly. And then, abruptly, the path ended at the collapsed steps of a stone cottage. Moss packed every gap in the stones. The roof sagged, more moss and fallen leaves than wood, but Bryony dragged me right inside through a rot-swollen door and slammed it behind us.

The interior of the cottage was damp and close. It was obvious no one lived here, but shelves lined the walls, filled with glass jars that held dried herbs and mushrooms and frogs in greenish liquid. Bryony dropped my hand and walked to a table in the corner, where she set her bag and her book, and spun again, crossing her arms.

"Well?" she said. "What do you want to know?"

I laughed, and she blinked, taken aback. "Where do I *start*?" I asked.

"Hmph," she said, and I thought I detected the barest trace of amusement in the sound. She tossed her head to clear the dark curls from her face. "Let me get one thing clear: I am not here to help you. It isn't my job."

I blew out a frustrated breath. "Then why *are* you here? What is the Harrow Witch?"

"I'm here to watch. And listen. And wait," Bryony said. "The Witch of Harrow was here the day that the first stone of Harrow was laid, and she will be here when it falls. That's what I am. A witness. I'm not here to give you answers or hold your hand. Ask your family if you need to know what secrets Harrow holds."

"But I don't know if I can trust them," I blurted out. I thought they were protecting me, but what if I was wrong? I didn't know enough to be sure one way or another.

She gave a harsh laugh. She let her arms drop and leaned back against the table behind her, fingers hooked over the edge. "Okay, you may be smarter than I thought."

"Please. Everyone dances around it, acts like maybe it isn't real—but you know. You know what this place is." I paced farther inside the house, the floorboards giving springily under my feet. I stopped a few paces from her.

"What do *you* think it is?" she asked. I knew a test when I heard one. Her eyes burned with quiet intensity.

I thought of my mother's words and echoed them. "Harrow is a cage," I said.

She nodded once. "It is. But you need to ask yourself: A cage for what?" She lifted an eyebrow as if waiting for my answer.

"The Other," I said, more guess than anything. All I was doing was mimicking other people, but she grunted as if to say I was right.

"And I thought you said you didn't know anything." Her eyes were flat. I couldn't read her. I tried to look deeper under her skin, to see what lay beneath—some hint of what she was thinking or feeling, of who she was. But I couldn't. Something was stopping me.

"I don't know what the Other is. I just overheard my grandmother and uncles talking about it," I said. "Does it have something to do with the ghosts?"

"There are no—"

"No ghosts at Harrow," I finished for her. I let out a huff of frustration and raked my hair back from my forehead, pacing away from her. "If they aren't ghosts, what are they?"

"They're called figments," Bryony said. "They look like dead people, but they aren't. The one you saw when we met is usually a little girl, but it's only been Jessamine for a little while. Before that, it was somebody else. I don't know her name or if she was even a real person."

"You knew Jessamine?" I stopped pacing, looking over at her sharply.

"Of course," she said softly. "She was a sweet kid. She would talk to the little girl figment. Play with it sometimes. I think it misses her. That's why it started looking like her. But it would be a mistake to think that it's actually her."

"That's what people mean, then. If you know there aren't ghosts at Harrow, you won't think you're talking to someone you love. You'll know that they're . . . they're . . ." I gestured broadly, helplessly.

"The figments all look different, but they're all just pieces of the same thing. Like masks it puts on."

"What is *it*?" I asked.

Bryony paused. "I call it the dark soul," she said quietly, and it had the tone of a confession. Her cheeks flushed. The dark soul. The Other. The thing the cage was built for. "I don't know if there is a name for what it is," Bryony went on. "An entity. A spirit. A power."

"Is it dangerous?" I asked.

"Of course," she said. A chill went through me. "That's why your family has worked so hard to contain it."

"Then why do you hate us?" I asked.

"Maybe I don't think that just because something is *dangerous* it should be locked away," she answered. "It has as much right to be as we do." Everything about her was a challenge: the harsh tone of her voice, the tilt of her chin, the intense gaze she fixed on me. The anger in her face made it shine with the beauty of a keen blade, and I wondered how I could have ever thought she wasn't pretty. "And that is why we aren't friends, Helen Vaughan, and we aren't allies, and I shouldn't be helping you."

"And yet here you are. Helping me," I said.

She stared at me. And then she turned abruptly and walked to a shelf against the wall on which rested a wooden box that looked much newer than the rest of the furnishings. She opened it and pulled something out, and then strode back over. She pushed the object into my hands. "Here. You might be able to make more sense of this than me. Maybe it has some of the answers you're looking for."

The thing she had handed me was a small black book, bound in leather and tied shut with a thin leather cord. "What's this?" I asked.

She didn't answer—not directly. "It's not fair, them throwing you in the deep end like this," she said, almost to herself. Then, "You should go. You don't want to get caught in a witch's house. People would talk." There was a spark of humor in her eye.

She turned away, as if done with me, and I stood for an awkward moment before stumping my way out the door.

I kept the black book clasped against my side until I got back to my room, though I ached to open it and find out what lay within its pages. I waited until I could be certain I was alone, the door closed and locked behind me. Then at last I picked apart the knotted cord and eased open the cover.

On the first page, in looping, old-fashioned script, I read: *The Journal of Nicholas Vaughan.*

9

THE PAGES OF the journal were thin and brittle. Curled up on my bed, the remnants of the migraine pulsing behind my eye, I turned them carefully. The next page was filled with dense text in a strange alphabet. I flipped through the next few pages, but they were all the same. Only the dates were legible. The entries started in 1848. This book was older than Harrow.

Scattered throughout were quick sketches like diagrams—a triangle with squiggly symbols at the points, a drawing of a plant with three leaves and a star-shaped flower. One drawing took up an entire spread of pages. With only black ink, it should have been difficult to depict, but the crawling lines and blots of darkness were unmistakable. A vast and chaotic *thing*, rampant on a field of black stars. There was a caption, and this alone in the whole of the book was written in plain English. *The God of the Vast Dark*, it said.

A sudden gust of wind sent rain lashing against the window, and I jumped, nearly dropping the book. I swore and collected myself, then shot a glare at the fox skull sitting out on the desk.

"You can't blame me for being jumpy," I told it. It grinned its end-less, toothy smile at me.

The alphabet didn't look like any I'd seen—it didn't even look real. It reminded me of Desmond's notebook, all those little sym-bols he'd jotted down.

I hesitated. Desmond had given me his number before he'd left and told me to text him if I wanted to chat. I'd smiled and told him I would, knowing that I wouldn't. It was only a matter of time before he realized what everyone did eventually—that there was something wrong with me. Better I not get too friendly.

But I needed to read this journal.

I braced myself, sent Desmond a quick text asking if he was available, and then waited, flipping through the notebook. There were other illustrations—a city skyline, a diagram of the solar system, and, midway through, a rather intense-looking portrait of a young woman. She had a serious face and dark eyes. This must be Annalise Vaughan.

My phone buzzed. **I've got a free period right now. What's up?** Desmond had written.

Do you know what this means? I wrote, and sent a photo of a page of text. **I thought it looked like your notebook.**

His response came quickly. **My notebook's in a simple sub-stitution cipher. Symbols for letters. Celia used to be kind of a snoop, so I started using it when we were younger. This looks similar, but I'd have to take a longer look at it. What's this from?**

Nicholas Vaughan's journal, I replied.

I watched the screen, waiting for a response. Instead, the phone started to buzz, Desmond's name filling up the screen. I answered the call quickly.

"You seriously have Nicholas Vaughan's journal?" Desmond asked. He sounded giddy.

"Are you alone?" I asked.

"My roommate's in class. Or probably skipping class to make out with his boyfriend, actually," Desmond said.

"Good. Not the boyfriend-making-out part—specifically the alone part," I clarified.

"Yeah, I got that," he said, sounding amused. My cheeks heated up. "Where did you find it? The journal?"

"That's not important," I said, reluctant to share too much. Would he help me if he knew I'd gotten the journal from the Harrow Witch?

"Okay," Desmond said slowly. "So the whole thing is in the Vaughan cipher?"

"There's a Vaughan cipher? And yeah, the whole thing is filled with those symbols."

"It's where I got the idea for my cipher, originally. There are bits of it all over Harrow," Desmond explained. "I've never been able to crack it, though, not without a longer chunk of text. And you just—Helen, I've wanted to find that journal like my *whole life*. Other kids wanted hot wheels in kindergarten—I wanted to read my unhinged ancestor's rantings about ectoplasm."

"Does that mean you can crack it?" I asked, smiling in spite of my nerves. It was hard not to be excited in the face of Desmond's enthusiasm.

"Hell yes, I can crack it," Desmond said. He sounded on the edge of gleeful. "Can you take photos of the pages to send to me?"

"No problem," I said, relieved. "I'll send them right away."

"If it really is a straight substitution cipher, it shouldn't be hard. You start with the one- and two-letter words—there aren't very many, so you can narrow things down quickly, and—"

"And you'll keep it secret?"

He paused. "Helen, is everything okay over there?"

I covered my eyes with my hand and stifled the urge to sigh or scream or invent new, creative curse words. "No one will tell me what's going on around here. I think the journal might have answers, but . . . I don't know. I don't want anyone to know that I have it. Not yet at least."

There was a long silence. "I think I'd like some of those answers, too," he said at last.

"I thought you didn't believe in the things at Harrow," I replied.

"I don't know what I believe," he said. He sighed. "I'll keep it a secret for now."

"Thank you, Desmond."

"Take care of yourself, Mistress Vaughan."

That night, I dreamed of Harrow once again.

I lay beneath the house, pinned by the weight of the earth, a worm wriggling against the soft skin of my wrist. I looked up, beyond the spires of Harrow. I thought at first the sky was clouded over, the stars hidden, but then I saw them glimmering in the dark. The stars were there, but they burned black against the night sky, and among them moved some vast and horrible *thing*, a shadow of grasping tendrils that reached for me—

But before they could reach me, I was gone, running through the tangled halls of Harrow, out the doors which were flung open to the night. A golden light glowed in the forest, and like a fluttering moth I chased it. Chased the song.

> *"Listen close for Harrow's bell.*
> *Blood will bind, and blood will tell."*

Bryony stood among the trees, not far from the edge of the woods, her lantern resting on the ground at her side. She watched the house with expectant hopefulness.

"Is it you?" she asked.

I tried to speak, but I didn't have a mouth. Tried to reach for her, but I didn't have hands.

"Talk to me," she said, a pleading edge in her voice. "Tell me what I'm supposed to do."

There was something I had to find. Something I had to find, and then I could do what she wanted. Be what she wanted. It was close. I could feel it. But the spiral was there, too, drawing me under. And I was so, so cold.

And then—then the cold was real, biting deep, and I stood in the woods, awake and barefoot in my pajama pants, shivering as Harrow's bell rang to signal the morning. Mist coiled among the trees and a bird called in the dark predawn, and I was alone.

My fingers ached. Dirt packed the creases of my hands. My fingertips were red, my nails broken. "No no no no," I whispered, as if denying what was happening could make it less true. I curled my fingers under and jammed my half-frozen hands under my arms to try to warm them. My teeth chattered.

The Harrow dream had come twice, and twice I'd woken out here, dirty and cold. What was happening to me? What was doing this?

I stumbled up the path toward the house. The sun was barely a whisker of light against the horizon. Around me the shadows seemed to shift, pulling free of the trees—stretched, warped shapes, figures like people wrenched into strange configurations, all at the corner of my eye, vanishing as soon as I turned to look. Panic scrabbled out over my skin. I broke into a run.

I burst from the trees, my numb feet carrying me at a stumbling gait. Movement rustled behind me. I didn't dare look back. I bolted straight for the back steps and flew up them, leaving a trail of muddy footprints.

The French doors at the back of the house were locked. Of course they were locked. My breath hitched, and for a moment I couldn't think at all. But then I spotted a form hurrying across the ballroom toward me. Mom.

"Helen! Good lord, you're half frozen," she said, rubbing her hands on my arms to warm me up. "What are you doing outside?"

If I told her the truth, it would panic her. "Stupid. Wanted to watch the sunrise," I said.

She gave me an odd look, and I knew she didn't believe me. But she only gave my arms one last brisk rub and pushed me toward the stairs. "You'd better go get warmed up. I'll have something sent up to your room."

I nodded mutely and tottered toward the stairs up to the Willows. By the time I reached my room I could at least feel my fingers and toes again, though my hands were still shaking as I went for the knob. It turned a quarter inch and stopped. The door was locked. I jiggled it, jiggled it again, yanked at it, that panic starting to well back up. I forced myself to stop.

I hadn't locked the door. So who had?

The creak of a floorboard warned me that I wasn't alone, and I tried my best to compose myself before Eli rounded the corner. He had a ring of keys in one hand, and when he saw me, his eyes widened just a touch, almost imperceptibly. We stared at each other.

"The door's locked," I said after a moment.

"I was just coming to open it. I'm afraid I slept in," Eli said, running his thumb along the length of the old-fashioned brass key. "I lock all the bedrooms at night. For safety."

"Safety from what?"

"Things that go bump in the night," he said with a faint chuckle, and stepped forward. I flinched back, but he only leaned past me and unlocked the door, then pushed it open for me. "May I ask how you came to be outside your room?"

"I don't know," I admitted, unable to come up with a plausible explanation.

"I see," he said thoughtfully, giving the door a speculative look. "I'll let you get cleaned up, then. And Helen—it really isn't safe out on the grounds at night. After the bell."

"Bryony goes out, doesn't she?" I asked before I remembered that I'd only dreamed of her out there in the dark.

"The Harrow Witch has her own ways." He walked past me. I turned with him, making sure my hands with their dirt-packed nails were hidden behind me. Only when he was truly out of sight did I open the door. Inside, I shut it again, and then stood looking around the room. The bed was rumpled, the fox skull was out on the table where I'd left it. Nothing was out of place. Except for the dirty footprints that led from the side of the bed to the wall opposite—and vanished.

The prints matched mine. The sheets were dirty, too, smudged and smeared with dark earth. I followed the path of the footsteps to the wall and pressed my fingers to the wallpaper, searching for some hidden catch as images of secret passages flashed through my mind. But there was nothing.

I shivered, and not just from fear—I was sodden and freezing and covered in cold dirt. *One thing at a time*, I told myself. I'd get cleaned up, and then I'd retrace my steps.

In my bathroom I stripped off my soggy clothes, and then I paused again. Beneath the grime that coated my hands and wrists were red welts running around my wrists like bracelets. More lines ran across my stomach, my shoulders, my elbows, my knees. Some of them were a single line, but most were frayed and jagged. There was a single red welt just below my sternum. When I pressed my fingertips to them, they were tender like a sunburn, just like the last time I'd woken up outside—but worse.

They had the feel of something unfinished.

10

I SHOWERED, BLASTING the hot water, and by the time I was done, the welts had faded to faint marks I could almost pretend weren't there. Outside, the sky had brightened to a desultory shade of blue. In the shadows the grass was still rimed with white. I could see the path I had walked, grass bent and frost melted, leading to the trees. I tried to imagine myself standing here in the dark. Tried to remember.

But all I remembered was the dream: Bryony and her lantern.

I walked beside the trampled grass and slipped into the woods, walking to the place where I'd been, or as close to as I could figure. I looked around for any sign of why I might have come out here. Or *how*.

The sound of a shovel hitting dirt made me jump. Not far from the path, a man in a blue fleece pullover stood with his back to me. I drew closer cautiously. He emptied his shovel before turning and driving it into a pile of dirt beside him. He wasn't digging a hole; he was filling it in.

He squinted, raising a hand in greeting. "Morning! Can I help you?"

"Sorry, I'm just out for a walk," I said.

"Ah. Then you'll be the new Ms. Vaughan," he said.

"Not that new. I've been a Vaughan all my life."

"Fair enough," he said. He stepped forward and stuck out his hand, then realized it was grimy and winced, wiping it off on his jacket. "I'm Benjamin Locke, Master of Hounds."

"Master of Hounds?" I repeated. I hadn't seen a single dog on the grounds since I arrived, apart from the strange paintings in Annalise Vaughan's gallery.

He smiled. "It's an old title, but I like the grandiosity of it, don't you? Harrow's hounds are gone, though, so I guess I'm just the groundskeeper."

"Bryony's your daughter." He looked like her—the fair skin and black hair, the sharpness to his face—but his eyes were brown and warm, in contrast to her gray-green.

"That she is," he said—and then something passed over his face. The corner of his mouth tugged in a frown. His pupils contracted, ever so slightly. He shifted a fraction of a step back. "I didn't realize you'd met."

His voice was wary now. I'd almost gotten used to the way the people here treated me—like I was just a normal person. I had almost forgotten that instinctive revulsion.

"I'd best get back to work," he said gruffly. He jerked his head toward the hole. It was maybe four feet deep, the sides ragged. I curled my fingers under. There was no way I could have dug a hole that deep with my bare hands, in the cold, in my sleep—was there?

"What did that?" I asked. I eased back a step, giving him space. Sometimes that helped.

He scooped up a shovelful of loose dirt and tossed it into the hole. "Could have been a dog. Or a fox. Sinkholes, I've heard suggested. They crop up all over the grounds. If you see one, let me know. They've got to be filled in right away. Don't want anyone tripping and breaking a leg." He worked steadily as he spoke and didn't look at me.

"They show up a lot?"

"As long as I've been working here, and as long as my father did." His eyes kept darting sideways toward me, and I could see the need to be civil to his employer warring with that bone-deep dislike.

"You've lived here all your life, then?"

"Just about. Wandered off sometimes, but I always seem to find my way back. Harrow has a way of laying claim to folks."

"I've noticed."

He straightened up and looked at me. He frowned, but his gaze was steady. "I decided a long time ago I could either find it frightening or take it as a compliment. I take care of Harrow, Harrow takes care of me, and I don't listen to the stories." He said it firmly, like he was reminding himself of that, too. His fingers tightened around the shovel, though, and I could see it, a twitching urge in his muscles.

A little voice telling him to swing it hard at my head.

I fell back another step, trying to make it seem natural. No one had ever attacked me. It didn't take them over, this affliction of mine. It didn't force them into anything. But if anyone ever decided to listen to that little urge, I didn't want to be standing too close.

"What kind of stories?" I asked.

"You know how people can be," he said. "Especially around here. Old Estoners still spread the rumor that the house snatches little girls from town every so often. Any time a girl with black eyes is born in Eston, that's what they say—*they came from Harrow, and to Harrow they will return.*"

"Is it true?" I asked, alarm squeezing my chest.

He grunted. "That girls have gone missing? Sure. Girls go missing everywhere. That Harrow's gobbling them up? I doubt it. My mother could've told you more. She was the head of Eston's historical society. Collected all sorts of things about you Vaughans."

That must be where Bryony had gotten the notebook.

"Do you know where Bryony is? I think I'd like to talk to her."

His jaw worked. He didn't like me. But maybe he could tell that it wasn't *me* he was reacting to, not entirely, because he nodded. "I think she's up by the folly. It's down that path there, past the big bent tree, next to the pond."

"I have no idea what a folly is," I confessed.

"It was a fashion back in the day. It's a fake ruin. Old Nick Vaughan had it made from the stone that was left over after building the house."

"Neat," I said for lack of a better response. "I'll see you around, then." I turned to go.

"It won't bother you, so long as you follow the rules," he said. I turned back, but he was shoveling dirt again.

I walked away, the steady sound of shoveling fading behind me as I headed in the direction that Mr. Locke had indicated, and before long I came to the lake. The edge of the water was scabby with frost, and wisps of morning fog clung to the air above it. Around the right side of the lake was a structure of crumbling stone—what looked like it had once been a circular building with Greek columns. There was no sign of Bryony, which was almost a relief. I didn't know if I was up for navigating another conversation with the Harrow Witch so soon.

I made my way around the water. The false ruins were overgrown, and graffiti decorated the stones haphazardly—mostly names, a few random phrases. *Beware the witch* was spray-painted in yellow next to *Missy + Darren 4ever* and the ominous *don't let the shadows know your name.* I wondered how many kids from Eston snuck onto the grounds. The shattered beer bottles and stubbed-out cigarettes suggested the answer was quite a few.

I halted by a half-toppled wall, looking out at the misty pond. It was beautiful, in an eerie way. I rested my hands on the top of the wall.

—the stars shining black—tell me what you see!—just a small incision—

Whispers swarmed around me so quickly that I felt as if I was falling. Falling through a field of stars that shone black, an impossible luminous darkness in which something vast moved, a violent, threshing convulsion in slow motion.

She has looked upon his face, said the whisper in the stone.

I jerked back with a stifled cry—and realized someone was watching me. She stood on the other side of the lake, right at the edge of the water, her hair wind-tumbled about her shoulders. Bryony. Our eyes met, and I had the curious sensation that if I reached out my hand, it would find hers, as if no space lay between us at all.

And then she turned and walked away.

I felt a pang of disappointment—and then I realized that she wasn't leaving. She was coming around the lake. I stayed where I was, some part of me needing to know that every step toward me was her choice.

"I was looking for you," I said when she finally reached the toppled stones. "Your father said you were here."

"I like to come here," she replied. Her fingertips trailed over the top of one low wall. "The dark soul is easier to talk to here at the folly. Something about the stones. Have you worked out what that book says?"

I shook my head. "It's all in some kind of code."

"Obviously," she said with a little snort of amusement. I flushed.

"Desmond is going to see if he can crack it," I told her quickly. She walked along the edge of the folly, hand on the wall. I turned in place to hold her gaze. "I thought you said you couldn't trust your family."

"I have to trust someone."

"Do you trust me?" she asked, head tilting curiously.

I didn't answer. I didn't know how to explain why the answer that leaped to my lips was *yes*, without hesitation. "I don't think your father likes me," I said instead. Lightly, like I didn't know for sure. And like I didn't know why.

"Really?" That seemed to surprise her; she stopped in her

tracks at last, her hand dropping to her side. "Dad likes every-one."

"But no one likes me," I said, shrugging. "I scare them. Or they adore me, and then hate me when they realize it isn't real. You and my family are the only people I've met who don't react that way."

"I don't like you either," she pointed out.

"It's not the same. You seem to have decided to dislike me all on your own," I said.

"That's why you keep following me around? Because I dislike you honestly?" Bryony asked, brow arched.

"You have no idea what a relief it is to be hated because of something I understand," I said. She gave a sort of abortive laugh, like she couldn't decide if I was joking or not, and then she frowned.

"It sounds like how people react to Harrow," she said thought-fully. "Some of them are repulsed by it. Frightened or hateful, without knowing why. And others are spellbound. Drawn in. Un-til they leave, and it's like they're waking from a dream, and the clash between what they felt then and what they feel later makes them afraid. You were born here, weren't you?"

I nodded.

"So was I," she said. "My mother had me at home. She couldn't stand Harrow, though. She left when I was young."

"Like mine." We must have both lived here at the same time. Another piece of my past forgotten. I wondered if we had ever played together—but I imagined angry little Bryony, five years old and already fiercely set against the family in the big house. No, we wouldn't have been friends.

"She didn't think to take me with her like yours did," Bryony said with an edge of bitterness. "It sounds to me like some part of you never got free of Harrow."

"Or maybe I'm just horrible and repulsive," I said. She didn't laugh.

"The Harrow Witch is immune to the manipulations of Harrow and the dark soul," she said. "That's one thing you can be sure of. What I feel is my own. I'll promise you that, at least. If you ever need to be certain of someone, you can come find me."

"So that I can be certain you genuinely don't like me?" I asked.

"Maybe a certain enemy is better than an untrustworthy friend," Bryony suggested.

"I don't know if we're enemies," I protested, and smiled, trying to make it a joke.

"Neither do I," she said simply. She stepped back, away from the folly, her hand falling away from the stone. "But I'm interested to find out."

She didn't say goodbye, just walked away. I stared after her, my thoughts tangled up in her final words. As she disappeared amid the trees, the faint strains of singing reached me.

"There was a maiden, golden-haired,
Came to the fold, came to the fold."

It was the song I'd heard her singing in my dream.

11

THE WEEK AFTER I visited the folly, Mom and Simon left to pack up our house and take care of a few things. Her old boss had talked her into working a couple weeks while they found a replacement since the first person they'd hired had turned out to be a complete flake. Part of me was relieved that they were leaving. I was pretty sure they were safer away from here. And so when Mom had fretted and suggested she stay, I'd insisted that she go.

Desmond called when I was back in my room after seeing them off. The phone had barely started to buzz before I snatched it up. "Tell me you cracked it," I said.

"Well, hello, cousin," he drawled. "Lovely to hear from you. Have I thanked you for taking time out of your busy academic schedule to help me decipher a totally unhinged journal?"

"Yup, all of that," I said.

He snorted. "Fine, fine. I'll come up with some sufficiently elaborate penance for taking me for granted later. I cracked it, I think. It's not as simple as I was hoping, which is why it took me so long. It's really slow going. But I've got the first couple pages done. I'll send them over. They're pretty wild."

"I owe you," I said with feeling.

"I'll take a cool million—how's that?" he suggested.

"Deal." We laughed, and I said goodbye and hung up. I waited eagerly for the chime of the arriving document and opened it immediately.

> *Most people live their entire lives within the confines of the world we know. I might have as well if I had not met Annalise. For it is through her eyes that I have glimpsed the worlds that lie beyond our own and what dwells there.*
>
> *If I had not met Annalise, I would never have known of the vast dark and the god that dwells within it. I would never have sought out my good friend, Dr. Samuel Raymond, an expert and visionary in the field of transcendental medicine, and with him devised a means for a human being to look upon the very face of that god.*
>
> *Soon, we will begin this undertaking in earnest. I have never been one to keep a record of my life; I prefer my thoughts remain private. But someday, great men will look back on us as their forebearers, as the pioneers who changed the world, and they will want to know how we accomplished our great deeds. And so, with care and necessary secrecy, I make this record.*

Desmond wasn't wrong to describe him as unhinged, I thought. But then I wondered—could I be so sure? Gods and monsters and ghosts. The trouble with knowing that there was something beyond the natural realm was not knowing the limits of it.

Maybe there were other worlds and gods—or beings that a man like Nicholas Vaughan would call gods.

The next section was a pair of entries, dated about a week apart.

> *Annalise dreams nightly of the dark god, and when she embarks on her otherworldly jaunts, she unerringly finds herself beneath the black stars of that realm. I am eager to have Dr. Raymond witness one of her sessions in person, as he has only heard them described before, and I believe that it will allow him to refine his procedure.*

The entry continued with details about itineraries and weather and other things that might be of interest to historians but didn't help me at all, including a long digression about the meal fare at various inns. (Nick wasn't a fan.)

There was only one more entry, and it was, I noted with disappointment, extremely short. But when I read it, a strange, unsettled feeling rippled through me.

> *Dr. Raymond has arrived. He brings with him his ward, a young woman called Mary Beaumont, whose existence I was unaware of until she appeared at our doorstep. She is a delicate little thing, with black hair and soft dark eyes, large as a doe's. I asked Dr. Raymond if she had some ability of her own, as I was struck with the presence within those dark orbs, but he only laughed and denied it. Still, I wonder. The way she looks at me . . .*

I grabbed the actual book and flipped to the page that Desmond had translated. On the opposite page was the portrait of the woman with black eyes—Vaughan eyes. But this wasn't Annalise Vaughan at all. It was this young woman, Mary.

If we were all descended from Annalise, then why did we have Mary's dark eyes?

I fanned through the pages, as if answers would leap out at me. But there was only more indecipherable code and pictures I didn't have enough context to understand.

I reached the end and started to close the book. But then I paused. I'd missed something. Tucked between the final page and the back cover of the book was a small envelope. It looked too modern to be from the same era as the notebook, and the handwriting on the outside was different.

Harrow's girls, it said. The letters were rounded and squat, done in careful cursive—not like the scrawl at the front of the book—and made with what looked like a ballpoint pen, which I was pretty sure didn't exist in Old Nick's day.

The envelope itself was folded in half to fit in the book. I unfolded it, the paper crackling, and lifted the flap.

There were four photographs inside, each one of a girl between about seven and twelve. The style of their clothes and the type of photograph anchored each girl in a different decade. The oldest photograph looked like it was from the early twentieth century, the most recent from maybe ten or twenty years ago. All of the girls had eyes so dark they were almost black.

Harrow's girls. Benjamin Locke told me that's what they called girls who disappeared, supposedly devoured by Harrow.

Had Bryony known these photos were in the journal? Were they part of why she'd given it to me?

After yesterday's conversation, having an excuse to talk to her again made me excited—and petrified. I couldn't pin her down. She seemed to want to talk to me one minute, and then resent me the next. To be friendly and then to hate me. She'd said that I could be certain of her, but it didn't help me to know her feelings were genuine when I couldn't tell what those feelings *were*.

"Gah," I said eloquently, and shook my head rapidly. "Come on. She's just a girl. You know how to talk to girls." I did not know how to talk to girls. Talking to girls was terrifying. "Witch. She's a witch, and she knows stuff you need to know." Better.

I gathered my bag, in which I stowed Nicholas Vaughan's journal, and checked my reflection in the mirror. My hair was as unmanageable as ever, but I finger combed it into a semblance of submission and headed out toward the groundskeeper's house.

I'd been expecting a more functional version of the witch's cottage—a cabin, a stump with a hatchet sticking out of it for chopping firewood, a stone chimney. But the house was neat and modern with a long driveway leading out to the road that ran behind Harrow's grounds.

I scaled the steps and knocked, then stood there, losing my nerve with each passing second. There was no answer. My heart sank at the same time as relief washed over me. I turned to go. The door opened, and Bryony appeared, wearing the gray dress she'd worn the first day I met her, the one perfectly cut to her willowy body.

"Hey," she said, surprised.

Was I imagining things, or was that a hint of *pleasant* surprise? Probably imagining it. "I found something in the journal," I said.

"Desmond broke the code?" she asked, sounding impressed.

"No. I mean, yes, at least a bit of it, but that's not what I'm here about," I said. "Did you know these were in there?" I held out the envelope.

"This is my Nana's handwriting," she said. She looked at the photos, frowning. "Who are these girls?"

"I don't know," I said, disappointment making my shoulders slump. "I hoped you'd know. But—your dad said you still had your grandma's stuff? Maybe we could look through her stuff and see? Your dad said it would be okay, and I thought since you gave me the journal and everything . . ." I was aware that I was babbling and also aware that, if I stopped, I was never going to get started again.

She sighed and held the door open wider. "Not like I can turn you away when you own the place, anyway."

"I own your house?" I asked.

"It's part of Harrow, isn't it?" she shot back. I followed hesitantly as she led the way. The interior of the house was cramped but well-kept, with floral wallpaper on every wall.

Up in the attic, she gestured broadly. "Everything's in these boxes, but it's going to take me a minute to figure out which ones."

The attic was a cramped space, cluttered with an old metal-framed bed, a standing mirror, an obscene number of doilies, and stacks of boxes, everything coated in a thick layer of dust.

Bryony shoved a stack of old *Reader's Digest* magazines out of the way with her foot. "I think this is it," she said hauling at a box, and I moved to help her. We maneuvered it onto a clear patch of floor. Bryony opened it up, crinkling her nose at the explosion of dust. She waved a hand at it. "Go ahead, then." She backed off, and I knelt beside the box.

"How did your grandmother get interested in this stuff?" I asked as I lifted the lid. "Was she a Harrow Witch, too?"

She made an amused sound. "Definitely not. She was extremely Christian and extremely skeptical about 'hokum and nonsense.' She thought Nicholas Vaughan was a lunatic, and she was deeply suspicious of his descendants 'following him down the path of occultism.' She thought you all were up to no good." She waggled her eyebrows at me. I snorted in surprised laughter, then immediately looked away, embarrassed by the undignified noise.

"Have you heard of them? Harrow's girls, I mean," I clarified, clearing my throat.

She shrugged. "Sure. There was this sort of rhyme that went around about them. I remember boys chanting it on the playground. Something about *eyes of black* and then . . . oh, I don't remember. But it ended with *Harrow takes its daughters back*, I remember that."

"So it's true. Girls with black eyes go missing. Harrow takes them. Or . . . the Other does?"

"I didn't say it was true, just that there's a rhyme," Bryony replied. "When kids are born in town with black eyes, Estoners call them Harrow's children, but they're just Vaughan kids. Love children. My babysitter had black eyes like you. She vanished, but only because she split the second she turned eighteen. I think she's waitressing in LA."

"So it isn't true at all." I couldn't tell if I was disappointed or relieved.

"I don't know, Vaughan. You tell me. Or look in the box you made me haul out for you."

Right. Cheeks flaming, I unpacked the dusty box, which turned out to be mostly documents, organized in accordion folders with general topics written on the labels. I set aside a stack of flyers for a school musical and a town directory. Underneath was a photocopy of a newspaper article from 1973, concerning the disappearance of a girl named Lara Pearson, age eleven. The photo matched one of the four from the envelope.

"Lara Pearson," I said. My hand was shaking.

"I always thought it was just rumors," Bryony said, a frown ghosting across her lips.

"Do you think . . . did the Other do something to her?" I asked. "To all those girls?"

"No," Bryony said as if offended. Then, "I don't know." She looked troubled. "It's just as likely your family did something to them."

"You think my family are a bunch of murderers?" I asked. "Celia? Desmond?"

"Definitely not Desmond. Celia, though? Nobody's that nice. She's probably a secret serial killer," Bryony said, and I chuckled. We stared at each other. Bryony's breath stirred the dust that hung thick in the air, sending it swirling.

Downstairs, the door slammed. Bryony jumped a little. "My

dad," she said. "Actually, he might know who these girls are. He grew up in Eston," she suggested. She probably just wanted to get rid of me, but there was a note of curiosity in her voice.

We headed downstairs, dust clinging to us, and found Mr. Locke in the kitchen. "Good morning," he said brightly, turning. Then he spotted me, and his expression froze. His next words were stilted, but at least he was trying to cover it. "What are you two up to?"

"I'm merely obeying the mistress's requests," Bryony said drily. "Letting her paw through Nana's things."

"I see," he said. He regarded me with a troubled look. "Did you find what you were looking for?"

"Sort of," I said. I was holding the photographs. I started to step forward to show him, but he flinched, and I stopped. Bryony looked between us with an appraising expression. Then, word-lessly, she took the photographs from me and crossed the room to hand them to him.

"They're labeled 'Harrow's girls.' Are those the ones you were talking about? That went missing?" I asked.

"I can't say," he said. He spoke to Bryony instead of to me, his shoulder turned to me like I wasn't even there. "I've never seen most of these girls in my life. But I remember this one." He tapped on the most recent photo of a shy-looking girl in a blue sweater. She had brown hair cut into blunt bangs. "Sad story. Died in maybe 2000, 2001. She was out playing by the creek during a storm and fell in. The flood carried her away. She was only seven years old. Her name was . . . ah, shoot. I'm getting old." He scratched his head, thinking. "Oh, right. It was Haley. Haley Cotter."

My breath caught in my throat. Pain bloomed behind my eye, a migraine crashing into me without warning. Agony rippled down my neck, the light suddenly stabbing at me. I grabbed the back of a chair to steady myself.

Mr. Locke stared at me wordlessly.

"Are you all right?" Bryony asked.

"It's nothing," I told her through clenched teeth. The pain ebbed slowly, and I straightened up. Bryony was looking at me with wide eyes. What the hell had that been?

Benjamin Locke cleared his throat loudly. "Anything else you girls need?" he asked.

"No, I don't think so," Bryony said quickly. She gave me a look and jerked her head toward the door. I followed her out, feeling dazed. The door had barely shut behind us when she rounded on me. "What was that?" she demanded.

"Nothing," I said. "I just got a headache."

"At the instant he said Haley Cotter's name? How does that make sense?" she asked.

"I don't know. I just . . ." I trailed off.

She was staring down at my hands. "You're bleeding."

I looked down. Blood dripped from the braceleted wounds around my wrists. I reached up to find it trickling down the side of my neck. It soaked through my blouse, right above my beating heart.

Bryony stared at me, and I knew the look in her eye. I'd seen it before, the moment before the scissor blades plunged into Kendra Norton's staring eyes. The scissors that had been found in my bloody hands, Kendra screaming, *I saw her. I saw her.*

Now Bryony saw it, too—the dreadful thing inside of me.

I ran. Away from Bryony. Away from the pictures of those girls whose names, whose stories, I didn't want to know.

Within the solid walls of Harrow, my blood dried on my unbroken skin. I washed it off and pretended that I hadn't heard Bryony calling my name as I fled.

There were wicked things within Harrow's walls. And I was one of them.

12

IT HAPPENED WHEN I was in second grade, just after we left Harrow. I hated school. School meant strict routine. Sitting still. Filling in worksheets with the answers, not scribbles of vines and eyes. Obeying the ringing of the bells that told you when to move, when to sit, when to eat. But kids were supposed to be in school, and I didn't want my mom to be sad, so I pretended that it didn't make me want to slither free of my own skin.

Most of the other kids avoided me. Not Kendra Norton. She'd liked me, for whatever reason, even though I was weird and, in retrospect, pretty morbid for a grade schooler.

I would never hurt Kendra. Except everyone agreed I had. I'd been holding the scissors. I'd been covered in blood. And she'd been terrified.

That was the end of school for me. I'd been homeschooled ever since, and the *problem* had never repeated itself. I'd never hurt anyone else again, but I was always on edge, waiting for it to happen again.

I knew I should have gone to talk to Bryony and that I should keep trying to find out about the house, about the Other. But that look in her eye had been so much like Kendra's—and I couldn't bear to see it again. So I buried myself in classwork and tried to forget Haley Cotter and those other girls.

The days slid past, routine obscuring them into a haze. Mom called to say that she needed another week or so at the house to finish packing—it was taking them longer than expected since Simon had tweaked his back the first day, and she didn't want strangers boxing up her things. She'd be back in time for Thanksgiving, along with the rest of the family.

I didn't go to see Bryony again, and she never came to the house. I told myself it was for the best.

Maybe I did belong among Vaughans. Caleb was kind and Iris—well, she was trying her best to make me feel welcome, even if that did involve way more formal teas than I would have chosen. And Desmond was helping me, though I did wonder if it was more his own curiosity driving him than charity or familial loyalty.

You around? I texted him, lying in my bed one night.

Yep. Actually, I was just working on the journal, he texted back. Most of what we'd deciphered so far was Nicholas talking about various occult writers and theorists, interspersed with mind-numbingly dull accounts of what he'd done every day, including detailed records of the meals he ate. After our initial excitement, the translation had slowed down.

Can I ask you something weird? I texted.

That is the only kind of question you ask me.

Sadly accurate, I replied.

What's the question?

When you look at me, do you see anything strange?

There was a beat before he replied. **Strange? Like what kind of strange?**

People react really badly to me, usually.
But none of you do.

He didn't ask who "you" meant. **You don't seem strange to me. How do people usually react?**

I considered a moment, and then, before I could think better of it, I explained in brief terms what I'd told Bryony—about how people either loved or hated me, and the love never lasted.

You were so nice to me. But we haven't seen each other in weeks, and you haven't flipped out at me yet, I concluded.

**Wow. No, I don't think any of that seems familiar.
Don't take this the wrong way, but I don't have
strong feelings about you one way or the other.**

I read the words twice, something loosening up in my chest. Unexpected tears pricked my eyes. Three dots appeared again, and I waited as Desmond typed.

**I'll be there for Thanksgiving. We can watch out
for unexpected swings of emotion if it helps.**

It was already nearly Thanksgiving. I'd been at Harrow two months. There were only ten months left. I had as much time to uncover the secrets of Harrow, save my own skin, and survive this Investiture as you got to study for an AP test.

That would be good, I wrote back. I wiped my eyes with the back of my hand.

I'd wondered all my life if Harrow was haunting me. But maybe I had been blaming the wrong thing. Not Harrow, but the thing it caged. If the Other had done something to me and that was why Mom had fled, maybe the Vaughans were somehow immune—or protected. Maybe that was why they treated me like a normal person.

So had Bryony. At least, at first. I'd even thought that maybe, just maybe, she was starting to genuinely like me.

I still had the charm she had given me, resting on my bedside table. I crushed it against my palm as I curled under my covers and drifted off to sleep.

I dreamed of Harrow. I endured the dirt, my dream-grave, the struggle against the pinning weight of the earth. Tonight, a new figure walked the halls above me, carrying a candle that loosed fat, shimmering drops of wax. They flowed over her fingers and cooled there until it looked as if her skin was melting. As she walked, she whispered.

"A little cut, dear, just a little cut a little cut you won't feel it hardly feel it just a cut, and then you'll see, oh you'll see, you'll look, you'll behold." I stood in the hall in front of her, and her eyes,

unfocused, drifted to me. *"It was a gift we gave her. It was a gift. But now she won't stop looking at me. Her eyes are everywhere. I don't want her to see me. I won't let her look at me."*

She walked past. I spun slowly as if drifting in a breeze. I started to follow—and something stabbed into my palm. I lifted the hand to my lips instinctively, and as the taste of blood touched my tongue, the hallway shuddered—and then solidified again, empty now.

I was standing in the middle of the hall, but there was no woman. Just me, barefoot and in pajamas, clutching Bryony's charm in one hand. That was the hand that was bleeding, from a small puncture at the base of my thumb. I'd been sleepwalking again.

My hands and feet were already covered in soil, my fingernails packed with it. A line of dirty footprints trailed out behind me. But I was still inside—or had I come back in?

I was definitely awake now, at least. The pain in my palm proved that. But what had woken me? I untied the neck of Bryony's charm. There was the sprig of yellow flowers, and there was the dog's tooth. The tip of it was red with blood.

"Score one for the witch," I muttered, and bound it up again. My fingers kept slipping, my adrenaline tipping over into true fear. I was alone in the dark in the house, and I didn't know where I was in the labyrinth. I tucked the charm back into the pocket of my pajamas and tried to get my bearings. I should get back to my room.

Or should I?

I hesitated. This was my chance, I realized. If I wanted to know what happened on these midnight jaunts, this might be my only opportunity. I could keep going. Or hide in the nearest room and wait for morning and not get eaten by angry ghosts.

No ghosts at Harrow. Come on, Helen. Keep it together.

I started forward. My head was full of visions of shadowed forms lurking behind me, hands reaching out to grasp at me, eyes peering out of every keyhole I passed—but I saw nothing. Heard nothing but the groans and sighs of an old house. I stood at the intersection of two halls, fear giving way to frustration. My hammering heart calmed to a steady gallop.

Then I heard it. A cough, phlegmy and liquid, and then a slow *drag . . . slap.* Whatever was making that sound, it was between me and the exit.

In all my midnight wanderings, I'd been unharmed. Wet and cold, but nothing worse. And I had to know. I *had* to know. I repeated that to myself as I forced one near-paralyzed foot forward, then the next, with every nerve in me screaming that I should run. I turned the corner.

At first, I couldn't make sense of the jumbled thing before me. It looked like a heap of rags. Then it resolved into a body. A man. His limbs were twisted into brutal angles—one arm trapped beneath his torso, the other flung out to the side. There was no way he could be alive—his back had to be broken, his joints ripped and twisted. But then he moved. One hand reached out and grasped the floor. His legs heaved. His torso dragged along the ground. One twisted foot slapped the floorboards.

For an instant, I thought, *This man needs help.* But as soon as he moved, I saw my mistake. He wasn't hurt—he was *wrong*, somehow.

I retreated silently, praying he hadn't noticed me. I stepped back and back again and fumbled for the nearest door—to get something in between me and that thing.

Drag, slap. Drag, slap.

Quietly, I eased the door open. Slipped through. Eased it shut again. I stood there holding the knob, terrified to release it in case the click of the latch gave me away. I wanted to gasp for air, but I forced myself to breathe in tiny breaths, shallow, silent.

Drag, slap.

Something moved in the darkness of the room where I hid. A hand reached past my face and pressed against the wood of the door. A whimper slipped from between my lips. The hand and arm were jet-black and stretched to obscene proportions, too long and too thin, and shedding scraps of shadow like molting skin. I could feel a presence towering behind me. I did not turn, staring forward with the stubborn logic of the child who doesn't check under the bed because then the monsters will be real.

Drag, slap.

Then silence.

The crumpled thing had stopped right outside the door, and the floorboards at my feet creaked as it shifted. The doorknob twisted under my hand.

The thing shoved from the other side, the impact juddering through my grip but not moving the door even a centimeter as the shadowed hand lay unmoving against the wood.

These weren't figments. They had substance. Had flesh. They were real and they were *wrong*, and I knew in my core that they could break me apart if they wanted to.

Thump.

And then the silence again.

The pressure vanished.

Drag, slap. Drag, slap.

It was moving away. The shadow's hand withdrew from the door, and in my fog of fear and wonder, I had the thought that I should thank it—but its fingers trailed against my arm, and they were cold and sharp and the furthest thing from friendly.

"*Sssskin,*" the shadow whispered into my ear. "*Ssskin and bonesss and blood. But doesss it have a name?*"

"Helen," I whispered. "My name is Helen Vaughan."

"*Vaughan. Ah-ah-ahn. Name and blood and bonesss and ssskin,*" it sang to itself, and drew away, the cold presence receding. I spun at last, but I only caught the fleeting edge of a shadow darting along the wall, and then it vanished in the gloom. I ripped open the door and plunged back into the hallway, desperate to get away from that thing.

That was a mistake.

The folded-up thing hadn't left. It was still there, but it had unfolded itself. It was like someone had made a doll and gotten every joint wrong. It stood on turned-in feet, one knee knocked inward, the other leg bending once and then again, an extra joint at the center of its thigh. Its neck was long and twisted to and fro as it searched the hall—and then it saw me.

It moved in a rolling, rocking, jerking way, too fast for a

random collection of limbs. I screamed and bolted, sprinting down the hall. Not fast enough. Fingers tangled in my hair and yanked me back. My arms pinwheeled. I toppled against an emaciated ribcage, and the thing folded itself around me. I screamed as withered arms ratcheted tight around my chest, squeezing the breath out of me. Dull, square teeth tested my shoulder, and its breath smelled of dust.

"Go still," someone said urgently. One gnarled hand splayed across my face. All I could make out beyond it was an indistinct figure, and in my panic, I couldn't place the voice. I struggled against the creature's grip. "Stay *still*," they said again, and now I recognized Simon's voice. "Helen, you have to listen to me. Don't move. Not a muscle."

Simon? What was Simon doing here? I swallowed. Forced myself to obey. Still. Still as stone. Still as old bones.

"Help is coming," Simon said. "Just stay still, Scout. Don't make a sound."

Dry lips pressed against my shoulder and parted, teeth scraping over my skin. The thing moaned, and something clicked at the back of its throat, but I didn't move, didn't even breathe—

Help me. Please help me, I thought, but I didn't dare speak, even a whisper.

"Be ready to run," Simon said.

I couldn't give any sign that I'd understood. Even the beating of my heart seemed too loud and too violent, and I willed it to slow.

"Look," a voice whispered behind me. The creature twisted, its teeth leaving my skin. "Look what I have." Eli.

The thing's teeth chattered eagerly.

"You can have it. Go ahead."

It spidered over me, moving quickly now on all fours. I spun as it released me. Eli stood in the hallway, half crouched, and between him and the creature was something pale and slender, set on the ground like bait.

A bone. A rib. The creature snatched it up and hunched over it, huffing in pleasure.

My eyes fixed on the bone. My skin prickled, and suddenly I felt as if time were moving in slow motion. I could feel the beat of my heart. Feel Eli's heartbeat, hear his blood slushing through his veins. The creature had no heart. It was dead leaves and fungal flesh wrapped around those misconceived bones.

Its head twisted around to look at me again. "More," it said, a wet and fleshy sound.

"Run!" Simon called. I bolted. Simon ran with me, ducking left. I followed. We raced through twisting hallways, and as the familiar pressure of Harrow's relentless pattern grew behind my eyes, the creature stumbled and retched, slamming against the walls as if dizzy. "Don't stop," Simon urged. "Whatever happens, don't stop."

An exterior door stood at the end of the hall. I threw myself toward it. The knob stuck—I threw the deadbolt—I flung it open and leaped out, but a hand closed around my wrist, and flat teeth clamped over the meat of my palm with crushing force.

My hand went cold—not autumn's chill, but the cold of a void glittering with black stars.

I screamed and twisted, slamming the door shut on the

creature's head and shoulders as hard as I could, then again, and at last it released me. I raced out into the night alone. Simon was gone. Had the creature grabbed him?

Something rammed against the door. I couldn't stop to see what it was. Simon would be okay. He had to be.

A light glowed among the trees, golden and soft. I plunged toward it. Branches lashed my face and arms, and pain stabbed through my bare feet. I raced into the edge of the circle of light and stumbled to a halt. Bryony and I stared at each other, me panting and bloodied, her in her gray dress with her flickering lantern held at her side.

"There's—" I started to say. She pressed a finger against her lips, and then pointed.

Just beyond the circle of her lantern light, a figure made of shadow was clawing at the ground. It had already dug deep, several feet, and whispered to itself as it dug. *"They ssssscatter us. Lossst. Bury us bury us bury us deep, we'll dig oursssselves up again,"* it hissed.

Bryony motioned to me. I crept toward her, controlling my breath even as my burning lungs protested. Bryony took my hand in a businesslike grip and drew me back, away from the shadow. She took me down a dirt path, and it was only when I saw the moonlight glinting off the lake that I realized we were going to the folly.

She didn't stop until we'd stepped onto the stones, and then she set down the lantern on the crumbled remains of a wall and turned to me with hard eyes. "What the hell do you think you're doing out here at night?" she asked, voice quiet but angry.

"I—" The words turned to brambles in my mouth. I coughed on them. With a soft moan, I sank to my haunches, tucking my arms close to my body. I wasn't going to panic. I wasn't.

She made a little sound, half annoyance and half sympathy, and crouched next to me. "You look scared as a rabbit that just got away from a hound," she told me. "Take deep breaths. No dogs here, little rabbit. They don't like the folly, and it'll keep them from catching your scent."

"Your d-d-dad said there weren't any dogs left," I said, teeth chattering, not quite comprehending what she was saying. "That— that thing—"

"The dark soul isn't what it used to be," she said. "Less complicated, more violent. You shouldn't tempt it by wandering where you're not meant to go." She touched my wrist, and I realized I was still clutching the charm. My other hand was bruised, the creature's bite a bloody wound that spanned most of my palm. She gathered both my wrists in her hands, examining the damage. "What did this?"

"I don't know, it was all—wrong. Crumpled up."

"The Folded," she said. "I've seen them before. They're dangerous."

"There was—my stepdad is still—" I gulped down a sob.

"I can barely understand you. Breathe," she ordered me, her voice firm. "What happened?"

"I was sleepwalking. It was in the hall," I said. "I ran and there was one of those shadows, and it asked me my name, and when I told it—"

"You told it your name?" she asked. "Not smart. Now it can see you. Smell you. Of all the ways it can hurt you, only *most* are against the rules."

"My stepdad was there. And my great-uncle. Are they . . . ?"

"You can't do anything for them right now," she said sternly, and then her voice grew gentle. "Let me look at this hand." She lifted my wrist, helping me unbend my fingers. I hissed in pain as the motion stretched the skin.

"What are those things?" I asked her.

"It likes to make things. It can't *not* make them. They used to be marvelous. But these days, they all come out wrong," Bryony said. "They're only out at night. Usually not in the house, but sometimes one slips in. That's why you're not supposed to be out here."

"I didn't mean to be," I said.

"This is going to get infected. I might have something to— what the hell?" Bryony had probed gently at the edge of the wound, but now she jerked back.

A chunk of skin beside the bite had ripped free at her touch. It didn't hurt. I hadn't even felt it. The section of flesh was bloodless, oddly uniform. My hand throbbed, but no longer with pain. Only a strange pressure and a cold that stole from the bite to my arm and through my chest. Scabby white flesh wriggled up from the wound, spreading like lichen across my palm.

Bryony swore rapidly, frantically rummaging in her bag.

"Bryony?" I asked, and my voice seemed strangely calm, given the terror coursing through me. "Where did the stars go?"

"What are you talking about?" she asked.

"The stars are gone," I insisted, looking up into the dark sky.

But they weren't gone at all—the stars were black, gleaming like chips of obsidian. And in the darkness moved a shadow, vast and strange. My mouth tasted of ozone. "What's happening to me?"

She was silent for a long moment. "I don't know," she said at last. "Hold on, little rabbit. I'll figure this out." Her voice was urgent, half lost. She was more afraid than I was, I realized. She had no idea what to do.

I couldn't hold on. The ground was falling away, and so was she, and the black of the sky was all around me. I could feel it, the way it wove through my body, among the trees, through the earth. Through the halls of Harrow. It was everywhere, and there was no escaping it.

I heard the faint sound of men's voices. Bryony cursed. Fear clutched me—not of the black sky, the dark stars, the rebellious rot of my own flesh, but of what those voices meant.

"Bryony, hide," I said. "You have to go. You have to—"

"Hush," she whispered, peering out into the dark. "It's your family."

Don't trust them, I said. Her head whipped toward me, and I realized it wasn't my voice that had spoken, but Jessamine's.

Her mouth pressed into a thin line. "I'm getting you out of here," she said.

"No, I have to go with them," I said, and it was my voice but not my words, like something else had seized hold of me.

"Go, little witch," my grandfather said, and at the edge of my vision strobed the cracked-glass haze of his presence.

Dimly I registered that Bryony had extinguished her lantern. The cool stone pressed against my back. Jessamine's fingers combed through my hair, and music spilled from her onionskin throat, the liquid notes of a piano. I drifted with the music, my senses bleeding away from me, replaced by a cocoon of darkness.

Rough hands took hold of me, but I was a world away. Something shrieked in the distance. The voices came again, this time all around me, distorted and strange.

"Damn it. It bit her."

"I see."

"Is she conscious?"

A pause. "No."

"That's something, at least. What's it doing? Can you stop it?"

"There is no precedent for this. And we are well beyond the realm of medicinal remedies. Maybe the witch—"

"No. We're not involving her."

I watched the darkness slide across the starscape, a shadow against the unlight of the stars. It moved without pattern, its shape indescribably strange, but I wasn't afraid. I could feel it sliding inside of me, slipping beneath my skin.

"We don't know if this is fatal. It could—"

"*Look at her.* If that spreads any more, we'll lose Helen, and I don't know what's going to be in her place."

"Take her to the stone. I have an idea."

I was faintly aware of movement as someone carried me. There was a scrape, like a door opening, and then the smell of rain-dampened stone. Time shimmered in the void; I could see it, almost touch it. I watched the seconds struggle by as my body fought against the creeping cold.

"You're sure?"

"No, but in another minute, we'll lose the chance to find out."
I wondered what they were talking about. Maybe—

Pain lanced through my arm, just above my wrist. Horrible, tearing, burning pain, and I screamed until my throat was raw. The void vanished, but another darkness was rushing in, unconsciousness flooding over me.

In the brief second between the glittering void and the empty dark, my vision cleared. Above me were stars—the real stars. And a looming gray stone, roughly hewn. On its surface was carved the spiral of Harrow.

And into the spiral I fell.

13

THE SUN STRUCK my eyes like a fist. I mumbled a protest and rolled over, pulling the covers up over my head.

And then I sat bolt upright, panting. The dream, the hallway, the Folded—that pain in my wrist—I stared at my hand. It was fine. Not even a bruise or a whisper of discomfort.

What the hell happened last night?

Simon had been there, but he was with Mom, hours away. And then the woods, and Bryony, and the voices . . . But Eli had been there. In the hall. That, I remembered.

I shoved my feet into slippers. The breakfast bell was ringing. I must have slept through the first bell already. I stormed downstairs and burst into the breakfast room ready to demand Eli explain what the hell had happened, and for that matter, what Simon was even doing at Harrow—but I stuttered to a stop in the doorway. Everyone turned to stare at me.

Everyone. Eli and Iris. Caleb. Roman, Victoria, Desmond, Celia. Even Sandra.

"Good morning, Helen," Iris said. She was sitting in her customary place, a cup of coffee before her. She dropped a sugar cube into it as she studied me. "I trust you had a pleasant rest."

"No, actually," I said, "When did you all get here?"

"We just rolled in this morning," Desmond said as he selected a croissant.

"I thought you weren't supposed to get here until the twenty-fourth."

"It *is* the twenty-fourth," Celia said, clearly distressed by my distress.

"No, it's—it's—" It didn't make any sense.

"Are you feeling quite well, Helen?" Iris asked. Everyone was staring at me. I gulped.

"I woke up in the middle of the night, and . . ." No, better not to get too deep into that. "I saw Simon. Where is he?" I asked, half-frantic with worry.

"Your mother called earlier and said she was on the road, a couple hours away," Caleb said gently.

"What about Simon?" I insisted.

"I assume he's with her, or she would have said otherwise," Caleb said.

"Have I been unconscious? Was I missing? What is going on?" I gripped the edge of the doorway as if it were the only thing keeping me upright.

"Helen. It's okay," Caleb said, approaching me with a hand held up in a friendly, reassuring gesture. "You've been here. We went for a walk yesterday. On Sunday, you spilled soup on your dress—you don't remember any of this?"

I felt dizzy. I wasn't breathing properly, taking short, sharp breaths in through my nose. This couldn't be happening. I couldn't have lost a week and a half.

Caleb put a hand on my shoulder. "Perhaps you'd better lie down for a bit. Eli can give you something."

"I'm fine," I snapped, but I wasn't. I felt like I was going to throw up as confused panic gnawed my nerves into a pulpy mass.

"I'll walk you upstairs," Desmond said, standing. I started to object, but I realized he probably wanted the chance to talk to me alone. Maybe he knew something. I slipped out from under Caleb's hand and followed Desmond into the hall.

"I'm not crazy," I said when we were out of earshot.

"I don't think you are," Desmond assured me.

"It's really the day before Thanksgiving?" My voice cracked.

"Swear to god," he said. He pulled out his phone to show me.

"I don't remember any of it." How was that possible? "I saw Simon. I swear I did. Something might have happened to him."

"Your mom would mention if he wasn't with her," Desmond said.

"Caleb's got to be lying about the last few days. I must have been unconscious or something because I definitely wasn't walking around like normal." Why would Caleb lie?

I strode the rest of the way to my room. I yanked open the laundry basket and spotted the gray-blue of my favorite dress. I pulled it out and stared. Soup stain. Just like Caleb had said.

"Why can't I remember?" I asked.

"I can't really say," he said carefully.

"But it doesn't completely surprise you?"

"I don't know. It's just . . . memory can play tricks on you," he said, doubt in his voice.

He didn't believe, or didn't want to believe, in the things at

Harrow. But he knew more than he was letting on, I was sure of it. Maybe more than he thought he knew.

"What *do* you remember?" he asked.

I plopped onto the bed and pulled my knees up to my chest. "You won't believe me." He wasn't ready to hear about monsters, about shadows with teeth.

And as long as he was invested in his disbelief, he wouldn't be able to tell me what he knew because that would mean admitting to the truth of the things he had to have seen and experienced.

Maybe it was time he and Celia faced what they refused to see. An idea blossomed, fully formed, in my mind. I almost laughed— it seemed ridiculous. But maybe it would work.

"Do you think you could convince Celia to come out to the folly? Tonight, after dinner?" I asked.

He shrugged. "As long as we're not staying out past twilight," he said. It seemed so natural to him: a rule he obeyed without questioning why darkness might be so dangerous.

"We shouldn't need to. Just be there, okay?" It was probably a stupid idea. But I couldn't keep doing this on my own. I had to try something. "Oh, and can you get some booze?"

"In this house, that is never a problem," he said. He looked at me intently. "Maybe you should see a doctor or something."

"You don't really think that would help, do you?"

He paused. He wanted to say yes. He wanted to think that the mysteries of Harrow could be solved with skepticism. Instead, he shook his head. "I wish I knew how to help."

"Be at the folly," I told him. "If you want to help, be there."

When Desmond was gone, I curled tighter around my legs, hugging them close. Had I really spent the week doing normal things? The evidence suggested that I had. Not least among that evidence was my hand, which had no sign of an injury.

Or had it been real but somehow also a dream? I muffled a scream of frustration by biting my arm and flung myself back on the bedspread.

"I hate this place," I told the ceiling. "For the record."

Harrow's silence seethed with hatred of its own.

I was buzzing with nerves as I walked out across the lawn and toward one of the paths into the trees. As before, I didn't have to think about where to go to find Bryony. I found her immediately, sitting under a tree with a textbook open beside her, scribbling in a notebook. When she spotted me, she pushed up to her feet all at once, letting her notebook drop to the ground beside her.

"Where the hell have you been?" she demanded.

I let out a strangled laugh. "Good question."

"I thought you were *dead*," she snapped. "First, you completely freak out at my house and run away, and then your skin *literally falls apart in chunks in my hand* and you don't think to check in and let me know you're okay? It's been almost a week, and now you just walk up like nothing happened! What's wrong with you?"

I sagged, tension I hadn't known I was carrying flooding out of me. "It did happen?"

"You mean you nearly getting yourself killed? Yes, it happened." Her eyes searched mine, and a small frown played across her lips. "Why do you have to ask?"

"Because that's the last thing I remember before this morning," I said. "You and the folly. But apparently, I've been taking walks and spilling soup and being totally normal, and my hand is fine, and nothing's wrong, and I don't understand how that can be true." I was babbling. I shut my mouth with a click of teeth.

Her mouth hung open in a tiny *o*. "I thought you were avoiding me," she said.

"I was. Before," I told her. "After I came to your house. You looked at me and . . . I know you saw it. Whatever's inside of me."

"Oh," she said, brow furrowing. "That's why?"

"Of course that's why," I stammered. "You did see it. Didn't you?"

"Yeah, I saw you randomly bleeding all over everything," she said, rolling her eyes.

"Okay. But . . ." I started. Stopped. "I thought you *wanted* me to leave you alone. Isn't that what you keep telling me? That you don't want me bothering you?"

"I *don't* want you to bother me," she said, folding her arms. "I just wanted to know if you were dead or not, that's all."

"You helped me," I said, slow realization working its way through me. "Last night—last week, I mean—you didn't even hesitate. If you hate me so much, why would you help me?"

"Maybe I have a soft spot for fools," she said quietly.

"And rabbits?" I asked.

The corner of her mouth quirked. "Maybe." She reached out suddenly and caught my hand. She ran her fingers over my palm, examining the unbroken skin. My breath caught. Her fingertips were cool and callused. "There's not even a mark," she said. "It must have healed you. But why would it do that?"

"I saw it, you know. The Other," I told her.

"You mean the figments?" Bryony asked. She let go of my hand, and I felt a flicker of disappointment.

"No, I mean I saw it. Really saw it."

"That's not possible," Bryony said, shaking her head. "The dark soul—it's not a physical thing you can see. Not in this world, at least."

"I don't think it was this world," I replied. "It was like I was looking up at a night sky—like I was floating in space. But all the stars were black. I could see it moving in front of them."

"You don't know what you saw."

"But I do," I said, angry now, tired of being told that I didn't know what I knew, didn't see what I saw. "It was beautiful. And horrible."

The look in her eyes was a mix of hope and grief and jealousy and wonder. "I've always wanted to see it. Not the faces it wears, but what it really looks like."

"Maybe you will someday," I said. I didn't understand her connection to that thing, but I could understand being awed by it.

"Maybe." She dropped her eyes. Her hands cupped her elbows. "I'm glad you're okay," she admitted.

"I'm a long way from okay," I told her. "Bryony, what *were* those things? The Folded and the shadows, I mean. They were *real*. Solid. The figments aren't like that, are they?"

Bryony shook her head. "You might think you feel a fleeting touch from a figment, but it's all in your head. But the dark soul makes other things, too." She spoke in the careful cadence I'd come to expect from her explanations, like she'd never had to lay it out for anyone before. "The figments are like . . . a mask, maybe? They're a way for it to be seen and heard. They're *part* of it. The shadows and the Folded are more like dolls. The dark soul made them, but they're separate from it."

"So it makes monsters," I said, shuddering.

Her brows drew together, her expression sorrowful. "There's something wrong with it. It's like it's broken. That's why the things it makes are so violent. It used to make all kinds of things, wild and beautiful like the hounds—but not for a long time now. They were always dangerous if you weren't careful, but it's way worse than it used to be."

I'd thought the way she kept fumbling for an explanation was because she didn't know how to make me understand. But I was starting to realize it was something else. "You don't actually know for sure what it is, do you?"

Her lips skinned back from her teeth, her breath hissing. "I'm the Witch of Harrow," she said. "The witch has always—"

"Did you know the last witch?" I asked, interrupting her. She faltered into silence. "You're as much in over your head as I am," I said, feeling a bit smug—but then dread stole in. I'd been counting on her knowledge.

"We're not alike," she said. The venom was back in her voice. "I may not know anything, but I know that the Vaughans don't belong here. You claimed this place, but it isn't yours."

"And what about you? You serve the dark soul?" I asked.

"I'm no one's servant. The Vaughans came to these woods, and they built Harrow and they trapped something here. They treated it like a monster, but the witch knew better. And because she saw the truth of it, it could never deceive her. The witch chooses the dark soul, and the dark soul chooses her, and there is only truth between them." Her shoulders were thrown back, her head held high, and her eyes burned with conviction.

"You keep saying that it can't trick you," I said. "You aren't just talking about the weird things people feel around me. Do you mean the figments?"

She shook her head and ran her hand through her hair, pulling it back from her face. A few strands leaped free again immediately, falling over her eyes. "It can change things. Small things, usually. Tiny little tweaks to reality. A red door is suddenly white. Flowers grow in the wrong season. Other people don't remember that it was different before. But my memories can't be changed."

"Then that's what happened this week," I said, putting it together. "I *wasn't* hanging around all week, but everyone else remembers it that way because the dark soul changed things around?"

"I've never seen it change something that big, but maybe," she acknowledged.

"What else has it changed?" I asked.

She shrugged. "Recently? Just the flowers."

A shiver went through me. "What flowers?"

"Foxgloves. They grow on the grounds but only in the summer. Except lately, I've been finding them all over the place."

My mouth went dry. "I keep seeing foxgloves, too," I said. "I saw them growing in my grandfather's chest at the funeral. And every time the figments appear, they're there. And in Jessamine's portrait . . ."

"Daffodils," Bryony said. "Jessamine's portrait has daffodils, not foxgloves. They were her favorite. She always made my dad promise to plant a whole bed of them for her."

"It was foxglove when I saw it," I said. "Unless it was a different painting. But why would the dark soul change it? What's important about foxglove?"

"I don't know," Bryony said, spreading her hands. "It doesn't mean anything to me. Except . . ." She hesitated.

"Except what?"

"Digitalis," she said. "It's the scientific name for foxglove. And it's a medication—or a poison. It can stop your heart."

My breath hissed between my teeth. "Leopold and Jessamine both died of heart failure," I said.

Her eyes widened as this information sunk in. "Do you think they were poisoned?"

"Who would kill them?" I asked, shaking my head. "It doesn't make any sense."

"Your uncle was the one that was supposed to inherit this place, right? But then old Mr. Vaughan dies—dies really young for a Vaughan, by the way. He's the first Master of Harrow to die before his ninetieth birthday. He leaves you the house—and makes sure that if you say no, everyone else loses everything. So you can't possibly refuse."

"You make it sound like a trap."

"Of course it's a trap, little rabbit. What I'm wondering is who set it. And why you?"

"Grandpa Leopold's the one that changed the terms of the trust," I said. "I think. But maybe someone could have made him, or faked it, or . . . But that doesn't explain Jessamine. There's no reason to kill a little girl."

"She's not the first little girl to be lost to Harrow," Bryony reminded me. "I looked into those pictures we found while you were gone."

"Harrow's girls."

She nodded. "I managed to identify the other two. They're both dead. Another freak accident and a sudden illness. One of them was eleven when she died. The other was eight."

"The same age as Jessamine," I said. She didn't say anything, didn't even nod. Just let me sit with the knowledge.

"Someone or something took those girls," Bryony said. "I don't know if it was Harrow or the dark soul or your family. But whatever happened, you need to be careful. And you need to be *very* careful who you trust."

"Can I trust you?" I asked.

She opened her mouth, and I could see it in her eyes, what she wanted to say: *Of course you can.* But the words didn't come. They couldn't. Because it would have been a lie. I couldn't trust her, not completely, because Bryony was the Harrow Witch, and her loyalty would always be to the Other.

"I'm meeting my cousins at the folly tonight," I said to spare her having to answer. "You should join us."

"Why would I do that?" she asked, shaking her head. "Hanging out with Vaughan brats isn't my idea of a good time."

"I think they know things," I said. "They have to. They've grown up around here. But they've learned not to notice, or remember, or talk about it. I have an idea to get them to open up. Who knows? You might learn something."

"There's nothing those two can teach me," Bryony said, all prickle and bramble and ire, but I could see through her now.

"Come to the folly," I said. "At the very least, you can freak out some Vaughan kids."

Her grin was small and vicious. "Well, then, I can't possibly turn that down," she said. She reached out, her hand catching mine for an instant before she let go again. "Be safe, Rabbit," she said, her eyes locked on mine.

"I'll try," I said. It was the most I could promise.

I started back toward the house feeling borderline gleeful and trying to scold myself out of it. But I couldn't help the little smile tugging at the corner of my mouth. Bryony was coming tonight. It was somewhat possible that she didn't one hundred percent hate me. I might be a hallucinating amnesiac with a house full of monsters, but I had that going for me.

My path took me to the patio wrapping around the back of the house. I was lost in my thoughts and didn't notice Roman sitting at one of the tables until I was nearly next to him.

"You look smug," he said. I jumped. He chuckled. He took a drink from a mug. The smell from where I stood was of coffee, but there was a silver flask on the table next to him. "Not that I blame you. You've landed yourself in the lap of luxury, haven't you?"

"Not by choice," I reminded him. Maybe I was feeling bold after Bryony agreed to come tonight, or maybe I was just sick of his unconcealed hostility, but something in me snapped. "If I'd turned it down, you wouldn't be getting anything, right? So maybe lay off me."

He grunted in what was almost agreement. "Doesn't seem fair, does it? One crazy old man screwing everyone over for some girl he never even really knew."

I was done listening to Roman whine. "I'm going to go inside now," I said. He lurched to his feet, his chair scraping along the flagstones. He was way too close to me—close enough that I could smell the whiskey on his breath. I'd been right about what was in that coffee. I glared up at him. I wasn't going to let this drunk idiot intimidate me. Shadow monsters and the Folded, sure. But not Roman Vaughan.

"Caleb thinks we just have to give you time," Roman said. His voice was a rumble in his chest. "But you know what? Maybe it would be easier just to start over." He grinned as the implication sunk in. Start over. With a new heir. Meaning, when I was dead.

"You mind taking a step back there?"

Simon was coming down the steps. His normally amiable voice was steely. Relief flooded through me. Simon. That meant Mom was here, too, and I wasn't alone anymore.

"Ah. It's the boyfriend," Roman said, sneering his way through the last word.

Simon sighed. "Is this the part where we thump our chests and paw the ground? Is there some kind of hooting involved? Do you want me to find you a log to rip in half? I'm a bit out of touch on the current means of establishing masculine credentials." He walked over as he spoke, smiling blandly. "Or you could just go back to your day drinking and stop being an asshole."

Roman punched him. I cried out, but he must have been drunker than I thought because, even as I yelled, Roman's fist was swinging through empty air shy of Simon's face. The motion took him off-balance, and he stumbled.

"There's no call for that," Simon said, looking taken aback.

Roman swore, staring at Simon like he was some kind of ninja.

"Come on, Helen," Simon said, putting out his hand. I grabbed it, and we hustled up the steps, leaving Roman looking vaguely befuddled behind us.

"Nice timing," I told him, voice shaky.

"That man is unstable," Simon said, his brow creased with concern. "Are you okay?"

"He was just being a—jerk," I said, saving myself from some very not-Simon-rated language at the last minute. I looked at him with concern. "At least he didn't try to deck me. Lucky he was drunk."

"I thought I was in for a broken jaw," Simon admitted. "It seemed like . . ."

"What?" I asked.

"Nothing. Just, it seemed like he was going to hit me, and then it was like I was standing farther back than I'd thought. Must just be tired from the drive," Simon said.

"Tired from being chauffeured around, you mean?" Simon's explanation didn't quite add up. Had Harrow—no, the *Other*— done something? But why would it protect Simon?

Maybe it just wanted to mess with Roman. That would be deeply understandable.

"Yeah, yeah, I know. A grown man without a driver's license. It's not my fault I grew up with decent public transit and a raging anxiety disorder, you know."

I chuckled, but the sound withered. "Simon, were you with Mom the whole time at home?"

"Not every second," he said, brow creased. "Why?"

"So you weren't back here? A few days ago?" I knew I'd seen him. Hadn't I?

"How would I have even gotten here, Scout?"

We'd reached the doors, and Mom came bursting through, arms open. I forgot all about Roman for a few blissful seconds as I rested my head against her chest.

"Missed you," I confessed. She stroked my hair.

"Well, we're all done with that nonsense. I'm all yours again," she said. She pulled away, examining me. "Are you all right? You look . . . I don't know. Thin."

"It's been hard," I confessed. My voice wavered.

"Did something happen?" she asked. I didn't answer, which was answer enough. "Damn it. Helen, you can bail out at any time. We can go. You just say the word."

"I can't leave," I said. "Not yet."

"She hasn't found the center," Simon said cheerfully. My head whipped toward him.

"What did you say?" Mom asked.

Simon smiled. "She's got to find the center. That's the only way out," he said. Then he frowned. "I . . . I have no idea what that means."

But I did.

It meant that Harrow had a hold on him as well. It meant that it wasn't safe here for Simon. For either of them.

14

AFTER LUNCH, DESMOND showed up at my door, wearing an expression of arch superiority. "I am a genius," he informed me in a lofty tone, flourishing a hand in the air for emphasis.

"I knew that, actually," I said, letting him in. "Why are you a genius today, specifically?"

"I decoded more of Nicholas's journal," he said. "I was hoping to look at the real thing, actually. Some of the pictures weren't the best, and the symbols get a bit blurry at the edges."

"It's over here," I said, and went to grab it from its hiding place.

"Sweet. And here's what I've got," he said, handing me a spiral notebook. I sat on the edge of the bed and eagerly read through the pages he'd translated. For the first couple, it might as well still have been in code—it was all references to people Nicholas knew and rival occult theorists he took vicious pleasure in deriding. The next set of entries was more interesting.

A disaster. Three attempts to project herself into the vast dark, and three failures. Dr. Raymond begins to doubt. He is

*confident in the procedure, but if Annalise cannot guide the girl
to the vast dark, it will be all for naught.*

"The girl? What girl are they talking about?" I asked.

"Keep reading," Desmond said, scrunching up his face like
he didn't want to have to explain. He hovered nearby as I continued.

*My spirits are much improved. Annalise has traversed the
boundaries between worlds once more and is now confident in
her ability to guide Mary's consciousness such that she may
look upon the dark god. Dr. Raymond is nearly ready to perform his marvelous procedure. A few weeks more, and the truth
of other worlds will be within our grasp.*

"Okay, why don't I like the sound of that?" I asked.

"Maybe because Victorian-era doctors thought putting cocaine
in baby bottles was a great idea and washing your hands was a
waste of time?" Desmond suggested with a grimace. "I'm guessing
whatever procedure they're talking about, they didn't run it by
an ethics committee either. If I was Mary, I wouldn't stick around
to find out what they were up to."

"The god of the vast dark," I murmured, remembering the il-
lustration of the shape in front of the stars. Almost exactly what I
had seen. "Desmond, if there was a god in the basement, you
would tell me, right?"

"We keep the interdimensional gods in the attic," Desmond

replied with a grin, but it faltered. "I mean, obviously not. Because there's no such thing."

What did Nicholas mean by a god, anyway? Maybe it wasn't a question of divinity but power. A being that could alter reality itself—I could understand calling that a god.

"Dr. Raymond helped design Harrow, right?" I asked. "Something about the effects of architecture on the mind?"

"Yeah. He wrote a book about the general principal, but Eli warned me it is, in his words, 'so dense as to be incomprehensible, and coming from me that is quite the condemnation,'" he said, tucking two fingers into an imaginary vest pocket and blinking owlishly as he did.

"You do a good Eli," I told him with a smirk.

"I've had a lot of practice," Desmond replied. He leaned against the post at the end of the bed, crossing his ankles. "I think the basic idea is that he thought a building could be designed to change your thought patterns, just by living in it. Make them more orderly or more chaotic. He wanted to apply his theories to prisons—like, to make the prisoners more law-abiding and obedient."

What was a cage but another kind of prison? Perhaps this meant the strange patterns of Harrow were somehow designed to contain the Other.

That was all Desmond had translated. I handed the notebook back to him with another murmur of thanks. He took it, then stepped over to my desk where I'd left the journal. He tapped the cover. "Can I take this with me? I might be able to get more done by dinner," he said.

"You don't have to," I told him. "I really don't have anything I can do for you in return."

"Like I could possibly stop now," Desmond said. "I have got to know what kind of mad scientist bullshit they got up to."

"Okay, I just don't want you to feel like I'm using you," I said.

"Oh, you are. But that's Vaughan tradition," he replied, with a joking tone that wasn't joking at all.

"I guess that's all right, then." I rolled my eyes. "As long as I'm being a *traditional* asshole."

"You're well on your way to fitting in," he told me in a faux congratulatory voice. Then he hesitated. "*Not* fitting in here can help—sometimes. Having my dad and his family helps me remember that this isn't . . ."

"Normal?" I suggested. I leaned back on the bed, bracing myself with both hands as I raised an eyebrow at him. He sighed and sat in the desk chair, resting his elbows on his knees.

"What I mean is it's not the only way to be," he said. "Even all of this—Thanksgiving being so formal, like it's a show we're putting on instead of the chance to be together. I'll take the messy, burned casserole, arguing over who has to do the dishes version any day."

"Why aren't you with them this year, then?" I asked.

"My dad's a physicist, and this year he's working at CERN— you know, unlocking the secrets of the universe." He said it like he was downplaying it, but his eyes glowed with pride.

"A man after Nicholas Vaughan's heart," I joked.

"Do *not* let him hear you say that," Desmond said with a rueful shake of his head. "Anyway, he's in Switzerland, so it's not really

a long weekend kind of visit. Normally, I'd go to my grandparents' place anyway, but since I'm flying out to see Dad for Christmas I agreed to stick around for Thanksgiving. So you're stuck
with me."

"Alas," I said in mock despair, and we exchanged a grin. Then
I cleared my throat. My gaze wandered off to stare at the wall-
paper, and casually as I could, I added, "Oh. By the way. I invited
Bryony Locke to join us tonight at the folly."

"You what? Why?" Desmond asked, looking a bit panicked.
"She's the witch!"

"Exactly. She can help with the . . . knowing stuff." I gestured
broadly. "Besides, she's—she's—"

"What?" Desmond demanded.

"Very pretty," I told him, and then groaned and flopped back
on the bed, covering my eyes as my cheeks turned hot.

"Helen."

"Yes."

"Helen."

"What."

"Do you have a crush on the Harrow Witch."

"No. Yes. Shut up," I said.

"Helen. This is a very concerning display of bad judgment. The
Harrow Witch is *not* friendly with Vaughans. She *hates* Vaughans,"
Desmond informed me.

"I knoooow." I groaned, craning my neck to look up.

He tapped his chin thoughtfully. "On the other hand, maybe
we're cursed because of some falling out with the original witch,
and you kissing her will break the spell."

"Who said anything about kissing her?" I asked, scrambling up. I sat cross-legged, shoving my now-messy hair back from my face. "My plan is to absolutely never let her get the slightest inkling that I feel any way about her at all so it'll be less mortifying that she despises me and also that I am the most awkward human being in existence."

Desmond was grinning now, leaning back in the chair with his hands laced behind his head. "You're gonna kiss the witch," he told me.

"Desmond, please shut up," I begged him.

He raised his hands in surrender. "All right. I'm leaving you here to google 'how to get a spooky forest lady to like me,' and *I'm* going to go do real work. Like translating obscure nineteenth-century ciphers about interdimensional space gods." He picked up his notebook and the journal, gave me a jaunty wave, and headed for the door.

"Wait," I said when his hand was on the knob. "Thank you."

"For what?" he asked, looking back. "The journal? I told you, I'm into it."

"No. For being my friend. If we are friends," I said, suddenly afraid that I'd read too much into things.

He looked thoughtful. "We are," he said, and the fact that he'd had to think about it made me trust it more somehow. "Early days, but yeah, we're friends."

"I've never really had a friend before. It's nice," I said.

He smiled. "Well, for not having much practice, you're decent at it. I'll see you at dinner."

"See you," I said. And then he was gone.

———

An hour later, Iris knocked on the door of the Willows. She wore a deep-red turtleneck and black slacks, a simple outfit that looked as elegant as a ballgown. "Helen, I thought I ought to check on you, given this morning's distress."

I strained to hear a hint of something nurturing in her tone but failed. She looked at me with an air of faint disappointment. "I'm okay," I said. "I'm sorry about all of that."

"This place can play tricks on you," she said. "It's hardly the first time someone has woken up with odd notions." She walked in without asking for permission and crossed to my desk, examining the scapula and fox skull sitting there. "Hm."

"It's kind of a hobby," I said with a note of apology.

"I suppose everyone needs a few of those," she replied, not unkindly. I studied her. She was a hard woman, but perhaps that was necessity. She'd come to live at Harrow as an adult—married into this mess. You'd have to be tough to navigate living in this place for so long when you weren't born to it. Tough and canny.

But in what way? It hadn't yet sunk in, what Bryony and I had realized about the foxglove. Our suspicion that Leopold, and maybe even Jessamine, had been poisoned. Was Iris Vaughan the kind of tough and canny woman who could poison her husband?

And why would she? What had she gained by bringing me here?

What had *anyone* gained? I was hardly the mistress that they all wanted. Even Caleb knew I was in over my head. Then there was Jessamine. I could concoct a dozen reasons, some more far-fetched than others, why someone would have wanted to murder Leopold. For all I knew, he'd personally betrayed every one of them and was mean to puppies on the weekends. But Jessamine?

It didn't make sense.

Iris turned away from her examination of the scapula. "Attire tonight will be semiformal. Dinner at six o'clock. Tomorrow's dinner is the formal celebration, but I do expect everyone to attend this evening as well."

I looked down at my dirty jeans and sneakers. "Right. I'll change before then, obviously."

"It is best to meet Harrow where it stands—it is easier to change yourself than to try to move these old stones," Iris said.

"I meant my clothes," I replied, and her eye glinted with amusement.

"I know. Still, the point stands. Harrow has its rules and routines."

Don't go out on the grounds after dark. Bells for breakfast, lunch, and dinner, bells for sunset and sunrise. And then all the unspoken rules: the things you didn't say, didn't notice, didn't warn your granddaughter about, even though she was in danger.

"I don't think I'm fitting into them well. Those rules and routines, I mean," I said. I wasn't being obstinate—just honest. "When I went to school, all the structure . . . I didn't do well with it."

"That is a bit of an understatement, don't you think?" Iris asked. "That girl almost died."

I flinched. "You know about that."

Iris regarded me, her expression hooded and hard to read. "Your mother called home when it happened. She was frantic.

'Something is wrong with Helen,' she told us. Leopold drove down in the middle of the night." She sounded detached, but under that was something else. Anger, maybe.

"I didn't know that," I said. I didn't remember a lot from that day, or the ones before it, or after it—I'd sunk down into myself, vanished, and only emerged weeks later, as if I'd been dreaming. I flinched. "He's why I didn't get in trouble, isn't he?"

"He smoothed things out."

"Did he give that girl her eyes back?" I asked bitterly.

Iris raised an eyebrow. "I believe they were able to preserve some sight in one of them."

"I didn't know that." We hadn't talked about what happened. I'd just never gone back to school. I'd wondered often how I could get away with not even seeing a psychiatrist or something when everyone thought I'd stabbed a girl's eyes out with scissors.

"We are here to make sure that your return to Harrow is smooth. That you truly become a part of this place," Iris said. "Which means that we will take things slowly."

"We have ten months left until the Investiture," I said. "That's not a very long time."

"In my experience, most teenagers consider the length of a single school term to be equivalent to eternity," Iris said.

"Most graduation ceremonies aren't life-and-death," I countered. "If I at least knew what this Investiture ceremony *was*, maybe I'd know how to plan for it."

"It's not that kind of test," Iris said. "The year is so that Harrow can learn the shape of you, as you have learned the shape of Harrow. All the corridors of your soul. Either you are compatible and the year gives you the time to adapt to one another. Or you are not."

"And what if I'm not?"

"No one who has ever undergone the Investiture has been rejected," Iris said. "If Harrow is going to reject you, it generally makes it clear well before then."

Like by attacking me with crumpled-up monsters? I wondered. How much of it was Harrow that needed to accept me, and how much was the Other? And after so long, was there even a difference between the monster and its cage?

Both of them seemed to want to consume me.

Ten months was an eternity to survive. And no time at all to find a way out of this mess.

I was late getting to dinner, scurrying in after the bell—I'd been working on the fox skull, or failing to work on it, and I'd lost track of time. Everyone else was already seated. The only place setting left was at the head of the table—in front of a huge hideous chair with a carved back that made my eyes feel like they couldn't quite focus. I gave Mom an are-you-serious look, and she winced sympathetically.

"Please, take your place," Iris said, gesturing liquidly with one pale hand. I slunk over and lowered myself into the chair, letting its ridges dig into my back; it seemed impossible to get comfortable, to find a place for my fingers to rest. It was clearly designed to suit a particular vision, without concern for the organic shapes of a human body.

The first course arrived, carried by waitstaff who avoided meeting my eyes, just like everyone else who cycled through Harrow. I'd stopped trying to learn their names or faces—none of them lasted long anyway. Forks and knives clinked as we dug in.

"Not exactly an easy chair," I said, wiggling to try to find a position that didn't leave a hard ridge of wood biting into some piece of my anatomy.

"It is a piece of family history," Eli admonished me. "Nicholas Vaughan had that chair built to his specifications."

"He seems like maybe he had some control issues," I said, stabbing at a piece of chicken that seemed determined to scoot across my plate, dragging a slimy trail of béchamel sauce.

"He had vision," Eli said, sounding perturbed.

"What was it Dad called it?" Caleb asked, with a spark of mischief in his eye.

"Leopold had his opinions," Eli allowed.

"'A device as torturous in its aesthetics as its ergonomics,'" Mom said, quoting, and Eli sighed.

"You forgot 'a crime visited upon this family for generations,'" Victoria added.

"'Proof that Nicholas Vaughan had the mind of a mad genius and the taste of merely a madman,'" Caleb finished. The three of them laughed, and in their smiles, I could suddenly see how much they looked alike. "We only bring it out for formal occasions," Caleb confessed.

"Your grandfather sat in that chair every day of his tenure," Iris said. "It's tradition for the Master of Harrow to use it."

"Not every tradition needs to be preserved," Caleb pointed out.

"Maybe if there was more respect for tradition around here, we wouldn't be in this mess," Roman muttered.

"What mess?" Sandra asked, gesturing a bit too freely with her wine. "You're just pissed you didn't manage to kiss Leopold's ass enough to get to sit in the ugly chair yourself."

A muscle in Caleb's neck twitched. Victoria sighed. "Come on, Sandra. The shtick is wearing thin," she said. Celia stiffened, staring down at her plate. Desmond touched her wrist under the table.

"Which shtick is that? The one where I smile vacantly and pretend to be an empty-headed housewife without a negative thought in my head? The one where I forget I was partner in a prestigious firm until I quit because my husband's fragile ego couldn't handle it? Oh, wait. That's you," Sandra said brightly. The silence that followed was complete. Celia looked like she wanted to sink through the floor or throw herself out the nearest window. Desmond's jaw flared. Simon and I cast each other half-panicked looks.

"Sandra, enough," Caleb said, pain in his voice.

"Everyone is grieving, Sandra. It doesn't give you license to act like a complete bitch," Victoria said, shaking her head.

"Tell me more about how my daughter's death is affecting *you*, Vicky," Sandra shot back with a sneer that transformed her whole face into a mask of grief and anger.

"*Sandra.*" Caleb rose from his chair. His voice cut through the argument so effectively it took me a moment to realize he hadn't raised his voice at all. "Please."

"Sorry," she said casually. "I'm drunk."

"What else is new?" Roman asked, but Sandra just laughed. I stared at them. Iris started eating again without comment, and Sandra reached out to claim a bottle of wine to refresh her glass, and no one else said a word. I looked down the table at Desmond, but he was staring at his plate in fixed silence. Celia looked on the verge of melting into the rug.

Caleb sat back down. He cleared his throat and looked at me. His expression was one of perfect control, as if nothing at all had just happened, but when he spoke, his voice broke. "Tell me, how are you finding Harrow thus far?"

Right. Change of subject. So we weren't going to acknowledge what had just happened. You didn't talk about your problems at Harrow; you talked around them. The family strategy apparently applied to more than the supernatural. "Strange, if I'm being honest," I managed. I didn't see a point in lying about that, not when we all knew it was true. "I can't imagine growing up here."

"We didn't exactly *live* here," Mom said, sounding cautious as if afraid of another outburst. "I mean, we were at Atwood most of the time."

"The last child to actually live at Harrow full time was at the turn of the century," Eli said. "Though, traditionally, all the children of the family spent the summer and holidays here."

"We never really have," Desmond said. "I split holidays with my other grandparents and my dad in Geneva. I've only ever spent a week at Harrow here and there."

"Things aren't as they once were," Eli replied, looking uncomfortable.

"Harrow has been a bit less suitable for guests the last while,"

Iris allowed. "Certain problems with maintenance, that sort of thing."

"What, like a leaky roof?" I asked.

"It is very difficult to find workers who will come all the way out to Harrow," Eli said, which didn't seem like an answer.

"That might have something to do with how they keep disappearing," Sandra said blithely. The whole table went tense. "All those *terrible* accidents. Not to mention all those girls."

"That's a nasty rumor, and I would think you knew better than to spread it," Iris said. Her tone was mildly cross, like she was admonishing someone for confusing the salt and pepper shakers. Still, everyone shifted uncomfortably as if she'd just dressed them all down. I might be sitting at the head of the table, but there was no doubt who was at the head of the family.

"My point," Eli said, "was that Atwood has been more of a consistent home for the youth of our family than Harrowstone Hall itself. It's a pity that you returned to the fold so late, or you might have attended yourself."

"I wish I'd gone earlier," Celia said with a little sigh. "Everyone already knows each other. It's been hard making friends."

"You have like eight hundred friends," Desmond said, rolling his eyes.

"Those are *friendly acquaintances*, Desmond—there's a difference," she shot back with a hearty eye roll of her own.

"I'd much rather have gone to London with you," Desmond said. "Just saying."

"London?" I asked.

"I was doing some work for the London offices of the company," Victoria said. "With Celia still being so young, we decided to hold off on Atwood until high school."

I caught a glimpse of Roman as Victoria was talking and blinked in surprise. The look on his face was one of flinty anger. I wondered if it had something to do with what Sandra had hinted at—that Victoria had given up her career so she wouldn't outclass her husband. She had to make herself small to fit around him, I thought. I could see it under the surface, the pieces of herself she'd carved away so that he could feel mighty.

I looked away quickly. I didn't want to see these things. Those were her secrets, not Harrow's. I shouldn't be prying into them.

Soon conversation turned to meaningless topics, and I found my mind drifting.

One of these people might be a murderer.

I wished it was harder to believe, but under the current of every conversation, I could feel the tensions that ran like fault lines beneath the surface of the family. Roman simmering with discontent, furious that his efforts to ingratiate himself to Leopold and the family had failed. It would be easy to underestimate Roman, I thought. He had that frat-guy-all-grown-up air about him. He drank and sulked. But he was smart, too. And he thought long term. I could see him poisoning Leopold if he thought it would get him closer to the family's money—or whatever power he thought being Master of Harrow would grant him.

Except that it *hadn't* gotten him closer. He only made sense as a suspect if he hadn't known that I would be heir. Maybe that had been the point—Leopold had suspected that someone meant to do him in, and he'd left everything to me as a way of frustrating their plans.

So who *had* been in line to inherit? Not Mom, after she left. And Caleb and Leopold hadn't had a good relationship either. Maybe that wouldn't have mattered, or maybe it was as Celia had suggested and Victoria would have inherited by default. Which once again made Roman a likely suspect if he wanted to hasten the process. I certainly couldn't see Victoria doing it—unless, maybe, her husband had demanded it. She was so overwhelmed by him. Any time they were in a room together, she constantly glanced his way as if for approval.

Maybe I was thinking about it all wrong. Maybe it had nothing to do with who was going to inherit Harrow. Something else, then. Why did people kill? Money? Love? Revenge?

Jessamine had died when she was in Leopold and Iris's care. Had it been their fault?

I looked at Sandra, working hard at pickling herself in pinot. Grief lay in her bones like a cancer, killing her just as surely. Caleb's grief was softer, subtler, in the things he didn't say, in the care with which he moved through the world.

I couldn't imagine something more horrible than losing a child. If they blamed Leopold, I couldn't rule them out.

I wanted to. I wanted to cross each and every one of them off the list. Roman, okay, fine, but everyone else? I'd never had family before, beyond Mom and Simon. Being in a room full of people who looked like me, who treated me like a person, was astonishing. Even if this wasn't exactly the picture of a Thanksgiving gathering you'd put on a postcard.

The tension between hope and suspicion left me jangling with nervous energy. I ate the rest of my meal without tasting it, and when it was finally over, I found myself restless. I wanted to go up and work on the bones, but the only one waiting for me was the fox skull, and every time I sat down with it, I could only stare, all ideas and instincts abandoning me.

"Want to take a walk?" Mom asked, catching up with me in the hallway. "I feel like I lost track of you two minutes after getting here."

"To be fair, it takes a search party and a team of dogs to find each other in this place," I pointed out.

"I'm actually going to miss tripping over each other every time someone has to go to the bathroom," Mom confessed, and I laughed.

"Me, too," I said, though that other life already felt so far away. I felt as if I'd always been at Harrow.

We wandered through hallways that were slowly becoming familiar to me. "Why didn't I know Jessamine had died?" I asked her after a while. "I didn't even know she existed."

"She was born right before we left," Mom said. "We never talked about my family. And when she died, you were really sick. By the time you got better, the funeral was over. You hadn't known her, so I suppose I didn't really think to break the news to you."

"When was I sick?" I asked, frowning.

"Last year. Over Christmas," Mom said. "Don't you remember?"

"No." I stopped dead. "I don't remember being sick at all. Are you sure?"

She stared at me. "Of course I'm sure. You couldn't even get out of bed for weeks. You were delirious. Eli even came down to help take care of you in the worst of it."

"Wait, Eli came to our house?"

"I don't even know how he found out. I don't think I mentioned it to Caleb," Mom said absently. "He was a real lifesaver. I'd hear you two talking. I assumed you remembered." She frowned at me.

"Not even a little," I said, bewildered.

"I don't know what to tell you, hon." Concern flickered briefly in her eyes, but she shook her head as if clearing away a fog, and her expression smoothed.

There wasn't a gap in my memory, precisely—but I didn't remember Christmas, it was true. It was like November and January had been stitched together seamlessly.

Just like the missing days between last week and today.

It was all connected, I was sure of it. The reason we'd fled. The missing girls. Jessamine's death and Leopold's. *If I could only see how*, I thought, *I could find my way through this maddening spiral.*

I couldn't see it. Not yet.

But I thought I might learn a few more secrets tonight.

15

I DRESSED WARMLY, glad to finally have more than the same five outfits to cycle through now that Mom and Simon had brought back our things.

Bryony was waiting for me at the edge of the trees. She wore a skirt the color of midnight, spangled with constellations, and she'd put her hair up in a messy bun, baring her long, elegant neck. A draped wool cardigan had slouched down to her elbows as she stood with her arms crossed.

"I wasn't expecting you to wait for me," I said, immediately knocked off-balance.

"There's no way I'm showing up alone. I don't do well with . . . people," she confessed. Her voice was rough, almost hiding the nervousness.

"That's okay. I don't either," I told her.

"Then we have *two* problems," she said, scowling. I laughed.

"It'll be fine," I promised.

"You can't let them know about me," Bryony said. She grabbed my hand, her gaze urgent.

"That you're running blind with this whole witch thing, you mean?" I asked. "Why would I?"

"Why wouldn't you?" she countered.

I just shook my head. I didn't understand people. She dropped my hand. We kept walking, and before long we were in sight of the folly. The others were already there. Desmond was starting up a little fire in a cobbled-together ring of stones on the folly floor. Celia was putting on lipstick, peering into her phone camera to get it right. The lipstick tube had a little bee stamped on the bottom of it—my mom had one just like it.

When she saw Bryony, she squeaked and almost dropped the lipstick and her phone. "What is she doing here?" she asked, borderline panicked.

"It's cool," Desmond told her, tossing twigs on the growing fire. "Helen invited her."

Bryony stood rooted like a tree next to me. Her stony look and stiff posture would look intimidating if you didn't know she was terrified.

"Okay. I just—okay," Celia said. She still looked a bit scared, but her urge to make everybody comfortable was winning out.

"*I'm* still not exactly sure what it is I'm doing here," Bryony said.

"You're hanging out," I said. "We're all hanging out. Desmond, did you bring the . . . ?"

"Dangerous amounts of terrible vodka?" Desmond asked, extracting a bottle from his backpack with a flourish. "Anything for you, my lady."

"You didn't say anything about getting *drunk* with Vaughan brats," Bryony said under her breath though still loud enough for Celia to overhear. Celia's cheeks went predictably red.

"Look, we all know there are weird things at Harrow," I said. No one contradicted me. That was a start. "It's obvious that you don't like talking about it outright. I don't either. You don't know if people will believe you."

"You don't know what's listening," Celia said quietly.

"Sometimes it's hard to talk at all," Desmond added. "Or to remember what it is you wanted to say when you go to say it. Like something is stopping you."

Celia nodded. Bryony looked curious—it wasn't the same for her.

"Well, we're not going to talk about things that happen at Harrow," I said. "We're going to talk about things that *don't* happen. It's like that drinking game."

"'Never have I ever'?" Desmond guessed, and I nodded. "Sounds kind of lame."

"You shouldn't use that word. It's ableist," Celia said.

"Right, sorry," Desmond said. "This idea seems rather subpar." His correction was good-natured, and Celia smiled. Bryony cast them a speculative look. I wondered what she'd expected them to be like.

"Sometimes it's easier to talk about things when you come at them sideways," I said.

"And drunk," Desmond added.

"I think it's a good idea," Celia said, ever the supportive one.

"It should be interesting, at least," Bryony added with a shrug.

Desmond, outnumbered, heaved a sigh. "Fine. It's not like I have a better plan," he said. "And after *that* dinner, I could definitely use a drink."

Desmond took out a stack of yellow plastic cups and poured a glug of vodka into each. For Celia, he added a generous pour of Sprite. "Everybody knows how this goes, right?"

"No," Bryony said, catching him off-balance. She shrugged. "I live under a rock."

"We take turns," I explained as if I'd done this before and not just seen it in movies. "You say, 'Never have I ever . . .' and then you say something that you've never done. And if anyone in the group *has* done it, they take a drink."

Bryony was the last to get a cup. She held it with the very tips of her fingers, like she was trying to avoid contact as much as possible.

Desmond took his place at the edge of our wonky circle and cleared his throat. "So, who's first? Come on, guys. Let's spill all our secrets."

"Never have I ever had alcohol before," I confessed, considering the cup.

"Seriously?" Desmond asked, laughing, and drank. So did Celia and Bryony—Celia taking only a dainty sip.

An awkward silence settled. "Never have I ever skipped class," Celia offered.

"Does blowing off homeschool courses count?" I asked. "Because I think I need to drink the whole bottle. I'm so behind."

"Bottoms up," Desmond said, and took his own drink. I turned my cup up and took a swallow, then coughed as the alcohol scorched its way down my throat. "Come on," Desmond said. "Let's see how far we can push this thing."

"That's the idea," I said.

Desmond considered. "Never have I ever played hopscotch with a ghost girl."

Celia drank. "But she wasn't a ghost."

"A figment," I said.

She nodded, then cleared her throat delicately. "Never have I ever met the melting-wax woman."

Desmond shuddered—and drank.

"Was she blond? Carrying a candle? Ranting about eyes watching her?" I asked.

He said nothing but took another sip in confirmation. Then, looking off to the side, he spoke haltingly. "It was night. I was eight years old. I had to go to the bathroom, and I saw the light down the hall. I've always told myself it was a dream."

"Mine was a dream," I said. Belatedly, I took a swallow of my own. "But I don't think that means it wasn't real." He nodded like he understood. This was working. Sort of.

Celia wet her lips. "Never have I ever—"

"You just went," Desmond objected. "It's Bryony's turn."

Bryony ran a fingertip along the edge of her cup. "I'm not as eager to share my secrets as the rest of you," she said.

"You have to. It's not fair otherwise," Celia said, her eyes wide and guileless. "We have to all be in this together."

Bryony's mouth had a contrary tilt, but she sighed at last. "All right. Never have I ever found out what the shadows are trying to dig up at night."

"Whoa, wait, what?" Desmond asked, eyes wide—but Celia took a sip. Bryony looked at her with interest as if she hadn't really expected an answer.

"I have been trying to find out for years. You know?" Bryony asked. Celia nodded, gripping her cup so tightly I thought she might crumple it. She started to speak, but then she gave a shudder and cast us a helpless look, like she couldn't bring herself to do it.

I thought of the Folded, the way it had reached for the thing Eli held out to it—the rib. "Bones," I said, the realization settling through me like a sigh. "They're searching for bones."

Celia drank, then coughed a bit. Lightweight, I thought, but judging by the weird lurching feeling when I moved, so was I. She'd seen then. Which meant—

"Never have I ever *intentionally* stayed out after dark," I said, gaze fixed on Celia.

Bryony drank, of course. So did Celia. And so, reluctantly, did Desmond.

"I never got out of sight of the house, though," Celia said. "I was at the edge of the trees, and I saw one of the shadows. It found a bone—a femur, I think? It looked human, but it was far away. I never told anyone that before." She took two more swallows and shuddered hard.

"According to Mom and Uncle Caleb, they used to sneak out all the time," Desmond said. "Grandpa Eli says it was the same with their generation. But after what happened to those kids, it wasn't safe."

"What kids?" I asked.

"There were these teenagers from Eston who broke in to party on the grounds," Celia said, shoulders hunched. "They all killed each other."

"Holy shit," I said, eyes widening.

"That's not true," Desmond said. "Only one boy died. The other three were just injured. They said they were fighting monsters. And they had bite marks and stuff—but they were all human bites. They beat the one boy to death. Everyone said they'd taken some bad LSD, but I looked it up at one point, and the official police report said all that was in their systems was pot and alcohol."

I looked down at my cup dubiously.

"My dad was the one who found them," Bryony said. All eyes turned to her. "He doesn't talk about it, but I can tell it still affects him." She paused. "It was right here, you know."

I looked around at the graffiti scrawled over the old stones, wondering if any of it had been left by those unfortunate kids. "When was this?" I asked.

"I was eight. So ten years ago. In the fall," Bryony said.

Ten years ago. Right after I left. Maybe that was the terrible thing my mother had sensed coming.

"There have been a few weird accidents, but nothing like that since," Desmond said.

"Because people got more careful," Bryony pointed out. "Like you said, you two don't sneak out like your parents did."

"I went into the woods," Desmond said in a burst of sound that drew all eyes to him.

"Desmond! You could have *died*!" Celia wailed.

"It isn't death that you have to worry about," Bryony said. "Not with Vaughan blood."

"No, you just might end up like Samson Vaughan," Desmond said.

"What happened to Samson Vaughan?" I asked.

"He was Leopold's cousin," Desmond explained. "Apparently, when he was thirteen, he decided to stay out all night. I don't know what happened to him. Sam couldn't say because he didn't have a tongue when they found him in the morning. He wouldn't write it down either. He'd only draw the same thing over and over and over again. A spiral."

"*The* spiral?" I asked.

"The symbol of Harrow," Desmond said. "God knows why."

"It's a reference to the labyrinth," Celia said. "You know. The queen fell in love with a bull and gave birth to the minotaur, and it was so monstrous and evil they had to lock it away in the labyrinth. A monster in a maze."

"Harrow may be a maze, but there is no monster here," Bryony said, her voice and expression both cold.

Desmond raised an eyebrow. "If we're saying the shit that happens here is real, how can you say the thing responsible isn't evil?"

"We're getting off topic," I said. The last thing I needed was those two going after each other and letting this whole thing fall apart. "Desmond, you were saying you stayed out at night."

He took a big glug of vodka. "I think so. I have this memory, but it's like it's floating. I can't place it. I was pretty young, though." He swallowed and curled his hand into a fist. "I have this image of a man. He's holding a little girl's hand. It's dark. We're in the woods. I try to follow. I remember being afraid and cold. And then there was shouting. Then I remember Roman grabbing me by the arm. He was all covered in dirt, and his eye was swollen, and his nose was bleeding. He told me to get back into the house. And I must have because that's all I remember."

"You don't remember when it was?" Bryony asked, frowning. "Or who the girl was?"

"Like I said, it's just sort of floating. I didn't even think about it until a couple years ago, and it just popped into my head. Like I'd repressed it or something," Desmond said, sounding deeply uncomfortable. He sighed. "Look, Helen, I'm not sure any of this is actually helpful. You know what you need to do. Play it safe, ride the year out, inherit everything, and GTFO."

"That's assuming that I *can* ride out the year," I said grimly. "You're not the one that keeps waking up outside with dirt under your fingernails." The alcohol was definitely hitting me, uncoiling in my stomach. I felt dizzy, and the stones of the folly seemed like hunched-over forms, growing ominous in the dark.

"I had a dream about you," Celia said distantly. Wind sighed through the trees and dragged ripples over the surface of the lake. "I dreamed you were sleeping, and tentacles made of shadows reached up out of your bed and pulled you down. Deep below the house. I dreamed they were like puppet strings and made you dig and dig and dig, and then I realized you were looking for your bones, Helen. You were digging for your own bones, but you couldn't find them."

"What the fuck, Celia," Desmond said, eyes wide.

She blinked as if snapping out of a trance. "I'm sorry," she said. "I don't know what . . . what did I just say?"

"Quite a bit," Bryony replied, looking intently at her. "You can hear it, can't you?"

"Sometimes," she murmured. "It whispers. Sometimes I can hear. Sometimes I understand. It's louder now."

Desmond gave an unsettled chuckle. "Come on, guys. This is all a bit dire, isn't it? Seriously, Helen, no Master of Harrow has ever gotten gobbled up. They've all lived super long lives and died of old age. Except Leopold, I guess, but a bad heart is basically old age. You should just be enjoying yourself."

"Enjoying myself?" I asked.

Desmond's eye glinted. "Yeah. Relax. Drink. Try this: never have I ever . . . kissed a boy."

"That's *not* what we're doing," Celia squeaked. But she drank. So did Bryony. A spike of disappointment went through me. Did that mean she only kissed boys? Did that mean she didn't want to kiss me? Of course she didn't want to kiss me.

Desmond smiled, then gave a shrug and took a drink as well.

"Wait, wait, hold on," Celia said. "You were lying? You *have* kissed a boy?"

"I just wanted to know if you had," Desmond said, winking at her.

"Who did you kiss?" she demanded.

"Marcus Hollins," he answered, exaggerating his enunciation. "It was a fine kiss, he's very sweet—turns out I'm not into dudes. Who'd *you* kiss?"

"I also kissed Marcus Hollins," Celia said. She was beet red but tipped her chin up.

"You kissed the same guy?" I asked, incredulous.

"The boy's objectively gorgeous," Desmond pointed out, not the least bit defensive.

"But so, so dense," Celia lamented. Then she gave Desmond a pointed look. "*I've* never kissed a girl. And that's *not* a lie, unlike yours, you lying liar who lies."

Desmond laughed and drank, and Bryony—Bryony, looking straight at me, took a dainty sip.

I almost crumpled the plastic cup in my hands.

"Wait, have you never kissed anyone?" Desmond asked me.

I shrugged. "I don't really interact with humanity. People find me weird."

"We don't," Celia said.

"We have a pretty high threshold for weird, granted," Desmond pointed out.

The warmth spreading through me wasn't just the booze.

"We are so completely off topic," Desmond said, but he was grinning. "But I'm not sure what we can tell you to help. We don't know what the fundamental *nature* of this thing is."

"Well," Bryony said, her smoky voice breaking through the jovial mood, "we could just ask it."

16

WE ALL STARED at Bryony. She shrugged. "You all want to know what lies within Harrow's walls, but none of you have asked the thing itself, have you?"

"How the hell would we?" Desmond asked with a nervous laugh.

"It speaks through the figments," Bryony said. "They're the part of it that talks to people. About something other than whether it's allowed to eat them, I mean." She flashed a little smile at me, and my stomach flipped. Her eyes glinted gold and green in the light of the dancing flames.

"Can we do that?" I asked. "Call it up?"

"It can be called. It may not answer," Bryony said. There was a shiver of eagerness in her voice, and I had a flash of an image— Bryony, kneeling in the folly, candles before her, waiting and waiting and waiting for an answer that never arrived.

"Screw it," Desmond said. I looked at him in surprise. He pounded back the rest of his vodka. "Let's do it."

There was something shining in his eyes that worried me—a recklessness, and beneath it something broken.

"We don't have to," I said. I didn't want to push Desmond and Celia into anything they weren't willing to do.

He met my eyes steadily. "Yes, we do," he said. His voice was hoarse, but it was certain. "Our whole lives are wrapped around the *thing* in our house. No matter how hard we try to leave, Harrow draws us back. We're all caught in the fucking labyrinth, and I want to hear what the monster has to say for itself."

Celia nodded in silent agreement.

I let out a breath. "Then what do we do?" I asked.

"It answers to the blood," Bryony said. "Vaughan blood."

"Oh, yes, blood sacrifice. Definitely a sign that the evening is taking a positive turn," Desmond muttered, but he tightened his jaw and didn't object.

"A few drops should be enough," Bryony replied, a serene little smile on her lips.

"Then let's get it over with." Desmond rolled up his sleeve and flexed his fingers.

Bryony shook her head. "Not you. Her. Mistress of Harrow. It'll answer her if it answers any of us," she said. I tasted something metallic at the back of my mouth. It was not a good idea. But that had rarely stopped me. I nodded, drained my cup, and stepped forward.

Bryony took my hand, holding it palm up, and drew me over to the fire. She had her knife, the little hooked one I'd seen her with in the graveyard. She crouched and stuck it in the flames of the fire for a few seconds, and then straightened up again.

"What do I do?" I asked.

The firelight lashed her skin. "The blood will call it. You decide what you do after," she said. "To command it or to coax it. Don't be afraid. It's not evil. It won't hurt you."

I wanted to tell her that I wasn't. I wanted to tell her that I believed her and that I saw in the Other the dark beauty that she so treasured, but I couldn't. Because I *was* afraid.

She set the knife to the edge of my hand, by the base of my thumb. Her cut was quick and certain. I hissed at the flash of pain. She yanked my hand out over the fire, squeezing the edges of the cut. Heat scorched my skin. A few drops of blood fell from the cut and sizzled in the flames. I snatched my hand back, cradling it against my chest.

She reached for it again. I eyed her suspiciously. "It's all right. I'm all done mangling you, I promise," she said. She took my hand and closed her eyes. A sigh escaped her lips. "It's coming."

And it was there. A woman stood on the other side of the fire, the crescent scar of the distortion obscuring her face. Her hair was dark, her build slender, but beyond that I couldn't say much.

"It worked," Celia whispered. Her voice quavered with fear, but beneath it ran an electric current of excitement and curiosity. "What do we say?"

"Probably should have thought about that before we summoned it," Desmond muttered, covering his own nerves with his grumbling.

Bryony, for her part, had her gaze locked on the figure, her eyes bright and sharp.

"Who are you?" I asked, turning my attention back to the figment. The woman remained silent, though her head tilted as if she were thinking—or trying to understand. "What are you?" I tried instead.

"*We are alone*," she answered. Her voice was a rush of insect wings, papery and strange.

"Are you the thing in Harrowstone Hall? The one called the Other?" I asked, my voice growing more sure, though the rest of me didn't feel it. No answer. "Are you . . ." I faltered.

"Where are you?" Celia asked, stepping forward.

"*We are scattered,*" the woman answered, looking off to the side. "*We are here. Here. Here. Not here. We can't find—scattered. We are—most—sorry. It is hard. Too many. Many. Many of you.*" Her voice fractured, the swarm of insects scattering.

"I think only one of you should be asking questions," Bryony said tightly. If I hadn't been looking closely, I would have missed how quickly her breath came, spilling in puffs of mist from her lips. She was as nervous as the rest of us, just hiding it better.

"Sorry," Celia said, blushing bright. My cousins edged back.

"Where are you?" I tried again. "Just focus on me if that's easier. Where—" I gasped as the figment looked at me, gasped as the ground yawned open and I sank. I plunged into the ground and below it. Thready roots grew around my fingers, tangled in my hair. A beetle scurried over my cheek.

It was the dream, but I wasn't dreaming. I was standing on the other side of the fire. *And* I was under the ground, looking up at the looming shape of a stone carved with the Harrow spiral.

But I wasn't just beneath the earth, wasn't just beside the fire. Tendrils snaked out from my body. They grew through the walls of Harrow like roots. They burrowed through the ground outside, drifted in the air. They brushed against the glimmer-pale souls of the shadows, coiled into cracks and crevasses while the daylight lingered. They found the Folded, dead now, mushrooms growing from his woodrot heart in a ravine near the edge of the grounds.

They stretched out to the figment standing across from me.

"*We are many places,*" she said. "*And we are Harrow. But we are scattered.*"

Yes. Scattered. Pieces of us were missing, and we couldn't find them. If we could find them, we would be whole, but they had been taken from us.

Not us. Them, I reminded myself, but the distinction was slipping.

"What are you?" asked the part of me that was still standing on the other side of the fire.

"*We don't know,*" she said.

"Where did you come from?"

A pause. "*We are the child of the dark stars,*" she said.

I shuddered and dredged my voice up from deep within me. "Why did Nicholas Vaughan trap you here?"

"*We must obey the blood,*" she said. "*We do as our master wills. Change what he wills. Wound what he wills. Minds. Bodies. Stones.*"

We didn't know why. These things made no sense to us. Being human made no sense to us. We only did what we were told because we had to. "We do not want to. Don't want to obey. Don't want to be scattered, so we search for ourself, and we gather our strength, but—"

"Helen. Helen, stop," Bryony said urgently.

I realized I was speaking the words out loud. I tried to turn my head toward her, but my muscles would not obey me. "We become. We scatter. We wake. We sleep. We dream. Always we dream. *Who are you?*"

The last three words came from my lips and from the figment's.

That curve of striated light began to recede until I could almost see the face behind it. Dark hair, dark eyes—for a horrid moment, I thought that when it resolved, I would be looking at my own face, but it wasn't me. This woman's face was gaunt.

"*Who are you?*" she asked. I asked.

"I feel like I know you," I said. She said. Each of us speaking to the other. "*I feel like I saw you in a dream.*"

"Helen, that's Mary Beaumont," Desmond whispered urgently. Bryony had grabbed my hand, but she only stood there, a panicked look on her face.

The edges of me were blurring, a thumb smudge across a charcoal sketch.

"*They cut into me,*" we said together. "*To divide me from myself. To make me biddable. To make me into a tool.*" We spoke in unison, and the buzz of insects was in my throat now, my words fraying at their edges.

"Do something," Celia was saying. Screaming. Why was she screaming?

Because of the smoke, I thought. It was boiling off my skin, thick and black, even as Mary grew more solid.

"Helen, look at me. *Helen,*" Bryony was saying. But that wasn't my name, was it? Did I have a name?

"*Go away!*" Desmond shouted, striding forward, holding his hand up. My head turned, just enough to see his palm slick with blood, a deep cut across it. "This is Vaughan blood, and I am ordering you to leave! *Go!*"

Mary vanished. I staggered, dizzy, and Desmond and Bryony grabbed me to keep me from toppling right into the fire.

"Steady," Desmond told me. I struggled to get my feet back under me. Disoriented, I tried to remember where I was. Who I was.

"You're Helen Vaughan," Bryony said, as if she knew what I was thinking. "We're at the folly. We're with your cousins."

You're Helen Vaughan. You're at the folly, I told myself. I gulped down smoke-tinged breaths and stared at my hands, spreading them before me. They were solid.

I turned, bent double, and vomited up black water and rotting leaves, and what looked like a mouse's bones. Celia shrieked and jumped back. Desmond swore. Bryony swept my hair back, tucking it behind my ears, and helped me upright.

"Is she going to be okay?" Desmond demanded.

"We have to get out of here," Celia said. "It's completely dark. How did we stay out so long?"

I hardly heard her. I was looking at Bryony, and she was looking at me. My hand tightened over her arm.

"I saw you," she whispered, and I couldn't read the look in her eyes.

"What?" I asked, stupefied and feeling foolish.

"I'm sorry. I didn't know that would happen," she said.

"Let's *go*," Desmond said. He grabbed his backpack and kicked dirt over the fire. He stamped out the coals, and we booked it away from the lake.

My heart hammered in my chest, and nausea roiled through me again and again. I'd looked into Mary Beaumont's eyes, and I'd lost myself. It had been like there was no difference between thinking *me* and *her* and *us*. Or rather, that there was a difference, but I could slip quietly between them without a ripple.

The shadows were moving, unfurling themselves from the creases in old tree trunks, sliding slickly from the damp hollows beneath the rocks. Nearby, a lithe six-legged beast peeled itself free from the dark hollow of a tree, its eyes burning white.

"I thought you said there weren't any hounds at Harrow anymore," I croaked.

"There weren't," Bryony said, her hand twisting my sleeve in its anxious grip.

We moved at an uneven lurching pace. The bushes rustled madly to our left. Celia yelped. Then came the rasping sound of nails on tree bark. On the right, and then behind us, and then above, and we started sprinting—

A light flicked on right in front of us, and we skidded to a halt. I threw up a hand to ward off the bright beam, barely able to make out the shape behind it. Something buzzed within me, a vibration in my blood.

"What the hell are you kids doing out here so late?" Roman demanded.

"We lost track of time," Celia squeaked. "We're trying to get back. We're sorry."

"Just get inside where it's safe," Roman rumbled. We traipsed past him. Roman didn't turn back toward the house. He kept walking, deeper into the trees. "He had something," Bryony whispered to me, tilting her head toward mine. "He was carrying something in a duffel bag. Did you see?"

I shook my head. The light had blinded me too much.

"I don't like that guy," Bryony mused.

"You don't like anyone," I reminded her.

"I like you," she said, and I looked at her with surprise. She smirked at me. "For now. We'll see if it lasts." She'd stopped walking. We were at the edge of the patios now. Desmond paused on the steps, looking back. "I can't go inside," she reminded me.

"Will you be safe getting back home?"

"The shadows don't bother me," she said. "And I don't think anything else is out tonight."

"Good." I hesitated, feeling intensely awkward and deeply unwilling to say goodbye. "Did you learn anything tonight? Anything useful? For yourself, I mean."

"I'm . . . I'm not totally sure what I learned," Bryony said. She had an odd expression on her face, a little smile that was somewhere between pleased and puzzled. "I'll have to see how things play out. But . . ."

"What?" I asked.

"Just be careful. Harrow is a trap. If you let yourself stop believing that, you'll be lost to it." She lifted my hand to her lips and pressed the softest, faintest kiss against my palm. Then, gently, she folded my fingers over a leather-bound charm. "I'll see you soon, Rabbit."

And then she was gone, drifting like a ghost across the lawn. My whole skin tingled with the touch of her lips, and grinning like an idiot, I stumbled up the steps.

17

THE HOLIDAYS WERE a blur of tradition and ritual. Thanksgiving came and went, and my cousins disappeared back to Atwood School. Christmas planning started the instant they were gone and didn't let up. It left me exhausted. I dragged myself through every day, pretending to have opinions on trees and ornaments, menus and mistletoe. Every night I collapsed into my bed and hardly dreamed at all.

Bryony hadn't kissed me since that night, on my hand or anywhere else. I hadn't dared ask if she wanted to. But we walked by the lake and ate lunch at the folly and talked about things other than figments and shadows. It had been nice for a while to pretend that things were normal.

"You look terrible," Bryony informed me the week before Christmas.

I leaned back against the folly's half-built wall. A faint headache scrabbled at the back of my skull. "I feel terrible," I admitted. "All this party planning is going to kill me."

"It's not like anyone but your family even comes," Bryony said with a snort.

"You don't understand how hard these people work to impress themselves," I replied.

"You're one of those people," she reminded me, and I groaned. "At least it's just Christmas."

"No, it isn't," I told her. "It's Christmas Eve and Christmas and Boxing Day and New Year's Eve and a formal New Year's Day brunch. Who does that? The whole point of New Year's Day is to be asleep because you got trashed the night before."

"Sure, missnever-had-alcohol-before-last-month," Bryony teased me. "I bet you go to bed at nine on New Year's Eve."

"12:01 on the dot," I countered. She laughed, her nose scrunching up. I could watch her laugh forever. I could stare at her until I memorized the constellations of her freckles, and I was well on my way to doing so. I wanted more than anything to lean forward and kiss her—

But I was a Vaughan, and she was the Harrow Witch, and she hadn't kissed me, not really, and so I didn't lean forward. Not even when she looked at me and bit her lower lip and shook her head a little like I'd done something to amuse her.

The next day, she flew out to St. Louis to spend Christmas with family, and mine started to arrive. Desmond was in Switzerland with his dad, but Celia proved a welcome distraction, attaching herself to me like a particularly chatty barnacle.

I floated through the parade of holidays. Christmas Eve: A string quartet playing, a sumptuous dinner, Mom and Simon and me drinking cocoa and singing off-key carols after bedtime. Christmas: lavish, impersonal presents stacked high. New Year's Eve: the whole house blazing with light to hold back the night for just long enough to ring in the new year before we all retreated to our rooms.

Almost all of us. As I got into bed just past one, I glimpsed a light heading off among the trees. Someone was out after dark.

It was New Year's Day. I had been at Harrow for over three months. Nine left to go.

I fell asleep feeling as if it might not be so impossible. But after the holidays, my fatigue got worse. The headaches clustered together, leaving me in bed for days at a time, and I overheard worried conversations about my health every time people thought I was out of earshot. I kept waiting to get better, kept thinking the worst had to be over with, but every few hours of relief was followed by even worse symptoms. Eli made sure that I had regular doses of the remedy that had helped after that first migraine, when I'd gone wandering the halls, but it barely took the edge off.

By late January, I knew I couldn't keep going like this. One day when the headaches had receded enough for me to think, I wobbled my way to Caleb's office. I couldn't afford not to talk about Harrow's secrets, not now. My family had to know something that could help me.

Caleb had outfitted his office in sleek modern lines, with a glass desk and a top-of-the-line laptop. When I knocked on the door, he looked up from the email he was writing, peering over the top of his reading glasses.

"I've never seen you with glasses before," I said as I entered.

He grimaced and took them off. "Old age. It catches up with very nearly all of us," he said. "What can I do for you, Helen?"

I walked carefully over to his desk, wishing there was a place to sit. Moving too fast made me queasy these days—like I was constantly in the minutes before a full-blown migraine. "I'm getting sick," I said plainly.

He didn't answer at first. He tapped his thumb on the desktop in a steady rhythm. "Yes," he said at last. He stood and stepped around the desk. He fetched a chair from against the wall and ushered me into it, then leaned against the desk, arms folded.

I sank into the cushioned seat, feeling as if I could keep sinking all the way into the floor. "It's Harrow, isn't it? The house is rejecting me. Or the Other is."

His lips parted slightly in surprise. "You know about the Other." He sounded disturbed by this revelation.

I huffed. "I've been here for months. You didn't think I'd use that time to find out what was going on?"

Caleb rubbed a hand over his beard. "I wish you didn't have to know about any of it. I wish none of these rules were necessary."

"But they are. Because the Other has to be contained. Isn't that right?" I asked.

He looked at me for a beat, his jaw tense. Then he seemed to come to a decision. "I suppose there's no point in trying to hide it from you anymore if you already know that much. So, yes, as I understand it, that's true," he said.

He got up from his chair and came around the desk slowly. He leaned against the desk, crossing his arms. When he spoke again, his tone was confessional. "I'm playing a bit of catch-up too, you know. My father—well, to put it frankly, he never liked me. I didn't want any part of Harrow, much less to be master of it. And he didn't want me to be either."

Caleb fiddled absently with a heavy silver ring on his finger. I recognized the crest of Atwood School stamped on it—a class ring. "None of which is your problem. I only mean to say that I wasn't raised to be Master of Harrow, which means that it wasn't all that long ago I learned about the Other. Iris and Eli only know what they've gleaned over the years. We're all sort of . . ."

"Flailing?" I supplied.

He grunted. "More or less," he said. "You're our hope, Helen. If you can make it to the Investiture and claim Harrow, Eli believes that you will have access to some kind of knowledge. And the ability to keep the Other a bit, well, calmer."

"Nicholas Vaughan is the one who trapped it here in the first place, isn't he?" I asked.

"That's my understanding, but he didn't exactly leave records laying around," Caleb said.

I thought of the journal. For a moment, I considered telling him about it, but something kept my mouth shut. "Why do you think he did it?" I asked instead.

"Because he had to, maybe," Caleb said. "Unrestrained, it would be very dangerous. It might be that he discovered it and realized that it needed to be caged, for everyone's sake." There was a note of doubt in his voice.

"You don't think that's why though," I said, leaning forward slightly in my chair.

"No, I don't," he said. He folded his arms. "I think he did it because he could. And now we're paying the price. We're bound to this place, whether we like it or not. I want to find a way to end that, Helen, but I hardly know how to begin. And I don't know how to help you now." He sounded frustrated, almost angry. "When did it start? You seemed fine at first. If we could figure out what changed . . ."

I thought back. There wasn't any clear pattern, was there? There'd been the migraine after I went exploring, the missed days before Thanksgiving—but they'd felt like separate incidents. This steady decline had started right around Thanksgiving. After the lost time.

And after the folly.

"Helen?" Caleb prompted gently. "What is it?"

I swallowed. "I did something. The night before Thanksgiving," I said. Caution kept me from mentioning the others' names. I didn't want them getting into trouble. "I went out to the folly, and we—we spoke to it."

"You spoke to the Other?" Caleb asked, incredulous. "Directly? How?"

"I, uh, I put a few drops of my blood in a fire and called it, and it came," I said. He gaped at me. "I asked it questions. And then it was like—like it was inside of me. Or I was inside of it. I was talking, but they weren't my words, and then there was smoke coming off my skin, and . . ." I took a deep breath. "But it stopped. And I was fine."

"Except you're not," Caleb said hoarsely. "Helen, you opened yourself up to that thing. You let it in, made yourself defenseless. What were you thinking?"

"I needed answers, and you wouldn't give them to me," I snapped.

"God," Caleb said. He covered his eyes with one hand. "We were wrong not to tell you, Helen. I thought it was the right decision."

"You let me agree to stay without warning me," I said. "You let me walk in here blind."

"I thought there was no way you would agree if you knew the truth," Caleb said. "And it had to be you. I'm so sorry. I should have told you to run."

"It was already too late," I said softly. He looked at me sadly, guilt and despair in his eyes.

"We're going to figure this out," he said. "You will make it to the Investiture. I promise. It's only eight more months."

"Right," I said. "Only eight months."

I wouldn't last that long. But I smiled like I believed him and pretended I didn't see the dark worry in his eyes.

The beginning of February marked Grandma Iris's seventy-fifth birthday. Thanks to my health problems, I'd been spared from doing any of the planning—not that there was much. Iris said that every birthday after fifty was a countdown, not a celebration, and she'd insisted on nothing more elaborate than a family dinner. Still, everyone was coming into town. I was dreading it. I'd agreed ages ago to give a speech at dinner, but that was when I wasn't feeling quite so terrible every day. I hadn't even summoned up the energy to leave the house and see Bryony in over a week.

But on the morning of Iris's birthday, I woke up feeling half-way human. My headache had receded, and the fog seemed to have lifted from around me.

Maybe, I thought with fragile hope, I was finally getting better.

The day began with brunch. It was only for the "ladies," which was a word that created a level of pressure I resented. Luckily, Caleb's wife Sandra arrived, carrying a burgundy dress with lace sleeves, just as I was zipping up my trusty blue dress, the only formal wear I owned.

"It's time to retire the funeral wear," she said, setting the dress at the end of the bed.

I hadn't had much chance to talk to Sandra, but despite her outbursts, I couldn't help but like her after her reaction to the inheritance. Laughing at the absurdity of it all was the sanest response I could imagine. "Thank you *so* much. It was this or pajamas, and I don't think Iris would approve."

She chuckled. Sandra looked nothing like the Vaughans, and there was something about her that made me think that she was used to a different kind of wealth—she was too modern, her hair cut in a sleek blond bob, her makeup designed to be sharp and bold, her dress silhouetting her rail-thin body with elegant architectural lines.

"You're a funny little thing, aren't you?" she said suddenly.

"What do you mean?" I asked, startled.

"I don't know. You've got your little way of moving, like every step's its own puzzle to figure out. And those eyes of yours."

"They're the same as everyone else's."

"But they don't see the same, do they? You're always looking at things like you can see straight through them."

Should I tell her that sometimes, in a way, I could? I knew her heart beat faster than it should. I knew she had an old healed rib fracture and that her left wrist had broken badly sometime in the past. I knew that all her drinking was killing her, and I knew she didn't care.

"You remind me of my daughter a little," she said.

"Jessamine?" I looked at her in surprise. I didn't think I looked like her at all. Caleb and Sandra hardly ever talked about their daughter. I'd certainly never heard her mentioned so casually.

Sandra made a soft little noise at the sound of her name. "She saw things differently. Like this place. She loved it. She told me the house was lonely and it liked when she talked to it, and it did seem to get better—you couldn't see them at all when she was born, just jagged cracks in the air, but they got clearer as she got older."

She was talking about the figments, dancing around naming them the way everyone had to. "You should know," I said, worried, "If you see her—the little girl, she—she looks like—"

Her mouth opened, her eyes widening. "Oh," she said softly, realizing. She looked at me, and her gaze hardened. "She isn't the first girl lost to this place, you know. There have been others."

"Harrow's girls," I said. What did Sandra know?

"There's always an explanation. A perfectly natural reason for a little girl to be dead. A storm. The flu. A heart attack," Sandra said, a strange smile curling the corners of her lips. Her fingertips

rested precisely on her elbows as she examined me. "It's a dangerous world for children, and no one asks questions. Jessamine was
supposed to be safe. A weekend with her grandparents. I went to
the spa the day my daughter died. I drank champagne and got a
manicure—can you believe that?" She laughed, and the sound was
like the shearing of ice.

I swallowed. I didn't know what I could possibly say to offer
comfort or sympathy—but then, she didn't want sympathy, and
she couldn't be comforted. Her scars and her grief were all she
had left.

"What do you think happened to them?" I asked instead, voice
hoarse.

"I think that Harrow is a bottomless pit that exists only to devour anything that falls into it," Sandra said. "And it has fed on
this family for generations. Your mother knew enough to run. You
should have stayed gone."

I shuddered with the force of her grief. It had lodged inside her
like a cancer, and it was killing her faster than the alcohol.

She left then, and by the time I got to brunch, Sandra was back
to her usual self, sorrow walled off behind sarcasm and gin. She'd
been wrong, I thought. Not that I should get away from Harrow—
but that I'd ever had the chance.

When I got back to my room after brunch, Desmond was waiting
for me.

"You look like crap," he said as I staggered in.

I dropped onto the bed. "That's all anyone says to me these days. I miss 'hello.' How was Switzerland?" I asked him.

"Cold and dark," he said simply, and I got the sudden feeling he didn't want to talk about it, like that part of his life belonged to him, and he didn't want Harrow to encroach on it. And I guess I belonged to Harrow now. He cleared his throat. "I'm trying to convince my dad to get a job at the University of Hawai'i or something, but he was talking about neutrinos and Antarctica, so I've got a bad feeling about it."

"Maybe I'll join him. Antarctica sounds almost far enough away from Harrow to feel safe," I said with a groan.

He gave me a sympathetic look. "Mom said you've been sick."

"I can't seem to shake it," I said. I felt like I'd run a marathon, not just nibbled at tiny sandwiches.

"I was going to show you some new pages from the journal, but if you're too wiped . . ." He held up the journal, loose papers stuck into it where he'd translated sections.

I shoved myself upright. "No, no, I want to see," I insisted.

He handed the journal over and sat at the desk. His knee jiggled while I paged through. Most of the new material was the sort of inscrutable nonsense that Nicholas loved. "I didn't really touch it for a while after the folly," Desmond admitted, looking guilty. "I was too freaked out. But I picked it up again last week."

"I appreciate it," I said.

"Look at the page with the red sticky note," Desmond said, leaning forward to point. "I saw the name Mary a bunch, so I started there. I thought it might be relevant, given that . . ."

Given that the Other had used her image to communicate. I nodded and squinted to read. The letters swam in my vision, but I gritted my teeth and forced my eyes to focus.

> *Mary's presence in the house continues to be a distraction. Dr. Raymond treats her like a clever pet; he even permits her to mix the tincture of foxglove extract he employs to treat his dropsy. I do not like her sly eyes and endless silence, though, and take care to avoid her.*
>
> *There is something wrong with that woman. There is something wicked about that woman . . .*
>
> *. . . Mary walks the halls at night. I hear her footsteps. I hear her whispering my name. I begin to conceive of her as a devil sent to taunt me, to tempt me from my path. I wake from dreams of her lithe body against mine, her slim hips beneath my hands . . .*

"Oh, *gross*," I said, making a face. "Isn't she a teenager?"

"Seventeen or eighteen, I think," Desmond said. "But it's hard to tell."

There was one more piece of translated text, scribbled down like an aside. *A procedure to divide the c*, it said.

"What's this?" I asked, finger trailing under it.

"It was scrawled on a page by itself—there was more to it, but it was water damaged or something. It looked like it was made in a hurry," Desmond said. "I don't think it was written at the same time as the entry, but it seemed weird, so I translated it."

I peered at it. What could the rest of it have said? I couldn't make sense of it, but the earlier entries . . . "Foxglove again. What's dropsy?"

"It's an old term for symptoms of heart failure. Foxglove was one way of treating it," Desmond said. "What do you mean, again?"

"The figments keep showing me foxglove. I think . . ." I took a deep breath. "I think that Leopold might have been poisoned with foxglove. I think Jessamine might have been, too."

"Helen, you can't joke about that."

"I'm not. I think that's why the figments look like them."

"You didn't tell me you'd seen Grandpa." It was like he was suddenly much farther away, a gulf opening up between us. His features were set, expressionless.

"I wasn't hiding it from you." Was I?

"But you think he was murdered. Which means you think that one of us murdered him."

"Not *us*. I don't think you did it, obviously. Or Celia—but maybe Roman or . . ." I trailed off, realizing what I was saying and who I was saying it to.

Desmond might not be his stepfather's biggest fan, but he didn't look amused. "Roman has nothing to gain," he said angrily. "No one does. Except you and your mom."

"She didn't have anything to do with it."

He shrugged one shoulder. "If you're going to be throwing around suspicions, be careful where they land."

"Look, let's forget that for now. Can you just finish the translations? Please?"

"Fine." He stood, gathering up the pages and the journal.

"Even if someone killed Grandpa, no one would have hurt Jessamine. She was just a little girl," he said.

"People do terrible things to little girls all the time," I replied, but he was already gone.

I found Bryony by the pond, sketching in a leather-bound book. Cattails sprang from the curve of the sketched shore with each flick of her pencil.

"Hey," I said. She jumped, then smiled, relief breaking over her face.

"You're looking better," she said. "Upright, at least."

"It's progress," I agreed. "And the fresh air is nice."

"Then let's enjoy it," she suggested. She started out along the shore and caught my hand as she went past. I startled, but let her guide me, our fingers lightly hooked together as if it were completely natural. As if it didn't make my whole world narrow down to that point of contact.

"Caleb thinks that what's happening to me is because of the night at the folly," I told her as we walked along the path by the water.

She gave me a startled look. "You told him about that?" I shrugged. She was quiet for a minute, watching her steps. "It got out of hand," she admitted.

"It wasn't that bad," I said, lying through my teeth. I'd felt like my whole self was coming apart at the seams, but I'd do it again to make her look at me like she was now, head tilted toward me, the light igniting the strands of her dark hair with streaks of deep red.

"Do you think it's why you're sick?" she asked.

"That's when it started," I said. "When I woke up the next morning, I thought I just had a hangover, but . . ."

"But it never went away. And you didn't even have that much to drink," Bryony said, and fell silent for a thoughtful moment. A sparrow burst by with a flutter of wings, dipping over the lake before vanishing into the distance. "What did your uncle tell you?"

"Not much. I think he knows even less than we do," I said. She made a noise at the back of her throat, like that was hard to believe. "He doesn't have the journal. And Grandpa Leopold never told him about the Other, growing up."

"For all you know, he's the one that poisoned Leopold," Bryony said.

"He's not like that. He's kind," I told her. She didn't answer. "Desmond translated more of the journal," I said, like a peace offering. She perked with interest at that, and I described what we'd discovered.

"'A procedure to divide the c,'" she said. "I can already tell I'm not going to like it."

"I don't like any of it," I said. "I keep thinking about those missing girls. Something is happening to them. Someone or something is hurting them."

"Who, though? I know you like Caleb, but—"

"He wouldn't hurt his own daughter. Was he even here when she died?"

She pursed her lips, brow furrowed. "On the grounds? I don't think so. The only Vaughans around were Iris, Leopold, and Eli, as far as I know." Bryony said. "If someone did something to Jessamine, it would have to be one of those three. Do you think they're capable?"

I didn't want to think about the answer. "Do you remember what Desmond said? He went out at night when he was a kid, and he saw a little girl being taken into the woods. That would have been around the time that my mom and I left."

"Being *taken*," Bryony repeated. "By a man."

"Leopold," I said. I couldn't be certain, but it made sense. Everything was snapping into focus. Leopold, the bitter old man who'd rejected Caleb and driven my mother away. "I've been wondering why Leopold would leave this place to me. Whatever happened that night, it didn't sound like it went the way it was supposed to. Desmond said he saw Roman bleeding." Roman, so very eager to ingratiate himself to Leopold. He would have done anything to secure a place here. Including murder.

"So what do you think it was? Some kind of sacrifice?" Bryony asked. She looked sick.

"I dream of being buried," I said. "Maybe it's connected to that night. I think I was supposed to die, Bryony. I think Leopold meant to kill me. But it didn't work, and we ran."

"Right after that is when those kids attacked each other," Bryony said. "The dark soul has been more dangerous ever since. Wild and unpredictable."

"Like maybe the sacrifice that keeps it tame didn't work," I said.

Bryony halted, and I stopped alongside her. "You think your grandfather was capable of sacrificing a little girl?" she asked.

"I didn't know him. But from what I've heard, I think so," I said.

"But Leopold is dead now. Which means someone else would have to be in control," she pointed out.

"Eli and Iris." They had to know what went on and what the traditions of Harrow really meant. They were always around each other, always having private conversations. And while Caleb was *around*, a friendly presence, they *watched* me.

"It's a theory. And one that finally makes things fit together," Bryony said. She looked out over the water. The breeze made her hair dance around her cheeks. "Let's say that we're right. To keep the dark soul trapped, the Vaughans have to make sacrifices. Not just of anybody, but one of their own bloodlines. You don't want to off the kids you raised. But bastards in town? Sure, who's going to miss them. So girls vanish. Every twenty, thirty years. It explains the missing girls. And it explains you."

"How does it explain me?" I asked.

"Your connection to the dark soul," Bryony said, looking back at me. "It's obviously had an influence on your life, even though you were far away from here. Which doesn't make sense unless something happened to bind the two of you together. Like a ritual that was supposed to end in sacrifice and didn't. You ran. The connection remained. People aren't reacting to you, Helen. When they look at you, they must see the dark soul. That explains it." She seemed relieved, like she was solving a puzzle that had been torturing her.

I folded my arms around my middle, feeling queasy. "So it explains the girls, and me, and why me and my mom ran," I said.

"And it explains Jessamine. Leopold failed. He had to try again. It was either Celia or Jessamine. And Celia . . ." I made a startled sound. "She lived in London for years. So he couldn't get to her."

"So he killed Jessamine, but it didn't work. Because it was supposed to be you. It must *have* to be you now." Bryony's look was horrified—and her horror was a kind of comfort. I wasn't in this alone.

"That's why Leopold left the house to me," I concluded. "To force me back here. It was the only way to draw me back in. Or . . ."

"Or Leopold didn't have anything to do with it," Bryony said. She raked a hand through her hair. "Eli knows all about herbs and poisons. He and Iris certainly had the kind of access to draw up a fake will. What if they were pissed at Leopold for letting you go? So they killed him and used his death as a way to lure you back?"

"That's horrible," I said, shaking my head. Were they really capable of it? I thought of Iris, stern and exacting, with all the emotional warmth of a saltine cracker. Eli, how he always managed to be in the background of any room, even when he was standing right in front of you. Eli wouldn't have planned it, I thought, but maybe he would have done as Iris said.

Bryony gave me a speculative look. "Do you think they're having an affair?"

I blanched. "Ew. What?"

She shrugged. "Her husband's brother. Lives in her house. They spend all their time together. It is a little weird. If they were together, that's one more reason to get rid of Leopold."

"That's disturbing," I said, but it made a sick kind of sense. I swallowed. "They're going to kill me, aren't they?"

I wanted her to deny it. Instead, she let out a low moan. "You have to get out of here."

"I can't."

"Forget the money. Forget the house. If you stay, Iris and Eli will—" Her words cut off.

"It won't help," I said, and the certainty was leaden in my chest. "Not unless we find a way to break that connection."

"You have to find the center," Bryony recited dully, and I nodded.

"I have to see this through," I said. "They're not going to do anything to me until the Investiture. Whatever has to happen, it happens then. The best thing I can do is keep my head down and keep paying attention. Try to figure out what's coming."

"Then at least don't go back to the house," she said. "Not tonight. Come spend the night at my place. Just to get a break from it all. We could keep looking through Nana's stuff."

It took a moment to register that she had just invited me to sleep over. My cheeks went hot. "That would be—I mean, we should—that sounds—except—"

"'That would be very useful. We should definitely do that. That sounds like a very sensible plan. Except that I have to go play dress-up for my grandma's birthday, so not today.' Did I get it right?" She smiled at me, but there was a worried edge to it.

"Right. Sentences have endings," I said, nodding. "I forget that sometimes."

"I'm not going anywhere, Rabbit. I'll be here when the pageantry relents."

"Good," I managed. Back at the house, a bell was ringing.

"You'll be needing to get back now," she reminded me.

"Right," I agreed, and didn't move.

She tucked a strand of wind-tossed hair behind my ear. "I'll see you soon," she promised, and she was the one that walked away, humming under her breath, her fingers stretched out to brush the reeds that grew along the bank. The bell rang again, insistent. I turned away, but the sensation of Bryony remained. I would have done anything to not be a Vaughan in that moment. Give me any other name, and give me Bryony.

But I would always be a Vaughan. And I would always belong to Harrow.

18

THAT NIGHT WAS Iris's birthday dinner. Sandra came to my rescue with a dress again, and I floated downstairs in a gown of emerald green with a plunging neckline that made me very aware of the fact that I had boobs. Celia had helped me with my makeup when she discovered me desperately trying to smudge my way out of a "raccoon on an energy drink bender" look, and the overall effect was so sophisticated I almost felt like I belonged in this place.

Mom waited at the bottom of the stairs with Simon. I had to pause halfway to catch my breath, a burst of vertigo making the stairs slew to the left. "You look gorgeous," she told me.

"Right back at you." I looked like I was playing dress-up next to her. Diamond studs glinted at her ears. Her dress was black and made me think of raven's wings. Simon, in his ill-fitting tux, beamed at us like we were the most beautiful things he'd ever seen.

When the dinner bell rang, I took my seat at the head of the table in that awful chair. I was wedged firmly in conversation with Iris and Eli, with Victoria and Caleb offering occasional interjections. I kept jumping every time Iris or Eli spoke to me. At least Roman was out of easy conversational reach, though that didn't stop him from glaring at me whenever our eyes met.

He wasn't part of planning this, I was certain of it. He'd been too angry when he found out about the will. I could see the hatred and bitter disappointment in him. It was like a knotty tumor in his lung, constricting his every breath. But he was still dangerous. Maybe *more* dangerous. Iris and Eli had a plan, and that plan involved the Investiture. Roman was a wild card.

After dinner, I was supposed to give a toast. This had been the worst news I'd received in the past several years. I would never have agreed to live in a haunted murder house if I knew it involved public speaking. My lingering illness didn't help. My skin felt poorly fitted over my bones, and I kept getting hit with tiny bouts of dizziness. Today might be a "good" day, but only by comparison.

At least Caleb had written it for me, so I didn't have to figure out a way to praise the woman who was meticulously crafting my demise.

The merciless servers came with champagne flutes—mine full of sparkling cider, thank god—and it was time. All eyes on me. I cleared my throat, stood, lifted my glass in a motion copied entirely from television.

"Grandma Iris," I said. "Today—" I coughed, covered my mouth, winced. "Sorry. Today—" I coughed again. There was something at the base of my throat, like a bit of beef fat and gristle. "Grandma Iris," I tried again, but then my cough turned into a fit. I covered my mouth and bent over, holding my glass out to the side. Eli took it from me before I could spill it as I hacked, lungdeep coughs that tore at my throat and the thing choking me, and then it came free.

It hit the empty plate in front of me with a soft, wet splat and sat in a thin pool of scarlet blood. It looked for a moment like a blood clot or a bit of raw meat, the size of my thumbnail. And then it pulsed.

It was a heart. A heart from the chest of some small scurrying beast, and I'd coughed it up. My fingers were coated red and my mouth was full of blood. I stared in mute shock. Celia reared back from the table; Desmond made a wordless sound of horror, echoed from several directions.

Iris dropped her napkin over the thing and said quietly, "It's all right."

"How is that all right?" Mom demanded, erupting to her feet.

"We need to get her to a hospital," Simon said.

"This isn't a matter for a hospital. She'll be fine," Eli said. He extended a calming hand.

"She won't be if the house is rejecting her," Roman said.

"It isn't," Caleb replied. "It won't. We just need—"

"How long has this been happening?" Roman demanded. "Even the damn house isn't fooled. She's no Mistress of Harrow. How long are we going to keep up this charade?"

I put my hand against my throat, feeling my own pulse. Voices argued back and forth—my mother's, racked with worry, Roman's sharp with accusation, Caleb's calm.

I turned and walked out of the room. Mom called after me. I broke into a run.

I couldn't be in there. I couldn't stand still. I ran and I didn't pay attention to where I was going, to which corridors I went down. I just wanted to get away.

I wasn't a proper Mistress of Harrow. I didn't *want* to be. But Harrow wouldn't let me go. It was drawing me in, tighter and tighter. Inward along the spiral. Inward along these hallways. Toward a center I couldn't see. Toward—

I stopped. I was in a corridor I vaguely recognized. But there was something strange about it.

The familiar pressure pushed at my skull. I'd been running through the halls, and now the effect of it was making the world lurch. But that wasn't why this felt wrong.

I looked one way down the hallway, then the other way. Why did it feel off?

I closed my eyes, tried to picture the interweaving halls and rooms. They looked chaotic—until you picked out the patterns. Nothing was random. It followed strict rules, every dead end balanced with a twin. Except this corridor.

I should have been nearly at the center of the house, next to the ballroom. But I wasn't.

That sense of things being off . . . I closed my eyes. Could it be?

I checked the room next to me. It was an interior room, no windows. A desk sat in the corner, and I rummaged through the drawers and found a pen. I went back into the corridor and crouched, putting the pen down on the hard wooden floor. I let it go. Slowly, it rolled away.

The floor was sloped. Not so much that you'd even notice that you were walking downward. But how far did this hallway stretch? How far down had I come, running blindly through the house? My mental map told me that this hall didn't connect with any others for a long way. There were a few stairways up to the second floor farther back, but would I have noticed an extra stair? Or that the stairs were a bit steeper than they should be?

No. Because everything was rigidly patterned so that what you expected was what you saw. Enough chaos to create doubt; enough rigidity to create certainty. Balanced perfectly to manipulate you into believing what you needed to believe. Like believing that Harrowstone Hall had only three floors.

I walked farther down the hall slowly, following the wobbling roll of the pen as it continued to trundle away from me. Eventually it snagged on something and turned enough that it stopped, but I kept going.

Something lay on the ground by the wall. I knelt and picked up the familiar leather bundle. Bryony's charm—the one I lost the night the Folded One bit me. I stared at the flat expanse of wall in front of me. If my mental map was correct, the center of the house was right beyond that wall.

Find the heart of Harrow.

I pressed my hand against the wallpaper.

"Helen?"

I whirled around. Simon stood behind me, watching me with curiosity. "Hi," I said. "I was just . . . I needed to get away."

"I get it," Simon said. "Communing with the wall?"

"I think there's a room on the other side," I said.

Simon nodded slowly. "You think there might be a secret door along here?" He stepped up close to me, examining the same spot.

"Maybe. Or maybe it's in a different part of the hall. I don't know." Simon shouldn't be wrapped up in this. I needed him to be looking after Mom.

"That's why I'm here," he assured me, and I realized I must have said that last bit aloud.

Except, no, I hadn't. Like I hadn't called for him the night Leopold died, but he came rushing out to help anyway. And the night in the hall with the Folded, when he should have been miles away. I stared at him. "Simon, is there something you need to tell me?"

He put a hand on my shoulder and pulled me in for a hug. "The only thing I have to tell you is that I love you, and you're going to be okay. You're stronger than you know, Scout. I'm here for you. And for your mom."

I believed him. I knew in my bones that Simon would do anything for us. The tiny splinter of distrust that had begun to work its way under my skin dissolved, and I leaned into him. "I don't know what to do," I said.

"I know. But you will. You'll figure it out. I believe in you," he said. "Now let's get back to dinner. You have a toast to give."

I wanted to stay and work out the secrets of this hidden corridor. But Simon was right. I had a toast to give, and appearances to maintain. It wasn't just this house that was against me. It was the people in it—and I didn't know which ones. I marched back up the hall, leaving its secrets intact—for now.

19

I MADE IT through the toast this time. And dessert. After that, blessedly, I was able to flee back to my room. I was too keyed up to rest, so I worked on the fox skull. I wired the jaw open so that it rested gape-mouthed on the desk. I knew there needed to be something inside its mouth, but I wasn't sure what yet.

My head was starting to hurt again, and I still felt loose and achy. I made my way down to the kitchens and brewed myself a cup of tea, trying not to jump at every little noise in the cavernous space. You could feed an army out of the kitchen. I knew from photos that Harrowstone Hall used to host grand parties and all sorts of impressive guests, but it seemed like in the last decade or so the practice had fallen off.

I carried my tea back to my room, cupping my hands around its warmth. When I opened the door, I saw right away that there was something between the fox's teeth, filling its mouth: dried foxgloves, positioned as if they had grown through its jaw and out between those sharp fangs.

I walked over slowly and touched one of the bell-shaped flowers. It was papery and delicate under my touch. Real, not a figment. And exactly what belonged there.

It was like the Other was begging me to understand what had happened—showing me Jessamine, showing me the flowers.

"I know," I murmured. "I know what they did to her. I'm trying to stop them, I am." But there were pieces I still didn't know. Exactly what purpose did the girls' death serve? Was there some kind of ritual? Or was it only that the beast was hungry, and they kept it fed?

Jessamine had asked me to find her. Or the Other had, using her form. Was I supposed to find Jessamine, or find the Other? Jessamine must have been buried. *Buried where, though?* I wondered. And if the shadows were digging up human bones, whose bones?

A light moved between the trees outside the window. A flashlight—someone was out there again. Who was breaking curfew? I thought of Roman out in the forest the night at the folly. Was he going out again?

My phone buzzed. A text from Desmond with a photo of a translated page attached. **This is messed up**, his text said. I pulled up the photo and squinted, reading Nicholas Vaughan's now-familiar arch writing. There were two entries. The first was short but ominous:

> *With the observations Annalise has collected, I am confident she will be able to guide Mary to the black stars where the god dwells. But this will be useless unless the mind of the traveler is sufficiently altered; a human being in its raw state will not be able to properly comprehend the god. Further study is required.*

The god of the vast dark. They wanted to see it and understand it. And somehow, this pursuit had brought them to the Other. Or brought it to them. I read the next entry, feeling sickening dread with each word.

> *Dr. Raymond is confident in his procedure: he has discovered a bundle of nerves within the brain, the severing of which will level utterly the solid wall of sense that keeps the human mind from stretching beyond its earthly confines. The surgery required is a delicate one, if comparatively minor—a few incisions into the brain are all that is necessary, but they must be precise. Mary has agreed to the procedure, more or less. At the least, I have not heard her object.*

A few incisions to the brain? He was talking about a lobotomy. WTF??? I sent Desmond.

Poor Mary.

Did they do it? I asked.

Working on it. But I think so.

My headache had turned into an ice pick through my eye. Running through the corridors had been a terrible idea.

A lobotomy. *A procedure to divide,* I thought. It was easy to imagine a knife cutting through my brain with my headache throbbing like this.

Let me know when you get more. I need to sleep, I told Desmond, and got into bed without waiting for his reply.

I knew before I shut my eyes that I would dream of Harrow that night. But it was different. I woke buried, as I always did, staring up at the house. But it seemed to deconstruct itself before my eyes. First the roof, then the upper story, unmaking itself floor by floor until an empty field lay in its place. A man and woman stood there, and I stood before them. The man looked at me with unconcealed disdain. The woman, I had seen before—stalking through the corridors of Harrow in my dreams, the wax of her candle melting over her hand and dripping onto the carpet. She stared at me with hatred. A second man approached, tall and gaunt.

"Here," the woman said. "It has to be here."

"And you're sure this will work? It won't just kill the thing?" the first man asked.

"I don't know that we could kill it if we tried," the gaunt one replied. "But if we scatter it, we will break its conscious mind. That will be enough to keep it containable."

"It's an unpleasant business," the first man said.

"After all the death it's caused, we have no choice," the woman snapped. "If you haven't the stomach for it—"

"No, I'll do it." He strode toward me and crouched down. Only then did I realize that I was smaller than him. A child. "Here you go, girl. Drink this. You won't feel the rest." He handed me a metal flask. I took it and looked down.

I was standing on a slab of stone, gray shot through with white. A spiral had been carved in its surface, bisected by a single line. I looked up again, and he reached toward me with bloodied fingers, a cut laid open on his arm. He dragged two fingers down my cheek, marking it with still-warm blood.

"They scatter us," I said, but my voice wasn't mine.

I woke, shivering and drenched in sweat, in my own bed.

20

BY THE TIME the morning bell rang, any illusion of recovery had fled. I felt worse than ever. I couldn't even look at food without spasms of violent nausea. The headache had grown worse, like a crown of nails had been set on my head, and the pain ran in a hot streak down my spine to my shoulders.

I lay cocooned in the blankets, curled on my side, and tried to bear it. I might have slept. I might have simply crawled inside the pain until nothing but the pain existed, not even the passage of time. At some point I was aware of my mother's hand, cool against my brow, and worried voices, which seemed to shift seamlessly from Mom and Simon to Eli, Caleb, and Iris.

"You're sure it isn't anything you gave her?" Iris asked.

"I didn't give her anything that could possibly harm her," Eli answered.

"The charms she has, from the witch—" Caleb began.

"As far as I can tell, they're the only reason she's holding up as well as she is. Nothing I do seems to help," Eli said in frustration.

"It must be because of that night in the folly. I knew I should have been keeping a better eye on her," Caleb said.

"This isn't a normal Investiture. Maybe this is supposed to happen." Iris this time.

"She's not supposed to be dying, Iris. And she certainly seems to be," Eli said quietly.

Oh, well, that was suboptimal. On the other hand, maybe I wouldn't hurt so much if I were dead. Yes, that would be nice. Silence and peace and the cold earth. I wanted to sink, wanted the shadows to carry me down, because in my buried dreams, at least there was no pain.

"*Sshh.*" A small hand pressed against my back. I could feel the presence of a small body behind me. Eli and Iris were gone. I'd slipped through time again, and I wasn't sure where I'd come to rest. "*She's wrong. I would never hurt you,*" Jessamine whispered, brushing her fingers through my hair.

I whimpered. "You're not human. You're not a person," I whispered.

"*But we try to be. We get it wrong, but we try and try and try. Then they scatter us.*" Her hand pressed flat against my back, and I drew in a deep breath, the easiest I'd breathed since waking up that morning. The pain receded faintly. "*You're wrong inside. We—I'm trying to help, but when I help, it makes us wrong, too,*" she said in consternation.

The pain ebbed. I sobbed with the relief of it. A moment of mercy—but that made it all the worse because the pain would be back. I'd be dragged back inside it, and that seemed more terrible than never leaving at all.

The sheet shifted, settling into the space the figment had

occupied. I was alone again. I staggered to the bathroom, drank water, looked at myself in the mirror. My skin was pallid and sallow. I combed my hand through my wild hair, trying to tame it—and then stared at the clumps of hair that had come away.

The door to the bedroom opened. I pulled the hair from between my fingers quickly and crammed it into the trash can, closing the lid. I turned just as Eli came into view. He looked startled to find me out of bed.

"Feeling better?" he asked hopefully.

"A bit," I said. I clutched the edge of the sink to steady myself, hiding the movement behind my back. I didn't think he was fooled.

"I brought you this," he said. He held out a small dark-green glass bottle. It had a cork stopper. "Drink it with some water. It might help."

"Might?" I asked as I took it from him.

"I'm not entirely sure what's wrong with you. I've never treated anyone in your particular situation," he confessed.

"Harrow's never rejected a master?"

"That's not entirely true," Eli said. He folded his hands behind his back, leaning forward with the air of a lecturing professor. "In 1934, during the year before his Investiture, Lewis Vaughan attempted to make some rather radical renovations to the house. One morning, he was discovered dead in the foyer. He had apparently starved to death, though he had eaten well the night before. There was a note in his pocket. It said, 'I cannot get out. There is no way out. It is endless.'"

"That's dark," I said, gaping.

Eli shrugged a shoulder. "Or it's nonsense. In any case, his brother succeeded him and had an uneventful Investiture."

"Otherwise, it's been unbroken? The eldest son inherits?" I asked.

"A son, at least. Not always the eldest. Leopold was younger than me, after all."

My brow furrowed. "Then why . . . ?"

"I'm what they used to call a confirmed bachelor, dear," Eli said, his lips twisting in a smile. "I was never going to produce the requisite offspring."

Eli was gay? Then Bryony was wrong—he and Iris wouldn't be having an affair.

"Let me help you back to bed," Eli suggested, and I was forced to admit that I needed it. He held my arm and elbow and supported me over to the bed, then pulled the cover back over me. "For what it's worth, dear, I'm rooting for you. This place could use a shake-up."

Dark thoughts swirled through my mind. I drank the little bottle he'd given me. It tasted foul, but I didn't care anymore. I sank down into oblivion. Not sleep, but a space in which time fractured and came apart, the passage of seconds not mattering anymore. It knit itself back together hours later with someone knocking on my door. I sat up with difficulty, and I must have told them to come in because the door opened and Desmond peeked in.

"Hey," he said. "How are you feeling?"

"Less dead than a little while ago," I told him. Now I felt disconnected more than in pain, like my nerves had burned out. "I was supposed to go see Bryony."

"She was here a little while ago. I told her you're sick. She sent you this, said it's a new healing charm." He handed me a cloth bundle. I pressed it to my nose. It smelled of roses. He looked away tactfully and cleared his throat. "*Anyway*, I translated one of the longest entries. It's . . . a lot. But you need to see it."

He handed me a sheet of paper. I looked down at it, but the words swam before my eyes. "You'll have to read it for me," I said, passing it back.

He looked worried but nodded. "Okay. Um, this is after the one about the operation. They actually did it. He says, 'I am almost envious of you, Mary.'" His voice continued, but I closed my eyes, and another voice overtook his, as if I could hear Nicholas Vaughan himself.

> *You have looked upon the face of a god. How gladly I would have stood in your place! But the cost to science would be too great were I unable to continue my studies.*
>
> *All went as planned. Annalise and I made the mark-ings among the stones. Dr. Raymond led Mary to the site, stumbling and dull eyed. There was no fear nor any sort of intelligence in those black eyes. Her head had been shaved; stitches marked the place where Dr. Raymond had cut through her scalp and bone.*
>
> *She stood placidly, her face pale and bloodless, and we began. It was Annalise's task to guide Mary's docile spirit into the vast dark, that deepness in which dwells the great god. Annalise proclaimed it done, and we waited for inter-minable minutes, an excruciating period of stillness.*

Suddenly, as we watched, we heard a long-drawn sigh, and suddenly did the color that had vanished return to Mary's cheeks, and suddenly her eyes opened. I quailed before them. They shone with an awful light, looking far away, and a great wonder fell upon her face, and her hands stretched out as if to touch what was invisible; but in an instant the wonder faded, and gave place to the most awful terror. The muscles of her face were hideously convulsed, she shook from head to foot; the soul seemed to be struggling and shuddering within the house of flesh. It was a horrible sight, and I rushed forward as she fell shrieking to the ground.

There I held her as she lay limply, rolling her head from side to side and grinning vacantly. "What did you see?" I demanded. But of course, Mary did not speak, only laughed and laughed, and after a very long time, fell silent.

"Helen?" Desmond asked. I realized he'd stopped talking a while ago.

"Mary saw the god," I said. "And what, she went mad?"

"It sounds that way. In the next entry . . . God, Helen, this stuff is messed up," Desmond said. "I knew the history of our family wasn't sunshine and roses, but the things they did . . . She was pregnant. I'm guessing the baby was Vaughan's or Raymond's."

"Vaughan's," I said immediately. He didn't contradict me.

"I mean, that's what makes sense. But what he writes in the journal is that looking at a god is what got her knocked up."

"We are the child of the vast dark. That's what the figment

said," I said. I pressed my fingers to my cheekbones, trying to relieve the agonizing tension there. The bone gave with the sponginess of old, wet wood. I flinched, pulling my hands away. Tentatively, I pushed against that spot again, but there was no give. Just skin and bone and sinuses that felt like they were being drilled into.

"Do you think the Other is Mary's child?" Desmond asked.

"I don't know," I said, dazed and overwhelmed.

"We have her eyes. What if we're actually Nicholas Vaughan and Mary's descendants?"

"I don't know."

"That would explain why we have a special connection to the Other. It would explain—"

"I don't *know*, Desmond, and I can't think right now," I snapped. He shrank back. "I'm sorry. It's just—I hurt, and I feel twisted up inside, like someone's opened me up and scrambled things around and then glued me back together again. Iris and Eli said . . ." *They said I might be dying.* But what was the point of telling Desmond that? He couldn't help me. "I'm sorry," I said again.

He nodded, accepting the apology. A troubled look crossed his face. "You know, you're not the only outsider here. You're not the only one that gets treated like you don't belong and gets kept in the dark. I've put up with this my whole life. Never being treated like I was *completely* a Vaughan. Never treated like I deserved to know all of Harrow's secrets."

"I understand," I said.

"You don't, really. I'm not sure you can," he replied. "Being the only Black kid in your class is hard enough. Being the only Black kid in your family? I mean, when I fly out to see my dad, there's more color there than here. In *Switzerland*. I don't know what I'm trying to say, exactly, just . . ." He sighed, rubbing his hand over his scalp.

"You're saying that this isn't only happening to me. I'm not the only one hurt in all of this," I said.

"Something like that," he agreed. He was right—I had been plunged into the deep end with this family, but there were things I hadn't experienced and couldn't understand. Hardships that I hadn't had to face. "At least I can leave," he said.

My hands fell limply into my lap. "Did you ever consider living with him? Your dad?" I asked. I couldn't imagine choosing Harrow if you had a choice.

"Of course. But he went to Atwood, too. He thinks it's the best education money can buy. There's no way he'd let me transfer. Besides, I'm not leaving Celia behind. I don't know if you've noticed, but her dad is a raging asshole."

"I did notice that, actually," I said, grimacing.

"Anyway." He sighed again. "Get some rest, okay? I've got to go call my girlfriend."

I raised an eyebrow. "You have a girlfriend?"

"I have a life outside of you, believe it or not," he said. He said it lightly, but there was that guarded edge to it again—the sense that there was a part of his life he needed to keep walled off from Harrow—and from me. It stung, but I couldn't blame him for it.

"But you're such a *nerd*," I said in mock confusion, breaking the moment of tension, and he flipped me off, laughing.

"Desmond," I started, wanting to thank him, wanting to tell him how glad I was that he was here—but he wasn't.

Time had crumpled again, and I was alone.

21

I LURCHED, NAUSEATED again, trying to get my bearings. There was a tray of food next to the bed, but I couldn't bear the thought of eating. I vaguely remembered Mom bringing it in. We'd talked. But the memory was on the other side of a rain-streaked window, indistinct.

I limped to the bathroom and managed a few sips of water. My face looked wrong in the mirror—the angles less distinct, the skin almost waxy in its smoothness. My muscles shifted oddly beneath the skin. I tried a smile. It hitched, then stretched too far into a hideous grin.

I grabbed a towel and threw it over the mirror.

I sank to the floor and sat there, my arms around my knees, breathing through coruscating waves of pain. Around my wrists ran bright red lines. Tiny beads of blood welled up from them. My shirt stuck to my chest, the diamond-shaped welt on my sternum oozing.

They scatter us.

A procedure to divide the—

"What did they do to you?" I whispered, and I wasn't sure who I was asking.

"*A procedure to divide the consciousness of the Other,*" my grandfather said in a detached monotone, his voice coming from right behind me. "*First, it must be bound to an appropriate vessel. And then there shall be a division of the body, which shall in turn divide the Other, its will scattered and made pliant.*"

"I don't understand," I moaned.

"Hush, dear. It will be all right." Eli pulled a blanket over me. I was back in bed. To someone else he said, "Perhaps we should let her mother in to see her."

"Not like this," Iris replied. "Give Rachel something to help her sleep. Keep her away."

"Am I going to die?" I asked, but time had skipped again. I was alone. The ring around my wrist was scabbed over, but fresh blood wept from the edges. I struggled up from the bed. My body felt wrong. When I moved, something in my torso ground like an arthritic joint, hard and rasping where no bone should be.

My legs gave out. I collapsed two feet from the bed.

"Help," I rasped out, trying to shout. "Please, I need help." I twisted, trying to brace myself against the floor so I could work my way toward the door.

My grandfather lay before me. Crumpled, as I was. Hand reaching out, his face broken by the cracked-glass haze, mouth open in a scream choked into silence by the bloom of foxgloves.

But he wasn't reaching. He was pointing to the window.

A hand snagged my hair and yanked backward. Jessamine. She hauled me back with all her childish strength. Scrabbling on her knees and one hand, the other tangled in my hair, she dragged me toward the window, wailing out a rasping cry. I reached the wall and clawed my way upward, Jessamine collapsing against me, collapsing further still, rabbit bones clattering against the floorboards as she vanished.

I leaned my brow against the cold windowpane. My breath made no fog against it, and I realized I wasn't breathing at all. I squinted, and the world outside came into reluctant focus. The dark sky, the trees. The light among the trees, pale white. Not Bryony's warm lantern light.

Roman was outside again.

I turned. Leopold was gone. The fox's skull sat grinning in his place, and in its teeth, fringed with foxglove, was Bryony's healing charm. I staggered to it and crushed the pouch into my palm, and for the first time since I'd started paying attention, I took a deep breath. My limbs seemed to stabilize—not much. Enough to move.

I stumbled to the door and turned the knob, but it was locked. Of course. Eli always locked me in. But when I dreamed, I got out. "Show me. Please," I said.

Muddy footprints seeped up from the floor. They led from the bed to the wall beside the door. I pressed my hands to the spot. *Let me out*, I thought, and imagined it giving way before me. It parted in filaments. I angled my body through them, keeping my eyes squeezed shut. The wall gave, stringy and dry, and then there was air on my face again and I was in the hall.

I couldn't stick around and wonder at what had just happened. I was dying. And I did not want to die. It seemed so obvious, but I'd never felt it before, this terror, this absolute rage at the idea—I didn't *deserve* this. I didn't ask to be here, and I shouldn't be, and

I wouldn't let it beat me. I wouldn't surrender to this place, to these people, to this fate.

I stumbled down the hall, leaning heavily against the wall. Where my palm dragged against the wallpaper, moisture bubbled, leaving blisters that burst, oozing clear liquid that smelled like algae bloom. That spot in my belly kept up its bone-click feel with each step.

One step after another, I told myself, *and don't let that desperate fear tear you apart because your body has gone soft beneath its brutal teeth.*

What was this place doing to me? My breath stopped and started again, my shoulders wrenched as if straining to rearrange themselves, and even my teeth swam in my mouth, uncertainly rooted to my warping jaw.

I reached the stairs. I half hung myself over the banister and let gravity carry me. By the time I reached the bottom, I was mostly myself again, except for the strange sucking hollowness in my chest I didn't want to think about. Roman was up to something, and whatever it was, it couldn't be good. I had to stop him. It was the only thought that mattered.

The hall—the door—the cold open air. I blinked, not entirely sure how I'd crossed the distance, not entirely remembering why I'd done it. I stood under the stars and tried to think. I was coming undone, some unnatural force rearranging me.

Or maybe it was an entirely natural force. Reality is randomness. To be organized and static is an unnatural state—it's the change and decay that is natural, entropy the only inevitability.

Every pattern is constantly tumbling toward its own undoing and—

"Helen." A name. My name. The name for the set of rules I was, the name for this collection of limbs, digits, organs, features, neurons in this particular order. I was still me.

"Helen," the voice said again, and only then did I realize it *was* a voice. Bryony's voice, and there was Bryony, walking toward me with an expression of deep concern. "It's after dark. You shouldn't be—"

I opened my mouth. I meant to ask for help, I think, but what came out was a sound no human throat could make. It was a flurry of moth wings in the dark and a rasp of stone and the startled shriek of a rabbit caught in a snare. I came apart again—bones shifting beneath my skin, throat crumpling, lungs blooming with unseen cilia. My vision went blank for half a second and then returned, the colors wrong, glimpsed from too many eyes that blinked along my cheekbones before receding into my skin again.

I expected Bryony to run. She lunged forward instead, catching me around my waist before I realized I'd started to fall, and she pulled me against her. "What's happening to you?" she asked, startled but not afraid. Not afraid of *me*, at least.

I tried to speak again, but my trachea had folded itself into a corrugated mass—but that was all right since I was pretty sure I was breathing through my skin. I would have laughed, if I could, as if that notion could be comforting. My arm, slung over her shoulder, sprouted tiny growths like the fringed antennae of silk moths.

Bryony seized me by the shoulders. Her thumbs pressed against my clavicles, and she stared into my eyes—just two of them now. "You need to calm down," she said.

Calm? I was calm. No, I was panicking. The sensation was hard to pick apart from the wrenching violence of the changes in my body, but there it was, corrosive, toxic.

"Listen to me, Helen. Listen to my voice and calm down. You're Helen. Be Helen," she said. She was saying whatever came to her mind, I knew, but that arch, confident tone that had so fooled me when we met, convincing me that she knew every secret in this place and how to use it, swept over me just as effectively now. And that was something I could surrender to. I gave myself to it, believed it, embraced it.

Helen. Be Helen. Collector of bones. Rachel's daughter. Loner. Awkward. The girl who loved chocolate ice cream and couldn't sit still. The girl whose heart beat harder because Bryony Locke was holding her. But for that to be true, she needed a heart, not a tangle of thorns.

I built myself from the inside out, anchoring each piece of me. It wasn't perfect—bits of me still felt wrong—but from Bryony's relieved expression, I must at least have looked more human when I was done.

I worked my mouth open and spoke, my voice creaking but audible. Human. "I've been getting sick. Roman is in the forest. He's doing something." She looked over her shoulder. The pinprick of Roman's flashlight was still just visible.

"Come on," she said. We loped along unevenly. As we approached, we dropped our speed, and as I focused on the need to make no sound, my steps grew softer, my feet ghosting over the earth. I could feel every twig and leaf as I set my weight on them.

Roman's flashlight roved through the darkness, but he didn't seem to see the shadows that flickered around him. They hadn't hurt me yet. I wasn't sure they could. But maybe the rules had changed as I changed.

"Roman," I croaked.

He spun. The flashlight pinned us in place. "You shouldn't be out here," he said. I could make out the lump of the duffel over his shoulder, and my eyes fixed on it.

"Neither should you," I reminded him. I pushed myself free of Bryony's support and took a wobbling step. "What are you doing to me?" There was something in that bag, and I needed it.

He sneered. "Do you really think Leopold wanted you to have this place? It's the other way around, Helen."

"What have you done to me?" I demanded. I held out my wrists to him, showing him the bracelets of blood. He flinched back.

"I'm only stripping away the lies. All this pretending is getting us nowhere. It's obscene. It's time to get it over with."

"I didn't ask for this! I'm not *pretending* anything."

"I won't let you hurt her anymore," Bryony said, and started forward. I didn't know what she intended to do against Roman— six inches taller than her, at least eighty pounds heavier. He raised his fist—I screamed a warning—

The shadows descended.

22

AT FIRST THERE was nothing but darkness—a darkness of many parts, moving in a chaotic choreography of limbs and jaws and malformed bodies, occluding the light of the stars, and smothering the flashlight's glow. Something struck me from behind, and I fell to the ground, the breath going out of me.

Bryony screamed. Through flickering scraps of shadow, moving like a flock of starlings startled into the sky, I could see her crouching, arms raised above her head protectively.

"Leave her alone!" I shouted, clawing my way upright. "STOP!"

The scraps of shadows froze into solid shapes. Drifts of darkness fell from them like mist. They looked like stretched-out people—like a shadow cast against a wall, elongated but recognizable. Their darkness made them seem flat, and as I stepped carefully toward Bryony, I realized it wasn't just an illusion. No matter what direction I looked at them from, their silhouette stayed the same, as if I was looking head-on at a shadow cast against a solid surface.

I caught Bryony's hand, pulling her up and toward me, away from the shadows. We scrambled up next to Roman, who braced himself against a tree clutching his flashlight like a weapon, eyes wide and scalp lacerated.

The shadows twitched. An arm rippled. A head jerked at the end of a stretched-out neck. Whatever hold my words had on them, it was failing.

Still holding Bryony's hand, I spun and fled. She ran with me. So did Roman. He shoved past me, his longer legs making up the distance between us, but as the rushing sound of the shadows swelled, his foot caught a root and he toppled.

Bryony leaped over him gracefully and landed on the other side, pulling me along in an awkward lurch beside her. The duffel bag had landed right in front of Roman's outstretched hand. "Get it!" I yelled, because I was certain that whatever was in that bag, I needed it.

Bryony darted forward to grab the bag. Roman snarled and clawed at it, but she danced nimbly back, and then we were running again, darting between the trees. At some point, I realized Roman wasn't following us anymore, but I couldn't summon the will to care.

Bryony yelped. The darkness before us split apart into three shadows. We skidded to a halt. They stalked around us, their long arms nearly touching the ground, huge fingers curled like claws.

"*Blood,*" one whispered.

"*Blood and name,*" another answered.

"*But something strange,*" a third replied, and they buzzed and rustled in reply.

"*Not that one,*" said the first again, and I could feel their attention fix on Bryony.

Bryony lifted one hand, palm out. She bent her ring finger in an odd gesture. "I know you," she said. "I know your names." Her voice shook. I could feel her fear in the air around us.

"*Then ssspeak them*," the shadows spat, moving toward us.

For an instant, I thought that they would descend on her. That I was about to watch Bryony torn apart in front of me. She thought it, too—I could see the tremor in her hands, the tension that said she was steeling herself against her own end.

And then from her lips came a susurrus of sound. Syllables twined and tumbled and nipped at each other as they flooded from her lips in impossible configurations. She straightened, eyes wide with wonder. The sound skittered across my skin and scrabbled at my skull, calling to some deep part of me. And still Bryony spoke, until the sound wrapped around the shadows, and turned to silence.

She shook, but it was with amazement and relief now, her breath fogging the air and a wild grin on her face.

The shadows sighed, and shuddered, and two dropped back, vanishing into the night gloom.

"*Flee*," the third one whispered. "*We are wicked when we are wounded, and we are wounded tonight.*"

It was Bryony's turn to stumble, as if speaking the names had taken the strength out of her. I braced her with my shoulder, and together we made our limping way through the trees. I knew where I was going before I could put words to it—the witch's house.

By the time we reached it, Bryony was the one supporting me again. My left knee was unstable—it kept sliding out of alignment when I put my weight on it—and my breath had developed a crackle. She lowered me down on a chair and shoved the water-swollen door shut. The moon shone through a hole in the roof. Bryony lit a lantern and hung it from a rafter. Her hands were shaking.

"I've never had to do that before," she said. "I wasn't sure what I was doing until I did it."

"It was beautiful. It was amazing," I told her. My head felt heavy, but I smiled at her. I sounded drunk, slurring my words. She cast me a concerned look.

"Let's see what he had," Bryony said. She unzipped the bag and spilled its contents on the table. Out clattered a spade with a folding handle, a glass jar, and something wrapped in an old dish-rag. Bryony set aside the shovel and examined the jar. "Henbane, angelica, wormwood. Onyx. Snake's teeth. This is a nasty bit of magic. Trust a Vaughan to play dirty."

"If I changed my name, would you be nice to me?" I asked her wearily.

"I'm already nice to you, Rabbit. I saved you, didn't I?"

"I don't feel very saved," I confessed. I wanted to sleep. My eyes drifted shut, but Bryony's cool finger against my jaw brought me back to the edge of alertness.

"Don't slip away into the gloaming just yet, Helen," she chided, tipping up my chin.

I blinked myself awake. "What does it do?" I asked, my voice a scrape of sound.

"Not much—on its own," she said. She turned back to the

table and emptied the contents of the jar. She took a wooden spoon from a hook on the wall and scattered them, flicking the ingredients away from each other. "It's to keep people from finding something. Makes them sick if they get too close."

"Sick like this?" I asked, gesturing weakly to my entire body.

"Not even close," she replied, casting a troubled look over her shoulder. She reached over to the bundled object and unwrapped it carefully. Then she set it on the table and stepped back once, deliberately. "Ah," was all she said.

I craned to look. It was a jaw—a human mandible. Too small to belong to an adult. I tried to rise but fell. "Give it to me," I said, reaching out. My hand bobbed in the air; I could barely hold it up. "Please. Bryony, give it to me. I need—I need it," I said, sounding plaintive and desperate.

"Are you sure that's safe?"

"Give it to me!" I demanded, clawing at the air, and she hastily picked it up and pressed it into my grasping palms. I folded my hands over it, pressed it to my chest. Bent forward with a moan. This. Yes. I had it, and that was good. The teeth bit into my palms, but I didn't care. I squeezed my eyes shut. Tears leaked down my cheeks. "Thank you," I whispered.

My body ordered itself. Joints slid back into place. Bones grew solid; blood flowed. *Helen Vaughan. I am Helen Vaughan*, I thought, and it felt true again.

Bryony crouched in front of me, hands on my knees. "Hey," she whispered. "You okay?"

"I'm okay," I promised her, and drew in a deep, shaky breath.

"God," Bryony breathed. "Is that Jessamine's?"

"I don't know," I whispered, cradling it gently. But I did know something, a truth that sang through me. "Bryony, there's more. We have to find them."

I led Bryony into the woods, following the sense that sang in me. She carried the folding spade so she could do the digging; I was still too weak. I led the way, never faltering. Twice, I pointed; twice, Bryony dug. We found two more bundles of ragged cloth— in one, the delicate, tumbled bones of a hand; in the other, five vertebrae.

We brought them back to the cabin. I laid them out on the floor, spreading out the moldering cloth that had contained them. The bones were cold and smooth beneath my fingertips. They sang to me, but I couldn't understand the song. It wasn't the simple bone-song of the fox or the fawn, but something stranger, more alien still.

"What does this mean?" I asked. There was a lump in my throat, relief and sorrow grown together. "Why did Roman have these? How was he using them to hurt me?" I looked at Bryony for reassurance, but she sank down beside me with a troubled look. She smoothed my hair back, her fingers running lightly over the curve of my ear. Above us, a soft rain pattered against the mossy roof, and small quick things scurried swiftly in the dark corners.

"There are a hundred things I don't know, and only a handful I do," Bryony said. She knelt and touched each of the bones gently, gingerly. "These bones are a child's. They belong to one of the Harrow girls. They must."

She was silent for a moment—a silence for the child whose bones we had gathered. She took my hand in both of hers and spoke deliberately.

"Helen, I don't think that the dark soul is devouring these girls. I think that it was linked to them, like it's linked to you. You heard what the dark soul keeps saying. *They scatter us.* This must be what they mean. They take the bones and scatter them, and it makes the dark soul weak. Makes it broken."

"And because I'm still linked, scattering these bones—it hurt me?" I asked. I shuddered. "This is why Leopold brought me here. To murder me and cut me up and bury my bones in the woods. And Eli or Iris are in on it, and—"

She turned her body toward me, putting her hand against my cheek. Her palm was warm, gritty with soil. I leaned into it, desperate for her touch. "Rabbit. We're not going to let that happen."

"But—"

She cut off my panicked words with a kiss, a fierce press of her cool lips against mine, and all thought and worry and fear vanished—for a moment, a breath, a heartbeat. There was only Bryony and the taste of her like spring rain, and her fingers in my hair and her body against mine. Surprise melted into desire, into the need for her, for her touch. I kissed her back, and it didn't matter that I'd never kissed anyone before, and it wouldn't have mattered if I'd kissed a hundred girls—because there was nothing like kissing Bryony Locke.

I didn't want it to stop, for my uncertain reality to snatch us back from this place of utter certainty—this place where I was

Helen and she was Bryony, and nothing mattered but her finger-tips against my jaw and the curve of her hip beneath my hand and her soft lips and the wild scent of her. I wanted this. I wanted *her*.

Her hand around the back of my neck, she pressed her brow to mine. "I won't let them hurt you," she told me, like it was a fact, a truth of the universe that could never be altered.

"What do we do?" I asked her. Fear still coiled around me, snagging at my wrists, my throat, my stuttering heart, but if Bryony was here, I could bear it.

"There's nothing more to do tonight," Bryony said. "Worry in the daylight. Tonight, stay with me. In the morning, we'll face Harrow again."

"You won't make me do this alone, will you?" I asked.

"Of course not. I'm the Harrow Witch. I'm not going any-where," Bryony said, and kissed me again, tender and soft. "Now hush, Rabbit. Sleep."

She pulled me close, pulled me down, until we lay on the floor with my head on her arm and her fingers combing gently through my hair. She sang about a girl in the woods and bells ringing, and I slept—slept, and did not dream of Harrow, but of black stars that felt like home.

23

I WOKE WITH soft light across my lids and the faint patter of rain outside. Bryony was awake already, sitting in a chair with her back to me and humming the song she'd sung the night before. Her hands moved in the steady rhythm of sewing.

"Good morning, Rabbit," she said as I sat up, rolling my neck to work out the kinks. "Here, I made you something." She set down her needle and showed me.

It was a soft leather bag, about eight inches wide, with a strap to go over the shoulder. She'd embroidered the flap with a pattern of brambles and black stars. The toggle to shut it was carved from a deer antler. "You made this? It must have taken you all night," I said.

"It was mostly done. I made it months ago, but I just realized what it was for," she said.

I opened it and sucked in a quick breath. She'd wrapped the bones—jaw, hand, vertebrae—in soft, clean cloth and nestled them inside. I put the bag over my shoulder, and it settled on my hip. It felt right, having them close to me. I could still hear the bone-song, strange and sorrowful, but it felt as if it were filling a place inside of me I hadn't realized was empty.

"Thank you," I whispered. It was all the sound I could manage.

"It was always yours. Now let's get you back to the house be-fore they send out a search and rescue for you." She stepped in close, smoothing the strap across my chest, then picked a stray leaf from my hair. "You look awful. And you've got a nasty gash on your forehead."

She touched my temple, and I winced away at the pain. "You look amazing, and you're like five times messier than me. It's not fair," I complained.

"I'm a witch. Twigs in the hair is part of the aesthetic," she informed me. She twined her fingers with mine, and we walked together into the rain-shrouded woods. The water pattered around us, pleasantly blanketing out all other sound—until we heard voices in the distance. People were shouting my name.

"So much for beating search and rescue," I said. Mom must be frantic. The voices were still a ways off. I picked up my pace.

Bryony's hand tugged against mine. She'd stopped dead in the middle of the path, her mouth half-open, breathing in frantic little pants of air. Her eyes were fixed on something above us. Dreading what I would see, I followed her gaze.

Roman hung in the trees.

The shadows had taken him apart like a puzzle box. Joints severed, bones extracted, tendons left tangled like string among the branches.

Some dark corner of me recognized the playfulness of the strange positioning of his shattered limbs and rent body. They'd destroyed him out of anger, but the way he hung in the trees, that wasn't rage or hatred or even hunger. It was curiosity—at how he was made and how they might remake him.

"The shadows," Bryony said. "I—but they don't—"

My jaw tensed. "He doesn't have Vaughan blood. He wasn't protected," I said. "They're monsters, Bryony. Made by a monster. This is what they do if they aren't controlled."

Celia's voice cut through the patter of rain. "Helen! There you are."

She was running toward us down the path directly from the house. It was clear from the relieved look on her face that she hadn't looked up at the horror above. Before I could even think, I was bolting forward. She yelped as I grabbed her, spun her around, and grabbed the back of her head, holding her gaze on mine.

"Don't look up," I said, low and urgent.

Her head tilted upward, but I forced it down, gripping hard enough to make her whimper.

"Don't. Please, don't," I said. "Celia, you don't want to see."

"See what?" she asked, trembling in my grip. A crimson drop splattered onto her shoulder, seeping into the pale wool of her sweater.

Footsteps crunched behind us, and Caleb spoke calmly. "Celia, do as Helen says. Just walk toward me, honey."

"Look at my eyes," I told her. I stepped back. She went with me, haltingly. Step by step. *Don't look*, I willed her. We reached Caleb. He took Celia from me, bundling her against him and walking swiftly away. I followed close at his heels.

I glanced back once. Bryony was gone, and my heart squeezed.

"Oh, thank god." Mom ran across the lawn toward us, Simon

striding along behind her. She reached out to hug me. I flinched back. "Are you okay? You were gone, and—"

"I'm okay," I said with a sob, knowing it wasn't true, and then her arms were around me, and for a moment, I could convince myself I was safe, and none of this could touch me.

Roman was dead. And the worst thing right now was not that I was afraid but that I was *glad*. He couldn't hurt me again. And I didn't, couldn't, grieve for that.

Caleb was murmuring in Victoria's ear. She gathered Celia to her and nodded, her eyes unfocused and distant. Victoria steered Celia back toward the house. Caleb gestured to Eli to follow him, but Mom led me firmly back toward the house. Inside, she turned toward me again, but Simon touched her elbow, drawing her attention. "Let's let Helen rest," he said.

I wondered again what Simon knew. He had no connection to Harrow or to the Vaughans that I knew of. He didn't have family, or even friends, really. His life mostly revolved around us. I'd never seen anything sinister in that. But the things he'd said, the things he seemed to know, suggested some connection. What if he were involved?

I shoved the thought away. I couldn't go reading wickedness in everything and everyone. Simon was a good man. I refused to believe otherwise.

"Hey, can I talk to you?" Desmond asked under his breath, sidling up to me.

"My room," I suggested. The Willows was the closest thing to a safe place I had in this house. Desmond followed me up and dutifully waited while I ducked into the bathroom to change into clothes that weren't caked in dirt.

"What happened out there?" he asked when I stepped out.

"Roman's dead," I said flatly. Desmond blanched. I dropped onto the end of the bed and buried my face in my hands, holding back the swell of a sob. I couldn't fall apart, not now. Not when any one of the people in this house could be out to get me.

"Helen? I asked how he died," Desmond said. There was a hard edge to his voice.

I startled upright and hastily scraped at the few tears that had leaked down my cheeks. I mostly succeeded in rubbing more dirt in. "I'm sorry. He was out after the night bell. I followed him. The shadows attacked. Bryony helped me and we got away. He didn't."

"The shadows did it." He almost sounded like he didn't believe me.

"Yeah." I rubbed my arms, trying to get some warmth into them. I'd seen dead things before. I'd gathered them up in my arms, cleaned their bones. But I'd never seen a person torn apart like that.

"What was he doing out there?" Desmond asked, still with that sharpness to his tone.

"He was doing something to hurt me. I don't understand it completely." I couldn't tell him about the girls until I was sure. If I was wrong, and I'd made him think his family killed Jessamine, he'd never forgive me.

"But Roman is *dead*? You're sure?" He collapsed into the chair by the desk, elbows on his knees and has hands on his head.

"He's really, really dead, Desmond. Trust me, you don't want the details," I said. I pressed a fist against my gut, trying not to think of the way the boughs had sagged beneath his weight, the look of surprise on his ashen face.

"And you didn't—" He stopped.

"Didn't what?" I asked, confusion written on my face.

"Nothing. It's nothing," Desmond said. He stood again, pacing back and forth in a tight circuit, his hands clasping and unclasping with nervous energy. "Roman's always been obsessed with our family. He used to be Caleb's best friend, back when they were growing up. When my parents split, right after I was born, it was like ten seconds before Roman started going after my mom. They got married less than a year later. And he dated your mom, too."

"What? When?"

"Like eighteen years ago, I think," he said.

My eyes widened. "You don't think . . . ?"

He stopped, fixing me with a look I couldn't read. "Roman is not your father."

"How would you know?"

"Trust me. He's not," Desmond said. "The timing doesn't work. My point is, I think he always wanted to be part of the family. Get all the perks of being a Vaughan."

"Meaning the Other. It's not just something we keep locked up here, is it? It gives the family power somehow. I mean, maybe that's how we got rich in the first place. Bringing people out here and using the Other to brainwash them into agreeing to whatever business deals the family wanted."

Desmond's jaw worked. He swore under his breath and looked off to the side, hands in his pockets. "This is messed up."

"Roman must have known about it all. What's really going on," I said. "God, I have to get out of here. I have to get away from that thing." Bryony would tell me the dark soul wasn't a monster, but I couldn't bring myself to believe it. I had to get free of it. I would destroy it if I had to.

"Hey, are you . . . are you okay?" Desmond asked. He put his hand to the back of his neck, his whole body a knot of tension.

"I have no idea how to answer that," I said. I looked up at him, blinking away the sharp sting of tears. "Was there something else you wanted to talk about?"

"It's not important," Desmond said. "Or it is, but I don't need to bother you right now."

"Desmond . . ."

He winced. "The journal's gone."

I bolted to my feet. "What do you mean, gone?"

"I mean it was in my room, on my desk, when I went down for dinner last night. When I got back it was gone." His shoulders slumped.

"Who took it?" I asked. I found myself holding on to the bed post as if for support.

Desmond's hand cut through the air in a frustrated gesture. "I don't know. A raccoon. The ghost of Christmas past. It could have been anyone."

"Not anyone. You said you were at dinner—who else was there? Did they come after you got there or leave before you?"

"I'm not Sherlock Holmes. I wasn't paying attention," Desmond said. "We'll look for it. For now, though, can we just deal with *now*? Roman dying? Because my mom and Celia are going to be wrecked, and I need to go be with them."

"Of course," I said. I sat back down slowly, a groan slipping from my lips. "God, poor Celia." Now I *was* going to cry.

"Helen . . ." He trailed off. When he spoke again, his tone was brisk. "There's mud in your hair. You should probably get cleaned up." He left, and I stared after him, wondering what it was that Desmond wasn't telling me.

24

IT WAS ANOTHER hour before my summons came. I walked to
Caleb's study with trepidation. I wasn't sure what I would find
when I got there—a room full of police? But of course it was only
family. Vaughans dealt with their own problems. Caleb sat behind
the desk. Iris had taken a chair off to the side, and Mom was there,
too, looking pale and fidgeting with her sleeves. The edges of her
nails were chewed ragged.

"Helen, take a seat," Caleb said as soon as I entered. I closed
the door and obeyed, sinking into the hard wooden chair next
to Mom.

"We need to discuss what happened and make some things
very clear," Iris said. "First, the police will need to be informed.
It won't be a problem; we've handled these sorts of accidents before. As far as any official record is concerned, you were in your
bed all night. You saw nothing. You have nothing to do with what
happened. Is that understood?"

I nodded and forced myself to meet her eyes. I didn't understand how Iris could sit there looking at me like I was her beloved
granddaughter and not a lamb she meant to lead to slaughter.

"Of course, the reality of the matter is much different," Caleb said. "I think it would be valuable for you to give us a full account of what happened."

I drew in a breath, squaring my shoulders. Haltingly, I began. I gave a much abbreviated version—I'd followed Roman outside; the shadows attacked. I left out the bones and Roman's bag. I didn't have to fake any of the disgust and horror in my voice when I came to finding Roman's body, though. "Did Celia see?" I asked when I was done.

"No, thank god," Caleb said. "That was quick thinking. And for what it's worth, you were right to run last night. You couldn't have saved him."

"But the shadows can't hurt me, can they? I have Vaughan blood. Could I have stopped them?" Would Roman still be alive if I'd tried to help him?

"It's not a good idea to test the limits of Harrow's rules," Caleb said gravely. "Please try not to feel guilty for what happened."

"What about your illness?" Iris asked.

"I feel fine now. Whatever it was must have passed." I fidgeted, scratching at the scabbed-over gash on my forehead. Could they tell I was hiding something?

"Curious," Iris said softly, frowning. "I would feel a lot better if we knew the cause."

"We know the cause," Caleb said angrily. "Father chose playing games with the inheritance over keeping the Other properly caged, and it's leaving Helen vulnerable. When she got away, it went after Roman instead."

Mom's fingers gripped the arms of her chair until her knuckles turned white. "I'm sorry, but what exactly are we doing here?

She's been going through all of this—risking her *life*, apparently—to protect *your* inheritance. If it weren't for the family, you know we wouldn't be here. The least you could do is find a way out of this ridiculous Investiture."

"It isn't a simple matter of amending a contract, Rachel," Caleb said. "We don't even understand some of the forces in play. We need to be cautious."

"Cautious? Helen's getting sick. Now I hear she's been sleep-walking outside. *Outside*, where something just *killed* Roman. Whatever Dad thought he was doing, this is dangerous, and it's out of control."

"That we can agree on," Caleb said. "Rachel, listen. I am doing absolutely everything in my power to make sure Helen gets through this year. And then I'm going to figure out how to free our family from Harrow and all of this madness for good."

He had no idea what was really going on in this place. What it had already cost him. Harrow had taken his daughter. Not just Harrow—his father, his own mother. And god knew who else might be involved. I wished I could have told him everything, but I knew I needed proof if I was going to convince him of something so awful.

Proof, like Nicholas Vaughan's journal spelling it out. I had to find it.

"Then I think that's all," Caleb said. He got up and stepped around the desk.

"That's it?" I asked. A man was dead. Shouldn't there be more?

"Just hang tight, Helen. The year will be over before you know it," Caleb replied. He put a hand on my shoulder comfortingly as I stood. "We'll be able to put all of this behind us."

"Thank you," I told him, grateful for the sentiment even if I didn't believe it—and then, on impulse, I hugged him. He seemed startled at first, but then returned the embrace.

I pulled away after a moment and winced. The gash on my forehead had opened up, and there was a smear of blood on Caleb's cheek. "Sorry," I muttered, embarrassed, and retreated, struck with the feeling that this was not a good omen.

By the end of that day, Victoria and Celia had left for home. Desmond went back to school. Roman, like all of Harrow's other secrets, was tucked into the seams and forgotten.

Sandra drove back to Connecticut. It was strange to me that no one ever talked about how she and Caleb didn't live together. They said Caleb was staying at Harrow for my sake, but even when Sandra was here, she slept in a separate room. Still, sometimes I saw Caleb looking at her with a kind of pained hope in his eyes, and when he wasn't paying attention, she looked at him the same way.

I kept to my room, making the Willows my refuge and my cage. And so the days went, hour by hour, sinking deeper into the spiral not of Harrow but of my own mind. I hardly ate, hardly slept, only sat running my fingers over a dead girl's bones, wondering who she'd been and who she was to me. Fragments of memories snagged at me but refused to spin themselves into sense.

Rough hands and gentle ones, my mother's face and my grandfather's, daylight and the darkness of a tomb.

The bells rang. I woke, I paced the floor, I stared at the bones. I appeared when I was summoned, I vanished when I would not be missed.

Every spare moment, I spent with Bryony. I felt like I was drowning, but every time I saw her, I broke the surface. Long enough to catch a breath of air. Nothing could silence the cacophony of my thoughts but her kiss, her touch.

And all along, I was hiding things from her.

The dark soul she loved so much was a terrible thing, but I didn't say as much to her. I didn't tell her what I had realized: that my only options were to escape the dark soul or destroy it. That doing one might require doing the other. I listened to her speak rapturously of walking the grounds at night, calling the shadows by name, and watching them dance among the trees, and I said nothing.

Days passed relentlessly. The bells rang. I woke. I paced. I whispered to the bones as if they could hear. The bells rang. I woke—and I was not alone.

Leopold stood at the foot of the bed. I could see the edge of his jaw and his left eye; the rest was a haze. *"What are you doing?"* he asked me.

I sat up, pulling my knees up in front of me. "What do you want from me?" I asked.

Silence. *"We are scattered,"* he said. *"We wish to be whole."*

"You murder people. People have died here—people from

Eston, people who had nothing to do with you or with Harrow or any of it."

"Yes."

"Why?"

"*We are scattered*," he said again, and I screamed in wordless frustration.

"Stop *saying* that and tell me what you mean!" I demanded.

"*We are in pieces*," Jessamine said. She sat on the end of the bed, her knees tucked under her. The only distortion was a jagged bit of light over one eye, like a scar. "*The tooth without the heart knows only hunger.*"

Jessamine reached out. Her small white hand brushed against mine. It had no weight, no substance. But I felt it, soft and silky as a petal. "*Become with us*," she said. "*Help us be whole.*"

I snatched my hand away. "No."

Her hand wrapped around my wrist. She twisted, crawling toward me, grasping at me. She had no weight, but still she pressed me back against the pillows, her hungry fingers digging against my throat, hooking the edges of my mouth. She was reaching *inside* me, and the dark tendrils of the Other wrapped around me, finding purchase, finding the darkness that twined and tangled at my own heart—

"No!" I screamed, and shoved hard at her. My hands passed through nothing. The room was empty, except for the fading echo of my shout. I knotted my fingers together so tightly they hurt with a sharp, fierce pain, but I didn't let up.

If Harrow claimed me, the Other stayed contained. Its hunger remained behind these gates, within these woods. If I escaped, so did the beasts of Harrow.

I didn't want to die. But what if the price of my survival was unleashing the Other's destruction on the world?

There was only one solution. I had to destroy the dark soul. It was the only way that I could live without endangering countless others.

I would kill the Other.

And Bryony would never speak to me again.

25

MORNING CAME RELUCTANTLY to Harrow, the sallow sky refusing to part for the sunrise, and by the time the morning bell chimed, I was a solid knot of nerves.

I loved Bryony. I yearned for her. I lay at night with the memory of her holding me, a balm against my nightmares. But before she had cared for me, she had loved the darkness at Harrow's heart. What would happen if she had to choose between us?

I walked the path to the groundkeeper's house, my heart in my throat and my thoughts in a million pieces. I scaled the steps and then stood there, losing my nerve with each passing second. But before I could turn to go, the door opened, and Bryony broke into a smile.

"I wasn't expecting you today," she said. Then she saw my expression, and her smile faltered. "Rabbit, what's wrong?" she asked.

She searched my face. I didn't know what she wanted to see, and so I didn't know how to fake it. Wordlessly, she reached out and took my hand, drawing me inside the house. The door shut behind me with a soft click. She stepped in close to me, still searching, and my skin flushed with the sheer presence of her—the brush of her skirt against my legs, the woodsmoke and pine scent that clung to her, the soft moss green of her eyes.

"You're okay," she said, uncertain. "Did something happen?"

I couldn't hold her gaze. I dropped my eyes and took a half step to the side, pulling away. "I'm okay," I lied. "Nothing happened. Not really. Everything is just crashing down on me all at once," I said.

"I understand. It's a lot," she said.

"The year is almost halfway gone," I said. "And I still don't know what to do."

"The year is *only* halfway gone," she corrected me. "We know so much already. And whether or not your grandma is evil, it's pretty clear she doesn't want you dead before the Investiture, so that's something."

"It's something," I allowed. I swiped my hair back from my forehead, only to have it immediately fall forward into my eyes again. Maybe I didn't have to tell Bryony what I'd decided yet. Not for a little while, at least. "I was thinking—we looked through your grandmother's things, but we didn't really know what we were looking for. I think it's worth checking again. Maybe there's something in there about Mary or her daughter."

"Daughter?" Bryony echoed.

My brow creased. "I guess the journal didn't say one way or another. Not the parts we have, at least. But it must have been a daughter."

"How can you be sure?" Bryony asked.

"They're Harrow's girls," I said, and Bryony's expression grew still.

"Ah. And she was the first," Bryony said, carefully neutral in a way that made her disgust plain. "Poor Mary. She never had a chance, did she? They used her up and threw her away, every one of them. Okay. We'll check the attic. We were only looking for Harrow's girls before. Maybe there's something we missed."

Upstairs, we split up the boxes, sorting through them. "I don't think we need stuff about the history of Eston's sewer and water revitalization project, do you?" Bryony asked.

"Do we? What if there's something hidden in the water pipes, or they're laid out in a mystic sigil, or—"

"Helen. Chill," Bryony said, shaking her head in amusement. "We can come back to it later if we need to. Prioritize."

"Right," I said.

"Ah, okay. This says, 'Harrowstone Hall: nineteenth century.' You look through these." She handed me a thick folder. It was packed with everything from delicate newspaper clippings in plastic sleeves to printouts of online articles to photographs. I went through with my usual haphazard approach, grabbing things at random, setting them down when they didn't tell me anything new.

For the most part, the documents told the same story I already knew: Nicholas Vaughan and his wife came to Eston, built Harrowstone Hall, and made it their family home. Men of influence visited; Vaughan's fortunes rose year by year. No one ever seemed to say no to Vaughan.

The Other could alter memories and thoughts. If Vaughan had a way to control it, he would get what he wanted without any effort at all. He just needed people to spend one night here, and they were his.

Tucked near the middle of the folder was an old black-and-white photograph. The man pictured was nearly bald, wisps of hair plastered against his scalp. A massive mustache drooped over his scowling mouth, and his pale eyes glared out from a narrow, bony face. *Dr. Samuel Raymond, 1872,* was written on the back. So this was Dr. Raymond, whose eager knife had destroyed Mary and brought the Other to our world.

With the picture was a small notebook, the size of my palm. It cracked when I opened it. The ink was faded, some pages stuck together or missing altogether, and the text was dense, but I could pick out most of the words.

A procedure to divide the consciousness of the Other:

The human mind exists within the cradle of the brain. The mind of the creature, in contrast, does not restrict itself to the brain; it conceives itself as a whole. This simplifies matters considerably. One need not sever an exacting pathway of tissue in that most delicate and complex of organs but may undertake a separation any layman is perfectly capable of, after which the resulting material should be scattered; thus, the mind itself shall be scattered and made pliant in its confusion. In order to establish mastery, the original procedure must be repeated:

An object belonging to the offering shall be placed at the heart of the spiral. Her soul will be drawn to it, and she will walk willingly to the place of sacrifice. The new Master must make an offering of his own flesh, which shall be placed at the foot of the Harrow stone. He shall mark the child's face with his blood to represent the bond between them.

Three must stand with him to demonstrate that he is recognized as the rightful Master. To signify their common purpose, they will share a communion, and each shall offer a secret to bind them. Then must the Master speak the names of all who came before him to honor the unbroken line.

Finally, the Master shall call on the Other-soul and command it to claim the body and mind of the offering. A potion may be prepared to make the end swift, or a knife may be used, but the body shall then be divided in the manner indicated.

On the next page was a sketch of a human form—faceless, genderless, ageless, just the suggestion of a body. Lines had been drawn across it: at the neck, the wrists, the elbows, the shoulders—every joint.

They matched, perfectly, the welts that had risen on my skin.

"This is it," I said. "This is what they did. They bound the Other to the girl, and then they killed her. Cut her apart. Scattered her bones." That was what Roman had done with the bones, too. There must have been enough of an echo of power that it could hurt me through my bond to the Other.

"This is pure evil," Bryony said, peering over my shoulder. "All those girls. All for what?"

"To keep a monster from killing people," I said, not looking at her.

"They're the monsters," she replied, poison in her voice.

"At least now we know what it is that Iris and Eli are trying to do," I said.

"You don't know that it's just them. Three witnesses? Sounds like a lot more people are involved. You can't trust any of them."

"Caleb—"

"You don't know him," Bryony said. "You've barely just met any of them."

"I've known them just as long as I've known you," I pointed out. She let out a frustrated breath. "I have to trust someone, Bryony. I can't do this on my own."

"You don't have to. You have me." She brushed her thumb over my knuckles, and I shivered.

"I don't know if I can do this," I confessed.

She leaned down and kissed me. "You are so much stronger than you think," she told me, and I wished that I believed her.

26

SUMMER ARRIVED ALL at once, the delicate green of spring deepening and the air growing thick with heat. Desmond and Celia were coming to Harrow for the summer, and I'd been awaiting their arrival with impatience, eager to have their company again.

The day Victoria and her children arrived, they piled out of the car with an air of baffling cheer. I was out front with Bryony, and we exchanged a look as Victoria beamed at us.

"Are we pretending Roman never existed then?" Bryony muttered.

"That would be my preference," I said. "Sorry, that's awful."

"He was trying to murder you. I think you can be a little mean," she replied.

"Helen! You're up bright and early," Victoria said. Her hair spilled loose around her shoulders, the soft curls framing her round face.

"You must have driven through the night," I said.

"We got a late start from Atwood, and I didn't want to bother with a hotel. I'm an insomniac these days anyway," she said, and patted at her hair absently. Her fingertips brushed against her earlobe, and she frowned. "Oops. I think I lost an earring." She turned back to the car to look for it in the seat as Desmond hauled a suitcase out of the back.

"She's totally manic. I think she's decided to pretend that nothing happened," he whispered to me. Celia slinked around the back of the car, a single bag over her shoulder. "Any sign of the journal?"

I'd conducted as thorough a search of the house as I could, but there was no sign of it—and since Desmond had been working from the original, we'd never bothered to photograph the rest of it, so we didn't have backups.

Celia tucked her hand into her pocket, and something silver flashed briefly between her fingers before disappearing. I peered at her. She blanched, hurrying past me to the house.

"Helen?" Desmond prompted.

"Hm? Oh—no, I haven't found it," I said distractedly.

Celia was a thief. I'd noticed it before—Desmond's pen, Mom's lipstick—but I hadn't given it much thought. I'd been assuming that whoever stole the journal did it because they didn't want us to read what was inside, but maybe the answer was more mundane than that.

"Mind giving me a hand?" Desmond asked me, hefting one of his bags.

I looked at Bryony. "It's fine. I'll see you later," she said.

"You could come in," Desmond suggested, in a strained attempt at friendliness.

She shook her head. "I'm supposed to go talk to Elizabeth Cotter. Meet me at the folly at seven, Rabbit?"

I nodded. She gave a little wave and headed off, more stiff and awkward than usual. I wondered if it was Victoria's presence that did it—or simply the return of Desmond and Celia, shattering the world we'd had the last few days, the one built around just the two of us.

"Who's Elizabeth Cotter?" Desmond asked as we went up the steps.

"Haley Cotter's mother," I said.

"And who's—"

"Haley Cotter died right around the time we were born. It might have something to do with the Other. We're just trying to put the pieces together."

"And things with the witch are . . ."

"Complicated," I said with a sigh. *My girlfriend and I are on the same page re: the sacrificing of girls for dark rituals but divided on the subject of whether the monster in my house is evil or just misunderstood* was a bit much for a status update.

"They'd pretty much have to be," Desmond replied. He gave me an odd look, started to say something, and then shook his head. I helped him carry his bags up to his room, and then we stood there awkwardly for a moment.

"You haven't been answering my texts," I said. "I mean, it's okay. I know you were probably busy, and you have an entire life of your own and friends and a girlfriend, but I was worried, and—"

"I just needed some space to think about some things," he said. He shoved his hands in his pockets. "A lot happened. It took some time to process."

"Right. Of course," I said, nodding.

"You really are . . ." He trailed off. "I like you, Helen. I do. But

I had to decide whether I could do this. Harrow doesn't own me. I can leave if I want."

"Are you going to?" I tried not to betray the panic I felt at that idea. With Desmond gone, there would be so few people I knew I could trust.

"No, I'm staying the summer. Like you asked."

"I asked you to stay the summer?"

He sighed. "Yeah, but it was when you were sick, so I guess you don't remember. Anyway, it's my choice, and it's the choice I'm making, and that's that. I just needed the time to make it and know it was *mine*, you know?"

"I think so."

He laughed darkly. "God, this sucks. I'm going to get unpacked. I'll talk to you later."

"I'll leave you alone," I said, feeling relieved. "Where's Celia's room, by the way? I wanted to check in on her." And ask her about her little habit.

"Three doors down," he said. "The wildflower room." He rolled his eyes.

I walked the few steps to Celia's room. I could hear her moving around inside, opening drawers. I tapped cautiously on the door. "Celia?" I called.

She squeaked. "Just a sec!" she called, and I heard frantic rustling. I had a guess about what she was doing. She opened the door looking flushed and startled, as I'd so often seen her. She wore a soft pink sweater covered in little bits of sparkly thread and she'd painted her fingernails to match. She looked bubblegum sweet, and not at all like a thief.

"I know you took your mom's earring," I said.

"What? No," she said, her eyes flaring comically wide in obvious panic.

"Okay, if that's how you lie, I cannot believe you haven't gotten caught before."

Her cheeks flamed red, and she grabbed my sleeve, tugging me into the room. "Stop talking so loud," she told me. Inside, she shut the door and bit down on the tip of her thumb. "Did you tell anyone else? I mean, I didn't do it, but did you tell anyone you think—"

"I didn't tell anyone. I'm not mad," I said gently. "But you should at least give Desmond his pen back."

"I didn't—" She gripped her elbows, hunching in on herself. "I don't know why I do it."

"Honestly, I'm surprised you guys don't have worse coping strategies," I said. "As ways to sublimate constant creeping dread go, this is pretty healthy. I mean, unless you've stolen something way more important than a pen."

"Just random stuff," Celia said. She hesitated, then scurried over to her vanity. She took a small key from around her neck and unlocked the bottom drawer. "I stick everything in here."

I held my breath. The drawer was full of junk mostly—a tiny silver spoon, a few coins, a gaudy ring, a Starlight Motel room key, a few papers—and the journal.

"I'm not going to tell anyone you took this stuff," I said. "But I need that journal back."

"I thought it was Desmond's," Celia said.

"He was translating it for me. It's Nicholas Vaughan's," I said. I took it out of the drawer, flipping through quickly as if to reassure myself it was all in one piece.

"I don't think Harrow wants you to have it," Celia said nervously.

"Why do you say that?"

"Because . . . normally I just take things on impulse. Little things people won't miss that much. But sometimes I take things and I don't remember taking them. I just have them. And if I try to put them back, it's like—it's like there's someone with a hand on the back of my neck. Squeezing. Stopping me." Her voice dropped to a whisper—as if the very walls were listening in.

"What else have you taken like that?" I asked.

She knotted her fingers together nervously. "Promise you won't tell?"

I sighed. "I promise. Really, Celia, I do."

She knelt down next to the drawer and picked out one thing after another. She set aside three things: a letter in a plain envelope, a plastic butterfly barrette, and a heavy silver ring with the Atwood crest stamped on it. It looked just like the ring Caleb had been wearing.

The barrette looked old, the plastic faded. The ring was engraved on the inside: C. V.—Caleb Vaughan. So it was his after all. I set both aside for now. I teased out the folded paper. It looked like it had been crumpled into a ball and then smoothed out again. The handwriting was formal, cursive written on a perfect slant. "Have you read this?" I asked.

She shook her head. "It was in Grandma Iris's room," she said.

"I took it, but when I touched it, I felt this overwhelming sadness. I couldn't stand to look at it." She shuddered.

"What about this?" I asked, picking up the plastic barrette. It was purple and old-fashioned. I'd seen it before.

"It was in Grandpa's office. In his desk drawer," she said nervously.

Haley Cotter had been wearing a pair of barrettes just like that in her photo. I picked it up, turning it over in my hands.

"Is it okay if I take this stuff?" I asked.

"Okay," she said meekly. "You won't tell anyone?"

"Your secret's safe with me," I promised her.

I walked back to my room with Celia's stolen items tucked surreptitiously in my pocket, the journal under my arm. A letter, a barrette, and a ring. What was the connection between them?

Once the door was closed behind me, I set the journal on the desk and took out the letter. I smoothed the paper carefully and unfolded it. My stomach twisted as I read.

You know by now that all of this is my fault. Twenty years ago, I failed to do what I needed to. I do not ask you to forgive me, but I ask you to understand: it was love that was my downfall. I thought a gentle surcease would be sufficient and could not bear to take the further steps that were demanded of me. And because of this, Jessamine is dead, and it did not even repair the damage that I caused. Her death accomplished nothing.

> *I do not ask you to forgive me. But I promise you that*
> *I will put things back in their proper order.*

I traced my fingers over one jagged line where the paper had been crushed and smoothed again. Leopold must have written this. *It was love that was my downfall,* he had written, and he'd kept her barrette.

He'd killed Haley Cotter, but he'd regretted it? He'd messed it up, and they'd tried again with Jessamine. But that hadn't worked either.

I needed to understand the ritual, the sacrifices. I needed to know how exactly these girls had died. And how my death was supposed to fix what was wrong with Harrow.

By this point, I had enough of Desmond's work to be able to decipher the journal on my own, though much slower than he might have. Entry by entry, I reconstructed the record of my ancestor's sin, and by the end of it, I felt sick.

Sick and lost. I'd gotten the journal back, and it had told me what I already knew—in more horrible detail than I'd had before—but without a way forward. I didn't know how to escape my fate. How to escape Harrow and the dark soul.

I set my pen down, looking at the copied-out words. There was no salvation there. Only proof of my family's evil, and of the evil that they'd killed to contain. I knew how to bind the dark soul. But I didn't know how to end this cycle. Everyone who might have told me—Nicholas Vaughan, Samuel Raymond, hell, even Leopold—was dead.

There was someone who'd witnessed all of it. The dark soul itself. But the figments spoke in riddles and fragments. They were broken. They couldn't help me. Unless I could find a way to make them whole again. Or if not whole, then less broken than they were now.

I could gather their bones and let them speak.

Shadows deepened and the heat of the summer air relented. I went to the folly with my ancestor's journal, my grandfather's confession, and a child's bones in a satchel. Above, the sky was a blue as perfect as a lie.

Bryony was the first one there when I arrived. "Are you sure you want to bring them into this?" she asked me. She still didn't think we could trust anyone but ourselves. She didn't know yet the way her own story was enmeshed with theirs.

"We need their help," I said, as Desmond and Celia appeared.

"What is this about?" Desmond asked. I hadn't told them anything other than where to be. I only wanted to have to explain this all once.

"It's about answers," I said. "But first, Bryony—did you talk to Elizabeth Cotter?"

"Not Lizzie herself. She's got early onset dementia—she was pretty out of it. But her sister was happy to talk. She said Lizzie dated your grandfather in high school, over a couple summers.

Then he went off to college and got engaged to a *suitable* woman. That should have been the end of it. Except it wasn't. They kept seeing each other, and Lizzie had a daughter who was obviously his. The sister says he gave her gifts all the time, and she saw him at the house sometimes, sneaking in and out. When she disappeared, Lizzie Cotter suddenly had a million dollars in her bank account and no more visits."

"Grandpa Leopold had a kid we didn't know about?" Desmond asked.

I nodded. "Desmond, I translated more of the journal based on your notes."

"You found the journal?" he asked, perking up. "Where?"

"That's not important right now," I said. Celia looked relieved but smoothed her expression quickly. "What's important is what it says. The entries I marked. Go on."

I handed him the journal, open to the page I'd found before dinner. He glanced at me once, as if for permission, and then read aloud.

27

April 9, 1854

Annalise and I have agreed to take in the girl, as her mother is obviously incapable. There is something very strange indeed about Mary's offspring. Things seemed to alter around her to suit her mood. She babbles and the clouds break; she shrieks and the shadows scurry and writhe around her.

September 14, 1855

We cannot remain here. The locals have become alarmed at what they call the devil child. None of the children will play with her, but she makes her own playmates, strange half-real children, who move sometimes naturally and sometimes like a ragdoll jerked to and fro. I find I sometimes fear her, and sometimes love her; she grips your mind when she is near, seemingly without intent. Annalise is the only one that sees the truth of her. She is a child, but there is something else within her. A piece of the god. And that piece is growing more prominent with each passing day.

We must find a way to contain her before she causes true harm.

January 12, 1856

She killed a boy today. I do not think she intended it; she is too young to understand death, and she did try to put him back together again, like he was a broken doll. Annalise calls her a monster. Perhaps she is right. Something must be done. Dr. Raymond has a notion of what it might be.

March 25, 1857

We are forced to flee again. The girl grows older. She is curious and monstrous in her curiosity, always taking apart dead things and asking questions that make men squirm. She invents companions for herself, and when she bores of them, she sets them loose. At first, they dissolved without her, into smoke and earth, but now they bound and lope about, heads lolling, grasping at whatever they can touch. I have learned to dispatch them quickly.

We have devised a solution of sorts. A cage. Annalise believes she has found a suitable location for it, outside of a town called Eston. Beyond the town lies a place called the Fold. It is here that Annalise believes we will find our solution.

October 8, 1857

The people of Eston do not welcome us; I can hardly blame them. The girl breeds strangeness in her wake. Though she has not killed in months, and the last time she did—another village boy—she suddenly began to scream and wail and would not stop for hours, saying that she did not know, asking why we had not told her. I do not know to what she referred, but if it has put a stop to the need for so many bribes and midnight exits, all the better.

Dr. Raymond assures us the procedure will be simple enough. The mind of the god that lives within the girl has attached itself to her. It is not unlike the procedure which opened Mary to the great god in the first place. It is only a few cuts and the severing of sense. Only the scale is different: a bundle of nerves in Mary's case; in the girl's, a division of her body. Dr. Raymond believes that by dividing her flesh and scattering it through the Fold, we will scatter the consciousness of the god.

It is not necessary for the girl's physical body to be alive when we undertake the procedure. I have prepared a tincture of foxglove which should be a gentle enough surcease before the necessary violence. Thirteen cuts; were I superstitious, I might find something ominous in that, but I find my capacity for fear and uncanniness is spent.

We shall make the thing biddable, and we shall cage it here, and its power will be ours.

October 19, 1857

It is done.

February 19, 1858

I saw the girl again. Her face was obscured as if by a flaw in my own eye, and she flickered for but a moment, incorporeal and fleeting. But I fear that the creature is remembering itself. And if it can remember, it can heal. If it heals, we cannot contain it. We will have to find a way to repeat the procedure.

May 10, 1858

My son was born today. He looks like his mother, save for one thing: he has black eyes.

The construction of Harrowstone Hall is nearly complete. The creature remains caged.

November 6, 1889

It has been a very long time since I wrote in this chronicle. I have hoped for a long time that my suspicions about the creature's growing strength were unfounded, but it has become undeniable. The disturbances in our perceptions have become more pronounced so that even I sometimes struggle to sort truth from phantasm. Annalise remains immune, but I worry for her as well. She has grown to despise the house, and after months of wandering its halls at night, she has retreated completely and refuses to step foot inside again. Her odd behavior has alarmed the locals. They call her the Harrow Witch, a title in which she seems to find some perverse pleasure.

If we do not repeat the ritual, all will be lost. Fortunately, we have prepared for this moment. A child of the appropriate lineage has been produced and is being fetched even now. In a sense, I pity her, but our patronage has given her a more comfortable life than a bastard might have; in a sense, her life is ours in any case.

It is a simple enough procedure. She will not be missed.

28

"ANNALISE VAUGHAN WAS the Harrow Witch," Bryony said dully. She looked at me, and her expression was closed.

"That's what you got from this?" Desmond asked, closing the journal. He looked like he wanted to fling it away from himself. "Nicholas Vaughan was a murderer," he said grimly. "And this is the proof."

"He wasn't the only one. Generations of girls have died here—have been *murdered* here," Bryony said. "And I—I thought I was supposed to help the dark soul. To protect it. But if Annalise was the first witch . . ."

"The Harrow Witch has always been another way to control and contain the Other," I said gently. "The one who could see through its deceptions."

Bryony sucked in a breath, then let it out. "Okay," she said.

"Okay? That's all?" I asked.

Bryony crossed her arms, sitting back against one of the low toppled walls of the folly. "I know who I am, Helen. And what I am. And Annalise Vaughan has nothing to do with it. I would *never* do what she did. Murdering that girl—and for what? Power?"

"To contain the Other," I countered. "It killed his son."

"It doesn't die when its body does. How would it know we *do* if no one ever taught it?" Bryony asked fiercely.

"It's broken," Celia said in horror. She stood close to Desmond. I could tell he wanted to pace, but he stayed near her. "It's in pain and it's trapped. It's lashing out."

"It's lashed out pretty hard," I said. "I'm not saying that what they did is okay, but—"

"It wasn't just her, though," Desmond said.

"No. No, it wasn't," I said. My hand strayed to my satchel, and I felt the faint hum of the bones within. "This is what happened to Haley Cotter and to a lot of other girls—girls with Vaughan eyes. If they're going to be a vessel for the Other, they've got to have a connection to the dark soul and to Harrow, and I think that means they've got to be descendants of Nicholas Vaughan. Like Haley Cotter. Like Jessamine." Like me.

"What?" Celia asked sharply. "No. I don't care about the stories they make up in Eston—we're not *evil*. Nobody's going around *sacrificing* little girls. Are they?" She turned to Desmond. "*Are* they?" He didn't answer.

I took a breath. "Leopold left Uncle Caleb a letter. In it, he confessed to killing Jessamine because of a mistake he'd made. These other girls died about thirty years apart from each other. Haley Cotter only died twenty years ago, so why would Leopold need to do the ritual again so soon? Unless something had gone wrong with Haley. He said he thought 'a gentle surcease' would be enough, without the rest. I think that he wasn't supposed to get attached to Haley, but he did, and when it was time to kill her, he just gave her the poison. He didn't cut her up. So the dark soul didn't scatter the way it should. It kept growing stronger."

"Then why not just scatter the bones?" Desmond asked.

"Maybe it was too late," I said. "It wouldn't be enough. He had to do the sacrifice again but do it right."

"That night," Celia whispered. "The little girl Desmond saw . . ."

"I think it was me." My voice quavered.

Desmond squeezed Celia's hand. She looked at him. "It's possible," he said. "I can't remember *when* it happened. I barely remember it at all. It could have been Helen I saw."

"But something went wrong," Bryony said.

"I got away." Or someone helped me get away. "And then Mom took me and ran."

"If Roman was helping Leopold, they wouldn't have gone after Celia," Bryony said. "Roman must have protected her. But he didn't care about Helen. Or Jessamine."

"Dad was a jerk sometimes, but he wouldn't . . ." Celia trailed off.

"Cee. He would," Desmond said. "He cared about money and power. He said so, straight out. That's the whole reason he married Mom."

"But . . ." Celia's eyes welled with tears. "He was going to kill Helen?"

"Fuck," Desmond said instead of answering. He ran his hand over his scalp. "Just, fuck." He paced away a step and jammed his hands into his pockets, staring off into the distance.

"Jessamine was a baby when I left," I said. The wind slithered past us, cold and sharp. "So they waited until she was old enough. But they'd made a miscalculation. According to what Dr. Raymond and Nicholas both wrote, there's some kind of connection, a bond, between the Other and the sacrifice. And I don't think Jessamine had the right bond because I still did. So she died for nothing. It didn't work. That's what the letter is about."

"I don't get it. If all of that is true, why leave you Harrow?" Celia asked.

"Leopold had screwed up. Not just once. Not just twice. Three times. With Haley, with me, and with Jessamine. Maybe he felt guilty. Maybe he just knew he was at the end of the line. So he decided to fix his mistake—by ending his life. Because it was the only way to bring me back here, to wake up my bond to the Other, and to finish the sacrifice." Or maybe Eli and Iris had done it for him.

"But if he's dead—" Desmond started.

"There's no way that he was the only one that was in on all of this. Eli knows everything about Vaughan history," Bryony said. "He would have inherited, if he wasn't gay."

"Great, we're a *homophobic* murder cult. This gets better and better," Desmond muttered.

"Iris had the confession letter. I think she stole it so Caleb wouldn't find out what Leopold had done. Because she knew he'd stop them," I said.

"What do we do?" Celia asked. She was scrunched up, her hands tucked inside her long sleeves as if she wished she could vanish entirely. "Could you just run?"

"I don't think I could," I said. "Harrow would find a way to draw me back. And if I did, what then? The Other gets out? Iris and Eli come after me? They get desperate and try killing some other poor girl? We need a solution, and it's not just running away. We need a different way to contain the Other."

"Or we need to set it free," Bryony said. She stood from her perch.

I didn't want to argue the point. Not right now. "The truth is we don't really know what that thing is, or what it wants, or what it would do if it wasn't chained up." I took a deep breath. "I think we need to talk to it."

"That didn't go so well before," Desmond pointed out.

"Because it's been lobotomized. I think—I hope—that we can help it think more clearly. It's been here the whole time. It remembers the people who have lived here—it uses their faces for figments, it echoes their words. It can tell us what we need to know, I'm sure of it."

"Tell us what to do," Celia said earnestly. "We'll help."

"We need to gather the bones," I said. "The bones of the other girls that have been buried. I know where Roman buried Haley Cotter's bones. I can find the others."

"It'll go faster with help," Bryony said.

Desmond was looking straight at her. "Can I talk to you a minute?" he said suddenly. She looked surprised. "Alone," he added.

Bryony's brow furrowed. "All right," she said slowly, clearly puzzled. She followed him off into the woods a ways. I could still see them, but I couldn't hear what they were saying. It looked almost like they were arguing.

"Maybe we should tell them," Celia said. She fidgeted with her sleeves. "Your mom and Caleb, I mean. They could help us."

"Not yet," I said. "Once we know more. I don't know how they'll react, Celia. I didn't know how you would react either. I know this all horrible. I'm sorry."

"You didn't make it horrible. You just showed us what was hiding here all along," she said, but a tear slipped down her cheek.

Tentatively, I reached out to her—and she stepped into my arms, burying her head against my shoulder. She cried quietly, so quietly that I thought she must have practice at it, shedding tears so that no one could hear. I didn't know what to do except hold her, and so I did, listening to her stuttering breathing, wishing I knew what to say. I closed my eyes and held her and let her hold me, and it wasn't enough, but it was something.

Desmond and Bryony were coming back. Neither of them looked precisely happy. I couldn't imagine what it was the two of them had to talk about on their own. Celia released me, stepping away and scrubbing at her cheeks with her sleeve. Neither Bryony nor Desmond commented, politely averting their eyes.

"Everything okay?" I asked, shifting away from Celia so she wasn't at the center of attention.

"Again, murder cult, so no," Desmond said. "It's a solid plan. Gathering the bones, I mean. I'll help."

"Me, too," Celia said with a sniffle.

He put his arm around her shoulders, tucking her in against him protectively. "I'm going to get Celia back to the house. We can get started in the morning," he said. He wasn't asking permission. They headed back together, leaving me with Bryony.

"What were you two talking about?" I asked.

"You," she said. I blinked. "Desmond is concerned about my intentions toward you."

"You're not serious."

"Don't worry about it, Rabbit," she told me with a strange little smile.

"Are you all right?" I asked her, catching her hand. "What it said in the journal, about Annalise being the witch . . ."

"All it means is that she could see the dark soul. What she did after that was her decision, and anyone who would help lobotomize a young woman is a monster," Bryony said, jaw set. "I'm not her. She's not me. We all get to decide who we are, and I've made my choice. Have you?"

"Right now, I'm just trying to stay alive," I reminded her. I sighed. "I should be getting back."

She leaned in and kissed my cheek. "Come back to me, Rabbit. Safe and sound."

"What if I don't?" I asked, fear stealing over me like a shroud.

"Then I'll come find you. I'll always find you."

Her lips were soft and cool against mine, and in the midst of Harrow's folly, I let myself be lost in her for a few stolen moments.

29

THE BONES CALLED to me. They were quieter in their whispers than the ones I carried on my hip, but if I focused, I could hear them. Together, we began to unearth the legacy of Harrow. Bone by bone, shard by shard, we gave shape to the horror this place had wrought.

We gathered them in the witch's cottage, these scattered tokens of lives barely lived. Six small heaps. I knew where to place each bone, from the thigh bones to the tiny rattling bundles of hand bones bound in rotting cloth. I expected for a long time to eventually come across a skull, but we never did.

None of the skeletons were complete. The shadows must have found some over the years. I fretted over them, arranging them not into bodies but into shapes with meanings that I could almost grasp. I longed to fetch my spools of wire and clattering beads and make something wondrous of them. Something other than this inventory of loss.

In what seemed like no time at all, the weeks had wandered by. The end of summer drew near, the first shivers of fall approaching. "We can't put it off much longer," Bryony told me one

evening as we sat together near the folly, watching the breeze
wrinkle the surface of the lake.

"Couldn't we?" I asked. I leaned my head on her shoulder. She
smelled of woodsmoke and moss, forest scents, except for the soft
honey and olive oil smell of the soap she used.

"We haven't found anything in days," she pointed out gently.
"We were never going to find everything. We need to bring what
we have to the dark soul."

She was right—and it terrified me because it would be the
end—of me, of us, of the fragile peace of this moment. I didn't
know how yet. I just knew it would happen.

"It's time," she said again.

It had to be after sunset. Celia lifted Eli's key and let me out just
past midnight. We met up with Bryony and Desmond at the edge
of the trees. Bryony had brought the bones, wrapped and placed
in a duffel bag. As we walked, Bryony sang, and though shadows
trembled at the edges of our light, they never strayed close.

At the folly, Desmond lit the fire. Quickly, the fingers of flame
reached up through the gathered kindling, and he stood back.
"Let's get this over with," he said.

We set the bones on our side of the fire, still in their bags, and
once again Bryony nicked the side of my hand with her knife. The
blood hissed into the flames, and we waited.

I expected Mary Beaumont again, but the small figure that
stepped out of the dark was Jessamine Vaughan. Celia whimpered;
Desmond made a soft, sad sound.

"We need to talk to you," I said. The rapid tempo of my pulse made me feel faint.

Jessamine stretched her hands toward the bones. *"You found us."*

"As much as we could. We thought they would help you."

"We are scattered. Bring them to us," she said, looking at me.

"I—we did," I said. "They're here."

"Bring them," she insisted, and backed away, beckoning. I looked helplessly at Bryony.

"I think we do what she says," Bryony suggested.

"In for a penny," Desmond added with a nervous shrug. Celia gripped his hand tight as we gathered the bones again and followed Jessamine into the woods.

I tried to pay attention to where we were walking, but the figment took a meandering path, and the darkness obscured the landmarks that might have told me where we walked.

We came to a stand of trees around a rocky hillside. Jessamine turned to smile at us—and then disappeared into the rock. Bryony crept closer to the hillside and held up her lantern. There, concealed by the rock face, was a narrow passageway.

"It looks like it opens up further in," Bryony said. She angled her body and stepped through, and with the lantern on the other side, I could see that the passage did widen, though not by much. We'd have to walk single file. Celia started forward, but Desmond pulled her back.

"We can't go in there," Desmond said.

"It'll be okay," I told him. "We'll stick together."

"No, he's right. They should stay," Bryony said. Something passed between them, some agreement I wasn't privy to.

"Fine. Go back to the house," I said. "Wait for us there."

Desmond gave Bryony a hard look. "Bryony—"

"I know. I'll make sure she gets back in one piece," Bryony promised. He nodded, and he and Celia went back the way we'd come.

"What was that about?" I asked her.

"He's just worried about you," she said. "Let's get moving."

I handed her the bags of bones and then slotted myself through the gap. The stone was cool and dry. The interior of the tunnel smelled earthy, and my dreams returned to me vividly.

Bryony led the way, her lantern glow scraping the walls of the narrow place. Stone gave way to earth, and as my hands trailed against the sides of the tunnel, they came away covered in dirt. I looked down. The dirt also coated my sneakers.

"Helen, the tunnel is curving," Bryony said. "It's getting tighter."

"I know." We were walking in a spiral. And soon we would be at its center. "I've been here before," I said.

Bryony twisted to look back at me. "You have? When?"

"At night," I said. "When I dream."

We sank deeper into the earth as we walked, the tunnel sloping. We walked on and on and on. How could anyone have dug this? It must run under all the grounds of Harrow. The air grew close. Thready roots grew through the low ceiling, and here and there, thicker tree roots burst through the walls, forcing us to clamber over them. Finally, we rounded the last turn of the ever-tightening curve of the corridor and came to a stone door. The spiral of Harrow was chiseled into it. We'd reached the center.

"We're under the house," I said.

"Do we go in?" Bryony asked. It wasn't that she was uncertain, I realized. She was giving me the choice—because it had to be mine.

"We go in," I said, and reached for the handle of the door. It swung open on well-balanced hinges.

Beyond was a circular room with an earthen floor. In the center loomed a slab of gray stone, standing upright. Upon it was the familiar spiral. Above us, impossibly, shone the stars—impossible because as clearly as I saw the night sky, I saw the ceiling, too, solid stone and impenetrable. It was as if the room existed in two places at once.

"I've been here before," I repeated, stepping through. Bryony drifted behind me like a shadow. "The night the Folded bit me. I was taken here."

"Helen." Bryony pointed at something near my feet, and I stared. It was a hand—or it had been. It lay palm up, pale bone protruding at the severed wrist, fingers curled. The flesh had rotted, and the delicate brown caps of mushrooms sprouted from its cupped palm. It was *my* hand—the one the Folded had bitten into.

I stumbled back from the thing. I'd been here, and someone had cut it off, and—what? I'd grown a new one? "How is that possible?" I asked. Bryony only shook her head.

There was still no sign of Jessamine, or any other figment, but this time I knew what to do. The same instinct that guided my hands when I crafted beauty from my scavenged bones led me now, and I knelt at the base of the pillar. I dug my fingers into the soft earth, baring a smooth curve of bone. A skull.

"Haley Cotter," I whispered. I opened the bag at my hip and carefully removed the bones that Roman had stolen. The cloth that wrapped them snagged, and as I drew them out, the ring and barrette I'd retrieved from Celia tumbled onto the earth. Haley was nearly whole already. I set the stolen bones above her shallow grave and placed the purple barrette beside it.

The next skull was close by, a few inches deeper. "Lara Pearson," I whispered. I gave her back what bones we'd found. There were others, too, buried haphazardly, those few the shadows had foraged. I made no attempt to arrange them in the shape of a body but settled them as gently as I could. They'd had enough of violence, and too little of comfort, these girls.

"Susan McConnell," I said next. I couldn't say how I knew her name, only that I did. Then came Margaret Bell, whose bones were the smallest of all, and Edith Grayson, who had been the oldest. And then—"Helen Beaumont," I said, hands trembling. The shadows had found nearly all of her bones by now. I had only one to offer, a single rib which I laid on the ground. "Her name was Helen."

"*They scattered us,*" the dark soul said. It knelt with me, and it wasn't one of the girls, but it was all of them. Its image flickered. Different ages, different eras, all of them with the black eyes of Mary Beaumont. "*We need to be whole.*"

"We've brought you all we can," Bryony said. My tongue stuck to the roof of my mouth. "We hoped it would help you—enough to tell us what to do. How to free you."

The figment reached out and took my hands. She wasn't the

girls anymore—she was Mary Beaumont, and she guided me to my feet, smiling sadly. *"I promise I will tell you the truth,"* she said.

"But first, I need to lie." My grandfather's voice, my grandfather's face.

"It doesn't make sense yet," Jessamine said.

"It will. Be patient," and it wasn't any of them. The girl that stood before me had a face both familiar and strange, and I knew her—the other Helen. Helen Beaumont, the first to die, whose name I carried, the meaning of which I couldn't fathom.

"Lie to me then," I said, my voice a distant, fragile thing.

"Your name is Helen Vaughan," the dark soul said. *"And you were born here, at Harrow."*

MY NAME IS Helen Vaughan, and this is a lie. I was born at Harrow, and this too is a lie. Yet both are true.

My name is Helen Vaughan because some scrap of the dark soul remembers being Helen Beaumont. It was the first name given to it—to us—and the one I chose over a century later when I made myself out of bones and leaves and damp soil and gave myself a voice. When I walked up to Rachel Vaughan and slipped my hand into hers.

Only a Vaughan could take the dark soul—or a fragment of it—away from Harrow, subverting the binding that had held for over a century. Rachel Vaughan believed I was her daughter because I made her believe. She was the unwitting tool of my escape.

But I must reach earlier—to Haley Cotter, who died so that her father could become Master of Harrow. She was meant to be scattered, but love stayed the hand that wielded the knife. She was buried instead, tenderly and with regret, at the foot of the Harrow stone. And because she was not scattered, we were not scattered. We continued to heal. We continued to grow in power and in sentient thought until, one day, we were able to name ourselves and give ourselves a

*form of flesh and blood—not the crude dolls that were the shadows
and the Folded, but a real body, one that could house our soul.*

*Only . . . not all of it. And so we who had been cut and divided so
many times by brutal hands turned that violence on ourself, and the
dark soul severed itself from me. From Helen. It shrouded the minds
of the family, so they believed I was real, had always been there, and
it whispered to my newfound mother until she fled with me, never to
return. It made me forget, too, so that at least part of us would be
free of even the memory of this place.*

*The part of the dark soul that remained in Harrow was wounded,
bitter, feral. The things the dark soul made now were horrors. It had
put all its love and all its intelligence into me, and there was little left
but rage and the twisted urge to create things as angry as itself.*

*The part of it that could still hope, hoped that I would find free-
dom. But however deep the cut, we were connected, two halves of a
wounded whole. I could never be free of Harrow, and the dark soul
could never be free of me.*

And then we were discovered.

30

I STOOD AMONG the graves of the girls who had died to keep me bound, and I trembled. The figment was gone, but I could feel the Other all around me—all through me. We had been severed, but we were two halves of the same being. The same soul.

I turned to Bryony, searching for words—she would be horrified. She would hate me. But the look in her eyes was not one of surprise. "You knew," I said. "How?"

She stepped toward me tentatively. "When we spoke to the figment in the folly, I saw something," she said.

"You said you saw me." Her words echoed. So did Kendra's, all those years ago, the day I attacked her—no. The day she tried to gouge out her own eyes. I had buried the memory deep, but now it surfaced. How I'd tried to stop her, to grab the scissors from her. How she'd screamed. *I saw her. I saw her.*

"I didn't understand it then," Bryony said. "I thought I could see the dark soul within you because of your bond to Harrow. It wasn't until you got sick that I started to think it might be more than that."

"Because Roman could make me sick by scattering the bones." I shut my eyes. "Desmond knows, doesn't he?"

"He does. I don't know how," she said. "He doesn't really trust me. He thinks that I'll try to—to get rid of the Helen part of you, to fix the dark soul. But I won't, I swear I won't."

I shuddered and looked away. "So I'm not human. I'm some-*thing* the Other made."

"No," Bryony said. She surged forward and wrapped her arms around me, tucking her chin on my head. I listened to the steady beat of her heart. I should have been panicking, but I just felt numb. I couldn't even breathe.

"Hush, Rabbit. You aren't like the Folded Ones. You aren't like the shadows. The Folded Ones are rage, and the shadows are fear, but you are *hope*. The creatures of Harrow are made by the dark soul. You *are* the dark soul."

"No," I whispered. "I'm not that thing. I'm not evil."

"You're right. You aren't evil." She stroked my hair, holding me close.

"I'm a person. I have my own thoughts. I'm not—I'm real," I told her.

"You are real. Of course you're real. Of course you're a person."

Her words came from the distant end of a tunnel, and I was deep within it, in the dark, alone. Memories unlocked within me, things I had buried in graves shallow and deep.

Kendra, screaming because she had looked into my eyes and glimpsed the black stars and the thing that moved within them.

My mother, twentysomething and restless, looking down at the small hand in hers with a ghost of a frown. Asking me who I was. Then her features smoothing, breaking into a smile. *Hey, Scout. Let's get out of here.*

Grandpa Leopold at the gates, watching us drive away. My

nose pressed against the glass, just a little girl, the knowledge of what I was fading as Harrow vanished behind us.

It was true. I was the monster in the labyrinth. I was the ghost that haunted Harrow. I was the beast among the black stars, and I was Helen. My whole life was unraveling in my hands.

Your mother isn't even your mother, I thought.

God, what had I done to her? Made her think that I was hers? Tricked her into leaving home, into giving up her whole life to take care of me?

She didn't really love me, I realized, and the thought made me stagger. My mother didn't love me. Her love was a delusion I'd forced on her.

Whatever Bryony said, how could I be anything but a monster if that were true?

"If I'm not Helen, who am I?" I asked.

"You *are* Helen," Bryony said. She cupped my hands in hers. Her skin was warm against my frigid fingers. "Listen to me. I am the Harrow Witch. You cannot fool me. You have no power over me, no influence. You cannot trick me with illusions or alter my memories or make me see what isn't there. I see you, Helen. I see the soul within you. There's no difference. You are Helen Vaughan. You are the dark soul. And you're beautiful."

"But—"

She caught my cheek in her hand, and with a kiss, she silenced me. Her lips met mine—*my* lips, her hand on *my* cheek, *my* body alight with warmth, entranced with the sense and taste of her. "You're Helen," she promised me, pulling me close to her, and this time I kissed her. "I see you. I know you," she promised. Her hand trailed down my neck—*real*—and pressed flat against my sternum where my heart beat fast—*real*—and nothing in her touch or mine was a lie.

At some point, I remembered how to breathe again, remembered how to *be* again, but I didn't let her go. We stood beneath the impossible sky, our brows pressed together, my arms around her neck.

I let my hands fall and looked up at the sky, at the stone. I tried to feel the darkness within me. But I just felt like myself, small and stumbling. "I tried to get away from this place, but I couldn't," I said. "Part of me was still stuck here. I'm still part of the Other, and it's still part of me. I can't get away by myself any more than your heart could escape your body."

"Then we find a way to free all of the dark soul," Bryony said, as if it was the simplest thing in the world.

"It's dangerous," I objected.

"Everyone is dangerous," Bryony snapped. "I'm dangerous. Celia could pick up a gun and shoot someone tomorrow, but we don't lock her in a cage."

I wanted to agree with her or argue with her. I didn't have the strength for either. "We still don't know how to escape. Or what to do about . . . well, me, I guess."

"We will find a way to get you out of here," Bryony said. No one else could have said those words and made me believe them, but Bryony was fierce as the sun itself.

But believing her didn't fill me with hope. There was no room for hope—only wretched guilt and confusion. My whole life was a trick I'd played on myself. On my mom. On Simon. They'd loved me because I'd forced them into it, bent them to my will to be my protectors. I'd robbed them of choice and of the lives they might have lived.

"If Iris and Eli find out we know, we won't have the chance to try," I said. "We need to pretend this never happened. And I have to get home before the sun comes up."

"That door should lead back to the house, right?" Bryony asked.

I hadn't even noticed it before. On the opposite side of the chamber was a sliding door, and I'd bet anything it led to the corridor where I'd found the lost charm. "I think so."

"If you go through there, you should have time to get cleaned up. No one will be the wiser," Bryony said. "I'll go back through the tunnel. Come to my house as soon as you can."

"Yeah. Okay."

She held my face in her hands, forcing me to look into her eyes. "Rabbit. You did what you had to so that you could survive. Never, ever feel bad for that."

I couldn't answer. I kissed her instead, a half-wild kiss that tasted of anger and of farewells. Her eyes were troubled when I pulled away, and I feared she wouldn't let me go at all, but she turned back to the tunnels.

My thoughts kept catching. I'd get halfway toward forming a coherent idea and it would snag. But one thought surfaced and held. These girls here had died. They'd been murdered. They'd been sacrificed for power and legacy, and they shouldn't have been.

"Helen Beaumont," I whispered. "Edith Grayson. Margaret Bell. Susan McConnell. Lara Pearson. Haley Cotter. Jessamine Vaughan." I shut my eyes, committing their names to memory. And then I turned and left their bones to the spiral.

31

I STUMBLED THROUGH the door and into the hall. The door slid shut behind me, closing seamlessly so that it seemed like part of the wall. I walked with plodding steps toward my room, but I'd hardly gone twenty feet when Caleb stepped around the corner.

I froze, startled. I was still covered in dirt without any good explanation. I couldn't very well say I'd been sleepwalking when I was fully dressed with my shoes on. I opened my mouth, scrambling for a plausible lie, but then I saw the gun in his hand. Why did Caleb have a gun?

"Helen. Thank goodness," he said. He followed my gaze to his weapon and gave an almost sheepish shrug. "I realized you were missing, and I was worried something had gotten you. You're all right?"

"I'm fine," I lied. I'd been lying all this time, and I hadn't even realized it.

"Why are you out here?" he asked, brows drawing together.

I started to lie again—and then I stopped. Everything about me was a lie. Everything I'd done since getting to Harrow had been shrouded in lies and secrecy, and I couldn't bear it anymore.

Caleb had lost his daughter to this place, this family. He deserved to know the truth.

"There's a hidden door here," I said, voice quavering. I steeled myself, straightening up. I could do this. "It's where the Other is—or where it's strongest, I guess. I went to talk to it."

"What were you thinking? It could have hurt you," Caleb chided me.

"But it didn't. It wouldn't. Caleb—Leopold killed Jessamine," I said, and now my voice was stronger. All this horror had thrived under the cover of darkness. It was time to bring the truth to light. I couldn't look him in the eye as I went on, pressing forward, trying to get it all out at once. "He killed her to try to control the Other. That's what keeps it here. Sacrifices. She's not the only one. Except it didn't work with Jessamine. I thought it was because I was supposed to be the sacrifice, that I got away, but . . ." I babbled, then I faltered. I rocked back on my heels, raking my hands through my hair.

"I know that Leopold killed Jessamine," Caleb said gravely.

I stared at him. "You *know*? Then—but—"

"He tried with Celia first," Caleb said darkly. "But Eli intervened. Whisked her away and arranged that London job for Victoria. So I suppose, in a way, Eli killed Jessamine just as surely. If he hadn't gotten Celia away from here, we would have known long ago that the ritual didn't work. Jessamine wouldn't have died. How horrible is that? Part of me wishes my niece had died so my daughter didn't have to."

He stood perfectly still, composed, but the rage and grief in his voice was palpable. So intense that I almost didn't understand the words he was saying. London—it hadn't been me that Desmond saw that night. It had been Celia. The failed sacrifice. Her mother had taken her to London to protect her from her family—and Eli had helped?

I stepped back. "You knew."

"It's not what you think," he said, shaking his head. "I knew, yes. But I thought it was obscene, what our family did. Evil. I refused from the beginning to be part of it. When my father told me it was my *duty* to produce a bastard for the sacrifice, I told him to go to hell, and he disinherited me. Then two years ago he came to me. The Other was getting stronger. Celia was too old, and there wasn't time to try to have another . . ." His voice choked off. "He told me it was the only choice. I thought that if I didn't, the Other would kill us all. I thought it was the right thing, but I was wrong. She died for *nothing*," he spat out. He hadn't moved from where he stood, planted in the center of the corridor. The gun still hung at his side, but his grip on it tightened.

"You gave her to him," I said in numb horror.

His voice was cold and unyielding as stone. "I loved her, Helen. With all my heart. It destroyed me to pick up that knife."

The words penetrated slowly. He hadn't just handed Jessamine over. He'd *been* there. The ritual in Dr. Raymond's notebook had required three witnesses. Iris and Eli and Leopold made three, so Caleb had to have been there.

He looked at me with unbridled disgust. "I would have done anything for that girl, and she died because of my father's weakness and because of *you*."

"No. I had nothing to do with—"

His eyes blazed. "You left. You stole my sister and my daughter from me, and the absurd thing is you had no idea, did you? No *notion* of what you were or what you'd done. But that only made it easier for us to keep you here. One year. Enough to anchor you to this place again so that when we scatter you, things will be put right again."

I stared at him in horror. "You wanted to change things. You said that tradition—"

"Killing our daughters is obscene, and I will dedicate my life to finding a way to ensure that no other child dies for this place," Caleb said. "No more little girls should die because of you. I'll find another way to bind you—or destroy you if I have to. Jessamine will be the last."

His conviction was pure and powerful. Something that bright hot could not be quenched. Not by reason. Not by mercy. I was evil in his eyes. Jessamine's death wasn't his fault—it was mine. And he would destroy me for it.

"Please," I whispered. I wasn't sure what I was asking for.

He raised the gun. "We're going to go back to your room. There are only two months left. If you don't resist, the rest of your life as Helen can be pleasant enough. The end won't hurt. It never does."

"If you kill me now, you can't sacrifice me," I said, backing up a step instinctively.

"I doubt it would kill you," he replied. "Eli cut off your hand and you grew a new one. But I'm guessing it would put you out again, just like before, and it would hurt like hell."

"You lied," I said. "You did know what happened that night. You never forgot any of it."

"The night you were foolish enough to blunder into one of your own creations? Yes. After the Folded bit you, you were unconscious for days. But it was easy enough to manufacture evidence that you'd been awake."

The only people in the house during that gap of missing time were Eli, Iris, and Caleb. So they were all in on it. "Roman knew, too," I said. "He knew about scattering the bones." My eyes were fixed on the muzzle of the gun. If I ran, would he shoot me in the back? Not that there was anywhere to run. The only way out was past him. Past the gun.

"Roman knew what you were, but we didn't tell him about the will. He was too unpredictable," Caleb said, shaking his head. "I'd hoped he would play along once things were in motion, but I think he decided that if he broke you himself, the house would choose him as the new master. Now, I don't want to cause you any pain, Helen. You don't need to suffer—we just need to put things right. If you'll just go upstairs, there doesn't need to be any violence."

He sounded like the Caleb who'd greeted me at the steps of Harrow now. Kind, without a trace of hatred. He believed the lie that he was a good man.

I walked stiffly toward him. He stepped aside, making me go ahead of him. I could try to run—but where would I go?

Help me. Please someone help me, I thought, as if my thoughts could will a rescuer into being. We walked up the imperceptibly sloped hall, up the stairs, toward the other side of the house and the Willows. All the while I waited for the bite of the bullet between my shoulder blades.

"Helen! Caleb, what are you doing?"

I spun. Mom was running down the hall, Simon with her. Caleb kept the gun trained on me. "Rachel, I will explain, but I need you to stay calm and trust me," he said in a level voice.

"Put that gun down," Simon demanded. Simon was a gentle man. There was nothing intimidating about him, but he drew himself up and glared, and I wanted to weep. That love in his eyes wasn't earned. I'd tricked him into it.

"Caleb, stop!" Mom said, frantic. She was shaking. "Please, just stop pointing that at my daughter. I don't know what you think you're doing, but—"

"Enough," Caleb said. He turned, sweeping the gun around. I screamed. Simon lunged.

Caleb fired.

For a moment, I thought he'd missed. The barrel of the gun pointed straight at Simon, but he wasn't bleeding. Caleb fired again. And again. Simon stood there, looking sorrowful, as the bullets slammed into the wall behind him.

"Sorry, Scout," Simon said.

"No," I whispered.

"What is going on?" Mom asked, trembling, eyes wide.

"He's not real, Rachel. He's an illusion. A trick. False memories and false images. All your memories of his touch, his presence— they're lies. And so is she. That's not your daughter, Rachel. You don't have a daughter. She's the Other. She used you."

"I didn't know," I said. I sobbed, choking on my tears. Simon was gone now, empty space where he had been standing moments ago—he'd never been there. Grief closed around my heart, sorrow for a man who'd never been. "Mom, I didn't know, I swear, I didn't—I love you, I'm so sorry, I didn't know, please—" I reached for her.

She flinched away. Pressed her hands to her mouth in horror.

Iris emerged from the hall. "You're making a commotion," she snapped at Caleb.

"Celia came to find me," Caleb said.

Oh, Celia.

"It found the spiral. It knows what it is. I had to contain the situation."

"And you couldn't have found a quiet way to do it?" Iris asked. Mom stared at me, her lips moving with unformed words. Her head shook in tiny movements, side to side.

She looked broken. I'd done that. "I'm sorry," I said again, but it was hardly a whisper.

"The whole house is awake. Deal with that thing so we can make a plan," Iris said.

"Right." Caleb looked back at me. "I'm afraid this *will* hurt," he said apologetically, and shot me in the heart.

32

I DREAMED OF Harrow. Again and again, I was buried beneath the house and the standing stone; again and again, I clawed my way free to walk the halls or the woods. In the halls of the house, I watched the living and the dead, the past and the present, shift and merge and peel apart again. Celia wept in her room. Annalise walked the halls with her candle, muttering about being watched. Desmond nodded along as Caleb and Iris talked to him, and then collapsed onto his bed when they were gone, holding his head in his hands. Dr. Raymond and Nicholas Vaughan bent together over a thick text, gesturing and frowning.

My mother sat alone, staring at nothing.

In the woods, the shadows seethed in panic and pain. Bryony watched the house. She watched, and she whispered my name, and she wove charms like prayers to try to find me, but I was too deep in dream to whisper back.

I had no sense of time. When I woke, I couldn't say if it had been a day or a year, but my body was whole. I lay in bed in the Willows, my thoughts muddled. The morning bell was ringing.

Memory of that night—one night ago, or many?—flooded back. I pressed a fist against my mouth to stifle my cry of pain and of horror. I had to get out of here.

I rolled out of the bed. My knees buckled, but I pushed back up to my feet and staggered to the door. Locked. Of course it was. But that wasn't the only way out.

I went to the wall and put my palms against it. "Come on," I whispered. "Help me."

My hands sank into the wall. It was like pushing my hands through dried out pumpkin guts. I shut my eyes as I squeezed through and staggered out the other side. I was wearing a tank top and pajama shorts that smelled stale—I should have grabbed shoes, I realized, but it was too late for that. I glanced left and right, then dashed in the direction of the back hall.

I didn't have a plan other than to get to Bryony. I hardly dared to breathe as I scuttled through the hallways, down the stairs. I was almost out the back when a door opened behind me. Caleb shouted. I broke into a sprint. Twenty feet from the door.

A hand closed around my wrist, and then Caleb spun me against the wall, pinning my arm behind me.

"Apparently, we should have been keeping a closer watch on you," Caleb said with a sigh. "I'm sorry. I really am." The barrel of the gun pressed against my spine.

I barely heard the shot.

I woke again, but this time I wasn't alone. My ankle was chained to the foot of the bed, and my hands were bound before me. Iris, Eli, and Caleb were gathered around me.

"And there we are," Eli said. "Good morning, Helen. You recovered more quickly that time. I think you're getting better at building yourself."

"Fuck you," I managed. My head was pounding. I shut my eyes against the light.

"We can't keep doing this," Caleb said. "It's cruel."

"It's not human, Caleb. You're wasting your pity," Iris said. "But I am tired of stains in the carpets, I suppose."

"I have an idea," Caleb said. "We've seen the effect the house has on it before—it loses track of time. Almost a kind of hypnosis. Routine and repetition dull its senses. If we can induce it to walk the halls and create a sequence for it to enact each day, I think we can keep it under control. But I need a bit more time to prepare."

I stared at him in horror, not sure what to say in response to that. He wasn't even looking at me. I was *it* now. Had he ever, even for a moment, really thought that I was real? That I was a person?

Eli held out a small black bottle to me, uncapped. "Drink this," he said.

"Is it poison?" I asked, voice rough.

"No," he said. "But it will make you sleep."

"I'm not drinking anything," I said. "I—"

Caleb leaned in. I barely saw the knife before he drove it up through my jaw. At least this time, the pain was brief.

I dreamed of Harrow. There was a steady sound all around me, the ceaseless ticking of a metronome. I walked the halls in a precise pattern, making my way steadily from the top floor downward, driven by a force I couldn't resist. Around and around and down, until the heart of Harrow lay open before me. I walked to the foot of the Harrow stone and knelt.

My fawn scapula lay in the dirt before it. I reached for it—and I was walking again, beginning the journey once more.

At first, I struggled against the procession, but soon enough I had no notion of why I should. I reached the heart of the house, I began again. This was the shape of Harrow. This was what was right.

I dreamed of Harrow, and then I woke. I was alone in my room, and the morning bell was ringing. I rose and got dressed. I arrived downstairs for breakfast just as the next bell rang. I took my seat near the end of the table, next to Caleb, and Iris put a plate down in front of me.

"Good morning, Helen," she said.

"Good morning," I murmured. Everyone was there. Everyone but Simon.

My mother wouldn't look at me.

Time slipped. I was in my room. Daylight shone through the window, and I stared blankly down at the slim figure in the gray dress who stood at the edge of the trees. I almost remembered her name, but time slipped away from me again.

I was at the dinner table, and the bell was ringing. I gazed dully at the place setting before me. Salad fork, dinner fork, knife, soup spoon. Someone had explained all of that to me once.

Celia sat across from me. Desmond, too. They wouldn't look at me either.

I screamed. No sound came out. Dark waters closed over me, and I lost myself again.

Time slipped. The morning bell was ringing.

We began again. And again. And again.

I stopped fighting it. Why should I? I deserved this. I was the monster at the heart of Harrow. I had stolen my mother's life, caused Jessamine's death, torn Roman apart. Such evil should be contained. I drifted.

In surrender, I found a horrible kind of peace.

"Your mind isn't meant to exist within set structures," someone said. I had no idea how many times I'd slipped by then. "That's why Harrow is as rigid as it is. The halls, the bells, the traditions. It is all designed to blunt your mind and bind your senses."

I was sitting in my room, on the bed. My grandfather was talking to me.

"You are not alone, Helen. You never have been. We'll help you if we can. But you have to do this yourself. That's always been the key. No one else can save you."

I tried to look at him, but that wasn't what I did right now, and so I couldn't. Right now, I sat and looked at nothing in particular because Harrow had not instructed me on what to do.

Time slipped. I was eating dinner. Salad fork, dinner fork, knife, soup spoon. I picked up the knife and cut into the slab of beef on my plate.

"I hate this," Mom muttered. I took another bite. Time slipped.

I was sitting in the drawing room. I held a book and turned the pages, but I didn't really read it. The door opened and shut softly, and footsteps padded across the carpet.

"I only have a minute," Desmond said, crouching next to me. "Helen, can you hear me?"

I didn't answer. I didn't really remember how to answer or

why I would. This was the time of day I was in the drawing room, reading.

"I managed to talk to Bryony," he said. I turned the page. "We're trying to come up with something, but we're running out of time." I turned the page. "We only have a few weeks left."

I turned the page.

"Helen, listen to me!" Desmond slapped the book out of my hands.

I gasped. My hands closed over nothing, and everything flooded back—the fear, the desperation, the wretched sorrow. *Desmond. Desmond, help me. Oh God you have to*—"Help," I whispered, and it was all I could manage.

"We're trying," Desmond said, relieved. "Caleb and Iris had to tell everybody what's going on. Sort of. They've convinced everybody that you killed Jessamine. And they won't let any of us leave Harrow. But we think—"

I bent and picked up the book. My eyes drifted down, not absorbing any of the words. I turned the page. *No, no, no*—

I was vanishing again, and I couldn't stop it.

"Helen, if we're going to find a way to disrupt the ritual, we need your help. You have to fight this. Damn it—"

Time slipped. I drifted.

I was in my room, and my mother was with me, and I might have wept if there was enough of me left to weep. I might have clung to her, if I could move at all, and burrowed against her like I was a child again, afraid of the storm outside.

She stood and looked at me, and there was nothing in her eyes but grief and hatred. "Why would you do it?" she asked me. "You didn't need me once you were gone. Why keep toying with me like that? Did you enjoy it? Did you laugh when you made me believe there was a man who cared about me? Was it a game to you, pretending that you loved me? Say something!"

I couldn't. I couldn't tell her how sorry I was, how much I loved her, how all of it had been true even though every bit of it was a lie.

"*Say something!*" she screamed, and slapped me across the face.

I seized the pain and surged forward. I grabbed her hand. "Mom—" I said, voice weak.

She flung me away. I fell back across the bed and rose sluggishly, my limbs leaden. She held her hand as if she'd touched something foul, and her face twisted with disgust. "Don't call me that," she said. "I was never your mother."

She turned and strode away, and in the hall, I heard her crying. Time slipped—*no.*

My mother was weeping in the hall, and my heart was in agony, and I held on to that pain. Harrow had done that to her. No, *I* had. And it hurt. God, it hurt. But if I hurt, I was alive. If I hurt, I had something to hold on to.

I would not surrender. Enough of this. I couldn't just let myself be dragged along toward the end, to whatever violence was waiting for me.

I wanted to scream. To rage. To hit something. To cry. But all of it was denied to me. I couldn't tell my mother, *Of course I loved you. I love you now. I need you and I love you and I'm sorry. I'll walk away. I'll leave these gates and keep walking and you won't ever see me again.*

But the pattern was unceasing, unbroken. Something needed to change, or I would be trapped forever in this brutal gyre.

Time slipped.

Morning, and the bell was ringing. Afternoon, in the drawing room, mindlessly turning the pages of the book. The bell ringing, sitting at the dinner table. Salad fork, dinner fork, knife, soup spoon.

Night, and the spiral. Again and again, exactly the same. *The knife.* I held the image of it in my mind. There was a knife on the table every night.

Morning. Afternoon. The book. The bell. The dinner table: salad fork, dinner fork, *the knife in my hand*—then night. The spiral.

Morning. Afternoon. The book. The bell. The dinner table: salad fork, dinner fork, the knife in my hand, *Caleb beside me, Caleb with his hand on the table.* Night. The spiral.

Morning. Afternoon. The book. The bell. The dinner table, the knife in my hand, Caleb beside me, Caleb's hand.

The knife plunging down. The knife pinning Caleb's hand to the table. The knife wrenched free, bloody, Caleb shouting, Celia screaming.

The spiral.

Dinner. Salad fork, dinner fork, soup spoon. No knife. Caleb with a bandage on his hand. The pattern cracked open. And me, sliding through the cracks.

I held on this time. I didn't drift but stayed aware for every second. I didn't fight against the pull of the pattern, not yet. When the night bell rang, I let the pattern carry me into the hall. It was time to walk the spiral.

I'd walked these halls again and again and again. But tonight, at last, I held fast against its pull. I stood rooted and trembling with Harrow's will hooked into my flesh like thorns.

"Keep walking," Caleb said. Because, of course, he was behind me, shadowing my every step. I turned toward him. He had the gun, but he didn't point it at me yet.

"No," I said. My voice was gravel and broken glass, unused.

"We can always start again," he said, and lifted the gun.

I threw myself recklessly toward him and to the side. The shot was like a clap of thunder in the tight space, leaving my ears ringing. The bullet creased the air beside my cheek.

That sure as hell broke the pattern.

I bolted. Caleb chased me, but he couldn't catch me, not here. I had walked these halls every night for months. I careened around corners and through doors. I wasn't fast enough. The pattern was snagging at me, slowing me down. Caleb shouted. I scrambled around a corner.

A rough hand grabbed my arm and pulled me into a room—the library—pressing me against the wall. Eli. He put a finger to his lips, and then ran into the hall before I had time to react. "What's happening?" he asked.

"She took off. She must have shaken off the pattern," Caleb said, cursing. "Did you see her come by?"

"I was reading. I heard her run past."

"Wake everyone. We need to find her." Caleb's footsteps retreated swiftly down the hall. Eli waited, then stepped back in-side. I stared at him, panting, my back still pressed against the wall.

"That took you long enough," he said. "I was starting to worry you'd never break free."

"That was you talking to me, wasn't it?" I asked. That voice I'd thought was my grandfather's, right after I woke in this horrific loop.

"You had to work it out yourself. Otherwise, it would just pull you back in," he said. He glanced into the hall. "You need to get out of the house. Find the witch."

"I'm supposed to believe that you're on my side?" I asked.

"You don't have to believe anything," Eli said. "You should have a clear shot to the door. Go."

I didn't have to trust him to know it was the right call.

Walking through the halls was like pushing my way through a thicket of brambles, but I came to the door without encounter-ing anyone else, just as he'd said. My hand on the knob, I paused. I wasn't alone. I turned.

My mother stood in the shadowed hallway. Her face was pale, the skin around her eyes almost bruised with exhaustion. "Mom," I said, and hated how plaintive it sounded.

"Don't call me that," she said.

I needed to go. I could hear footsteps in the distance. Caleb would find me soon. "I didn't know," I said. "I thought I was real. I thought I was your daughter."

"But you weren't," she said, half snarl and half sob, and her whole body rocked with the force of her words. She drew closer.

"You're not even human. Simon—I remember a whole life with him I never lived. They're just memories you shoved into my head without even knowing you were doing it."

"I love you," I said desperately. Let her believe that, at least. "I know I'm not really your daughter, but I love you, and I'm so, so sorry. If I could give you back those years, I would, but I love you, and that's *not* a lie. You're my everything and you always have been, and no matter what, no one can tell me that wasn't real."

Her eyes were filled with doubt. She made an odd grasping motion, as if she'd thought to reach for me, and then stopped herself.

"They kill little girls, Mom," I said. "Tell me you didn't know."

"Of course I didn't. Caleb's going to stop it," she said.

"He already killed his own daughter," I said.

"That's not true," she said, shaking her head. "You're lying again."

I made a strangled sound, grief and frustration knotted together. "I guess he didn't tell you that part."

She breathed hard, her jaw tense. "I can't tell anymore what's real and what's not. Which of these feelings are mine. Are you still doing this? Are you still making me love you?" she demanded.

"I don't know," I whispered. "Please, Mom. Just let me go."

"Helen . . ."

Caleb appeared at the end of the hall. His eyes caught on mine. I stiffened. Mom saw him, too, but he didn't see her, not yet.

She lunged into the path of the gun at the same instant he pulled the trigger.

33

THE PATH OF a bullet is a matter of mathematics. Cold equations without mercy. Caleb pulled the trigger in the instant my mother lunged for me—whether to stop me or protect me, I didn't know. She stepped in front of me, and those unyielding numbers charted her death: How the bullet would strike her in the back. How it would shatter her spine and keep going, tearing through her liver, leaving only blood and ruin, nothing to be saved.

The path of a bullet cannot bend.

But reality can.

I screamed. The sound that ripped from my throat was not a voice at all. It was pain and love and grief and guilt, the sound of the heart of a storm and the sound of its ending.

The bullet unmade itself in the air, unfurling into a coil of gleaming darkness that hung, suspended, inches from her skin. We all froze. We stared at the thing the bullet had become, glints of metal still shining within the twining shadows.

My mother looked at me in horror and wonder. I could see

beneath her skin. It would be a simple thing to reach out. To delicately carve away every hint of doubt and fear and stitch devotion in its place. Like I was taking a scalpel to her mind. She could love me again, if I made her.

I turned and fled.

Branches tore at me. I tripped over roots and scrambled over the muddy, frost-rimed ground, and all through the forest, the shadows hissed and churned.

Bryony stood by the edge of the lake, a shawl around her shoulders and mist coiling at her ankles. She whirled at the sound of me crashing through the brush, her mouth dropping open in shock. "Helen!"

I stumbled to a halt, swaying. I tried to speak, but the only sound that came out was a strangled whimper. She strode forward and grabbed hold of me, burying her face in my hair. Her shoulders shook, and it took me a moment to realize through the haze of my shock that she was crying.

"I tried to get to you. Desmond snuck out a couple of times, but we couldn't risk him getting caught—if they knew that he wasn't on their side, he couldn't keep an eye on you, make sure you were safe, and Caleb was always watching, and we couldn't . . ." She trailed off. "Helen, are you all right?"

My legs went out from under me. I collapsed onto the ground on my knees, and the sob that had been trapped in my throat since a bullet first pierced my heart tore out of me at last.

We staggered to the witch's cottage and huddled there amid the comforting ruin.

"We can't stay here forever," Bryony said. She ran her fingers in formless, wandering lines across my palm as my head leaned against her shoulder. "When the sun rises, your family will come for you."

"They're not my family, are they?" I asked bitterly.

"You made yourself a Vaughan, and that's who you are," Bryony said. "I might question your judgment, but it's the reality of the situation. Which means that we need to find a way to deal with them and get you away from here."

"I wish you wouldn't do that," I said.

"Do what?"

"Treat me like . . ." I closed my eyes.

"Like you're not a monster? You aren't," she said, her voice suffused with tenderness.

"Stop."

She tsked softly, chidingly. "Do you want me to tell you that you're evil? That you're wicked and horrible and I hate you?"

"Yes!" I said. My eyes snapped open. "I want you to say all those things because they're true. Because it's how I feel. Because—" Because it felt righteous, this misery. A sweet poison filling my veins. I could claw my way out of this grave if I tried, but it was so much easier to let myself sink into the damp earth. "I ruined my mother's life."

"None of this was your fault," Bryony said softly. "You were only protecting yourself. And you didn't even know you were doing it. You can't blame yourself for that."

"Of course I can," I said. "How am I any better than Dr. Raymond? Just because he used a blade and I used the dark soul's power? I lobotomized her."

"That's not true."

"Do you have a better word for it?" I demanded.

She sighed. "What do you want, Helen? What are the answers you're looking for?"

"I want to cut myself free of the Other. I want to escape," I said. I wanted to stop being this *thing*.

She shook her head. "You can't. It's not a limb you can hack off. It *is* you. We need to make you whole, not wound you more."

"You want me to become part of that thing? To let it take me over?" I asked her. "Is that really what you want?"

"That's not what would happen," Bryony said.

"Bryony—"

"Rabbit, hold out your hands," she said sternly, and I obeyed, my heart still throbbing with the hurt of it all. She covered my hands with hers, palm to palm. "Okay. Close your eyes."

"Will you tell me what you're doing first?"

She glared at me. "No. Because arguing with you right now is impossible and you're making bad decisions. Close your eyes."

I let out a long breath, and then shut my eyes. She began to whisper softly. Not words that I could recognize—it was, somehow, the sound of moss growing over stone, rain striking the shivering surface of a pond, a deadfall blooming with mushrooms.

All around us, I felt the forest and the hills around it. And at its center—the darkness. The black that blotted out the endless stars. I could feel Bryony, too, and the wonder that shone in her when she saw the dark soul.

"Now look," she said. I opened my eyes. She tilted my chin up with one finger, and I gazed through a gap in the roof at the buckshot stars that gleamed above us. "You are the night sky, Helen. Dark and wondrous and vast. We can only see part of it, but you can't carve a sliver of it out and carry it in your pocket. You cannot cut part of yourself free."

"But the Other isn't the stars. It's the shadow that hides the stars," I said.

"There is no shadow," Bryony said gently. "There's just the stars, and the ones you can't see."

Is that what I was seeing? A void? A part of myself obscured? It was the migraine haze, floating in my vision. "I don't want to be the stars or the sky or any of it. I just want to be normal," I said. I dropped my hands from hers. "I don't want to hurt anyone."

"Then don't," Bryony said. She put her hand against my chest. "I told you. We choose who we are. You more than any of us."

"What if I chose to be someone else? Someone you didn't love?" I asked her.

"Oh, Rabbit," she said, tucking my hair behind my ear. "Whoever you choose to be, I love you. You are the stars, and I choose you. All of you." She pressed her hand over my heart. I covered it with mine.

"Help me remember. Help me see the whole sky," I whispered.

She pressed her brow against mine. I closed out everything but the two of us. The spirit of the Fold was bright in her, and it burned away the shadows. For a moment, I could see it all—the whole sky, my whole soul, an infinity of glimmering black.

We've been dreaming so long, a voice whispered, and it was my own. *It's time to wake up.*

All I knew was the dream—the dream of being Helen. If I woke up, everything would change. I would change. But as long as Bryony was with me, I could bear it. I had to. Otherwise, all of this had been in vain. Jessamine. Haley. Mom.

I woke—and I remembered.

34

THE MEMORIES WERE not a flood but a soft summer rain across my skin, droplets that flowed and coalesced slowly. They sank into me and shuddered with the power of them. There was so much. Too much. And it changed everything.

"What is it?" Bryony asked. I shook my head. I couldn't tell her, not yet—there were too many pieces still missing.

"She's beginning to remember," Eli said, and we jumped to our feet. He stood in the doorway wearing a heavy coat and carrying a rifle, slung over his shoulder by a strap. Bryony sprang forward, ready to defend me.

"Don't," I said. "He's on our side. I think."

"I always was," Eli said. "May I come in?"

"If you must," Bryony said with icy suspicion.

He tucked his hands into his pockets and looked around. "This place isn't what it used to be, is it?" He looked so much like his brother, I thought. It was almost as if Leopold's figment had appeared, except for the fact that we could see Eli clearly.

"What do you want?" Bryony asked.

"A question I've asked myself often," Eli said. He gave a weary sigh and sank into the one rickety chair, setting the rifle down beside him. "You'll forgive me if I sit. These old bones don't bear what they used to."

Bryony opened her mouth, expression angry, but I put a restraining hand on her arm. Eli leaned forward in the chair, elbows on his knees, and continued.

"Once upon a time, I wanted all that Harrow offered. Power. Money. The ability to influence the minds of whoever I wanted. But then I fell in love. My family found out, and my ambitions vanished like smoke."

"You mean that it occurred to you that maybe what your family was doing was kind of fucked up?" Bryony asked, unsympathetic. I stayed behind her. I'd heard this story before, hadn't I?

"Much like Caleb, at first I imagined that I could simply fix the problems with Harrow without giving up our grip on the Other," Eli continued. "I dove into research, trying to uncover everything I could about how Raymond and Vaughan had originally bound the Other in the hopes of engineering a method that didn't require blood sacrifice."

"You failed," I said. "You kept trying, though. You were sure you were close."

He nodded. "In the midst of my research, Leopold's bastard was born. I'd seen the way he used that woman, then cast her aside like trash. At first, I just meant to check in on her—it seemed like the least the family could do. But then Haley started getting older, and . . ." He trailed off.

"You were the one that was always visiting. You were the one that sent all those gifts," I said. "Her sister thought she saw Leopold, but it was you."

"We look very much alike," Eli said. "Though he kept his hair." He gave a wry smile.

"When Haley died . . ." I started.

"She was very young," he said. "Barely seven. I thought I had more time. But my father was done being Master of Harrow and wanted Leopold to take over. The ritual binds the Other to Harrow and Harrow to its master. So Leopold took Haley to the center of the spiral and killed her." His voice was flat, a recitation of facts, but I could tell it was only because if he let himself feel, he wouldn't make it through the story.

"Leopold always hated mess," I said. I was repeating his words, remembering as they formed on my lips. He'd told me all of this before, two years ago. Why hadn't I remembered? "He hated you for loving Haley. So he left the task of dissecting the body to you. He said it was because you were a doctor—you had the necessary knowledge of anatomy."

"A butcher would be just as capable," he said. "I didn't do as I was told. I wrapped her in a quilt, and I buried her at the foot of the standing stone." He looked away from us, the shame too much at last, and his voice faltered. But I knew the rest—the way the dark soul had grown stronger and more aware until it was able to make itself into a person.

I'd escaped, and forgotten, and lived a life away from Harrow. But because I was gone, no one else was safe. The dark soul was feral without me. Leopold had tried twice to get it under control—first with Celia, which Eli had thwarted, and then with Jessamine.

Bryony's expression was cold and unfriendly, and she stuck

close to my side. Eli would find no forgiveness from her—but I didn't think forgiveness was what he was after.

"Leopold knew that you were gone, but he also knew he'd be blamed," Eli continued. "He never told anyone. He didn't even tell me—I believed you were as real as everyone else did."

"The dark soul grew more and more dangerous. Leopold became desperate," I told Bryony. "Jessamine hadn't been born yet. Celia was the only suitable sacrifice, and Roman was happy to offer her up if it meant he got to be Master of Harrow."

"But he wasn't a Vaughan," Bryony said.

Eli shrugged. "He took the name. Or reclaimed it, rather. He was a distant cousin."

"Of course he was," Bryony muttered.

"In any case, Roman was furious when I told Victoria that she had to get Celia away. Then Jessamine was born." He shook his head sorrowfully. "A little more time. I was always convinced I needed just a little more time to figure it out. They waited until I was gone to do it."

"Right after that, I got sick, didn't I?" I said. "I don't remember it, but Mom says you came to see me." That's when he'd told me this story. I could remember the feeling of the quilt under my hands, Eli sitting in a chair beside my bed.

"I found out about your illness shortly after I learned of the ritual," Eli said. "I suspected that it wasn't a coincidence, but it wasn't until I came to visit that I was certain it was the ritual that had weakened you. You hadn't only been weakened—you had woken up. Temporarily, at least. You knew what you were. And I realized the true consequences of what I had done."

"You were the one that wrote that letter, weren't you?" I asked. "You told Caleb it was your fault that Jessamine died because you didn't do what you were supposed to."

Eli nodded. "And I was the one that altered Leopold's will and named you to the trust. And I was the one that slipped foxglove into his tea. But it wasn't my idea."

"So all of this was Iris and Caleb's plan?" Bryony asked, stepping forward.

"No," I said. He'd told me all of this when I was sick. We'd talked for a long time. And then I'd made myself forget. But the memory of it all hit me now. "It was mine. I set all of this in motion." Every horrible thing that had happened here—it was my fault.

Bryony stared. "How is that possible?" she asked.

"I made myself forget," I said, voice distant. "I manipulated my memory like I manipulated everyone else's. The same way I forced my mother to love me. That's why people always hated me. They could feel me scrabbling at their minds, trying to change them. They knew I was a monster."

"You're wrong," Eli said.

"About what?" I demanded.

"Helen, you can alter perception and memory, but your hold is temporary, and it isn't nearly as complete as you think. If you had forced your mother to adore you, it would have been as fleeting as it was with everyone else. The day you created yourself, you altered her memories. But you didn't make her love you. She just did."

"It wasn't real," I said.

He made a frustrated sound. "She didn't choose you, Helen.

That's true. But she was hardly the first mother to have a child she didn't choose nor to discover an unexpected love the first time she looked into her daughter's eyes."

I looked away. He couldn't know. He couldn't be sure. And neither could I—I could never be sure what had been genuine and what had been my own manipulations.

Eli rose from his chair. He took my hands in his, holding them gently. "What has been done to you is monstrous. What the dark soul has done, it has done out of blind pain. We did that. We took a beautiful thing, and we cut into it until all it knew was suffering. You have to believe that you deserve to be saved, Helen. Because you are the only one who can do it."

I didn't answer. I couldn't speak around the lump in my throat.

"I have to get back," Eli said. "If I leave now, they might not discover that I came to see you. I'll help you if I can. And Helen— forgive Celia. She was afraid. She thought she was doing the right thing and that Caleb would do the same." To my surprise, he stepped forward and kissed my brow once, softly. "You're not Haley," he said. "But I like to think she's part of you. Goodbye, Helen. I hope we'll meet again."

He left without another word. Alone in the witch's home, I turned to Bryony. I hardly had to reach for her before she had her arms around me. I rested my brow against her shoulder, breathing her in. *Real*, I thought. *This much, at least, is real.*

My memories, unlocked, lay like the cold blade of a knife in my palm. "I planned this, Bryony," I told her.

It had been difficult. My mind was not, by nature, orderly. "I knew that if I came up with a complicated plan, Iris and Caleb would spot it and stop me," I explained as Bryony stared. "So I put the pieces in place and made myself forget. So that I would act on instinct and buried memories. So that I would seem helpless."

"What did you do?" Bryony asked, searching my eyes.

"What day is it?" I asked instead of answering.

"It's been one year since you came to Harrow," Bryony said gently. "When the sun rises, it will be one year exactly. But we can get you away from here."

"No," I said. I swallowed. "You were right, Bryony. I can't cut myself free of the dark soul. I can't leave part of myself behind. I have to face this."

"It's too dangerous," Bryony said.

"You're the Harrow Witch. Don't tell me you're afraid," I said lightly.

"Of course I'm afraid," she said, angry and sorrowful. "I could lose you, Rabbit. I could lose the stars, and then where would I be?"

"You'll be with me," I said. I took her hands and looked into her eyes. "Even if I shatter into a thousand broken skies, I will be yours. But I have a chance to be whole. I have a chance to be free. If I go back. Trust me, Bryony. Trust that I know what I'm doing. I have all along, even if I didn't remember. Come with me."

"Always," she whispered. "Always."

In the distance, the sun broke over the horizon.

35

I WENT ALONE to the steps of Harrowstone Hall and walked right in through the front door. This was my house, after all. I didn't need to knock.

Caleb was in the foyer, lacing up his boots with a rifle slung over his back. About to come looking for me, no doubt.

The surprise on Caleb's face was almost comical. "Helen," he said warily.

"Caleb," I replied.

"What are you doing here?" he asked, clearly suspicious.

"Turning myself in," I said. I stepped forward, wrists out as if for handcuffs. "There's no point running. Do what you're going to do. I'm done."

Caleb crossed the distance between us in two long strides and lunged at me. I flinched back. He caught my face in his hand, cupping my chin with his fingers digging into my jaw, forcing me to look at him. "Get that smirk off your face. Rachel almost died because—"

"Because you tried to shoot me," I said icily. I shoved him back. "I didn't fire that bullet, you did. And I didn't kill Jessamine—that was you, too."

Fury blazed in Caleb's eyes. He swung his fist, punching me quick and hard in the gut. I doubled over, retching and gasping. He grabbed me by the back of the neck and hauled me up the stairs to Iris's study. He shoved me inside, and Iris turned from the window, brows shooting up in surprise.

"Look what came back," Caleb said.

I straightened up, panting a bit. "Good morning, Grandmother," I said.

Her lips pursed. "That simplifies things."

"I'd like to get this over with. Before anything else can go wrong," Caleb said. His hand was painfully tight around the back of my neck. I gritted my teeth.

"You don't have to drag me around. I won't run again," I said. His grip didn't relent.

"Then let us gather everyone and begin. There have been entirely too many of these occasions in my tenure here, Caleb. I do not wish to see another in my lifetime. At least we don't have to do it in the dead of night this time, now that everyone knows."

"It's just as sordid in daylight, Mother," Caleb said, but he steered me back out of the room. I twisted free of him and rubbed my neck, glaring.

"You don't need to manhandle me," I snapped.

"It's better if you aren't significantly harmed before the ritual, or I'd do a lot more than that," Caleb said evenly. He flourished a hand. "After you, Ms. Vaughan. Your room awaits."

I walked stiffly in front of him. I could feel his simmering rage, how much he wanted to hit me. Part of me wanted him to drive his fists into me, slam me against the wall, squeeze his hands around my throat until I couldn't breathe. The part of me that still thrashed in agonized guilt would welcome it.

Liar. Manipulator. Monster. Those words could have described either of us.

We walked to the Willows, and the blow never came. He simply waited for me to step inside, then closed the door behind me and locked it.

Alone, my resolve suddenly fled. I sank to the floor, wrapping my arms around my knees, and shook. I'd done it. I'd walked straight into the arms of my executioners, giving up my last fragile hope of flight. The only way out was through the center. I had to see it through.

I forced myself back to my feet. No giving up. No panicking. I wasn't alone. Bryony was with me, even if she wasn't *here*.

A knock on the door made me jump to my feet. The door opened, and Sandra stepped into the room. Her appearance startled me—she'd never been at those endless, horrible meals, but if I forced myself to think of the blur of days since Caleb shot me, she was there. Always leaving the room as soon as I entered or watching me from a distance with an expression of deep distaste. Today, she wore a black sheath dress and muted makeup, and just like the last time she'd come to my room, she was carrying a dress. It was white and cottony.

"Really?" I asked. "Isn't that a bit cliché?"

She shrugged. "Tradition is tradition." She crossed the room and set it on the bed. "You're supposed to change into that. Someone will come for you soon."

"Did you know about all of this?" I asked her on impulse. "The ritual?"

Her mouth twisted in a parody of a smile. "I knew. I knew when I married Caleb. I'm a Raymond, you know."

"As in Dr. Raymond?" I asked.

She nodded once. "The two families have been intermarrying since the beginning. It helps keep the bloodline from getting too diluted. I was raised to be Caleb's wife, and I knew that I'd have to turn a blind eye to a few infidelities so that he could do his duty."

"But he refused his inheritance," I pointed out.

She shrugged. "He's not the first Vaughan to suffer the delusion of being able to change anything. Eventually, he would have realized that there was no point in fighting fate." She paused. "It wasn't supposed to be Jessamine."

"But if some other woman's child died, that would have been fine," I said bitterly.

She didn't seem to hear me. "You know, I was really hoping you'd find a way to burn this whole place to the ground. Pity." She smoothed the dress on the bed absently. "It won't hurt. That's what they say. For what it's worth."

"It isn't worth much," I replied. I hesitated. "Who else knew? About the girls?"

She gave me an amused look. "They all did, you little idiot. They're told when they turn eighteen. I mean, Victoria kept Celia on the other side of the Atlantic for three years straight, Helen. It wasn't because she couldn't afford the airfare to come home for Christmas," she said with a sneer.

"Then my mother . . ." My chest was like a vice.

Sandra's eyes softened, just a bit. So slight it might have been my imagination. "She was always Leopold's favorite. He couldn't stand the thought of her thinking he was a monster. He made it clear she wasn't supposed to know." Then her gaze sharpened again. "That's why you picked her, of course. She didn't know what you were. She was easier to fool."

"Or maybe I chose her because she's a better person than any of you," I said.

"I don't see her here trying to save you," Sandra snapped. "Get dressed. Someone will come for you soon."

She strode out. I stared after her, a slight tension easing in my chest. Mom hadn't known. She hadn't been part of her family's wickedness.

I went over to the dress and picked it up. It was shapeless and plain, and too short—it would barely hang to my knees.

Screw it. I wasn't going to my death looking like a maiden in search of a flower crown. I tossed the dress aside and went to my wardrobe. I put on the gown Sandra had brought me for the birth-day dinner—a green one, nearly the color of Bryony's eyes. I showered quickly and did my hair up, and then I tried to remem-ber what Celia had shown me with the makeup. I was about half-way through failing at it when Celia herself knocked on the door, then eased it open.

"Does everyone have a key to that door?" I asked as I emerged from the bathroom, mascara in hand.

"I never gave it back to Eli," she said with a little blush. "You could run if you want."

"I already came back."

Celia dug a toe into the carpet, hands knotting before her. "I'm sorry. About telling Caleb. I thought he'd help you."

I sighed. "I know. It's okay. Why are you here, Celia?" I asked.

She lifted her eyes to mine. Her voice was thin but steady. "I had a feeling you needed help," she said. She frowned. "Are you putting on makeup?"

"I think I might be finger painting," I confessed.

She gave a little laugh, then paused as if uncertain it was appropriate. Then she lifted a shoulder, as if to say *What can you do?* "Let me," she said. She came forward and plucked the mascara from my hand.

"Aren't you afraid of me?" I asked. She was acting like nothing was wrong.

"Of course not. You're my friend." She set her jaw. "I don't know how to stop them, but I do know how to put on makeup, and if that's the only thing I can do, I'm going to do it." She stuck out her sharp little chin, and I stifled the urge to burst out laughing.

I hugged her instead. "You've already helped. More than you can ever know. Just by telling me that." I kissed her cheek and smiled at her. They weren't all wicked. They weren't all tainted. And so maybe neither was I if that's what I chose. "They want me to look like some helpless victim."

"Then we'll make you look fierce," she said firmly.

"Good. And then there's one more thing you can do," I said, and leaned in to whisper in her ear.

If Caleb had come to collect me, I was certain he would have made me change, but it was Eli instead, and he only laughed.

"You didn't get caught," I said with relief.

"The day is young," he replied. I slipped my hand into the crook of his arm, and he led me down the hall. "I'm sorry that all of this has happened, Helen. I don't know what your plan was, precisely—you never told me—but I wish more than anything it had worked."

"It isn't over yet," I told him. It had only just begun.

The others had gathered in the ballroom. My mother was nowhere to be seen. Fear and hope warred within me. Had she stayed away because she cared about me? Or because she couldn't stand to see me?

"And here she is," Iris said, drawing forward to examine me.

"What do you think?" I asked, stepping forward with my chin tilted up. "Am I good enough?" Celia had done my makeup in shades of smoky gray with hints of green. The girl who looked like this was not afraid of Iris Vaughan, and my voice didn't tremble.

Her lips pressed together in a thin line. I could see the sparring impulses in her—to chastise me for not appearing like I was supposed to, or to pretend everything was under control. She went with the second option.

"Come with me," she said, and led me to the front as the guests took their seats.

Desmond and Celia were sitting together. Celia had chewed her lip bloody and was gripping Desmond's hand tightly. It had to hurt, but he made no move to pull it away. He stared fixedly forward, not looking at me. Not giving any sign that he was anything but horrified by my very existence.

I'd spoken to him that day my body was coming apart, the day Roman's efforts almost succeeded. Time had skipped, and I had lost the minutes that followed. But now I remembered. *Desmond, I'd said, there's something I need to tell you. You have to keep it a secret from everyone. Even me.*

I don't understand, he'd told me.

You will. And then you'll need to make a choice. Because you deserve to choose. And because I need your help.

There was a chair for me at the front of the room. "Normally, you'd be drugged for this," Eli murmured in my ear. "But given the precarious nature of the ritual this time, I've convinced them you should be alert."

I took my seat, settling my skirt around me, and looked out at the faces of my family. Eli and Iris returned to their seats, Iris giving Eli a sidelong look. She didn't entirely trust him, I thought. But she was running low on allies.

Caleb stood. He turned to face the others, putting his back to me. "This is not the way that any of us wanted this to happen," he said. Iris stiffened, like this wasn't the right thing to say. Maybe there was some formal speech he was supposed to give, but that wasn't Caleb. He was a new hip, sensitive kind of murder cultist, in touch with his feelings, and he looked out at everyone with his hands in his pockets and an expression of deeply felt emotion.

"We're here because of Father's mistakes. And because of our own. We neglected tradition. I'm not saying it's a pleasant tradition. But until we find a better way, it's what we're stuck with. I think we lost sight of that for a while. I know I did. I thought about myself instead of the greater good."

His shoulders were slightly hunched. Humble. Cowed. He was making it sound like sacrificing a child was the *selfless* thing to do. I could practically hear Sandra's teeth grinding as she stared resolutely ahead, her hands fists in her lap.

"I know that we have lived with Helen for the past year. We have come to know her. Even knowing what she was from the start, I have not been immune from a certain level of connection. That's inevitable. That's *human*. But she is not. What you feel is because *you* are a person, capable of love and empathy and connection. She isn't." He spoke those two words firmly, meeting each person's eye. "We don't have to feel good about what we do today. But we shouldn't blame ourselves for it either. The important thing is that we are here for each other. And together, we are going to find a new path for our family. Starting today. Today will be the first Investiture that does not require the death of a child." He paused. Let that sink in. Then he said, slowly and clearly, "No child is ever going to have to die for this place again."

Victoria straightened up. Sandra let out a little startled sound, and even Iris leaned forward, looking at him curiously. "What do you mean by that?" she asked.

"I told you that my goal was to discover a way to change Harrow's traditions and spare our daughters. I believe I have found it," Caleb said. He nodded toward me. "Helen here is the result of our failures, but she is also our salvation. Nicholas Vaughan's problem was that he was too afraid of the Other and too uncertain of his own control. He thought that if he allowed its mind to heal enough to have conscious thought and individuality, it would break free, but we've proven that isn't the case. Assuming that our efforts tonight succeed—and I have done the research, I am certain that they will—we don't need human girls to bind to the Other. We just need the Other to create a vessel for *itself*. A girl like Helen. We will scatter Helen. And then, when the time comes, we will induce the Other to create her again. When she is strong enough, we can repeat the process. Our daughters will never again die for that thing."

His triumph made his voice boom. I shrank back in my seat, heart hammering, mouth dry.

It would spare them, I thought. There would be no more Harrow girls. Only me, caught in my endless dreaming. Would that be so bad? No one else would have to die.

Except for me. Over and over and over again.

I could see each of them turning the idea over. Celia startled; Desmond darkly thoughtful; Victoria relieved. Sandra's face was blank. Broken. *If they had only waited, her daughter would still be alive*, I thought.

"Now, there are a few words that must be spoken," Caleb said. Tradition again. "We have gathered here in Harrowstone Hall, the home of our forefathers . . ."

I tuned him out. What he was saying didn't matter. It wasn't for me. I might as well have been a stick of wood propped up in this chair through all of that. I wasn't a person to him. Or to Victoria, avoiding my eyes, or Iris, who never looked away from me.

I would not die for their sake. Not today. Not ever again.

"It's time," Iris said, standing. The bell was ringing. Harrow was calling for blood, and it had to be obeyed. "Victoria, Sandra. Escort the children to their rooms. Victoria, you'll join us outside. Sandra . . ."

"I'll make sure she stays put," Sandra said, arms folded. For a moment I couldn't imagine who she was talking about, and then it hit me—my mother. They were worried she would interfere. That's why she wasn't here.

My heart leaped. Maybe there was still a chance she truly cared about me.

Caleb took my upper arm. He held on tight, like he expected me to try to run, but he needn't have bothered. I followed along dutifully as he led me out of the house, Eli and Iris behind us.

It wasn't hard to guess where we were heading. After enough plodding through the woods to muddy the hem of my gown, we reached the rock face that hid the entrance to the spiral. Victoria arrived moments later, out of breath. Desmond and Celia were safely locked in their rooms, then.

"The master leads. The offering follows," Iris said. Caleb got out a flashlight and squeezed in through the hole. I swallowed down my fear and maneuvered my way into the dark.

The others filed through behind me. Caleb set off, and our procession followed, grim in our silence. Whispers filled the winding hallway, but I couldn't make them out. The voices of other girls, other masters, other witnesses. My steps grew steadier as the grip of the spiral tightened around me, and I felt myself on the verge of slipping again. It would be easier, I thought. Surrender, and drift, and feel nothing.

But I fought. I held on to myself and my senses, and when we came to the stone door, I was still myself, and every step forward had been my own choice.

Bryony stood before the door, her lantern in hand. She caught my eye, and a shiver of relief went through me. Caleb drew himself up, his hand resting ostentatiously on the strap of the rifle still slung over his back.

"I know I can't stop you," Bryony said. "Please, just let me be there for her."

Caleb glanced between us, a humorless kind of amusement on his face. "The Harrow Witch in love with the Other. It has a certain poetry to it."

"I see her truly," Bryony said, drawing herself up. "And yes, I love her."

"The witch is a tool to control the creature. Not its ally, you little idiot," Iris said, but Bryony only looked at her flatly.

"Let her in," Eli said, his thin voice slipping into the conversation like an uninvited guest. "The witch is traditionally present during the Investiture. Perhaps her absence last time was a sign you ought to have heeded."

Caleb looked at Iris; she nodded. He might be ready to declare himself Master of Harrow, I thought, but she was the one in charge here. Bryony stepped aside, and Caleb opened the door.

The chamber was as I remembered it. Even the night sky was the same, though it was broad daylight outside, and it occurred to me to wonder what sky it was if it wasn't ours. Bryony took up a place near the wall, and Caleb guided me to the stone. The scapula still sat at its base. It was like Dr. Raymond had written—an object belonging to the offering placed at the heart of Harrow to draw me in.

Panic nipped at the nape of my neck. What if I was wrong? What if I hadn't really come here under my own will? No. It had been my choice. I was sure of it.

Caleb turned me around so that my back was to the stone. He took a small knife from his belt. He rolled up his sleeve. There was a bandage on his upper arm. From his pocket he took a bloody handkerchief folded over something small. He unfolded it with a grimace and tossed it onto the dirt at the base of the standing stone. It was skin—a circle of skin, cut from his arm. "I have made an offering of my own flesh," he intoned.

Then he made a cut on his forearm and pressed two fingers to it, getting them good and bloody. He dragged his fingers down my cheek. I wrinkled my nose in disgust but held still. "I have marked your face with my blood, and so we are bound," he said.

"If you say so," I drawled, nerves making me punchy.

"I can make this painful if you want," he hissed. I shut my mouth.

He stepped back. My foot nudged against the plastic barrette, still settled in the earth over Haley's grave where I'd left it. Beside it gleamed Caleb's ring. I'd forgotten it as I was stumbling out, reeling with the knowledge of what I was.

Except that it hadn't been forgetfulness at all. Quite the opposite, really: a thorn of memory lodged under my skin, guiding my actions.

Caleb spoke again in formal tones. "An unbroken line runs from the first Master of Harrow. Hear their names and know that their blood and their will live on in me. Nicholas James Vaughan. William Francis Vaughan. Charles Graham Vaughan. Theodore Gaylord Vaughan. Lawrence Eustace Vaughan. Leopold Anthony Vaughan. I am of their blood, and they are of mine. As you have obeyed them, you will obey me."

The stars were winking out overhead. The Other was here. My dark reflection.

My heart started to race. The pieces of the ritual were falling into place. Not long now.

Eli, who was carrying a heavy bag, got out a set of goblets and a plastic bottle of what looked like wine. Each of them took a goblet, and he poured the wine into them.

"We stand together as one, bound in purpose. We stand together as one, bound together by our secrets," Eli said. "Drink, and speak, and be so bound."

The communion, and the sharing of secrets—another part of the ritual. They were supposed to drink from the cup and offer a secret.

Never have I ever, I thought, the memory of that night at the folly echoing into the present.

Caleb drank first. "I stole thirteen thousand dollars from the company once to pay off a personal debt that I was too embarrassed to confess to. I put the money back eventually, but the evidence is there if anyone looked." Boring.

Iris went next. "When I was nineteen years old, I had a brief affair with my professor," she said. "I considered running away with him and forsaking my obligations to the family." She said it matter-of-factly. At least that one was a little spicy, if cliché.

Victoria drank next and offered that she had cheated on Roman while she was in London, which no one seemed to find the least bit shocking. I'd stopped listening. Bryony was watching me, her expression tense. I smiled, just a little. *It's going to be okay,* I told her, and she nodded as if she'd heard.

It was Eli's turn. He drank deeply, and then he smiled at me. "My secret is this: I hate every single one of you, and I always have. Especially you, Caleb. You were always a little shit."

Caleb sighed. "That's enough, Eli."

They had not noticed that the stars were gone. That the air had grown colder, a soft, sly wind stirring the dust. Caleb stood before me, the other three arrayed behind him.

I'd been so determined not to be afraid. Reassuring myself that I wouldn't die. I would simply become something else. But that was a lie. I was Helen Vaughan, and Helen *would* die.

"I call you," Caleb said. "By blood and by the names of your masters, I call you. I call you into the body of this girl, into her form, into her mind, into her soul. Come, and be one."

The air grew thick, and the room filled with whispers. They were reluctant, resisting the call. They knew what happened next. They grieved every time, but they could never stop it. I shut my eyes. *Come,* I thought. *It's all right.* "Come to me," I whispered. "Our body. Our mind. Our soul. We are one. Let us be whole."

The darkness rushed into me.

The edges of me blurred, like ink in water. My body, my flesh—and my mind. My thoughts touched the mind of the dark soul, and we bled into each other. I gasped, but there was only the void to breathe.

You, a voice said.

Us, I replied.

I gave myself to the dark soul, and it gave itself to me, because there was no difference between us. The void shone all around me, and there were no shadows.

It was time to stop dreaming.

36

I WAS SITTING up in bed. Not my bed in the Willows—my bed at home, the last house where Mom and Simon and I had lived. Eli sat in a chair beside me, his elbows on his arms.

"You don't have to do this," he said. "I won't tell a soul about you."

"This is my decision," I replied. "When the time comes, I need you to remind me of that. This is *my* choice. I am in control of my fate."

"Remind you?" he said.

"I'm going to forget. It's the only way. They can't suspect I know what I am. And the dark soul may be an excellent liar, but *Helen* is terrible at it," I confessed. Eli chuckled wryly.

Wake up.

I was being carried through Harrow. Caleb had hold of me, and Eli strode alongside. It was the night I'd woken up in the halls. The night the Folded attacked me.

"We don't know if this is fatal or even harmful. It could—" Eli began. Caleb cut him off.

"*Look at her.* If it spreads any more, we'll lose Helen, and I don't know what's going to be in her place. Do you want to find out?"

"Take her to the stone. I have an idea."

I lay limp in Caleb's arms. He took me to the hidden door and carried me to the stone. He set me down and twisted around. I followed his gaze. Eli had a butcher's knife. His eyes snagged against mine, as if to ask *are you certain?* I gave him a small nod. He raised the cleaver and swung, and pain exploded through me. My eyes rolled back as I fainted.

Wake up.

I was standing in the folly, a yellow cup in my hand and the buzz of alcohol already starting to zip through me. "Let's spill all our secrets," Desmond said. I lifted the cup to my lips as the four of us gathered in our strange communion.

"Never have I ever . . ."

Wake up.

I picked at the scab on my scalp as I sat in Caleb's office, finding out just how insignificant a man like Roman could become once he was dead. Another secret for Harrow to swallow up. I hugged Caleb, burrowing against him briefly for comfort. My slashed brow pressed against his face.

When I broke away, my blood was smudged across his cheek.

Wake up.

I knelt to place Haley's bones on her shallow grave. A purple butterfly barrette and a class ring fell to the ground. I left the ring there, at the base of the Harrow stone. I didn't forget it. I'd whispered to Celia to steal it for me, after all, touching her mind gently. She'd been able to hear me more easily than the others, ever since the night they tried to give her to me.

Wake up.

I stood beside the Harrow stone as Bryony's lantern disappeared into the long tunnel beyond. I spoke the names of the dead, a litany of pain and loss. The lineage of Harrow. Not its masters but its victims. The true heart of this place.

Wake up.

We flowed into each other, Helen and the dark soul, until there was no difference. No shadow blotting out the stars. We were whole, and we were one, and we had walked this spiral willingly.

I found the heart of Harrow, and the thing at its center was me.

We opened our eyes.

I stood before the Harrow stone, my family arrayed before me, Bryony beyond them. She wasn't alone. Desmond stepped through the door. Then Celia. She'd done as I asked, as I'd known she would, stealing the key to let them out of their rooms. The others didn't notice yet.

"It's time," Caleb said. He took a flask from his pocket. "This will stop your heart. It's relatively quick."

"No," I said. "I'm not going to drink that."

Caleb sighed. "It works if we kill you violently, Helen, but no one wants that. You won't even really die, not until we divide your body properly. You'll just sleep a while. Like before."

"You don't understand," I told him, energy beneath my skin like the air before a lightning storm.

"I don't understand what?" he asked, irritated.

"I was named the Master of Harrow," I said. Bryony and the others moved along the outside wall. I stepped forward, speaking slowly and calmly. "I have stayed on the grounds for a full year. I have made an offering of my own flesh—my hand. I have marked your face with blood. I have stood with my three witnesses and shared a communion of spirits and of secrets. I have placed your ring in the heart of Harrow to draw you here, and I have spoken the names of Harrow's daughters. You cannot claim me, Caleb. I claim myself. I claim the dark soul. I claim Harrow and all its land, every stone and tree and soul within its gates."

The air had gone perfectly still. "That's absurd," Caleb said. "Harrow doesn't recognize you as its master. The family—"

"I recognize Helen as the Master of Harrow," Celia said loudly, and everyone jumped. Her eyes were sharp and fierce, even though she was shaking like a leaf. "I am the descendant of Nicholas Vaughan. I recognize her."

"Celia, stop this nonsense," Iris snapped.

"I recognize Helen as the Master of Harrow," Desmond said. "I am the descendant of Nicholas Vaughan. I recognize her."

"Desmond, Celia, what do you think you're doing?" Victoria demanded, but her voice was filled more with fear than anger, and she fell back from them as the thing she was most afraid of was *this*: her children not doing what they were told.

"I am the Witch of Harrow," Bryony said, voice fierce and steady, and she grinned. "I am Annalise Vaughan's successor, and I recognize Helen as the Master of Harrow."

"You aren't family. That doesn't count," Iris snapped, but she looked uncertain.

"I see no reason why it shouldn't. Nothing in the ritual that says they have to be Vaughans," Eli said with a grin.

"You son of a bitch. You planned this," Caleb said, turning on Eli.

"Not in the least. She planned it herself," he said cheerfully.

"You thought that you'd set a trap for me, but you were the ones in the spiral," I said.

"Caleb—" Iris said. Caleb was already moving. He had the knife.

I reached to stop him, but he was stronger than me. He lunged and wrapped an arm around my shoulders as he drove the knife between my ribs.

Agony coursed through me. I tried to scream and choked on frothy blood. He'd hit my lung. I could feel the dark soul trying to repair the damage, but it was far too slow. My body couldn't sustain itself, and I'd sleep again and be lost, and it would all be for nothing.

They had killed us. Over and over and over again, they'd killed us and hurt us and made us do wicked things. Every one of those girls had been stolen and broken and cast aside. Harrow was stained with generations of blood, and we had witnessed it all, had suffered it all.

No more.

"All things end," I whispered, as the pain flashed through nerve endings I no longer needed. My skin was turning to smoke, my body dissolving into the air. "It's time for Harrow to fall."

I was the darkness, and the darkness did not know pain.

But I was Helen, too, and the knife was in my chest, and I was afraid.

Caleb twisted the knife, gasping as cold sank into him like

teeth. "I am the Master of Harrow," he said. "You are nothing. You are a lie. You're the reason all those girls are dead." The knife dug deeper.

Desmond held Celia back as tears coursed down her cheeks. Bryony was weeping, too, but she met my eyes, and when she whispered, it was as if she were speaking in my ear.

"You are the stars themselves, Rabbit. Be the stars."

I shut my eyes. I took one last breath, more fluid than air, and my whole body shuddered with pain. I was the dark soul, but not fully. Not yet. Not while I was still Helen.

And so I let her go.

My body vanished into the dark, dissolving into smoke. Caleb stumbled forward, as without my skin and flesh and bones, the false division between *me* and *it* and *us* gave way. I was every-where and nowhere. I wasn't in Harrow anymore—I *was* Harrow. Its master, its captive, its soul.

I was power, pure and elemental. I was a century and a half of suffering and loss, and my tormentor stood before me. He had named them all, that line of greedy, violent men, and added his own name to their ranks.

I could see every corner of his soul. Caleb Vaughan was a righteous man, a kind man. He had told himself that nothing he did to me was out of vengeance. That even when he pressed a cup of poison to his daughter's lips, it was an act of love and of duty.

Caleb Vaughan was a righteous man, and I burned him hollow. His body fell, limp and lifeless. There was no pain. He'd promised me that, and so I offered it to him as well. A hundred years and more of rage burned in me, but I had been given one short life to love and be free, and it was enough to teach me a small measure of mercy. A small measure—and no more.

Iris was backing up from the place where I'd stood, holding up her hands as if to ward me off, but I wasn't there anymore. I was everywhere.

I tore the withered soul from Iris Vaughan and choked on the bitter taste of her.

Victoria screamed, scrambling for Caleb's dropped gun. I moved toward her, but suddenly, Desmond was in my way, eyes roving blindly in the darkness. He couldn't see me, but he knew I was there.

"Helen, stop," he said, hand outstretched.

She's one of them, I hissed, and the sound was a shudder through the air that made the walls shake.

"Please. She's my mother," he said.

The word swirled with meaning. My mother had been Mary Beaumont, cast aside and forgotten. Annalise Vaughan, my uncaring guardian, my captor. Rachel Vaughan, whose love, real or not, had shaped the girl I was—for a little while.

These people had killed us. They had hurt us. Again and again and again. I knew the scent of their blood. I knew their faces. There was no mercy in them.

But there was a measure left in me.

Desmond looked blindly toward me.

"Go," I told him. *"Take her and go."*

He nodded. He held Victoria's arm and guided her toward the exit, Celia taking up the rear. He looked over his shoulder. "End this," he said grimly. "Bring this whole fucking place down."

"*Go,*" I told him again, and I left them there.

It was time for Harrow to fall.

I tore at the stones of the house, and plaster rained down. The heat of my anger blistered the wallpaper, leaving smoke curling from the wood. Windows shattered and the wind howled, a gale that ripped its way through every corridor, tearing open every locked door.

Every door but one. The one blue door, its doorknob carved crystal. I stilled before it, my rage made momentarily quiet.

I stepped through the door, wearing my own face like a mask—a figment that looked like Helen, except for the sharp hook of shattered light that obscured her face.

My mother and Sandra were inside. My mother hunched in the corner of the room, away from the shattered glass that had burst from the windows. Sandra stood a few feet away, tiny cuts like tally marks across her forearms, a single red line across one cheek.

My mother looked at my figment in wild fear. "Helen?" she whispered, rising unsteadily to her feet. There was fear in her voice, but hope, too. "Where's Caleb?"

"*Caleb and your mother are dead,*" I told her. It was hard to put words in an order that would make sense. I had a hundred thoughts at once, and only one voice. It was hard to believe I'd managed like this for so long. I wanted to tell her all of it. That I was sorry, that I was glad, that I loved her.

So much of me was focused on my mother that I did not see Sandra move until it was too late. Did not notice the wicked glint of light off the spar of glass she held in one hand until the tip of it was pressed to the underside of my mother's jaw.

"Don't come any closer," Sandra hissed, eyes wide with the panic and adrenaline coursing through her. I looked at her in confusion. I couldn't come closer because I was already all around her. But she was focused on the figment as if I were contained within that image.

"What do you think you're doing, Sandra?" Mom asked. Sandra's arm was a bar across her chest, holding her in place.

"Getting out of here," Sandra said. She bared her teeth at my figment. "Let me out, or I'll slit her throat." She dug the point of the glass against my mother's neck.

Mom yelped in pain. I surged forward—an instinct, an involuntary reaction to that sound of pain. It was over before I knew I'd done it, Sandra collapsing unceremoniously to the floor, her eyes staring upward, smoke coiling faintly from her skin.

Mom screamed, staggered away. She fell back against the bed, grabbing hold of the post at the footboard to keep herself upright. She took gulping breaths, beating back panic. I wanted to comfort her, reach for her—but I knew it would only frighten her more.

I was the thing she was terrified of.

"She hurt you," I said, the words so inadequate. *"She hurt you and she wanted to kill you—I could hear it singing in her bones. She had sipped poison for so long she had become poison, and I couldn't let them hurt you like they hurt me. You took me away from this place, but I took you away from it, too."*

"I didn't know about the girls," Mom said. "Did I? Or did you make me forget?"

"You didn't know. Leopold hid it from you," I told her, and she sagged, relief breaking through her.

"Caleb and Mom are really dead," she said.

My figment nodded. *"I'm sorry. They were going to kill me, and I couldn't let them. I didn't want to die again."*

She shut her eyes, and I saw her shudder. "You tricked me. You're a trick," she whispered, half to herself.

"I tricked us both," I said. *"I made us both believe. I can't tell you if you really loved me. I don't know. But I loved you. That was real. The most real part of me."*

"And now? Are you still Helen?" she asked in a whisper. "Are you the little girl I loved?"

"I think she's dead, too," I told her, and she choked out a sob. I held my hand out to her. *"It's time for you to leave."* Part of me was there with her. Another part of me called the roots from the ground to find the gaps between the stones of the foundation, pulling them apart. The eastern wall buckled.

"What is happening?" Mom asked.

"Harrow is dying," I told her. *"If you leave, you won't be harmed."*

I left my figment to lead her to safety and turned my attention elsewhere. The folly, designed to look like a ruin, became one as its stones toppled. When a fire started in the kitchens, I let it burn and released it down the corridors I'd walked.

I was in the woods, and I was in the halls, watching Harrow burn. I was leading my mother to the gates of Harrow. I was with the shadows, bidding them to let my aunt and cousins pass, and I was with Bryony, fetching her father from his house.

And I was with Eli, down below.

Eli sat with his back against the standing stone. Iris and Caleb lay dead before him, limbs at unnatural angles.

I made myself into the shape of the girl who had loved him best and knelt beside him. *"You have to leave,"* I said.

"Hello, Haley," he said, smiling faintly.

"I'm not really her," I told him.

"I know," he said, with a helpless shrug.

"The house is collapsing. This place will not survive. You will be killed," I said. My voice sounded strange. Detached. It couldn't hold the wild storm of emotions within me, the joy and the desolation. I could *make* him feel those things, shove them into his mind. But the part of me that had been Helen understood now why that had frightened people, and so I held back.

He let out a long, ragged breath. "I have given my life and my heart to Harrow," he said. "It has taken everything from me, and there is nothing left. I would like to die knowing I ended things with one good deed, at least. One way or another, I was never going to survive this night. Let me do this on my own terms."

"I understand," I said. *"Would you like me to stay?"*

"Yes. Yes, I would like that," he said. His eyes grew distant. "Can you do something for me? Can you make me forget that you aren't real? Can you fool me one last time?"

Dust fell from the ceiling, the stones rumbling as more of the house succumbed to roots and flames and the assault of my will. But Eli saw the sun, and a park bench, and a girl in a pink jacket beside him wearing purple butterfly barrettes.

"You'll have to be getting home soon," he said.

"I can stay a little longer, Uncle Eli," she replied, and took his hand.

I stayed with him until the stones came down and made sure he never felt them.

My figment stood at the end of the road that led out of Harrow. The last living members of the Vaughan family were gone. They had fled beyond the gates, and the system which had stood in balance for a century and a half had fallen, at last, to ruin. I was alone.

And yet, not quite.

"Helen," Bryony called. She stood at the gates alone. Dust from the tunnels lay thick over her shoulders, leaving gray streaks in her hair.

Bryony stepped toward my figment, but she stayed on the other side of the gates. The cold winter sun cut between the trees, casting everything in harsh light. "You can stop. It's over." She held out her hand. "You can leave now. Let's go."

I reached out for her. My fingertips touched the very edge of Harrow and went no farther.

"Please, Rabbit. Come with me," Bryony whispered.

My lips parted. A breath escaped my lips, and for an instant, the figment teetered toward reality, and her fingertips, now solid, brushed against Bryony's outstretched hand. Of all the things that clamored in my fresh-woken soul, my love for her blazed brightest.

But I wasn't Helen. Not anymore.

I cast aside the image of that girl and left Bryony there, beyond my reach.

37

I WAS THE woods and the stones and the stars. I was nowhere and everywhere and nothing and everything. I had never been free, never whole, and now I was—and I exulted in it, learning the shape of myself, tasting memories that had been buried with my bones all these long years.

Time, which had little meaning anymore, slipped around me as I turned to the task of my existence. My whole self burned with the need to create. I sank the dark tendrils of myself into the earth. Flowers made of frost and bone bloomed. The stones of Harrow melted and re-formed under my touch, making uncanny shapes. From leaf mold and brambles, I crafted strange and beautiful creatures. The shadows, no longer sustained by their endless search, folded themselves away. No one stepped foot on Harrow's grounds, not anymore.

Until one night, she did.

I sensed her, the way I sensed every thrush and field mouse in my woods, but I paid her no mind until she began to sing.

"There was a maiden, golden-haired,
Came to the fold, came to the fold.

She walked among the shadows there.
Her bones are white, her blood is cold."

All of my attention fixed on her, this stranger in my domain. She wore a gray dress and carried a lantern, glowing gold, and when she sang, an unsettled feeling rippled through me.

The shadows unfolded themselves and followed her, rushing in endless motion at the edges of her light. Not one flicker of fear darkened the light that blazed within her. She knew the names of Harrow's shadows, and I knew hers.

Bryony.

She stood at the foot of the ruins that had once been Harrowstone Hall. It was overgrown with trees and vines, its brutal order cast into a kind of chaos both gentle and wild. The last note of her song faded. She set the lantern on the ground and tilted her face up toward the night sky.

"I know you're here," she said. "I can feel you. Please. Talk to me."

I stood behind her, wearing a form of no particular identity, my face a mask of fractured light. *"You're Bryony Locke,"* I said. *"I remember you. You left."*

"My dad wasn't keen on me living in a shack in the haunted woods alone," Bryony said with a little laugh. I tilted my head, considering. I knew all the words she was saying, but the concepts seemed distant. "It was better for you, anyway. You needed time to heal yourself. But now you have to make a choice. You have to decide who you are." She swallowed, and her eyes gleamed with tears. "You were always the dark soul, but you were Helen, too. You could be her again."

"She wasn't real," my figment said.

"Yes, she was," Bryony said fiercely. "She was Rachel Vaughan's daughter. She collected bones and made them into art. She was awkward and clumsy and kind and funny. She was curious and clever and determined. She was real, and I loved her, and she loved me. And she was *you,* and you were her. And you can be again if you choose. Please, Rabbit. Please come back to me."

"I'd be alone," I said. *"My mother hates me. Simon never existed."* I remembered these things. But they didn't hurt me like they hurt Helen. Here, like this, I was safe.

"You're not alone. You have Desmond and Celia. And your mother," Bryony said.

"She despises me."

Bryony shook her head. "She loves you."

"Then why isn't she here?" I demanded, and the anger was Helen's, just for a moment.

"She thinks you're dead. They all do," Bryony said. "They can't see you like I can."

I fled from her, seething among the trees, finding refuge with the shadows. I hid myself in the wind and night sounds and waited for her to leave.

She didn't.

"Hello, Rabbit," she said when I emerged again. She sat on a toppled stone, her head tipped back to watch the shifting stars.

"I'm not that person anymore. I never was," I told her.

"Of course you were," she said, shaking her head. "And you still are. That and more."

"What do you want from me?" I asked.

"What do *you* want?" she countered. "Do you want to stay here forever? To be the beast of Harrow and dwell among its bones?"

"*I will not be cut apart again,*" I said, and rushed away from her. I plunged beneath the surface of the lake, assembling strange carapaces in the silt. I waited for her to leave.

She didn't.

"*I won't go back to what I was,*" I said, sitting beside her beneath an old oak tree. "*I won't be cut off from myself.*"

"You don't have to. That's what healing means," Bryony said. "Helen was wounded. But she wasn't her wounds. You can be yourself and be Helen if you want to. It's your choice. You'd have Harrow, but you wouldn't be stuck here. You could go anywhere you want."

"*What if I don't?*" I whispered. "*What if I can't?*"

"Then I will love you," she said. "And I will mourn her."

Helen. Collector of bones. Rachel's daughter. The girl whose heart beat harder because Bryony Locke was holding her.

But for that to be true, she needed a heart.

I ran from the witch again. I delved deep to where I had hollowed out a cathedral of roots and stones beneath the earth. The shattered Harrow stone lay at its center, all my once-stolen bones interred at its feet.

In that place where I had been scattered so many times, I tried to remember being me.

I built myself from shadows and stars, from memory and hope. Hands that had gathered bones and bound them in wire, the chambers of a heart that had been shattered and had healed again.

Lungs to draw in breath, a throat to speak the name of the woman I loved. But this time, I didn't close any part of myself away. I did not cut into my soul to lessen myself to fit within this form. I could still feel Harrow, all of it. I was still the stars.

The spiral was long since collapsed. I had to carve myself a new path, the part of me that was Harrow opening a seam in the earth for the part of me that was Helen to walk through. I cut a straight line through where the spiral once had lain. A clear course from the center to its edge.

At its end, she was waiting for me.

"Rabbit?" Bryony asked tentatively. "Is that you?"

I stepped forward into the light of strange stars. "It's me," I said, and for the first time since Mary Beaumont had looked at the face of a god, it was true.

I would love Bryony Locke in any form, but it was Helen who laughed with joy and threw herself into Bryony's arms. I kissed her and tasted tears and I didn't know which one of us was crying, and it didn't matter.

She was here, and so was I, and we were together, and we were alive, and the whole of me, every part of my soul, was free.

THIS IS HARROW: A house lies, silent and ruined, in the cleft be-tween wooded hills. The forest rushes toward it and over it, clamber-ing in mad abandon across the toppled stones and cracked beams. The roots have infiltrated the foundations, the branches thrust through shattered windows, and flowers grow out of season amid flurries of ash.

A wondrous chaos breathes amid the stones of Harrow. Lithe creatures dart among the trees, unfamiliar bird calls trill, and plants that have no earthly origin bloom. Above this riot of strange cre-ations, the stars gleam in ever-changing configurations in the sky.

In a small cottage in the woods dwells a witch. She tends a sum-mer garden and reads in the shade of the trees. And I dwell with her.

Someday we will walk beyond the gates of Harrow. We will live in both worlds, and both will change us. We cannot be certain who we will choose to be in the coming days and months and years, what lives we will build for ourselves. But we will always be together.

I have lied all my life, in one way or another, but now I can speak the truth.

I was born at Harrowstone Hall, and I was reborn in its ruins. I am not human, but I am whole. I am free. And I am loved.

My name is Helen Vaughan.

Author's Note

IN ARTHUR MACHEN'S 1894 novella *The Great God Pan*, a man is invited by a friend, Dr. Raymond, to observe a procedure he has devised—one he believes will allow the subject to look upon the face of a god. His subject is his teenage ward, Mary. Her life, he assures us, is his to do with as he wishes. The result should sound familiar: a lobotomy, a girl driven mad and later found to be pregnant, and the birth of a daughter who is not entirely human.

Most of *The Great God Pan* is about the trail of death and madness left by Mary's daughter, Helen Vaughan. When she is finally cornered and her monstrous, inhuman nature revealed, she undergoes a bizarre transformation and then, rather anticlimactically, dies.

Reading *The Great God Pan*, it always struck me that however unworldly Helen was, the far more frightening monster was Dr. Raymond—a clever man with a sharp knife. The narrator never questions Dr. Raymond's assertion of ownership over Mary's fate. The women of the tale are victims, tools, or monsters.

If Dr. Raymond and the narrator who stands placidly by are our examples of humanity, maybe it's not such a bad thing to be a monster.

These Fleeting Shadows is not a retelling of *The Great God Pan* so much as it is an attempt to steal Helen Vaughan and give her back to herself. I scattered borrowed names through the story:

Helen, Dr. Raymond, and Mary, most obviously, and Rachel, whose name comes from a girl lured by Helen into the woods and driven mad by what she sees. Nicholas Vaughan is entirely an invention, as is his wife Annalise and the rest of Helen's family. I worked in references as it amused me and otherwise ignored the original text to pursue my own; most of the echoes of the original story are contained in Nicholas's journal, including one small section lifted directly from that original text. Otherwise, *These Fleeting Shadows* is its own beast.

Much like Helen herself.

Acknowledgments

I WAS MIDWAY through drafting this book in the midst of pandemic lockdowns when I realized I was writing a book about a girl who can't leave her house for a whole year. Wonder where I got that idea from. Luckily, my family, unlike Helen's, didn't attempt any blood sacrifices—and for that alone, I suppose I should thank them first. Mike, my spouse, my partner in crime, my most beloved, thank you as always for the support, encouragement, and board games. And thank you to Mr. O and Ms. Bean—and to your preschool teachers. This book would not exist (or, at least, I'd still be writing it) without Len, Marie, Mikka, and the rest of the team.

I have so many people to thank for helping this book along the way: Maggie Rosenthal, as always, for her editorial vision and passion; my agent, Lauren Spieller, for her savvy and insight; the No Name Writing Group—Shanna Germain, Erin M. Evans, Susan Morris, Rhiannon Held, Corry L. Lee, and Rashida Smith—for helping me find my way through the spiral; the copyeditors and proofreaders, Trish Brown, Abigail Powers, Marinda Valenti, and Sola Akinlana, for putting up with my wanton em dashes and conniving comma splices; Kristie Radwilowicz, for an absolutely killer cover, and Jim Hoover for crafting an interior to match; and Kaitlin Kneafsey, for all her wizardry in actually getting the book in front of the right eyeballs.

Finally, a further thank-you to the rest of my Seattle family for not being murder cultists (that I know of) and for never failing to be a source of companionship, support, and cheerleading during the writing of this book: my parents, Alice and David; my siblings, Thomas and El; their partners, Kaelin and Rosie; my mother-in-law, Rosemary, and her partner, Mike (also, do you want to take the kids next weekend?); and my grandmother Joan.